vice & VIOLET

vice & VIOLET

SARAH A. BAILEY

Page & Vine
An Imprint of Meredith Wild LLC

This is a work of fiction. Names, characters, places, and incidents either are the product of the author's imagination or are used fictitiously, and any resemblance to actual persons, living or dead, business establishments, events, or locales is entirely coincidental. The publisher does not assume any responsibility for third-party websites or their content.

The author acknowledges the trademarked status and trademark owners of various products referenced in this work, which have been used without permission. The publication/use of these trademarks is not authorized, associated with, or sponsored by the trademark owners.

Paperback ISBN: 978-1-964264-21-9

Author's Note

Dear Reader,

Thanks for visiting Pacific Shores. If you've been before, welcome home. If this is your first time, I want to remind you that *Vice & Violet* is the second book in a duet and should be read *after* finishing *Reckless Roses.* For the best reading experience, I strongly recommend going back to complete *Reckless Roses* if you have not already.

Vice & Violet is intended for readers 18+ and contains sexually explicit material, as well as themes of grief, trauma, and mental health that may be difficult for some. For a full list of content warnings, please visit my website: sarahabaileyauthor.com

Lastly, for those of you who have been around from page one of *Heathen & Honeysuckle*, who have found a home in Pacific Shores and with this family, thank you for being here with me. I created this world at a time I needed comfort most, and I never could've imagined that it would be possible for these words to reach so many. I never could've imagined the healing I was searching for myself could be found for many of you, too. Thank you for always reminding me why I do this, and for loving these characters as much as I do.

Trust me, I'm not ready to say goodbye, either.

With love,
S.A.B.

For those lost in the darkness:
May you find your ultraviolet to guide you through.

And for the ones who say, "I can fix him,"
Augustus is all yours.

Prologue

Violet

Four Years Ago

"hoax" - *Taylor Swift*

I was under the impression that March equaled the start of spring—blooming flowers, sunshine, the hope of a new dawn. Shit like that.

However, the frigid gust of wind that stings my cheeks as I climb out of the Fourth Street and Washington Square subway station feels like an omen of despair.

I use two fingers to zoom in on the map on my phone screen, figuring out which direction I need to take to find my dropped pin. I have to go three blocks north, then take a right down Tenth Street, and that should lead me right to her door. Though, I've gotten lost three times so far today, so I'm not overly hopeful.

I asked Monica for the address in passing, making it sound like I was going to send her a card of some sort. Thankfully, Monica didn't press for the occasion, because it's nowhere close to her birthday or any other card-worthy holiday we'd be celebrating.

That was three weeks ago. I quietly booked my flight out here and then told my friends—her family—that I was going to spend the weekend with my parents in Palm Springs. I knew nobody would ask questions about that, because my parents don't speak to them anymore. They don't speak to anyone, including me.

Somehow, I make my way to the address Monica provided me. It's a charming red-brick building with steps leading up to one entry, but numerous black fire escapes and white-framed windows looking out onto the street tell me they must all be apartments.

I walk up to the front door, finding a metal panel with unit numbers—each one paired with a circular button. I recheck my information, confirming that she's 313, and press the buzzer for her apartment.

It goes unanswered.

"Come on, Elena. You fucking coward," I growl, buzzing her again after a minute passes.

The wind picks up, and I wrap my coat tighter around myself. I definitely should've worn more layers. I didn't pack for an extended stay, because hotels in Manhattan are expensive as fuck, and I have no idea how this interaction might go with her. I wanted to prepare myself for pain—more than the pain she already caused me when I woke up that morning months ago—and somehow, it felt like if all I had was a carry-on when I ran back to California with my tail between my legs, it'd hurt less.

Despite expecting this to all go poorly, I couldn't not try. I gave her time and space. Six months' worth of it, really, but I know her better than anyone on earth knows her. She's been brewing and hiding and letting her emotions build. Eventually, the adrenaline and the shock are going to bottom out, and the grief and guilt will set in, if they haven't already.

Partially, I'm fucking angry at her for isolating herself from me. Another part of me is fucking terrified that she blames me, and that she'll never look me in the eye again without seeing him. Most of me, though, is just desperate to know exactly what's going on inside her head so I can fix it. I've always been able to see her in ways others can't. I've been able to read the words she can't express, and I think that's why she ran from me. She's not ready to address this, and she knows the moment she looks into my eyes, all that she's been suppressing is going to rise to the surface.

So, I'm angry with her, but more than anything, I fucking miss her. I've been destroyed without her, and I'm fearful of the guilt that comes alive when I look at her—the kind I felt that night when she was sleeping in my arms—but I'm not afraid enough to never see her face again.

I gave her three months to run and hide in New York, and now I'm cashing in. She's going to see me, she's going to talk to me, and she's going to hear me out. I'm going to fix this, fix us, because even after everything, I still believe we're meant to be.

Fate makes it hard to feel like it's on my side when I realize she isn't home right now, though.

I sigh, backtracking down the steps and taking a stroll around the block. I pick up a scarf, a sandwich, and a Coke from the bodega on the corner before I return to her building. I ring her buzzer three more times with no answer before I settle in on the bottom step and wait.

Either she's inside right now and ignoring me—in which case, I'll wait her out. Or she's not home, and that just means I'll be right here when she shows up. Even if I end up sitting here all night, New York is the city that never sleeps or whatever, so I don't need to either. All I know is that I didn't fly three thousand miles not to see her fucking face.

I put in my AirPods, bundling the scarf around my neck and chin, and tuck my hands inside my coat as the sun sinks low on the horizon, causing the temperature to drop further. Hozier blasts inside my ears, and nerves swirl in my bones, but I settle in to wait, feeling hopeful for the first time since that late night in January.

The sound of laughter startles me from the daze I must've dozed off into. My eyes fly open as I sit up straight, realizing I was leaning against the handrailing of the stairs. I check to ensure my backpack is still on the ground between my legs, thankful it didn't get swiped.

It's completely dark now, though the illumination of the city around me makes it feel damn near daylight. There are still dozens of people strolling along the sidewalks, dipping in and out of apartments, bars, and restaurants on the street in front of me. It's lively and cheerful. I can understand why people love New York so much, though I'm not sure I'd ever be able to justify living somewhere where I can't see the stars.

I wonder if that's why this is the place Elena ran to. I wonder if she's trying to avoid the sky I remind her of.

That laugh chimes again, closer this time. I know that laugh better than I know my own heartbeat. I can still remember the way it racked against my chest the first time I heard the sound when I was just a kid. The way I'd do anything to hear it over and over.

I stand up, swiveling my head down both sides of the street in search of that laugh, of her. I don't know how she's going to react when she sees me, but I hope it's enough to get me through her door and give me a chance to explain why I'm here.

I finally catch sight of her rounding the corner of a nearby alley. She's not paying attention to where she's going, arms linked between two people. A girl with short, platinum-blond hair and a blue beanie, and a tall, lanky man who gazes down at Elena like she hung the goddamn fucking moon.

She skips between them, dark curls bouncing, her beautiful face bright with carefree laughter.

What the fuck?

Two other people follow behind them, and the tall man says something I can't decipher before the rest of them burst into laughter again. Elena lets go of the girl's arm, allowing the man next to her to twirl her in circles right there on the sidewalk. She giggles the entire time like a fucking schoolgirl before he tugs her into him, snaking his arm around her waist.

I feel sick.

I hop off the bottom step and duck behind the staircase that leads to her building, listening as she makes conversation with this group of strangers, her voice growing louder with each passing second. My mind reels and my stomach drops because she sounds clear. Happy, even.

For months, she shut herself away from not only me, but from her brothers, her parents—every fucking person who loves her. For months, she didn't eat, she didn't sleep, and wouldn't speak.

She missed the goddamn funeral, for fuck's sake.

According to Everett, she claimed she was falling behind on deadlines, that she needed a fresh place to focus, and what better setting for a writer than New York City? I assumed she was using it as an excuse to rot in silence, because while Elena may be fine falling apart herself, she doesn't like to watch others worry for her. I assumed it was the mask she always wears, pretending she's okay when she's breaking inside. I assumed that she'd tumble into darkness on her own out here, and I've laid awake every night in the three months since I discovered she'd boarded that plane, wondering if she was okay.

I put my own grief on the back burner to prioritize hers. Stopped caring for my well-being because I needed her to be okay, and when she wouldn't let me fix her, I wrecked myself in solidarity, even if she wasn't there to witness it.

Because when she came back home, I wanted her to know that I waited to heal. Waited for her, because I've been determined to do it together.

But as I hide behind a brick wall in the middle of Manhattan, listening to the love of my life laugh with another man, I realize that I've been crumbling all on my own.

I bite my fist to quell my scream as I hear her unlock the main door to the building, the shuffle of multiple footsteps leading inside. Clearly, she's made a pretty new life for herself here in New York, out on a Thursday night with friends while I've been waiting for her in California, destroying myself in the process.

When our world burned down around us, I thought she was lost in the flames right beside me. Now that I'm standing in the ashes of the house we built together, I realize I've been alone the whole goddamn time.

Chapter One

Vice

"Liability" - Lorde

The only thing worse than falling into unrequited love is grieving it.

It is the human condition to romanticize life, even the most far-fetched fantasies. Like unconditional love. We spend our time daydreaming about those who refuse to give us anything, finally offering everything. Greener grass and brighter skies and the grasp of strong hands catching us when we fall.

Even when you're not loved, you can live in reveries of realities where you are.

Except for the reality of death. Because death can't be romanticized.

The finality of it is suffocating. Forgetting and forgiveness are no longer options.

Time stands frozen.

Your last words echo through eternity, becoming permanent. Like tattoos upon the soul.

And we're buried with our ink.

I watch the cursor blink in the blinding brightness of my computer screen. Wiping the exhaustion from my eyes, I reluctantly let them fall onto the clock in the corner of my laptop: 3:46 a.m.

Sighing, I highlight the entirety of what I just wrote and press delete. "Nobody's going to read a fucking romance book that starts like that," I mutter to myself in the dead of night. My head falls into my hands, fingers massaging my temples.

I shut off my laptop and turn on the small lamp on my desk, illuminating my room in a warm glow. My body instantly settles at the change in lighting.

I'm not afraid of the dark, but I do fear the calamitous spiral my mind will send me down if I think too long about all the lives I'll never get to live. An unfortunate side effect of being a romance writer in the harsh, unendingly torturous reality I now find myself inside. Darkness and creative attempts tend to bring out the demons I spent nearly four years burying—the ones so briskly brought back into my life when my twin brother unexpectedly turned up at my Brooklyn apartment and hauled me home to California.

I'd left for a reason.

It's easier to ignore the ghosts that haunt me when I'm not face-to-face with a childhood of memories those ghosts left behind. Especially on days like today.

I never think of him. Not consciously. It may be his face in my nightmares, his voice screaming when I remind myself of all the parts of me worth hating, his absence that made the place I once called home a barren wasteland. But I don't think of him.

Except on October second.

October second is the worst day of my life.

It's weird now that I can compartmentalize it. If I think about that moment too deeply—the smell of the emergency room or the look on my brother's face, the vomit I spewed along the concrete outside or the sound of his mother's scream, the way the sheets in my guest bedroom had still smelled like him or the mug in my sink from the coffee I poured for him that morning—it comes roaring back.

I'm not sure how long it took me to reach the point where I could pluck each of those triggers and place them inside their own box, teaching myself to acknowledge the reality of those memories, but pretend they don't exist at the same time. A few months, maybe.

I was able to function after that, by all appearances, at least. I attempted to get back to work, knowing my publisher had provided me extensions on all my deadlines due to extenuating circumstances, but I quickly found that while I was surviving the day-to-day again, deep-seated depression and suppressed grief cause writer's block. Who would've thought?

My move to New York was supposed to be brief. Get my family off my back about therapy, fresh air, and the lifeline I forcibly cut my ties with. I was going to go out there, sublet a cute apartment in Greenwich Village, and live out my Carrie Bradshaw dreams.

Instead, I failed. At everything. And for some reason, it was comforting.

It's so much easier to be sad because you're a failure than to be sad because you lost all the love you'd ever known.

I wallowed in that. The failure, the depression, the one-night stands, and the heavy drinking.

Then Everett knocked on my door.

I could cover up well enough if I had notice. Nothing motivated me to clean my apartment like a call from my parents or my brothers letting me know they were going to come visit. I could play the part of hopeful writer and New York tour guide, happy and optimistic to be living in the City of Dreams.

I wasn't expecting Everett that day, though. He showed up uninvited, took one look at my dead eyes, the stranger in my bed, and the mess I was living in and hauled me back home.

He was convinced that the smell of the ocean, my favorite West Coast coffee, and my mother's arms would heal whatever demons I spent those years fighting. I hate to be a disappointment, but six months after moving in with my twin, his girlfriend, and her ten-year-old daughter, I can say with confidence that I am.

A disappointment, an imposition, and—still—a massive fucking mess.

So, I resolve to stay up all night, staring at a blank computer screen and attempting to form words. I think the only reason my brother hasn't kicked me out yet or forced me to get a job is because I've been convincing him that I'm writing again. I hate being a liar almost as much as I hate being a disappointment, so I try my best, but my brain is perpetually empty, I think.

It appears that I can't stop being both of those things.

My routine is to be up when Everett and Dahlia start their day at four in the morning because they're *go-getters.* I check in with them and make conversation before either of them is fully awake. They assume I'm working away at my manuscript, and I've always been a late-night writer.

Then, when they get home from work at the end of the day, nobody questions why I'm still in bed, and nobody asks me to have dinner with them so we can talk about our days and pretend like I'm as fucking happy as they are.

I throw an oversized cardigan over my shoulders, rising from my desk and sneaking down the stairs. I put my tea kettle on the stove as I hear the sound of the shower turning on above my head. I sort through the pantry in search of my favorite tea, grabbing the honey too.

A few moments later, I hear what resembles pounding horse hooves more than footsteps descending the stairs, just before my massive, six-foot-something brother turns the corner. He's got only a towel slung around his waist as he runs a hand through his wet dark hair.

"Motherfucker!" Everett gasps, rearing back when he flips on the light and finds me standing at the kitchen island. "Christ. You're like a goddamn cat."

"That's a compliment to me."

"Up early or haven't slept?" he asks as he walks over to the coffee maker and gets a pot brewing.

Everett doesn't have to open his businesses until after ten o'clock, but since Dahlia has been taking a baking course at a nearby culinary institute and has to be there by six, Everett gets up with her every morning. He makes her coffee, sees her off, and then gets her daughter ready for school.

"Haven't gone to bed yet." I yawn, knowing he's aware of my sleep schedule. I think he's still hopeful I'll get my shit together, that one morning he's going to get up and find some kind of productive, motivated, ambitious version of me who's ready to take on the world.

"How's the book going?"

The kettle begins to whistle, giving me the perfect opportunity to avoid the question. I snatch it off the stove and pour my tea. My brother watches me as he waits for Dahlia's coffee to brew, leaning back against the counter with his arms crossed.

I put everything away and creep toward the staircase. "Well, I'm going to try to get a few more words in." A few words I won't delete. "And then get some sleep. Have a good day."

"Lele." My brother's voice is stern, and the tone makes me pause, turning to look at him. "You know what today is, right?"

My stomach bottoms out. "Yes, Everett," I murmur through clenched teeth.

"Are you okay?"

I sigh, throat suddenly tightening. "I am fine. The only thing that makes me not fine is when everyone is asking me if I'm fucking fine."

Everett lifts his eyebrows, entirely unconvinced. "I ask you so much because you lie and say you're fine when you're clearly"—he waves his hand in my direction—"not fine."

"I don't want to talk about it today." I glance down at my feet because I don't like the guilt that shoots through me when I look at his face.

"You don't want to talk about it ever, but you need to. Today, especially."

What the fuck is there to talk about? I loved someone. He broke my heart. I said terrible, horrible things to him that I can never take back. He died. The end.

"Good morning," a tired voice sounds from behind me as Dahlia hops off the bottom stair and strolls into the kitchen, smiling.

Everett gives me a look that says he's not done with this conversation, but when his eyes flit to his girlfriend, they turn molten, his face so bright, it's like I'm not even in the room. He smiles at her, and it's like the world goes from darkness to daylight.

I never thought I'd see my brother in love like this. I never thought I'd see him in love at all. It was weird to leave Pacific Shores knowing him as an emotionally unavailable playboy who loved to party, and come home nearly four years later to find him not only in a committed relationship, but also giving total dad energy to his girlfriend's daughter.

Wild.

Watching them together is borderline repulsive, but I still can't stop myself from smiling as he pulls her against his chest and drops his mouth to her lips. The soft moan that escapes Dahlia is definitely my cue to leave.

"Okay, well, you two have a good day. I'll see you this evening."

"Good night, Elena," Dahlia sings, laughing into my brother's neck.

I turn the corner, heading up the stairs just as Everett calls out, "Elena?" I pause halfway up, waiting for him to continue. "Do not get upset with Mom and Dad, or with Leo, if they come to check on you today."

I don't respond as I continue to my room, shutting off my lamp and drenching myself in darkness, crawling into bed and letting it swallow me whole.

Chapter Two

Violet

"I Always Wanna Die (Sometimes)" - The 1975

Sometimes, I daydream about killing myself.

Not even because I want to. I don't think I ever would. Maybe I should and I'm a coward, or maybe deep down I still believe there is something to live for, but regardless, I think about it.

I dream about it because I'd like to know that my last act was perpetual torment on my father. I'd get satisfaction knowing that it'd likely destroy him, that maybe he'd follow me into the depths of hell too. I'd hope that he would feel the pain, guilt, and hopelessness that he's been causing me for the last four years.

Not that I don't deserve it. I do.

But I fucking hate my father anyway.

Though, killing myself in spite of him would destroy my mother in all the same ways. It'd destroy my friends—the few people left in this world who still give a shit about me. And I love them more than I hate my dad. So, I won't kill myself.

I can't pretend I don't sometimes think about it simply because I yearn for her reaction. There are parts of me convinced she'd celebrate, other parts of me that think she'd curl up right beside me and die, too, because that's how I feel about her. The biggest fear I have—arguably the thing truly stopping me—is the undiluted fear that my death wouldn't ruin her the way his did.

What a fucked up thing to envy.

If I died, I'd be freed from the shackles attached to her

affections. It wouldn't fucking matter who she loved most at the end of the day, because I'd be swallowed up by the darkness that I can't help but sometimes feel would be a reprieve.

Yet, that fear pricks at my skin all the same. I can't live with the possibility of confirmation that I meant nothing to her, even though she's been confirming that sentiment herself with each passing day of silence since the morning she left my bed.

One thousand three hundred and sixty days of silence, to be exact.

Despite the fact that she's been living four blocks from me the past six months, or that I have dinner with her family every Sunday. Dinners she never joins.

That day felt odd. Operations at work were normal. The weather was fine. But something was rattling my bones; something didn't feel right. Or maybe it did, for the first time in a while, and that's what felt wrong.

Nobody told me that Everett left town. I was none the wiser. Yet, somehow, when my two childhood friends showed up on my doorstep in the middle of the night, I wasn't surprised. When Everett told me she'd returned to Pacific Shores, I wasn't taken aback.

Because somehow, I already knew.

That bone-rattling awareness, that odd unease, it was her. She was coming home. Her ghost was descending upon my world—here to endlessly haunt me.

One thousand three hundred and sixty days of silence, and one hundred seventy-eight days of haunting me from half a mile away.

I've only seen her once in those one hundred seventy-eight days. Sitting on the opposite side of the aisle at Darby and Leo's wedding. She arrived on her own not long before the ceremony started. After taking a moment to herself with the bride and groom directly after, she was gone. Like a goddamn apparition. Just a glimpse, a reminder that she's real, that the reckoning and ruining and irreversible damage she'd caused my soul wasn't something I made up inside my head—as I often attempt to convince myself—it was true.

But she disappeared too quickly for there to be any chance at closure.

I've yet to see her since. Not at the boardwalk her brother owns, and not at family dinners. Not on her birthday, and not on mine. I certainly don't expect today—of all days—to be any different. I don't expect she'll get out of bed today, if I still know her the way I used to.

I'm surprised I got out of bed today, too. But I wanted to work. I've found that being at the shop is better than being all alone.

But leaving the house led me to the room I sit in now, daydreaming about killing myself again. It doesn't happen all that often, but if there is any date I'm going to sit around and ponder death, I suppose October second makes the most sense.

"I'm doing fine," I tell Kelsey, my therapist, shifting uncomfortably on the leather couch.

She stares at me over her glasses, unconvinced. "I know what today is, August."

I sigh, looking down at my hands, trapping them between my thighs. "Yeah."

Except I don't really want to talk about it. About that day, or about him. I've gotten to a point where I can think of my brother fondly. I hyperfocus on the positive memories and our childhood together, and I don't allow my mind to wander past that. I don't want to address that day. I don't want to think about what I saw, or the call I had to make to my mother—my friends.

I don't think it serves me, and I know it won't change a goddamn thing.

Kelsey told me I can't reverse my trauma, but I can learn to process it and move forward. In my opinion, thinking deeply—visualizing—that day on repeat until it's processed, whatever the fuck that means, only causes me more pain. I want to focus on the moving forward part.

"So, you don't want to talk about your parents. How they're

spending today. How about yourself, and how you're feeling?"

I don't want to talk about my parents, because they don't give a shit about me, but I don't want to tell her that, either.

When I don't answer, she continues. "We can talk about that day, or everything that came after. Or, we don't have to talk about it at all. If you need this hour to sit in silence, or to talk about something completely unrelated, I'm here for that. Whatever makes today feel less heavy."

I let out a breath of relief, settling into the couch and expanding my lungs.

This is only my third time seeing Kelsey, and I keep having this fear that she's going to force me to talk about all the emotions I know I hold in. In our first session she said it's not healthy to hold back the way I do, and that's why I'm having trouble finding closure.

I want to tell her that I can't get closure, because my brother is dead, and the last thing I ever said to him was awful. I want to tell her that my parents fucking hate me for it. I want to tell her that I can't get closure, because the love of my life cried in my arms just hours before she moved three thousand miles away and never spoke to me again. I want to tell her that thinking about those facts, and the little-to-no control I have over changing them, makes closure impossible.

Not thinking about it is what keeps me functioning.

Because I'm thinking about it right now and fuck, I'm shaking.

I swallow, looking up to my therapist. "Day-to-day I'm doing fine, really. Work is all right, fall and winter are pretty slow, but I'm getting by. I've decided not to sell my house."

Kelsey nods attentively, listening to everything I say. She doesn't seem disappointed that I refuse to talk about the real reasons I'm here. Our conversation drifts into my childhood, and I realize she only asks basic questions about my brother and family, not diving deep enough to trigger me. By the end of the session, I'm laughing, telling stories about my brother as a kid.

Fine. Whatever. Darby was right, as per usual. Therapy isn't that bad.

I head down the stairs from her office and out onto Main Street in downtown Pacific Shores, where Darby's blue Mustang is parked against the curb. She insists on driving me to make sure I actually attend, and grabs us lunch while I'm in my session.

She's been asking me to start therapy for months now, claiming that it was immensely helpful to her and her sister, Dahlia, when they began going at the start of the summer. After that conversation, Leo, Darby's husband, admitted he'd been seeing a therapist since he was twelve. Then, Everett, Leo's brother and Dahlia's boyfriend, agreed to go to therapy too. He told me that he had the least reason to seek counseling out of all of us, and I had the most, which meant if he was going to do it, I had to do it too.

"Hi! How was it?" Darby asks before taking another bite of her food as I open the passenger door and slip inside. "Sorry, I tried to wait but I'm fucking starving." She holds a paper bag out to me. "I got you a sandwich. Turkey and cranberry with bacon, which is disgusting, by the way. Please eat it before I vomit."

"It was good." I snort. "And I only say this because, unlike your husband, you're not one to gloat. You were right. I think it could be helpful." She opens her mouth, but I cut her off before she can say anything. "And, no, I don't want to talk about today. I got it all out during that appointment, and I'm going to return to work, eat my sandwich, and then go home and watch *Dazed And Confused*." My brother's favorite movie.

She nods slowly, turns on the ignition, and takes off toward the boardwalk at the end of Pacific Shores' main drag as I eat. We're quiet, the roar of the wind and the smell of the ocean taking over as we make the short drive.

There were times I thought about moving away. There are memories here that will always be painful to bear, but I can't imagine not living near the sea. I can't imagine not looking up at palm tree-clad sidewalks or smelling salt in the air at all times.

I can't imagine life without the pier, the surf, and the sprawling cliffs along the ocean's edge. The world-famous sunsets that we residents have the privilege of witnessing nightly. My brother ran away from Pacific Shores once, too, and he came home because he realized there was no place else he'd rather be.

I think he'd be disappointed in me for a lot of things, but most of all, he'd be disappointed in me if I left the place he loved most. So, I refuse to do that.

"You sure you don't want to stay for the event?"

I shake my head. "I know you guys are doing it for me, and I appreciate it, but I don't think I have the energy to handle it tonight."

Darby nods.

"Maggie will stick around the shop, though. She'll have candy for the kids, and I still have two artists dropping in to do the fall and Halloween-themed presets for anyone who donates to the Foundation."

Her blond hair catches the sunlight, making it appear truly golden, matching the smile that stretches across her freckled cheeks. I know her hazel eyes would be bright if I could see them behind her sunglasses. "I'm proud of you for going today," she says, squeezing my arm.

I smile back. "Thanks for forcing me against my will."

She chuckles as we both climb out of her car parked behind the building she and Leo own. I take a left, toward Boardwalk Tattoo. My business sits on the far end, closest to the pier, while Darby's, Honeysuckle Florals, is two doors down from me.

"I'll see you Sunday for dinner."

"Oh, I'm sure you'll find a way to see me before then too, Darby." I grin. "You're basically obsessed with me."

She flips me off. "Careful what you say around my husband. He gets jealous."

"Trust me, I'm well aware."

Darby laughs, strolling through the back door to her flower shop.

Leo's fucking crazy over her, has been since we were kids. It'd only been a number of weeks that they'd known each other before he had me tattooing her nickname across his chest in the garage of my childhood home. Leo wasn't her husband then, of course. They were just two seventeen-year-old kids who met on a whim and fell deliriously in love over the course of a summer before falling apart. Ten years later, they found their way back to each other. Darby moved to Pacific Shores permanently from Kansas—and became my best friend.

It was about this time last year that she found me floating on my back in the ocean, fully clothed on a rainy Monday morning. It wasn't a cry for help, and it wasn't a suicide attempt—I don't think. I hadn't touched the water since the day my brother died, and we were swiftly approaching the third anniversary of it. I wish I could explain to anyone—to myself—what compelled me to walk down to the beach that morning and wade into the waves.

I don't know what came over me, like my head was stuck in a fog I can no longer see.

I don't know why Darby was walking in the rain. She said it's just something she enjoys doing. She happened to find me and pulled me from the water, thinking I was drowning. I begged her not to tell anyone, and she promised she wouldn't, so it's our secret now. But after that, she never really left me alone again. I know it scared her shitless, and I feel bad about it.

But out of all my friends who could attach themselves to my hip in the spirit of my own well-being, Darby is definitely the least annoying, so I can't complain much.

I think we're kindred spirits. I think we hide behind ourselves the same way. Pain becomes numbness, and we have a tendency to become content with feeling nothing, rather than allow ourselves to feel anything unpleasant. I appreciate her for trying to pull me out of that.

Her husband likens her to flowers, but I think she feels like sunshine.

The shop is quiet as I step inside. I have a small office behind the front desk, but I don't spend much time there. My least favorite part of owning a business is actually running the business. Sometimes, I almost wish I hadn't opened my own tattoo parlor and instead continued working in a space owned by someone else, merely managing my clients. I'd prefer to spend my time creating art, not fostering the environment that allows us to create it.

Luckily, my only full-time staff member and piercing artist, Maggie, also helps balance the books. I'm certified in piercing, as well, but I don't enjoy it as much. I'd rather ink.

May through August are our busiest months, with tourism slowly tapering off into the fall, and the winter being very slow. I've got to sit down and set my budget, utilizing the high profits from the summer to ensure I can keep the lights on through the winter, but doing so feels overwhelming, and for some reason, that therapy session exhausted me today.

"I'm back!" I call out to Maggie, who's sitting at the front desk, playing solitaire on the iPad that doubles as the cash register.

She tosses me back a thumbs up as I slide into my office and inhale the remainder of my sandwich. Ignoring my laptop—and the spreadsheet opened on its screen labeled "September," which I know I need to go through—I close it. Instead, I pull my sketchbook from the bottom drawer of my desk and a pencil, letting my hand glide across the page.

I don't think when I draw; I just let the design flow through my veins and out of my fingers. I wish I could say I was visualizing something, and I just had an uncanny ability to bring it to life on paper, but I don't. I'm not envisioning anything. I'm letting my hands work. Spilling out whatever subconscious thoughts and fears are plaguing me.

I don't know how much time passes before Maggie calls out, asking if I'm heading home. The late afternoon sun has fallen behind the building, casting my office in shadow. I look down at my sketchbook, taking in the sight of roaring whitecaps and floating violets across the page.

Chapter Three

Vice

"chemtrails" - Lizzy McAlpine

"Why are you staring at me like that?"

"Hush," my brother murmurs. "She's analyzing."

He stands across the breakfast bar in his kitchen, his girlfriend's daughter next to him as they both study me. Lou tilts her head, strawberry-blond hair falling over a shoulder. Her arms are crossed, and her eyes narrowed. "Yep." She nods before looking to Everett. "She's a tortured poet."

He lights up with laughter, like she's the most endearing thing he's ever witnessed, before planting a kiss to the top of her head. "You're so intuitive, *mi lucecita.*"

"What the fu—" My brother shoots me a warning glare. "Fudge does that mean?"

Lou smiles knowingly, and my brother chuckles again, scratching his beard. "Go upstairs and tell Mama to hurry up, or we're gonna be late."

"She doesn't like it when you rush her."

"That's why I'm sending you, Luz." He smiles, and she huffs, slipping off her barstool and bounding up the stairs.

I simply came downstairs to grab a snack, but instead stumbled upon my brother in the most ridiculous fucking outfit I've ever seen, eating enchiladas—my dad's recipe, I'm sure—with Dahlia's daughter.

"Are those all chicken?" I ask, nodding toward the pan.

To my surprise, he smiles. "Nope. I made two cheese-only. Just in case you decided to eat a real meal tonight."

He turns to the stove, plating the enchiladas and adding a scoop of Mexican rice on the side before setting it down in front of the chair Lou just vacated. I don't eat dinner with Everett and his family all that often. For two reasons: I don't want to feel like I'm imposing on the little life he's built for himself, and I don't want to make anyone feel like they have to go out of their way to accommodate my vegetarian diet.

I don't have the energy to cook for myself most days, so I end up living off snack food, which I'm fine with. But my dad's enchiladas are the ultimate comfort food, and Everett is the only person who can make them almost as well as Dad.

I know my brothers have an event down at the boardwalk tonight, raising money for the Foundation. I'm not attending, obviously. Even on a good day, even for a different reason, it wouldn't be my cup of tea. But when you're the villain in the story, and everyone else is living in their epilogue, it's probably best not to show your face around the memorial events of the horror you helped cause.

The house was quiet when I woke from my afternoon nap, so I figured they'd already left to begin setting up, and I'd have the place to myself for a while.

The front door opens, and my brother and I both peek our heads around the narrow corner that leads from the kitchen to the front entryway, finding our mother stepping through the door. She sets her purse and keys on the table next to it, sliding her large sunglasses off her face, brown eyes—a twin shade to mine and Everett's—lighting up as she looks at us both.

"*I miei bambini!*" she exclaims, reaching me and wrapping me in her arms. "*Siete entrambi qui. Bella ragazza, mi sei mancata.*"

"*Ciao*, Mama," I murmur against her cheek. Both of my parents are on the shorter side, so it's no surprise I match my mother's height at barely five feet, my dad reaching five-seven on a good day. Nobody knows where Everett's obnoxious height and body mass came from. If he wasn't the spitting image of my dad and hadn't come out of the womb just four minutes before me, I'd tell everyone he was adopted.

Mom pulls back from me, and then freezes, I'm assuming to notice my brother's outfit for the first time. I turn with her, taking him in. A jacket I can only describe as a dark blue, sparkly pom-pom, accents his chest and shoulders over a black T-shirt and dark jeans. Though, his belt appears to be...bedazzled? Hand-glued with multicolored rhinestones, and he's wearing a pair of white sneakers that look the same. His nails are also painted a sparkly, electric blue.

"What's going on here?" my mom asks, circling her finger through the air in front of him.

"You look like Tom Sandoval," I snort.

"Who?"

"Is this what the kids are wearing nowadays?" Mom asks. "What's Dahlia dressing up in tonight? Fishnets and a coconut bra?"

"God, I'd love that." My brother laughs. "Speaking of, can Luz hang at your place for a while after the event tonight?"

"Why?" Mom asks.

"Give it like two minutes, and I think that question will be answered for you."

Our mom rolls her eyes, digging through the fridge. "Is this your way of letting me know you're trying to make me more grandbabies?"

"Oh, they're trying their damndest," I mutter. I don't think Everett realizes how loudly his headboard slams against the wall that I sleep on the other side of. Nodding toward my brother, I continue, "So, what is going on tonight that's got you all..." I trail off, unable to find words for the getup.

He rolls his eyes at me before answering, "We're doing a Fall Crawl. We've got it all decked out in Halloween decorations and converted the empty suite between the tattoo shop and Wicked Wildflower into a walk-through haunted house. It's a soft launch for the bakery, where Dahlia will be handing out samples of menu items to get people excited about its opening next year. Darby is selling pumpkins and autumnal flower arrangements, and August's workers have set up drop-ins where customers can get a pre-designed tattoo done during the event."

"Why aren't you guys going to the banquet anymore?" I ask.

"August isn't invited to it. Things haven't been good between him and Alex since Zach passed."

I physically flinch at those words, and my brother pauses, no doubt noticing it too. I break our eye contact, glancing down at my abused nail beds, picking the skin away.

He continues, "They've never allowed him to be involved, and he's never allowed us to support him, so Leo and I went every year, thinking it was better to do something than nothing." I see my mother wipe her eyes from my periphery. "But after last year, we decided we couldn't be complacent in their shitty parenting, regardless of what it's doing for the community. I can't approve of someone treating their son that way, so we decided to do something ourselves."

I don't even allow myself to conceptualize my thoughts on that.

Instead, I ask, "Is he going to be there? At the boardwalk?"

I can't decide which answer I'm hoping for. Part of me hopes he's as miserable as I am, and that he doesn't deserve to be celebrating with pumpkins and haunted houses. Another part of me—the larger part, I think—hates myself for having that thought, and wants to know he's healed.

Everett shakes his head. "No. He's not ready for that yet, but we wanted to do something to show him we support him nonetheless."

"Great." I force a smile. "Well, I hope you have fun. Sounds like a phenomenal time."

I suddenly feel the intense need to leave. I don't want to be around any of them. I don't want them to know I'm not numb. I don't want them to know I still care. That I still can't say either of their names or think about their faces without wanting to scream. I don't want my family to know how affected I am by the simple title of a summer month.

I don't want anyone to know how comforting it is to realize that while I lie in bed tonight, replaying the worst day of my life, he'll be doing the same. I don't want to address that, even to myself. The solidarity I feel in it. The heavy burden only the two of us bear—and how, although we don't speak, I'm somehow relieved to know I'm not feeling it alone.

I toss my dirty plate into the sink, refusing to make eye contact with my brother as I pass him, hugging my mom quickly and heading toward the stairs.

"Elena, what's—" Everett begins, but we both pause as a door shuts at the top of the staircase. I take a step back, waiting for Dahlia and Lou to come down. Lou comes first, smiling as she bounds down the stairs and grabs my mother by the hand. She's wearing a giant pink suit jacket with silver sparkles, a pair of matching boots, and pink streaks clipped into her strawberry-blond hair. "C'mon, Mom said we have to load all the desserts in the car, and then we can eat one."

"Well, it's hard to argue with that offer," my mother chimes.

Dahlia comes down next, wearing sheer black tights, a glittering black leotard, and thigh-high red boots. Over her shoulders, she has on what looks like a...ringleader-type of jacket? Red, white, and gold, with a matching top hat. Her lips are painted a bright cherry.

"Is that the answer to my question?" Mom asks Everett, popping her brow.

He grins, bottom lip between his teeth. "She kills it every time. Every-fucking-time, Wildflower."

She tosses him an eye roll, but the color in her cheeks gives away the effect of his words. My brother steps into the entryway, the space now feeling incredibly crowded with the five of us here, myself the most out of place. Like this is another family entirely, and I'm watching them live their lives within the walls.

Everett helps Dahlia down the last step, kissing her cheek as he pulls her in, whispering something against her ear that sends a fit of giggles bursting from her lips. She slaps his chest, pulling back. "Okay, y'all. Let's get the car loaded up before we're late."

As she shuffles her daughter out the front door, my mom plants a kiss on the top of my head, pulling me in for a hug. "*Te amo, tesora*," she whispers, eyes misting. "Have lunch with Dad and me this weekend, please? We miss you."

I nod, earning a smile before my mom follows Dahlia and her daughter outside.

That's the guilt that burns the most. Watching my parents try to fix me when I know that they can't. They were so happy to have me home, but I think they—my brothers too—were shocked at the person who stepped off that plane. I'm not who I was before I left for New York, not who I was before that day four years ago. I'll never be that girl again, and I hate seeing my family attempt to revive her when I know she's long been dead.

I'm sure a therapist would tell me it's why I'm so avoidant.

My brother makes no move to leave, leaning against the doorway with his arms crossed. "I would've invited you. If there was any chance in my mind that you'd entertain the idea, I would've invited you. Begged you to attend, actually. I want to be with you on this day. Every day. But when you don't let me..." He shakes his head. "It makes it hard to continue trying."

"How do you do it?" I ask. "Move on. Celebrate. Be...happy."

My brother sighs, running a hand through his hair. "His life ended, but mine didn't."

I bite back a gasp, and Everett throws his hands up in surrender.

"I know you think that sounds fucked up, and maybe it is. I wish he was here. I wish that he could meet my kid. I wish he could meet Dahlia." His eyes flick toward the closed front door, like he can see them through it. "I wish he knew Darby came back and that they ended up happy together, or that his brother finally opened up his dream business and kept the house Zach loved. He should be here, and it'll never stop being gut-wrenching that he's not, but the fact is, I can't do a damn thing about it." He shrugs. "I know it sounds cliché, but I think he'd want more for all of us. We know Zach loved attention, and we know he wouldn't want to be forgotten. He'd fully expect us to mourn; he'd be pissed if we didn't." Everett laughs, scratching his beard. "But I also think that if we all spent the rest of our lives walking around like lifeless zombies, he'd be real disappointed. If he's somewhere else watching us right now, the least we can do is entertain him." Everett points at his ridiculous outfit.

A snide laugh escapes me. "So, what you're saying, is he'd be disappointed in me?" I mimic my brother, pointing at myself—the pajamas I still have on at 4:00 p.m., or the stain across my Grand Canyon T-shirt because I honestly can't remember the last time I washed it.

I don't put much thought into what I said, and I know neither Everett nor I are surprised that it was my takeaway from his spiel. I can't bear to listen to people speak of him, so I zone it out. I only allowed myself to absorb the part that made it clear my brother was referring to me when he mentioned lifeless zombies, because we both know that's exactly what I am.

"I didn't say that, Lele." Everett sighs defeatedly, tossing open the door. "You did."

"If you let me borrow your Jeep, I'll go hang out at Mom and Dad's so you can have your sex. I can bring Lou back with me later," I say. "I'm not really keen to hang out here and listen."

My parents will be at the event for a while anyway, so I'll get a few hours to myself. Plus, my dad is the only person who doesn't pressure me to talk about my feelings or be a productive member of society. He'd rot on the couch with me all day watching *Real Housewives* if my mom would let him. That safety is a comfort that's rare to find.

I don't mind being around Lou, either. She doesn't know who I was before I became a ghost, and she doesn't seem to mind the fact that I'm painted in shades of gray now. She's a little spitfire, and I get thorough enjoyment watching her humble my brother. While I'm terrible with children, she's ten, so she's kind of like a mini-adult. At the very least, she can read, so we never run out of things to talk about.

Everett nods. "Home by nine thirty?"

"Sure."

He's halfway through the front door before he pauses at the threshold, turning back around so quickly I don't register what's happening until I'm wrapped in his massive, tattoo-clad arms. "Love you, Lele," he whispers.

"I love you too."

Chapter Four

Violet

"I Look in People's Windows" - Taylor Swift

"I don't know, man. She said she had a headache, and she'd call you to have lunch later in the week."

"I told her I needed her to be here tonight, specifically. I don't give a shit about later in the week."

"She can't control when she gets headaches."

"You know that's bullshit. You know she doesn't want to show because—" Leo doesn't finish his sentence, pausing as I bump my hip on the dining room table, making my presence known. He and Everett whip sideways, looking at me from where they stand in Leo and Darby's kitchen, their arms crossed, both leaning against the island in the center of the space, forcing smiles. "Hey, Auggie. You're early."

"Yeah, sorry. I just thought I'd come straight here from work, and it was unlocked." I awkwardly hitch a thumb over my shoulder, pointing toward the front door.

"Don't apologize," he says, stepping into the dining room and pulling me in for a hug. "Door is always open for you."

"Just be careful, or you might get an eyeful of his ass," Everett mutters under his breath.

I rear back, giving them both what I imagine is a perplexed look.

"I'm going to fuck where I want in the house I own." Leo shrugs. "Doesn't mean you're not welcome anytime, but I won't be held responsible for what you witness if you show up unannounced."

"Noted," I murmur.

"You are such a menace," his wife chimes from behind me, and I turn to find Darby stepping off the bottom stair. "Hi," she whispers to me, wrapping an arm around my waist and kissing my cheek before she continues into the kitchen.

"Am I wrong, Honeysuckle?" Leo asks, watching her pass him and snapping out an arm to pull her back against his chest.

"No." She laughs as he tickles her ribs and kisses the top of her head. "But you could be less...graphic about it."

"Oh," he scoffs. "I'm sorry. Augustus"—he looks at me—"I like to make love to my beautiful wife on the dining room table sometimes, and I won't apologize for it. I mean, how could I not? Look at her."

Darby shoves out of his embrace, smacking his chest as she continues into the kitchen.

"You know what? Nobody answer that. I'll fucking kill you."

Everett chuffs, muttering something about him being insufferable. Leo follows his wife down the hall, and I follow Everett into the living room where their mom, Monica, sits on the couch, braiding Lou's hair. The ten-year-old is on the ground, eyes growing wide as I enter the room.

"Hey, Mama," I say, sinking down beside Monica. "Hey, Lou."

"Hi," she responds quietly. Monica laughs to herself.

Everett is glaring at me, and I don't know why, but I fucking hate being on the other side of that look of his.

I spend ten minutes chatting with Monica about the tattoo shop and how business is going. She politely asks about my parents, and I pretend like I care. We're both full of shit.

The front door opens and closes, two distinct laughs echoing through the house. One booming and loud, one melodic and soft. I assume it's Carlos and Dahlia, who must've pulled up at the same time. Monica and Lou both stand and scurry into the kitchen to greet them, while Everett takes his mother's spot next to me.

"She's not coming because of me, right?" I ask through clenched teeth. I know it's what he and Leo were discussing before I arrived, but I need the confirmation.

Everett settles into the cushions, crossing his arms as he assesses me. "You tell me."

I sigh, shrugging.

"I can't fix it if neither of you will tell me what happened."

"Not asking you to fix it," I say.

He's quiet for a moment, staring at the television—but I know he's not seeing the football game on the screen. Finally, he turns to me. Brown eyes that match his sister's are soft and sad. "I need to fix her."

I nod. "I don't know how to help you with that, though."

"I keep trying to show her that I see her. I see her broken, and I want to put her back together, and she only gets defensive about it. I don't know how to get through to her."

"She gets defensive because she masks her pain," I tell him, all too familiar with the workings of her brain. "When someone can see through that mask, she feels like she's failed. She gets defensive."

"Why does she mask?" Everett asks, his eyes desperate as he looks at me.

"To protect the rest of you, and probably to protect herself, too."

"Protect us from what?"

"Her darkness." I sigh. "You have to make her think she's not failing at hiding her hurt, because she'll feel like she's failing all of you. She'll get defensive, and she'll push you away."

He runs a tired hand down his face. "See? You're the only person who can get through—"

"No, I'm not," I interrupt. "I don't know her anymore. And there is a good chance all that advice I just gave you won't apply here." I look down at my hands, interlacing my fingers and flexing them. "But based on the person I used to know, that's what I can tell you."

Everett looks hurt by that. I know it's confusing to him that I can't explain why I don't know her anymore, but if I've learned anything over the last four years, it's that I've got to protect myself first. I let her destroy me for far too long.

"So"—I clear my throat, attempting to change the subject—"what's the big news?"

Everett lets out a breath, running a hand through his hair. "I have a feeling about it." He smiles softly. "But I think it's best we let them be the ones to spill."

"Maybe I shouldn't have come," I murmur, the thought escaping my lips before my mind has time to put reins on it. "It sounds like a family thing, and she should be here."

"You're our family too," Leo's voice carries from across the room, startling both Everett and me. He's leaning against the door frame that leads to the kitchen, arms crossed at this chest and his blue eyes narrowed. "You should be here."

I throw him a shallow nod, unable to help the fact that I feel out of place. I always feel out of place with them—because whether it's valid, whether or not they understand it, I am the person who destroyed their sister beyond repair. She may have broken me, too, but the blame she places on my shoulders is still mine to carry. I can't look my two childhood best friends in the eyes, knowing that if they understood the entirety of our story, they'd never speak to me again.

Leo smiles, and I can tell it's genuine. I can see the flash of disappointment in his eyes that his sister didn't come tonight, but the smile on his face tells me that he'll allow nothing to take away the excitement of whatever it is he's gathered us to share tonight.

Clapping his hands together, he calls the two of us into the dining room where the rest of the family is already dishing up their plates. We don't talk about the empty seats at the table, or the missing souls in the room.

I feel empty, and I wonder if my soul is missing too.

Chapter Five

Vice

"this is me trying" - Taylor Swift

"Missed you at dinner on Sunday," my brother says as I step into the kitchen, condescension dripping from his voice, and passive aggression apparent on his face.

"My PMDD was acting up."

"Thought you had a migraine."

I pause, staring into the fridge before snatching a jar of pickles from the door. I slam it shut and turn to face Leo. "Migraines are a symptom of PMDD, asshole."

Truth be told, I was through the worst of the week by Sunday evening. On Thursday, I was so anxious I wanted to set the world on fire. Friday, it was myself I wanted to set on fire. Saturday is when the migraine set in, and after twenty-four hours of wishing I could dissolve into nonexistence, I sort of began feeling myself again on Sunday.

Except, what does feeling myself even mean at this point? I have no idea who I am.

Those thoughts of dread aren't linked directly to my PMDD, I don't think. But they are impossible to explain to the people around me, so telling Everett I had a migraine when we reached Sunday afternoon felt like the easiest explanation.

"Fuck. I know. I'm sorry. That was insensitive." Leo sighs, his blue eyes warring between guilt and disappointment as he looks at me. "We had news to share with you."

"I know. It's okay." Sometimes I think I'm lying to myself too.

After popping the lid on the jar, I fish out a pickle. Both of my brothers eye me suspiciously from the other side of the kitchen as I take a bite. Bitter juice slams into my tongue, and my entire body clams up before I'm leaning over the sink and spitting it down the drain. "Ah fuck." I spit again, desperate to get the taste out of my mouth. "These are dill."

I hate dill pickles. They're evil incarnate.

Leo snorts, holding out his hand. I set the pickle in his palm, and he immediately takes a bite, moaning. "Goddamn, I miss these."

"All that money and you can't afford pickles?"

"My wife doesn't like the smell," he deadpans.

"Marriage woes," I hum, sitting up on the counter and letting my feet dangle off the edge. "So, what's this news you have to share with me?"

Leo opens his mouth, but Everett speaks before he can. "Actually, Lele, I have something I'd like to talk to you about first."

Fuck. Here we go.

You're too messy.

You're not pulling your weight.

You've overstayed your welcome.

We don't want you around.

All things I expect him to say.

I swallow. "Yeah?"

"You know the bakery is set to open in a few months, and Dahlia needs some help in the cafe. She's great, you know? At literally everything." He smiles to himself. "But believe it or not, she's never worked an espresso machine before. She wants to be known as much for her coffee as for her baked goods, and since you worked at the coffeehouse years ago, I thought maybe you'd be able to help out?"

He looks nervous, and I wonder if that's how everyone who talks to me feels when they ask me for a favor. Like they're walking on eggshells. Ironic, considering it's also how I feel about myself.

"She needs help curating the menu, setting up the coffee bar, and training new staff. We'd put you on payroll, of course." He gulps, glancing at Leo before his eyes find mine again. "Plus, we... We think you need to get out of the house. You need something to wake up for in the mornings. Need something to—"

"I'm writing," I snap back defensively.

"Where's the book, Lena?" Leo asks. Sighing, he looks away from me, blinking hard. In a calmer tone, he continues, "Maybe having something else to do will...I don't know? Help the creativity flow for you? It's clear you're stuck, and you can't live off those dwindling royalties forever."

My nostrils flare as I attempt deep breaths to calm myself down.

I don't even understand why I get like this. I know it's apparent to everyone around me that I'm a dysfunctional mess. I'm a pathetic, twenty-nine-year-old woman with no job, no money, no friends, and no future. I rarely leave the house, and I never do my laundry. I can't remember the last time I ate a meal with all the major food groups included.

Still, I attempt to live in delusional ignorance, where the elephant that follows me into every room is unseen by those around me. They can't know I'm struggling if I pretend I'm not, and when they call me out on it, when they address the two-ton animal sitting on my chest, I get defensive. I don't want to be helped. I don't want them to care. I want them to pretend it doesn't exist and let me rot. In exchange, I pretend I'm not falling apart when I'm around them.

"I'm fine," I mutter.

I'm not. Yeah, I'm still making minuscule monthly royalties from my old works, but three years of no new publications, getting dropped by my agent, and not marketing myself in any capacity, means I'm basically living on a wing and a prayer that someone stumbles upon my titles at the bookstore, or they're recommended *that book I read a few years ago* by a friend.

So, financially, I'm not doing well. But I make enough to

cover my basic needs: food and the minimum on my maxed-out credit card.

"It's like you're not even trying." I think Everett said that, but I'm staring down at my hands braced against the counter.

"What's left to try for?" I murmur, admitting a truth that I've long kept bottled inside.

I don't want to be better, because I don't think better exists for me, and I don't want to address it with my family because I can't fucking stand the look on their faces when they realize what a failure I've become.

I don't raise my head, not until I see a flicker of movement in my periphery. Toned arms, and a wide-chest stand in front of me, and I glance up to find my brother's blue eyes bright with unshed tears. I hear him reach into his pocket, I know his arm is extended out toward me, but I'm too afraid to look away from his face.

The smile he gives me is forced and heartbroken. Finally, I look down at the small black-and-white image in his hand.

"Her."

I don't realize I'm crying until the heat of my tears runs down my face. My hand trembles as I take the sonogram from him, studying the outline of a head, a small body, and two tiny feet.

"Her?" I ask, my voice breaking on the word.

That heartbroken smile turns wide and real as I look back up at him.

Leo nods. "My daughter."

It's unadulterated happiness that reflects on my brother's face. The kind of expression that says all his dreams are coming true right before his eyes. The contented smile Everett gives us both is full of hope and pure joy, but as I look back down at the sonogram—at the niece I'll soon have—all I feel is broken.

Chapter Six

Violet

Three Months Later

"Fuck it I love you" - Lana Del Rey

"Why can't he do our piercings?" the young woman asks from the front desk, pointing at me.

I chuckle under my breath but pretend I didn't hear them as I continue sanitizing the bench where I just finished a six-hour shin piece.

It's nearly nine o'clock, and I'm ready to go home. I opened at ten this morning, and I don't foresee myself being able to go home anytime soon. I don't set hard-and-fast business hours for the shop. I won't keep the lights on when no one is around, but I don't want to close up when the boardwalk is busy, and there is a chance of walk-ins.

I planned on leaving after my three o'clock appointment, but my drop-in artist, Lilly, just left, and the boardwalk is much busier than usual for this time of year.

Three women who can't be over the age of twenty-one stand at the desk, asking about belly-button piercings. Luckily, Maggie stuck around this afternoon to help out when I realized how many walk-ins we were getting.

"You have to be careful with that one, anyway. He's a heartbreaker," she says.

The woman raises a brow, giving me a once-over and smiling like she doesn't mind what she sees. "What makes you say that?"

"Oh, you know. Broody and noncommittal." Maggie tosses her head back, winking at me. "He's one of those shy, broken, emo boys."

I scoff, rolling my eyes.

"Bet I could fix him," the woman purrs.

That makes me laugh out loud. "I'll be in my office if you need me."

I toss my cleaning supplies in the cupboard behind the front desk before turning toward the hallway that leads to the back. The group of girls are beet red as I pass them, offering a smile. They definitely didn't intend for me to hear that conversation.

I fall into my desk chair, shutting the door with my foot. I won't leave until Maggie does—I don't want to leave her alone this late at night, so I pass the time with an audiobook while I budget for the upcoming year.

January is the worst month for me. Winter is always hard, but people at least vacation during the holidays, and we maintain some business while schools are on break and people are off work. When the new year comes along, seasonal depression hits, everyone goes back to work, and nobody wants to spend a dime following the holidays. It's well known that many small businesses struggle at the start of a new year, but as I compare numbers, I realize just how much my fucking mortgage is taking a toll on my finances.

I don't need four bedrooms, a den, or a wraparound porch. I don't need all this space I can't afford, but after considering selling last year, I couldn't go through with it. I can't let go of one of the only happy memories of my brother I have left.

I've thought about getting a roommate, but the idea of living with a stranger wigs me out, and living with someone I do know wigs me out even more. I considered asking Leo to move in last year when he was still staying in the studio above Heathen's. Though, it doesn't matter now that he's a married homeowner with a baby girl on the way.

I smile at the thought. That pure, unfiltered happiness on

both their faces when they told us. Darby had a rough time getting pregnant, and I know she was close to giving up hope entirely, so I couldn't be happier for the two of them.

It really goes to show how incredibly different lifestyles can look for those of us in our late-twenties. Some are married and have families. Fuck, even Everett has a kid at home, when only a year ago, he was the biggest bachelor I knew. Then, there are those like me: hardly able to pay our bills, emotionally unavailable, estranged from their parents, and likely to die alone.

The morbid thought is broken up by the sound of Maggie knocking on my door. "I've got my station all cleaned up. Register is closed too. You cool if I head out?"

I stretch, lifting out of my chair. "Yeah, go for it. I'm going to lock up, and then I'll be out of here too."

"We could just leave together, if you want?"

I know there are underlying connotations to that question, and like every time she's propositioned me before, I maintain a professional boundary.

"Nah, you're good. You can head out."

She swallows hard, and I know that disappointed her, but I've made it clear that I'm not interested in her that way. Maggie's sweet. She's cute too, with her pixie cut and her pin-up look, but I'm not about to fuck my only full-time employee.

"Have a good night," she mumbles before shutting my door behind her.

I wait long enough to know she's gone before I leave my office and head toward the front of the shop. I unplug the neon lights strung around the space, tie off the trash, and set the bags by the back door so I can toss them on my way out. Just as I'm finishing up, I hear the bells on the door chime.

Fuck. I should've realized Maggie didn't lock up the front before she left.

"We're actually closed!" I call out.

I need the business, but I'm not staying here all night for some random, drunk asshole.

The response I get back is a laugh, loud and raspy.

My blood runs cold at the sound of it, my flesh turning to ice as it rakes across my skin. That laugh is implanted in my bones and stamped upon my soul; my entire body freezes as it echoes through my hollow chest.

I'm standing at the back door, staring at my feet because I'm fucking petrified to turn around. There is zero explanation for her being in my shop at eleven on a Saturday night, laughing. I'm not prepared to address this, so much as look at her.

I don't fucking want to.

What's worse is that the sound of her is accompanied by another. A lower, deeper, male voice. An intense sense of déjà vu washes over me because this isn't the first time I've hidden behind a wall, listening to her laugh with another man, and allowing her to wreak havoc on me. In fact, I've been in this position so many goddamn times I lost count.

Sucking in a swift breath, I spin on my heel and head toward the front of my store. My business. What I built—alone, without her. She fucking left me. She does not get to show up whenever the fuck she feels like tormenting me.

"You cannot be here..." My words die on my tongue as I turn the corner and find her standing in front of me. It's been months since I last saw her face, and even then she rendered me speechless all the same.

She wore a black dress to her brother's wedding. The kind that clung to every curve like it was painted on. Her face was sad and withdrawn, she was thin and frail, but like every other time I'd looked at her throughout the duration of my life, what stood before me was the most beautiful woman I'd ever seen.

This moment is no different.

Except, rather than a black dress that molds to her body like it was made for her, she's wearing cut-off shorts, a black Glass Animals tee, and a worn pair of Vans. Her hair is thrown into a knot atop her head, with wild, dark strands framing her like a lion's mane. The tail of the serpent I tattooed around her thigh on her twenty-third birthday peeks from beneath the hem of her shorts. The septum piercing I gave her when she was nineteen catches the overhead lights, glinting. If she turned her head right now, I'd catch a glimpse of the constellation on her neck—my constellation.

She's covered in me, and yet she's spent years pretending I don't exist.

I want to fucking hate her for it.

She's still the most beautiful woman I've ever seen—and I want to hate her for that too.

Time seems to suspend itself the moment her eyes meet mine, like the room warps around me at lightning speed, and completely freezes at the exact same time. I suddenly can't make sense of the floor or the ceiling, of where I am or what I'm doing.

It's all her. It all revolves around her.

I don't know how to make it stop—especially now, because I can see the panic in her eyes. That's what has my feet stuck to the ground and words lodged in my throat. Her eyes are moving too quickly over my face, a type of desperation I've seen in her most fearful moments.

Everything settles then. I clock the trembling of her bottom lip and the slight tremor in her hands. There is a lazy smile on her face as she stares me down, but I see the unspoken expression there, because I know her better than anyone else on this fucking planet.

She's terrified.

I glance at the guy next to her. He's tall, lean, and covered in tattoos. Dark eyes, and what appears to be long, dark hair beneath his green beanie. I almost laugh. Guess she has a fucking type, then. He snakes a possessive arm around her waist, tugging her against him, and I don't miss the way she flinches at the contact.

"Hey, man. Sorry, we thought you were open."

He shuffles her sideways, and Elena opens her mouth like she wants to say something, but no sound escapes.

"Elena," I say roughly, her name like acid on my tongue.

There is no way she's been dating this guy for an extended period of time. Her brothers would've mentioned that, and based on the information they have shared, she hardly leaves the house.

It was only three months ago that Everett begged me for advice on how to get through to her. From what I heard, he'd asked Elena to help with Dahlia's bakery and was turned down. After that, the updates from her family dwindled, almost as if nobody wanted me to know what was going on with her, but I'm fairly certain someone would've mentioned her having a boyfriend.

Both Elena and the man turn back to me, fear on her face and confusion on his. She tucks a stray strand behind her ear, eyes fluttering to the ground. "Yeah, hey," she murmurs.

"You know him?" her date asks, glancing down at her.

"Well, I told you my brother owns the boardwalk, right? Augustus is a friend of his."

Augustus.

A friend of her brother's. As if I hadn't known her first. Loved her first. Given her every fiber of my fucking being until there was nothing left of me at all.

"I didn't realize you were closed," she continues. "Elliot was just telling me how much he liked my arm piece, and I explained that I had it done here. Thought we'd pop in."

She's lying. Why the fuck is she lying? I painted her in violets in my parents' garage, long before I owned this place.

She swallows, that lip trembling again, as Elliot—the fucking asshole—roughly spins her toward the door.

"It was good seeing you. Sorry to bother," she offers quietly as Elliot pushes the door open.

I don't know who the woman standing in front of me right now is, but I know it's not the same one I spent my entire childhood loving. Elena would take one look at a man touching her without consent and snap his wrist in half. She'd never flinch beneath the weight of someone else's presence, or lower her voice to a timid whisper as if she's afraid of waking some sleeping beast.

I don't know what happened, but she's scared, and there is no fucking way I'm letting her walk out that door right now.

"Actually, while I have you," I cut in, sighing in relief when they both stop at the threshold. "I've got some cash I owe Leo in my office and we've been working opposite schedules lately, so I'm not sure when I'll see him next. Would you mind passing it along for me?"

I don't know this Elliot guy, but the grip he has on Elena's shoulder sure makes it easy to assume he's a piece of shit. It's enough that he's taken the outspoken, fierce, spitfire of a woman I used to know and turned her into some kind of trembling doe, so I don't think it's a stretch to assume he's not above stealing. If anything is going to make him pause and give me thirty seconds alone with Elena, it's the potential to get some money in his pocket.

"Oh," Elena breathes, her eyes closed with relief, tension dropping from her shoulders. "Yeah, sure. I can do that."

"It's in my office if you want to come grab it." I nod my head toward the back.

Elliot stiffens, like he's not willing to let her go, and I casually toss my hand in my pocket, gripping my phone, ready to call the police. Thankfully, he steps back inside the building and lets her slip out from under his arm.

"Be right back." She smiles at him, offering a seductive flutter of her lashes like she'll be rewarding him for the act of grace later.

My stomach hurts at the sight of it.

I let her pass me, putting myself between her and Elliot before following her into my office. I leave the door open, not wanting to raise suspicion. Elena walks to the farthest corner of the room behind my desk, and I step in close, just enough for her to hear me whisper, "Did he hurt you?"

"No." She shakes her head. "I don't think so."

"What do you mean you don't think so?" It's my body trembling now, eyes desperately raking over her, searching for any sign of harm. "How long have you been dating him?"

"I just met him tonight."

"Tonight?" I rub my face, far too tired to be dealing with this right now. "What the fuck is going on, Elena?"

Her eyes go wide, and we both freeze, realizing I raised my voice. We're silent for a moment, listening for footsteps, but thankfully all remains quiet.

"I met him on a dating app," she hisses through clenched teeth, grabbing my arm and tugging me closer as she lowers her voice. "Tonight was our first date, and he got...aggressive."

"Aggressive how?" I ask, far too focused on the way her skin feels against mine.

It's been over four years, down to the week, in fact, since I've last felt her touch. I abhor the way my body reacts to it. Like something dormant awakening again.

"We went on the Ferris Wheel and he..." She shivers. "Touched me. In a way I was not totally cool with."

Red clouds my vision, and as if she can sense it, she tightens her grip on my wrist, bringing me back to her.

"When I asked him to stop, he..." She sighs. "He started yelling at me. He called me a tease for the shorts I was wearing and said I should've known what I was getting into when I signed up for the app."

I could grind my molars into fucking dust right now.

"First of all, that's not true. You don't owe a goddamn man anything. Ever," I growl. "Secondly, I know that you know that. Why didn't you tell him you'd slit his throat?"

She loves threatening to slice a man's neck open.

Her face falls, gaze dropping to the ground. Almost as if she's disappointed in herself. I want to touch her, pull her against my chest and cradle her head like I've always done when comforting her.

But I don't.

"I let him pick me up in front of the house." She lifts her head, and I swear I can see the faintest veil of tears in her gaze. "He knows where I live"—her voice breaks in a near silent whisper—"where Lou lives."

Fuck.

This guy really shook her up. She's afraid of him following her home. I don't know why her concern for Dahlia's daughter humanizes her in my eyes. She's always been human. Empathetic to a flaw...almost. I spent four years turning her into a heartless succubus inside my head.

"Stay in my office and lock the door behind me."

Her brows furrow as I step back toward the door. She shoots out, grabbing my arm before I can reach it. "What? No–"

I pull myself from her hold, unable to fathom the heat of her touch. "For once in your goddamn life, just listen to me, Elena. Lock the fucking door."

I leave my office, shutting the door behind me, letting out a breath when I hear the lock click into place. My steps echo down the hallway. Elliot mutters, "Took you long enough," before he halts, cocking his head with a furrowed brow when he sees I've returned without her.

He stands by the front door, arms crossed at his chest. I quickly walk behind the front counter, putting it between us. He frowns beneath his porn-stache. "Where's Elena?"

"She'll be going home with me tonight."

He scoffs. "The fuck did you just say to me?"

"You need to leave." He doesn't move. I lean against the counter like I'm bored. "There's a panic button beneath this desk. I've already pressed it. Police will be here in two minutes. You can walk out that front door right now, and I'll conveniently forget what you look like by the time they get here," I say, feigning calm, though I know damn well I don't have a panic button. "Or you can stay, and you can speak to them about touching your date without her consent tonight."

He rears back, genuinely shocked. "What the fuck are you talking about? She's a fucking liar, dude. I didn't do a goddamn thing!"

He steps toward me, which I think is intended to be menacing, but it only makes me laugh. "My best guess is that you're so used to copping a feel without permission that making women uncomfortable is second nature. You don't even realize what you're doing." I shake my head, chuckling again. He stiffens, unsure how to react to my lack of fear. "I know it may be a struggle to get this through your dull fucking head—past that fragile ego and sense of entitlement—but she's not interested." I nod toward the door. "Now get the fuck out."

He leans around me, eyes scanning for Elena, before shaking his head and turning away. "That bitch isn't worth this shit, anyway."

My hands curl into fists at my side, wanting to pummel him for those words. It takes all my composure to keep my feet planted on the ground. I watch him walk to the door, waiting until he's pressing against the handle before I call out, "Elliot."

He glances back, dark eyes narrowed to slits.

"Elena doesn't live alone. She lives with her six-foot-four, three-times-your-size brother, and the only thing he hates more than creeps fucking around his sister is creeps fucking around his wife and kid." He rolls his eyes at me. "Her other brother owns this boardwalk and would happily trespass your ass for the rest of time if he knew the way you scared her tonight. Do not ever contact Elena again."

He smiles at me. "What? You're not going to threaten me yourself?"

"It's not my place to make threats for her," I respond. "But if it were, I wouldn't bother. I'd just hunt you down and split your skull open for calling her a bitch like that."

He looks me up and down, a smirk accenting his lips. "Whatever. Good luck to you, man." He shoves open the door open and strides out.

I need it, honestly.

I follow, locking the door behind him, shutting off the lights, and stumbling through the dark back to my office. I knock on the door lightly. "It's me. He's gone."

Only a second later, the knob clicks, and she's swinging it open, revealing the endless brown eyes I spent my whole life lost inside. They're bloodshot and hooded, a faraway look on her face. "He left?"

"Yep." I nod. "Do you need me to drive you home?"

Her gaze drops. "No, it's fine. I'll order a ride."

"Sorry, let me rephrase that," I say. "You're going to let me take you home. Do you have all your things?"

She lifts her head, brows pinched, eyes blazing. Of course, she has no problem getting a fucking attitude with me. "Don't tell me what to do."

I swear to God, this woman.

She ghosts me after the worst tragedy of my fucking life, breaks my heart and destroys my soul, disappears for literal years, and then shows up to my business on a Saturday night with another guy, expecting me to rescue her from her creepy fucking date?

"You're not in a position to argue with me right now," I snap. "And I won't have your brothers on my ass for abandoning you late at night after whatever disaster that just was."

She scoffs, rolling her eyes as her arms cross at her chest. "That's why you're insisting? Because you're scared of my brothers?"

"Yes," I lie. "And I'm not scared of them. I'm easily annoyed by them."

"Whatever." She slings her purse over her shoulder, hips swaying as she disappears into the hallway. *Goddamn hips.* It's infuriating that I can still remember how they feel around my face.

"You're welcome," I mutter under my breath, flicking off the light.

She stops in the hallway, turning around. The building is dark now, only the faint glow of the pier filtering through the windows. Her face is a wall of stone, unwilling to let me see behind the mask she's wearing. If only she hadn't spent years teaching me how to read her eyes. There's emotion there, emotion she's working really hard to hide.

"Thank you," she says flatly. "Sorry I'm not showcasing my gratitude in a more appropriate way for you. I'm a little fucking embarrassed, if you couldn't tell. Kind of wishing I was literally anywhere else."

At least she's honest.

My instinct is to comfort her, reach out and touch her, tell her it's okay, and I'm glad she found me. That part is true. Seeing her right now is fucking torture, and this isn't anywhere near the kind of reunion I imagined for us, but I'm goddamn grateful she walked through those doors tonight. That Maggie hadn't locked them when she left.

I don't want to think about the lengths Elena might've gone to keep that man from bringing her back home where her family is sleeping.

But I've been living in self-preservation mode since the moment I woke to an empty bed four years ago. Having her stand in front of me right now is the epitome of the kind of destruction I've been trying to avoid in my life.

My brain shouts *Danger! Run while you can!*

Meanwhile my heart screams *Touch! Feel! Home!*

I need to get away from her.

"I get it" is all I say.

She nods, spinning around and heading toward the back door. I follow, locking up behind us and wordlessly climbing into the driver's side of my Bronco. Elena hoists herself in, slamming the door.

I used to think the way she did that was adorable. How such ferocity could fit inside the tiniest of people. The way she'd glare at the height of my truck like it personally wronged her, and the huff she'd make—that she still makes, apparently—when she throws herself inside.

She wobbles slightly, letting out a whoosh as she slumps against the seat. Her head droops, and she rubs her eyes before reaching for the seatbelt.

"Are you drunk?" I ask, thinking back to her bloodshot eyes.

She only shrugs.

I turn the ignition, engine roaring to life before I back out of my parking spot behind the boardwalk and take a right on Main.

Elena groans, rubbing her temple beside me. "Don't turn so aggressively. I'm nauseous as fuck."

"Elena, did you drink?" I ask, taking my eyes off the road to look at her briefly.

"A little."

"It doesn't seem like a little. Is it possible he put something in your drink? If so we need to go to the hosp—"

"No, no," she groans, swatting her hand in my direction. "I only had two cocktails at the restaurant, and I didn't leave the table at any point. There is no way he could've spiked them."

Unless she's been sober the past four years, she's definitely had more than two drinks. The Elena I knew could toss them back with the best of them and didn't often get sick until her fourth shot, at least.

"Did you have anything to drink other than the two cocktails at dinner?"

She winces when I hit a pothole. "I had a little something to calm my nerves before I left the house." She huffs a laugh. "Meeting strangers on the internet is no joke, clearly."

Christ.

"You were drinking at home before your date...by yourself?" I attempt to keep the judgment out of my tone, but her muttered "go fuck yourself" says I failed.

The remainder of the ride is silent. Thankfully, it only takes a few minutes before I'm pulling next to the curb out front of Everett and Dahlia's townhouse. We sit uncomfortably for a moment. Elena simply stares at her hands and makes no move to get out.

"Do you have your keys?"

"Nope." She drums her fingers against her thigh. "Just realized that I forgot them, and I'm waiting until I find the courage to call my brother."

I sigh. "C'mon. I have a spare. I'll let you in."

We climb out of the Bronco, walking quietly up to the door, and as I slip my key into the lock, I realize that Elena's about to walk away from me, and I have no clue when I'll see her again. I have a rare moment of honest vulnerability here, and for once in my goddamn life, I might have the upper hand.

Maybe it makes me an asshole, but I can't stop myself from asking, "Why did you seek me out tonight, Elena? Why'd you come find me? You could've called your brothers, or your parents, or the police. Why me?"

I glance behind me. She's chewing on her lip, rocking back and forth on her heels. "I wanted a tattoo," she lies.

"You know I wouldn't have given you one."

I don't ink drunk people, but more than that, I won't ever touch her skin again.

"Hmm. Funny." She brushes past me, planting her hand on the door, lifting her head to give me big brown eyes, fluttering lashes, and that innocent smile that used to—nope, still does—make me rock fucking hard. "You used to love painting my skin."

I close my eyes, breathing through my nose and willing my body to calm the fuck down.

Elena presses on the door, not realizing I haven't unlocked it yet. Her head snaps up, and it's fury in those eyes now. I turn to her, blocking the entrance.

"You don't get to fucking do that. You don't get to show up, cause chaos, and then walk away with a smirk on your face and a comment like that." I cross my arms, leaning against the door with my shoulder. "You never sought me out before tonight."

"You've never sought me out either," she whispers.

Yes, I did. And I found you beneath the arm of another man.

"I'm not the one who left."

Her eyes flash with something like regret, but I don't have it in me to believe her.

I step away from the door, deciding I won't get the answers that I need. I flick the lock, pulling my key out and slipping it into my pocket.

Elena grasps the handle, murmuring, "I was desperate. You seemed like the best option to get out of the situation. That was all."

Well, that's a searing knife through the center of my fucking soul.

"Figures." I laugh roughly, backing away from her. "That's all I've ever been to you, right? An option. A safety net. A reliable doormat to wipe your fucking feet on." I turn, walking back toward my truck, mind racing and heart pounding, but I only make it to the end of the driveway before I spin back to her, raking my hands through my hair. "You don't get to do this to me anymore, Elena!"

I'm shouting now, but fuck it.

"It destroyed me, you know?" My voice cracks. She doesn't even look at me. She's still facing the door, head down, but she makes no move to step inside. "Losing him broke me. But you? You fucking destroyed me." I take a step toward her, my body begging to close the gap between us and take back everything I've already said, and all that I'm about to. "And I don't want any part of whatever you've—"

The front door swings open, and Elena stumbles back, gasping. Everett's hulking figure fills the frame. He's wearing nothing but a pair of black sweats, his hair sleep-mussed as he runs a hand through it.

"What the fuck is going on?" he hisses.

He takes one look at his sister, and I know she can see the disappointment morph his features just as clearly as I can. His eyes then lift to mine, and it's anger I see there. I wonder how much he heard, knowing he wouldn't be able to understand it.

"She got drunk at the boardwalk and wandered into my shop. I gave her a ride home."

I don't give either of them a chance to say anything else as I walk to my truck. I don't look back at the house as I start it up and drive away.

The smell of fresh bread and a hint of sweetness assault my senses as I push open the front door to Dahlia and Everett's townhouse the next morning.

It's honestly the last place I want to be, but the text I woke to from Everett that read: *My house. Now* left little room for argument.

Their kitchen is directly off the entryway, so I walk right into it, finding Everett, Leo, Dahlia, and Everett's friend Ryan standing around the island as Dahlia slides a tray of steaming croissants across the counter.

Slipping off her oven mitt, she says, "I'm taking Lou to your mom's this morning, and then we're meeting Darby at Honeysuckle and getting brunch after."

She lifts to her toes, kissing Everett's cheek before stepping away. He doesn't let her get far before he grabs her wrist and tugs her back into him, smashing his mouth against hers. She smiles, planting a hand on his chest and letting out a small whimper as she pulls away.

"Love you, Wildflower." He gives her a dopey smile, the stern expression he flashed me when I walked in immediately wiped away.

"Love you," Dahlia drawls. She calls for her daughter from the bottom of the staircase, and the strawberry-blond eleven-year-old appears a moment later.

Everett sees the girls off, cheerful and lovesick, before slamming the front door shut and turning to me, fury on his face. Pointing to Ryan in the corner of the kitchen, he growls, "Tell him everything."

Ryan is the County Sheriff, and one of Everett's best friends. Normally, I don't think this kind of complaint would go through the sheriff's office, but knowing Elena, she'd be unwilling and uncooperative when it comes to the authorities. Which tells me we may be speaking off the record right now.

"Where is she?" I ask.

"Still asleep," Leo says.

I've got to get the fuck out of here before she comes downstairs. When I lift my head, my gaze clashes with Everett's across the kitchen, and he nods as if I spoke those words aloud.

I give them the spiel about Elena showing up last night with Elliot. Ryan asked for a physical description and what he was wearing. They asked me to recount my conversation with Elliot and what Elena had told me about him touching her, being aggressive, and her fear of him following her home had she tried to leave.

I reach the point where we made it back to Everett's house when Ryan asks, "And how much did she say she had to drink?"

"What the hell does that have to do with anything?" Leo snaps.

Ryan shakes his head. "Not like that, man. Just helps me get an understanding of what her headspace was like, that's all. Plus"—he nods at me— "you mentioned she seemed fairly intoxicated but claimed to only have had two cocktails with dinner?"

I almost tell them what she said about drinking alone before the date, but I stop short, snapping my mouth closed.

"She said she was sure she never left her drinks unattended with him" is all I say instead.

Everett tilts his head at me. "No. What else were you going to say?"

Fuck.

"I don't think it's my place."

I think Elena would kick my ass if I told her brothers what she said to me in confidence while she was under the influence. But I think she'd go ballistic if I shared that secret in front of Ryan, too, someone she hardly knows.

Leo must read my face when my eyes flitter to the Sheriff, because he says, "Ryan, can we talk to August alone for a second?"

"Yeah." He nods. "I've actually gotta go. My shift starts in half an hour." Walking over to the sink and dumping his coffee mug, he continues, "Look, there isn't a whole lot we can do. I've got a description and his name recorded. If Elena is willing to share his dating profile with me, I can take that down too. We can keep the information to aid if someone else comes forward with a similar report, or if we can catch him in some sort of act." He looks at Leo.

"And you can trespass him from the boardwalk. He'll be fined if he's caught down there again."

"Already done," Leo says.

Ryan nods again, clapping Everett on the shoulder and thanking me once more before he leaves. I'm left being stared down by my two hulking best friends, knowing Everett must've heard every ounce of vitriol I spewed at his sister last night—without any of the context.

Because we never had the chance to tell them—tell anyone—all that had happened in the months before my brother died.

"Listen..." I run a hand down my face. "About what I said to her last night..."

Everett shakes his head. "That's a conversation for later. A conversation you need to have with her first."

I nod, leaning back against the counter and bracing my body weight on my forearms. "She just...seemed like a shell last night," I admit. "She was cowering under that guy. Shaking, and timid and terrified. You both know that's not like her."

Leo scratches the back of his neck, looking sad. "I think she lost her voice."

"What do you mean?" Everett asks.

"She can't write. She can't talk about her feelings to anyone. I'm not surprised she's forgotten how to stand up for herself too."

We're all quiet after that.

I feel out of place. This isn't my problem to solve or my concern to have. Elena cut clear ties with me years ago, and despite last night's minor hiccup, we're not speaking. It's not my business to be involved with her well-being...or lack thereof.

Yet I can't stop myself from asking, "Everett, do you keep alcohol in the house?"

His brows furrow, mouth tilting downward. "Some. Why?"

Fuck. I sigh. "I think she'd really fucking hate me for telling you guys this. I'm positive she didn't intend to say it to me last night."

"If her safety or health is at risk, you need to speak the fuck up, August," Leo says.

"She seemed a lot more intoxicated than two cocktails would have suggested, especially with her tolerance. I came to the same conclusion last night that Ryan did this morning. I thought he might've put something in one of her drinks, so I asked about it." I run a hand through my hair. "She said she'd been drinking here at the house before the guy picked her up. She claimed it was to calm her nerves, but I don't know, man."

Leo leans his elbows on the kitchen counter, head falling into his hands.

Everett stares at his feet, brows drawn, chest heaving. After a moment of silence, he opens the cupboards above the fridge, revealing a few bottles of liquor. Two fifths of vodka, one of which is less than half-full, and a bottle of whiskey that looks mostly untouched.

"They're all pretty full," he says. "We really only drink at home on holidays, but...I don't remember buying this vodka. I... I don't think this is mine."

I wish I hadn't been looking at Leo when Everett said the words, because the devastation that engulfs his face is gut-wrenching. It's like watching someone give up hope in real time. It makes my stomach hurt and my soul ache. As much as I want to hate her for all she's put me through, all she's putting her family through, I can't help but feel like this is my fault.

I'm the catalyst that put all of us here. The one who couldn't stop lusting after his brother's girlfriend, the one who insisted on keeping secrets, the one who walked away from that beach in stormy weather, leaving my only sibling to the raging waves.

My chest constricts, and suddenly it's hard to breathe. Lungs seizing, throat closing, I mutter the words, "I need to go" before stumbling out of my best friend's house, offering no other explanation.

My vision tunnels as I climb into my truck, and I hardly make it home before that darkness swallows me completely.

Chapter Seven

Vice

"making the bed" - Olivia Rodrigo

Well, fuck.

I stare at the bottles sprawled across the counter in front of me. The liquor I've been hoarding for months, thinking nobody would notice.

It's not like I drink all the time. Just whenever a spiral takes me down a particularly dark path. Or before I meet up with a stranger from the internet because I'm craving human connection—and that's usually paired with guilt-drinking, since my family doesn't know about my online hook-ups. They think I joined a writer's group that I meet with at the library once a week.

The lying makes me sick to my stomach, so I take a shot or two to dull the nausea.

So, I don't drink all the time, only when I really need to, which might be damn near every day. But it's not like I'm getting shit-faced. If I were that bad, it wouldn't have taken so long for anyone to notice...right?

The look on my brothers' faces tells me they won't believe my excuses.

"How long, Lena?" Leo asks.

"The drinking or the fucking strangers?"

My twin tilts his head back, groaning.

Honestly, I don't know why I fell back into these habits.

In New York, it was so easy. I met a few fellow writers through recommendations from my agent, and when I went out drinking with them six days a week, I found it incredibly easy to forget the way my life crashed down around me, what a terrible person I am, and how achingly lonely I was. I missed every deadline, I lost all of my deals, and my savings plummeted. I'm fairly certain I spent an entire year without being sober for a single moment.

Once I hit that rock bottom, I figured it best to just stay there. It made the most sense—it felt like what I deserved. I lived off credit cards and moved from my cute Washington Square apartment to a shoebox in Greenpoint, barely scraping by. At that point, the depression wasn't from trauma, wasn't from the horrible things I'd done to the people I loved, or the guilt that ate me alive day-by-day. By then, I was depressed because I was unemployed, poor, and drunk.

That's a lot harder to do in a small town. A hometown where everyone knows you, knows your past and your mistakes and your tragedies. At first, I didn't have the urge to drink or fuck strangers, but it was like I wasn't just sad because I'm pathetic; I was sad because I was grieving again. I couldn't carry the weight of both at once, and I feel lighter when my head is buzzed and my body is touched.

"Around the holidays, I guess," I finally answer.

The timeline is somewhat accurate, though the trigger may not be, but I'm not ready to address that with myself, let alone with Leo.

Late afternoon casts a shadow over the house, but I'm having my first coffee of the day. I tried my hardest to avoid the conversation I knew I'd have to have with Everett after last night. I think I'll avoid thinking about last night for the rest of my life.

I don't want to think about Elliot, about how stupid I am. I used to be careful. Met up only in public places, always took the guy back to my apartment so I could maintain control. I used to trust my intuition and would bail on anyone who gave me cause for concern.

Elliot was a walking red flag, but I'd already been drinking, and I didn't want to go home, so I pushed past the discomfort. When he slipped his hand between my legs, every alarm bell in my mind set off.

If he was willing to do that in public without my consent, how far would he go in private?

I'd braced my hand on his arm, attempting to push him away, and he pinched my thigh, gritting his teeth and snapping that I was a tease, and that I should've been expecting it. There was a fury in his eyes, and I think it's written into the biology of all women to recognize that look of fury when they see it in a man. I don't know why I clammed up or why I froze. I used to have teeth too. I used to consider myself a predator when it came to men like him.

Instead, I cowered. I pretended I was fine, convinced him I was just cold and preferred to wait until we were alone. He wasn't happy with my response, but it got his hand out from between my legs. Though, that doesn't change the fact that I can still feel his touch there, even now.

I don't know why I didn't text one of my brothers or call my parents. I guess I hoped I'd be able to get out of the situation unscathed, that they'd never find out, though I should've prioritized my safety over my humiliation. I don't know why I walked into Boardwalk Tattoo when I saw the lights were still on. I didn't even know if August would be there, but it was like some sense of knowing or guiding wind told me to step inside, told me I'd be safe there.

Maybe it was the alcohol, maybe it was the fear, but facing him was the aspect of the evening I'd been least prepared for. After we got off the Ferris wheel and began down the pier and back toward the boardwalk, my skin was buzzing with need to escape—to seek safety. At first, I wasn't sure what I was searching for. I was only driven by the compulsion to get away from Elliott, but when I spotted Boardwalk Tattoo, it felt like a light clicked on. A beacon.

Even without confirmation of his presence, when I saw the illuminated sign of his shop, an aching familiarity surged in the pit of my stomach. The same feeling I can still recall from my youth—when I'd seek him out in the halls at school or sneak into his room after a fight with Zach. It's something settling, the casual intimacy of his eyes meeting mine, the soft smile of deep understanding, the warm touch of comfort. I hadn't felt it in years. I don't know if it was hope or fear or some innate sense of knowing when he's near, but my feet led me straight to him. For all the familiarity my body seemed to feel, there was so much about him that was anything but.

It's like...I know what he looks like. I spent the best days of my life staring at his face. I've spent hours cataloging his features: emerald eyes, roman nose, pillow-like lips, the faintest hint of freckles that dot his cheeks—only visible if you stare closely enough. I've soaked in his touch and slept on his skin. I've loved him so deeply and fiercely, that description of the sensation doesn't exist, because nobody's ever garnered words for it.

I used to think his face was the reason I felt so compelled to write love stories—always searching for some way to express how he felt to me.

So, I know what he looks like, but last night, the face staring back at me was a stranger's, and while I would consider myself an expert in heartbreak, that devastation was something new.

He had more tattoos on his arms, a new piercing on his eyebrow, and if I'm not mistaken, his tongue is pierced now too. He was wearing a different pair of glasses than the last time I saw him. Black browline frames with gold wiring. I've still never met a man who pulls them off quite the way he does. I saw him at Leo's wedding, briefly and from across the aisle, but it wasn't enough to study those tiny changes—to realize all that I've missed.

I lay in bed all night replaying his words to me when he took me home.

You fucking destroyed me.

Once I started, I couldn't stop. Replaying every interaction I've ever had with August on a loop. All of the best days of my life. All my favorite moments.

"Violets are my favorite."

"That's because you're a violet too."

"You're my person."

"You've always seen me with the utmost clarity."

"I've waited an eternity to have you like this, and I don't want to let it go."

"So don't."

"Why are you doing this to yourself, Lele?" Everett asks, breaking me from my reveries. "All we want to do is help you. We can't do that if we don't know what's wrong. What's causing this."

I sigh into my coffee mug, because I ask myself the same damn question every day. Depression doesn't run in our family, it's never been something I've struggled with before, at least not chronically. Not outside the week per month that my uterus decides I'm its worst enemy.

I wonder if guilt can cut that deeply, or if this self-hatred was always swimming beneath the surface of my skin, and all it took was the right amount of regret to slice me open and allow that hate to begin seeping out. I know grief moves in stages, and I know it's something the human spirit is meant to overcome.

I was one person before that day, and I became someone else after, but I refuse to blame all of my mess on that. I refuse to acknowledge that I may have ruined myself over someone who, when it came down to it, didn't truly love me. If the roles were reversed, I don't think that he'd be in my position all these years later. He'd have moved on; he'd have been okay.

Sometimes, I hate him for that. Then, I hate myself more because how can you loathe someone who died? What kind of person does that make me?

Enough time has passed that I can compartmentalize those thoughts. The grief and the guilt. They're not eating at me every second, not an active parasite attached to my skin the way it once was. They say time heals all wounds, and maybe that's true, but for me time is nothing but a bandage. I'm still bleeding beneath the fabric.

And it's that blood loss that causes the bone-deep exhaustion I'm not capable of escaping.

I am so fucking tired.

I'm not so sad I can't get out of bed. I don't cry over him anymore. I may live in a perpetual state of self-deprecation, but even that active hatred—those final words I spewed at him—doesn't echo through my mind the way it used to. I'm just exhausted.

I fail to see the purpose in doing much of anything, and maybe where motivation and ambition die, depression thrives.

I'm not about to voice all that to my brothers. I don't know how.

I don't want to see the disappointment on their faces, so I glance out the window instead. It's foggy. Cloudy. Like it may rain. This used to be my favorite type of weather, but dark skies are the equivalent to bad omens for me now, and I fear the storm raging has nothing to do with the air outside, and everything to do with tension in this room.

"You can't ignore the question anymore, Elena," Everett says. "I've let you do that for too fucking long. I've tried being patient. Supportive. Offered you a job and let you stay here and rot when you refused to accept it. Yet, you continue to shut me—us"—he references Leo in my periphery— "out. I'm not doing that anymore. Not only are you putting yourself at risk, but you let that man know where you live." His voice breaks, and it's enough to pull my eyes back to him. His gaze blazes through me, and I can tell he's fighting to stay calm. "Where my fucking daughter sleeps."

My eyes flutter closed as the sentence slams into me, reverberating through my chest. A familiar sting builds behind my lids, and all I can do is whisper, "I'm sorry."

"I don't want you to be sorry. I want you to get better."

I can't. I want to fucking scream.

I cannot be better. That doesn't exist for me, and while I know it's wrong and misplaced, I'm so goddamn angry at them for refusing to let it go. For refusing to accept whatever I've become now. Even my parents have given up on me. I don't know why my brothers won't.

"I don't think I should stay here anymore," I find myself saying before I'm able to give the sentiment much thought.

Do I have anywhere else to go? Not really. My parents don't have a spare bedroom.

"Do you want to come stay with me, Lena?" Leo asks.

I shake my head.

I can't stay there either. My relationship with Darby is strained—nonexistent would be the better word for it, actually. Plus, they're about to have a baby.

I don't have enough money for a place of my own, and I have no prospects of a job or a finished manuscript in the near future.

In short, I'm fucked, but I can't be here anymore.

I can't handle being the outsider in this family dynamic. I can't handle breaking my brother's heart every time I fail at being anything other than dead inside. I can't promise I won't keep fucking up, and now that my messes are a threat to the ten-year-old girl I've become quite fond of, I can't bear that guilt either.

"Where are you going to go, Elena?" Everett asks. "I want you here, I promise you, I do. I just need you to try and be better."

I shake my head, my vision tunneling, darkness closing in around me. The room feels like it's shrinking—the ceiling falling down, the walls closing in. My breathing is labored, I know it's a panic attack, and I need to get away.

"I need..." I set my coffee on the counter next to the bottle of vodka I really wish I could take with me. "I need air."

Brushing past both my brothers, I don't bother grabbing a coat as I toss the front door open and step out into the rain. It's the kind that falls in sheets with the wind, like a constant mist blanketing the world. A chilled sheen of moisture coats my skin as I take off down the driveway and start running.

Running from my issues like I always have. A familiar burn emanates in my chest, a brief reprieve from the emotional pain I'm trying to outrun. Breath escapes my mouth in short, rapid bursts, which are preferable to the choked sobs of panic.

I'm wearing cotton shorts that are already soaking through, and a *It's always sunny in Pacific Shores* crewneck I got from Heathen's, which is hilarious considering the weather right now. My worn-out Converse have no business slapping against this slick pavement, but I don't stop.

I don't know where I'm going or why, only focusing on the rain on my skin, sea air in my lungs, the ache in my legs, and the burn in my chest. I welcome them as I close my eyes, hitting a comfortable rhythm and allowing my body to take over my brain, leading me wherever it wants to be most.

Water drips into my eyes, causing me to squint. I'm hardly able to see where I'm going, but I can just make out the street sign ahead of me that reads *Strand*. That same aching familiarity erupts in my chest again. The intricate sense of knowing that if I turn right at that corner, I'll be led to the safety I so desperately need.

It's not safety I deserve.

It's a selfish craving, and it'll inevitably lead to the ruin of more than just myself. Yet, as I reach the intersection of Pacific and Strand, I make the turn. I continue running, faster. More urgently. Until I finally stop, hands on my knees as I heave and swallow gulps of air. Heavy drops of water form on my lashes, still dripping into my eyes and blurring my vision further, but I know exactly where I am.

I've been here before, just once.

Just like the last time, I hate myself as I do it, but my feet move of their own accord. Up the drive and to the steps, until I'm in front of that olive-colored door. I'm soaked to the bone, a puddle already forming at my feet, my hair a mop in front of my face.

I rap my knuckles against the wood, waiting with bated

breath as footsteps echo on the other side, but that same sense of knowing—that guiding wind—wraps itself around me. A word that's become foreign in recent years flashes through my head—safe. It rings clear as the lock turns, the hinges creak, and his face appears in front of me again.

Chapter Eight

Violet

"exile (feat. Bon Iver)" - Taylor Swift

She looks like a drowned rat.

I have to bite back a laugh at that intrusive thought because the look on her face tells me right now is clearly not the fucking time.

Her depthless brown eyes look even darker with the purple circles beneath them, telling me she didn't sleep last night. Her clothes are soaked, clinging to her skin, water cascading down her face and legs. Her hair hangs in heavy, wet clumps around her shoulders, drops falling off the ends and into the puddle she's now formed on my doorstep.

She's a mess.

Her eyes are red-rimmed and swollen. I can't tell if she's actively crying or if it's just the rain falling down her face in heavy rivulets. Her gaze bleeds desperation, and her soft mouth parts, breath huffing like she can't quite find the words.

I don't have them either. I'm too fixated on those lips. Fixated on every inch of my skin they've brushed across, on all the words they've ever said. In the way they moved as they whispered my name that night just before she left me. How goddamn badly I long to hear them beg for my forgiveness.

I'm still staring at them as they begin to move, and my eyes snap to hers.

"I didn't have anywhere else to go," she whispers, voice raspy like she's been running.

"Did you walk here?" I ask.

"Ran."

Her soul-snatching gaze meets mine, and I'm immediately swallowed whole, drowning within her. Cursed by those endless brown eyes.

She's like a fucking enchantress. A goddamn demon, harboring my being.

"So I'm your last resort?" I ask.

She sucks in a swift breath, eyes falling to the ground, and it's like I'm being let free. "It doesn't sound like you're particularly interested in being my first these days."

Because you ruined me.

"I'm not."

"I can't stay with Everett anymore," she whispers.

The tone doesn't invite much room for argument, and I wonder if he kicked her out after discovering her drinking. I wonder if she finally pushed him to the edge. My stomach twists with a pang of guilt. I didn't think he'd give up on her when I told him about it.

"I can't stay with my parents, or with Leo. I don't want them to see me like this." Her voice is so broken, and knowing the aspects of Elena's personality that haven't changed, I imagine that sentence was a hard one for her to admit. Especially to me.

"Why me?" I ask.

She raises her head, and now I know for sure that the moisture brimming her eyes is tears. "I don't want to keep hurting them, and my personal implosion doesn't hurt you. You don't care about me anymore."

You are so fucking blind.

Somehow, I remain stone-faced.

For reasons beyond my control or comprehension, I open the door wider and step aside. She's timid as she enters my house, slipping off her shoes and refusing to leave the entry rug as she drips water all over my floors.

I shut the door, leaning against it. "I don't have it in me to take care of you anymore, Elena. I have nothing left to give you."

She closes her eyes like she can't bear to look at me, and it's a quiet moment before she clears her throat, finding her composure. "Can you let me crash on your couch tonight?" She forces a smile that is so unconvincing it's like she's forgotten how to smile at all. "For old times' sake? I need space from my family to figure some shit out. I'll be gone by morning. I swear."

Her bottom lip trembles as she crosses her arms over her chest, nails digging into her forearms. I don't know if she's fighting back tears, or if she's so cold she's shivering, but I can't fucking stand the sight of it.

I nod toward the staircase in front of us. "Upstairs, take a left. The room at the end of the hall has an ensuite. Take a shower and crash there tonight. I've got spare clothes in the dresser and towels in the closet."

She nods, and that goddamn lip is shaking again as she whispers, "Thank you."

A rogue tear escapes her eye, falling down her cheek in slow motion as she turns toward the stairs. She's halfway up before I call out, "Five hundred."

She pauses, keeping her back to me.

"Five hundred a month and you can rent the room. It's cheaper than anything else you'll find in Pacific Shores."

She spins, tilting her head as her dripping hair falls over her shoulder. "Why?"

I don't like the idea of trading vulnerabilities with her. I never want to lose the upper hand again, but considering she's homeless, wet, and begging for a place to sleep, I figure it's safe for me to say, "I have trouble staying afloat in the winter when business is slow. I've been considering getting a roommate for a while to help with the mortgage."

"But you didn't want to live with a stranger?" Elena asks.

"I don't want to live with anyone." I shrug. "But I was starting to believe a stranger would be better than someone I do know."

She leans against the railing. "So, why me?"

"Because you are a stranger to me, Elena," I say, cementing the boundary I'll need if I'm going to share any kind of space with her at all.

Her features explode in shock before morphing into something like despondency. She swallows, giving me a shallow nod, her gaze fixed on nothing in particular, like she's completely lost inside her own mind.

"I don't have that much money on me right now," she admits quietly.

"Pay it by the first. That's two weeks."

Her eyes lift to mine, and all I see is hopelessness in her gaze before she nods once again. I turn on my heel before marching through the living room and into my bedroom off the den, leaving her standing on the stairs, dripping wet and in tears.

I listened to the shower run, the sound of her footsteps above my head as she padded around the spare bedroom, and the creak of the bed as she climbed inside of it. Only then did I allow myself to attempt sleep, only when I knew she was too.

It evades me as I lie on my back, staring at the ceiling. My mind plays our interaction on a reel, glitching and pausing at the broken look on her face when I walked away.

My skin itches with the urge to fix her, a dawning realization that I may let her destroy me over and over again, because somehow, it feels like home. Parts of me want to welcome it, thinking that the pain she brings is better than the numbness I live in now.

Elena Ramos is my purgatory.

My bones ache for her touch, my soul screams her name, and I'll never fucking escape it.

Chapter Nine

Vice

"We Hug Now" - *Sydney Rose*

The stairs creak beneath my feet as I tiptoe to the lower level of the house. A lot of homes in this neighborhood are older, but many have been updated to match the modern, beachfront dream buyers seek along the California coastline.

August's resembles something homier—charming and warm. Almost academic in its use of dark wood along the floors and molding, the soft cream and beige walls, and the way it's draped in earth-toned furnishings. The stairs end just in front of the door, with the kitchen to my right and the living room to my left. I turn that way, stepping onto the massive geometric-patterned rug that covers the space. A crimson couch sits beneath the front bay windows. A cream recliner is next to it, both facing the TV mounted to the wall above the dark-stone mantel.

Beside the chair is an open doorway, and I'm rendered speechless as I step through it. The floor sinks down into a den, showcasing the age of the home. The den is softly carpeted, with two reading chairs in the center of the room. Bookshelves line the walls from top-to-bottom, each one crammed full.

A home library.

It smells like paper—comforting and familiar. I walk the perimeter of the room, slowly running the tips of my fingers over the spines, cataloging the way August has everything organized. First, by genre. Then, by author name. His selection of mysteries is by far the largest, which isn't surprising. I know they're his favorites. Followed by fantasy, thriller, and paranormal. His nonfiction section is the smallest, of course.

He even has a few shelves of romance—including every book I've written.

I don't let my eyes wander on those too long. It's like a stab through the chest to remember how passionate and motivated I used to be. How lovely it felt to live inside the worlds I'd developed all on my own. The liberation of creating something that you know could not exist without you. The name Violet Rose, foiled on the spine of one of my black hardback editions, winks in the morning light like it's taunting me.

I don't know if I'll ever publish a book again, and when my entire identity was built off my ability to do exactly that, it's a harsh reminder that I have no goddamn clue who I am anymore.

"I can make space here if you need a place for the books you have at Everett's."

I jump, knocking into one of the shelves, startled by the sound of August's gruff voice. I turn, finding him standing against a door I hadn't noticed. He's wearing the same thing he was last night—sleep-mussed curls, glasses, a black T-shirt, and gray sweatpants that leave nothing to the imagination. Not that I needed the stark reminder of its size staring me in the face, I'm well acquainted with the man's magnificent fucking cock already.

He clears his throat, and I realize I've been staring.

My eyes flitter up his body, landing on his face. He pops a brow behind his black frames.

"I... Thanks. Most of my books are actually in storage with my parents. I only keep a few boxes with me, and I'll probably store those in my room, if that's all right."

"Actually, those books are right here."

My mouth drops, and I glance around the room. August and I have always loved a lot of the same titles, so while I recognized many of them, I assumed they were his own copies. "What do you mean?"

"Your parents got rid of their storage unit a while ago, and Monica felt bad about giving away all your books but didn't have space to keep them, so I offered to take them off her hands."

"Oh..." I don't know how else to respond. I would've been disappointed if my mother had given away all the books I've read and collected over my life, but I wouldn't have been angry with her. I left home on a whim. I've never had a place to store them. I've never had anywhere to truly call my own. I couldn't expect her, or August, to find space for them. "Thank you."

He only shrugs, hands in his sweatpants pocket, like he couldn't care less. "Everett called me last night, looking for you. Repeatedly." I wince, having nearly forgotten the disaster that was this weekend—and yesterday's conversation with my brothers. "He insisted on coming to get you. I told him to give you space, but you should text him or something. Don't let shit fester."

His tone is devastating—words laced with some kind of pain I don't quite understand. I don't want to look at August, so I turn, studying the spines of the books on his shelves. I run my hands across them again, finding comfort in their texture.

I don't want to see my brother yet. I need a plan first. August offered me a room, and my initial reaction was absolutely the fuck not. I can't stomach that—living with the ghost of my grandest sins. But continuing the dance of fallacy with my brothers has officially crashed and burned. Hiding in Everett's home will no longer be tolerated, and the crushing weight of my family's disappointment is a suffocation I can no longer endure.

Fully aware that I'm wearing a pair of August's oversized joggers, a sweatshirt that damn-near swallows me whole, and last night's rat's nest of matted hair I failed to brush through, I exit the den and head toward the front door.

August follows me, and I realize the door he'd been standing in front of must lead to his bedroom. At least we'd be sleeping on two separate floors. I slip my shoes on, murmuring, "I'm just going to take a quick walk and clear my head. If Everett shows up while I'm gone, let him know I'll be back soon."

"Will you?"

"Yes?" I grit, lifting my head to glare at him.

"You don't have the best track record when it comes to walking out that door."

My eyes close, guilt washing through me. Shaking off thoughts of that night, I finish tying my shoes, toss open the front door, and head out into the bright morning without a word.

The air feels fresher now that the rain has passed, like it cleared the radicals clinging to the oxygen we'd been breathing, leaving only purity behind.

I did intend to walk, knowing I'm not wearing the most appropriate clothing for a jog, but as my feet hit the pavement, I crave that familiar burn and rhythm of running.

I used to run often, before the mere effort of getting out of bed was too tiresome to attempt most days. Running felt like a good form of punishment for my never-ending sins. It fucking hurts. It makes me ache and sweat, makes me feel like I can't breathe.

I deserve to feel like I can't breathe.

I used to run often after Zach died. It helped convince my family I was okay, because technically running is good for me. For my body. Others could be convinced that the fresh air is beneficial for my head and my soul, though both of those things are diseased without hope of cure.

But at some point, I no longer felt like running. In New York, there was no way for anyone to know whether I was keeping up with it, and it was then I realized what a fraud I was. I didn't care if I was hurting and had no hope of ever feeling better.

After the confrontation with Everett last night, I felt the need to bolt. My masks were ripped off my face, and all of my ugly, unhealed wounds were exposed for all to see. When I hit the pavement, I had no idea where I was going—until I ended up in front of the house I've only been inside once, but still know all too well.

It was a moment of weakness to ask August to stay the night, the same kind of comfort I've sought out all my life when I was hurting. Like a lighthouse upon the rocky cliffs of my soul's sea, he'd been a beacon—but I know better than to keep believing he still operates for my benefit.

He let me stay out of pity. I bet if it hadn't been raining, he wouldn't have even let me come inside. That understanding made me bolt again this morning.

Running with no destination in mind, I head west from August's, toward the ocean. The smell of salt and the sound of seagulls amplify the closer I get, until I'm jogging up Oceanside Avenue. I stop at the familiar white house with blue shutters and honeysuckle bushes lining the front windows, placing my hands above my head as I breathe through the seizing pain in my chest.

I'm so fucking out of shape.

I shuffle up the walk that leads to the covered front porch, climbing the steps and rapping my knuckles on the door. I've had far too many tense confrontations via front door in the last twenty-four hours—I don't imagine I'll be getting out of bed for several days after this. But, at the very least, I need to have options before I meet Everett. I need to have a plan ready, even if I fail at following through with it.

It only takes a moment before Darby opens the door. There's a soft, tired smile on her face, and I realize it's far too early on a Sunday morning to be bothering them like this. That smile on her lips morphs into an "O" as her eyes go wide, and her body rears back at the sight of me. Her tumbling, straight golden hair sways with the movement, like she's a fucking animated Disney character.

One hand falls to the ever-growing bump beneath her tank top, the other hand clasping her throat. "Elena," she gasps. Huffing a laugh, she continues, "Sorry. I wasn't expecting you. Hi!" She eagerly steps aside, motioning for me to enter.

"Sorry, I know it's early," I murmur, shutting the door behind me and following Darby to the kitchen.

"Oh my gosh, no worries at all. I'm so happy you stopped by." She stops at the island in the center of the kitchen. "Do you want coffee or anything?"

"Do you have tea?" I ask, immediately feeling like an asshole for making a pregnant woman shuffle through her pantry when I'm not even supposed to be here.

"Oh, of course." She opens the door in the corner of the kitchen, lifting onto her toes to slide out a massive jar filled to the brim with a dozen types of tea. "Take your pick."

She flicks on an electric kettle before grabbing two mugs from a cabinet next to it and setting one in front of me. "Leo's surfing down in the cove right now, but he should be back any minute."

How do you do it? I want to ask.

How do you watch him wade in the waves with faith he'll escape them?

Swallowing down the words, I ask instead, "Dahlia's still preparing the bakery for opening, right? She's in there almost every day?"

Darby's brows knit together, confusion flickering across her face as she places a teabag in each of our mugs. "Yeah." She nods, swallowing. "The grand opening is March first, but they're in there every day getting things set up and ready."

"What time does she normally arrive?" I ask.

Darby grabs the kettle off the stove and pours steaming water in each mug. "I don't know. Around seven or so most mornings now that she's finished her baking course at Golden State."

"And you have a spare key?"

Her hands fall to her stomach, making idle circles as she eyes me warily. "Yes?"

"Could I borrow it?"

She only blinks.

"I'm not going to like...cause destruction, and I swear I'll give it back. I just... It's for my brother, mostly." I shrug. "And for me, I guess. I need to prove something to him. Both of them."

Darby takes a deep breath. "Is there a reason you're asking me and not Dahlia herself?"

"I can't tell you that yet, but I swear it's nothing bad."

She gives me a wistful smile before disappearing down the hall. Returning a moment later, she hands me a small cupcake keychain with one key on it. I hold my hand out as she drops it into my palm.

"Thank you," I breathe. "Please don't tell my brothers. I mean...they'll find out, but I'd prefer that be through me."

She opens her mouth to say something, giving me that same apprehensive look as before, when suddenly her eyes squeeze closed and a hiss escapes her mouth. She groans, dropping her head to glare at her belly.

"You okay?" I ask.

She huffs, shaking her head. "I'm fine. She's just kicking up a goddamn storm."

"Do you like being pregnant?" I find myself asking, unsure if it's an appropriate question after it's already left my mouth.

"I do, I swear." Darby laughs, smiling longingly at her stomach. "Things I thought I'd care about, like stretchmarks and weight gain, don't bother me in the slightest. But other things I didn't expect to be afraid of like my blood pressure or her heart rate, freak me out at all times. It's a very odd experience, but I wouldn't change a thing."

"You're still beautiful. I promise."

She smiles up at me. "And I know you mean that, because you don't bother lying for the sake of anyone's feelings, even a pregnant woman."

I shrug. "True. You look like you wipe your ass with sunshine and let singing birds pick out your clothes for you in the mornings."

Darby bursts into laughter, and the sound makes it impossible not to join in. We're interrupted by the distant sound of door hinges, and a moment later, my brother rounds the corner in a black wetsuit, the top half folded down at the waist and his bare chest on display. His hair hangs in front of his face, still wet with seawater.

"As I live and breathe." He creeps into the kitchen with a hand clutched to his chest. "Is that my sister? In my kitchen? Drinking from my coffee mug?" Leo crosses the kitchen in two long strides, closing the distance between us and taking my face between his hands. "Are you okay? Did you get hit in the head?"

I roll my eyes, frowning as he squishes my cheeks between his hands. "You're annoying."

He smiles, dimples popping. "Well, I can see you're fine."

He wraps his arms around me and tugs me into his chest. I return the hug before he takes a step back, grinning brightly as he spins around and faces his wife.

Leo pulls her into him, planting a kiss to the top of her head. "My honey." Then, squatting to his knees, he lifts her shirt, placing both hands on her bare belly. "My baby." Pressing his lips against her skin before lifting his head to her, my brother's gaze clashes with his wife's—the love and adoration so blinding it seems to block out everything around them. "How's she cookin' today?"

"She's playing soccer this morning, actually," Darby says affectionately.

Leo chuckles. "C'mon, baby girl." He spreads his palm over the front of her stomach. "Give Daddy a kick. Show me how good of a surfer you're gonna be someday."

"She's going to be whatever she wants to be."

He chuffs. "Says the one who decorated her entire nursery in florals."

"Everyone loves flowers," Darby argues.

"You're right, baby," Leo concedes.

A moment passes before my brother begins laughing again, rubbing his hand across his wife's stomach. Darby winces, but it doesn't take away the pure joy on her face as she watches him on his knees in front of her.

"Elena, you've got to come feel this," Leo says with astonishment.

I'm fairly certain it's incredibly rude to touch a pregnant woman's belly without her consent, so I keep my feet planted exactly where they are. Darby lifts her head and meets my gaze.

As if she can read my mind, she nods. "Do you want to feel?

It's kind of weird."

"It's not weird," Leo gasps. "It's beautiful."

I hesitantly step toward them, stopping beside my brother where he squats at the floor. Darby reaches out a hand, wrapping her fingers around my wrist and placing my palm at the center of her stomach. She readjusts me, knocking Leo's hand off her belly.

A second ticks by before I feel it. Like a ripple beneath Darby's skin. It moves across my palm, the flutter of confirmation that someone else is in this room with us.

I rear back, shocked by the sensation. "Oh, my God."

I immediately drop my hand back to her stomach, eager to feel it again. Darby and Leo laugh at me, and my brother rests his palm against mine. Sure as shit, she kicks again, the tiniest little wave against our hands.

"Hi, sugar," Leo whispers, glancing at me. "You can talk to her."

Darby nods. "She really acts up when Leo's talking to her. Lou too."

I have no explanation for it, but tears spill from my eyes. I mean, I knew Darby was pregnant. Leo gave me that ultrasound photo a few months ago, and he's been keeping me updated ever since. But it's suddenly very real now. My brother and his beautiful, kind wife—whom I've tried to convince myself I hate—have created a whole new life, and I've been missing the entire goddamn thing.

Leo, with Darby's permission, finally told me their whole story not long after I moved home. The truth of why she left, and why it took ten years for her to reach out again. He told me he never got the letters she wrote him, and the restrictions her father kept on her to prevent them from having contact.

All that hate I harbored for Darby transitioned right onto her piece of shit father, who's currently rotting in jail and awaiting trial for a plethora of offenses that Dahlia had him charged with earlier this year. He's to be sentenced in the next couple of months, and with luck, will spend the rest of his life behind bars.

Regardless, I felt there was too much damage done, too much distance and space and silence, for any attempt at reconciling the brief yet strong friendship Darby and I once had.

As her growing daughter's little foot presses against my hand again, I don't know how to feel. "Hi," I whisper to her belly, my voice breaking beneath my tears. I don't know what else to say. I don't feel qualified to introduce myself as her aunt yet.

As soon as he realizes I'm crying, Leo stands from the floor, turning me sideways and pulling me into his arms. I'm swallowed up by his chest, but vaguely hear Darby whisper something about excusing herself.

"You okay?" Leo whispers against the top of my head.

"Yes," I murmur, the sound muffled against his chest. "I don't know why I'm crying."

"It's okay to cry, Lena. It's always okay to cry."

For some reason, his assurance causes me to weep harder, tears fully soaking my brother's bare skin as I realize he's still wearing nothing but a wetsuit.

"Do you ever think about how he'll never know?" I whisper, pulling away to look up at him. "He'll never know you two made it back to each other, or that you're having a baby. He'll miss all of this."

"He knows," Leo says confidently, rubbing his hand over the back of my head.

"It feels like my fault." The words fall from my lips without thought. I hadn't meant to express them aloud, to let my brother hear that truth that I've kept so deeply hidden.

He pulls back, placing his hands on my shoulders, leveling his gaze with mine and staring into my tear-stained eyes. "What do you mean by that?"

I shake my head, wiping at my face as I drop my head, refusing to look at him.

I glance around the house, taking in Darby and Leo's furnishings and decor. All the changes they've made in the past year since they bought it, and the small details I recognize from when Darby's grandmother owned the home. I still remember sitting upstairs, in what is now their daughter's nursery but used to be Darby's room, doing her hair and preparing her for her first date with my brother over a decade ago.

I spoke to her with so much authority on love. What it means and how it feels. Thinking I'd had it all figured out, when in reality, I had no fucking clue what was coming for me. Both of us were falling for the first time way back then, convinced it'd last forever, and for them it will.

Their first love made it out alive, but mine didn't.

Chapter Ten

Vice

"The Cut That Always Bleeds" - Conan Gray

Can we talk about everything tomorrow? I need some time.

I love you.

I send the text, slipping my phone into my pocket as I begin walking back in the direction of August's house. Leo didn't press about where I'd spent the night, didn't bring up the conversation we'd had before I ran away.

I think he was so happy to have me in his home, happy to see me having a conversation with Darby, and to watch my reaction to his baby girl, he didn't want to ruin the moment. I'm thankful for that. I needed to feel normal, even if just briefly. Maybe that's the real reason why I ended up at their front door.

Everett's always been the confrontational type. He believes in laying things out on the table and taking care of them immediately. He wears every emotion on his sleeve, he always speaks his mind, and he makes sure those around him know how he feels.

It's a strength, but it isn't what I need right now.

I know I'm disappointing him, I know I'm scaring him, and I know he feels helpless. Being unable to help myself is hard enough without knowing that it's hurting him too. Call it twin telepathy, or the forced proximity of living in his house, but we've been feeding off each other's pain and sorrow, and I don't think it's healthy for either of us.

Somehow, I think Leo sensed that, too, so he gave me the escape I needed today. I love my brothers equally, but I'm more deeply connected to Everett, and I don't think it's always a good thing. With Leo, I can express myself without the worry that every emotion I'm experiencing is going to be absorbed and reflected back onto me.

Everett is a caretaker by nature. His purpose is to make everyone else around him feel safe—to make them smile and to help them feel whole. I'm not capable of giving him that right now, and I hate that he feels like he's failing me because of it, so maybe space is better for us.

Everett

I love you too.

He doesn't respond with anything else, and I can't remember the last time I initiated that expression. Sometimes, I don't want to love anyone at all, because people I love tend to die. My family is exempt from that absence of feeling—love. It's innate. I have to love them, but sometimes I fear that my love is dangerous. A death sentence. So, I don't often say the words.

I don't run back to August's, feeling entitled to my own breath for the first time in a while. It's not triumphant, it's no breakthrough, but for the first time in recent memory, I don't feel like I'm choking. I'm sober, and I'm breathing.

I stroll, letting the sun beat down on my face and the sea air caress my skin. I don't like to look at the ocean. I don't want to see waves violently break and crash against the shore. It reminds me that life is painfully fucking short.

But I can't ignore the bone-deep peace that the smell of it brings, the calming rustle of palm leaves in the wind, the sound of birds above my head. Home will never truly be home again, because I don't think I'll ever dig my toes into the sand or feel the current against my shins as I sit atop a surfboard. I'll never again watch the sun sink below the horizon, because waves and sand and the color blue are tainted with death for me now.

I don't know how my brothers do it—I certainly don't know how August does it, if he even does. All I know is that I can't look out at the Pacific and not think of the last breath Zach ever took, the last thought in his head, and if it was of me. Of my shortcomings and my betrayals that—at the time—I felt so secure in. I was confident I wasn't capable of hurting him, and I'd been cut so thoroughly that, when I finally healed those wounds, I didn't care if my treatment methods caused him pain.

I thought he was indestructible, until I saw the look on his face when he uttered those final words and slammed the door. Left me standing in my kitchen, in his brother's T-shirt, with tears streaming down my cheeks.

You are impossible to love.

Sometimes, I consider tattooing that sentence on my forehead so everyone can see my shame.

I'd take back that entire morning and the night before it, the venom I spewed in his direction. But I wouldn't take back the choice I'd made months prior. Despite all the destruction it caused, I can't bring myself to regret the love I experienced, and maybe that's the worst part.

By the time I make it back to August's house, I'm thoroughly drained, my brain so sunken in a pit of despair I can hardly make sense of my surroundings. I suddenly realize that I have no idea if I should just walk in, or if I need to knock. I don't even know if he's home.

If he is home and hears me trying to open the door...that'll be awkward, so I resolve to rapping my knuckles against the wood instead.

Sure enough, August swings the door open a second later. He's still dressed casually, though not wearing the same thing he wore earlier. He looks like he's showered. He looks beautiful, despite the worn and tired expression on his face. Wordlessly, he steps aside to let me in. I kick off my shoes before standing helplessly in the entryway.

August leans against the banister with his arms crossed. "Everett was here. Then he left. Said you didn't want to see him."

"I just wanted more space," I murmur. "Do you think I could stay one more night?"

"I offered to rent you a room."

"Right." I nod. "And I'm undecided on that, so I'm hoping to milk one last free stay while I make my decision, and I'll let everyone know what my plan is tomorrow."

"You've been milking me for years already, Elena. What's one more night?"

I attempt to swallow my laugh, but it comes out through my nose. I clamp a hand over my face to cover my snort. August scoffs like I'm ridiculous, but when he rubs his jaw, I can tell he's fighting a smile too.

My eyes snag on the fading ink stretched across the back of his wrist. Dotted stars, connected by straight lines that outline the Leo constellation.

"You still have it?" I ask, chasing the thought aloud before I can stop myself.

His brows knit, following my gaze as he twists his arm to look at the tattoo. "Yeah?" He frowns. "Why would I get rid of it?"

I'm never going to look at a representation of you on my skin and wish it wasn't there.

Words I'd said to him years ago, words drenched in naivety by a young girl who believed the foundation of her most cherished friendship was unbreakable.

"I don't know," I whisper. "I assumed you'd regret it by now."

August's eyes drop as he chews his inner cheek. He runs a hand across the ink, saying more to himself than to me, "I don't regret them. I don't regret any of it."

"Any of it?" I ask.

"The relics on my skin." He drops his arm. "The friendship." Lifting his head, he meets my gaze. "The love. And perhaps I ought to, perhaps that's half the guilt, but I don't."

August pushes off the banister, and my breath halts in my lungs, holding itself hostage as he closes the distance between us, towering above me with fierce emotion raging in his green eyes. "I don't regret loving you," he whispers, and my eyes fall shut as the depth of his voice rattles my bones. "But I do believe I'd regret ever doing so again."

If his voice rattles me, his words crumble me, grinding those very bones to dust.

"So, as long as you live here, we are roommates. Ships passing in the night. Nothing more." The bite in his tone latches onto my being, tearing through whatever fragments of my soul might've been left intact.

My instinct is always to hide my emotions, swallow back my tears, but I don't do that this time. I open my eyes, forcing him to watch as a rogue bead slips down my cheek, the aftermath of his destruction.

I force him to see the effect only he has on me, because while his most lethal weapon is his words, mine is reflecting the pain they cause.

Chapter Eleven

Violet

"Looking Back" - Lord Huron

"That's really not necessary," Elena mutters from behind me.

I don't turn around, and I don't stop emptying out my liquor cabinet and placing the few bottles I keep into a box. Mostly wine I've been gifted over the years, and a bottle of rum Leo left here after his piña colada phase.

"I'm not a fucking alcoholic, Augustus," she all but growls, appearing beside me when I don't stop.

"Maybe, maybe not. All I know is that you were using alcohol as a coping mechanism, and at the very least, that's concerning. I won't enable your behavior while you're staying here, and I don't drink anyway."

I finish packing the box, lift it into my arms, and turn to face her. She's scowling at me, lips curled into a perfect pout that's a little too goddamn reminiscent of the way they once looked covered in my cum.

I scowl back.

I brush past her, carrying the liquor out to my truck and tossing it into the bed. When I re-enter the house, Elena's prattling in the kitchen. She's stomping, slamming cabinet doors, sulking as I know she does. Finally, she throws open the pantry—I'm assuming in search of tea—and stops short.

She frowns, brows knitting together in confusion, as she stares down the pretzels, Oreos, peanut butter, and Earl Grey tea I stocked the pantry with. Once she opens the fridge, she'll find that I also filled it with baby carrots, sweet pickles, and the microwavable chow mein she loves.

"I don't believe that you keep your house stocked with peanut butter, Oreos, or Earl Grey on the regular."

I shake my head. I don't like any of those things; I just know she does.

"I ran to the store yesterday. It's no big deal."

She tilts her head, revealing a glimpse of the tattoo behind her ear. The first tattoo I ever gave her, stars connected by lines that form the shape of the Libra constellation. My sun sign, and the complement to the tattoo I have on my wrist.

"I don't want a handout from you, August," Elena mutters, snagging a teabag and shutting the pantry.

"Interesting, considering you show up on my doorstep whenever you need something."

She gives me those pouty lips again, and I hate the way the disdain on her face makes me half-hard. "I can get my own groceries."

"I mean...you're writing, right? Figured you'd want your favorite sustenance." My tone invites challenge. We all know damn well Elena isn't writing a goddamn thing.

I know her brothers mean best when they care for her the way they have been, and for a while, that might've made sense. Only I can relate to the depths in which my brother's death affected us both, and sometimes I'm not even sure I understand how heavy it weighs on her, even after all these years.

But I also know that Elena doesn't respond well to soft love. She needs to be pushed. She needs her intensity, stubbornness, and fierceness to be matched. She needs to be challenged, because that unbreakable will to rebel and land on top is what propels her forward, and the last four years of coddling have done nothing but hurt her more.

I'll fill my house with her favorite writing snacks, I'll charge her rent, and make her feel compelled to get her ass out of bed every day and work or write or do anything at all. I don't even know why I feel the need. Part of me is convinced I should yearn to let her rot, but the broken look on her face that night she showed up at my doorstep, the fear in her eyes when she walked into my business on that date—hurt more than any of the pain she's ever caused me.

"I'm taking a break," she murmurs without facing me, eyes glued to the kettle like she's willing the water to boil.

"How do you intend on paying rent?"

That gets her to turn around, frowning at me. "Why the fuck does it matter so long as I pay it on time?"

"You shouldn't stop writing."

The kettle screams, giving voice to the tension in this room. Elena ignores me as she flips the burner off and fills her mug. "Why do you care about this?" she finally asks, leaning against the counter, facing me as she brings the tea to her lips and blows on it, her eyes on mine.

My cock jumps.

"Why'd you leave?"

Her features turn solemn, and I have no idea why the fuck I let the question leave my mouth. Her eyes darken with something like torment, a fitting description to the sensation inside my chest.

I want to blame her so badly. I want to hate her. It should be easy. I have valid reasons. But when her face twists with agony and morphs into something far too close to regret, I'm left conflicted.

"It was what we both deserved," she whispers. Without another word, Elena pushes off the counter, steaming mug in hand, and walks past me without a second glance. I stand still, listening to her ascend the stairs, the silence of the late night taking over when the bedroom door at the end of the hall clicks shut.

I've spent four years believing Elena placed the blame for my brother's death on my shoulders—because I left Zach alone on that beach to go looking for her. I chose her over my brother that day—I've chosen her over everyone else. Always. I hated her for it. Sometimes, I still do. It destroyed me to carry that guilt alone, but the look on her face just now, the hollowed and haunted whispered words, makes me wonder if maybe I haven't been the only one carrying this load. Maybe it's so heavy it's crushed us both, and we're so suffocated by it, we've failed to see the other beneath the rubble.

Chapter Twelve

Vice

"Where's My Love" - SYML

I check the time on my phone. It reads 7:02 a.m., perfect timing as I pour the steaming milk into a glass filled halfway with equal parts espresso and chai tea, topping it with two pumps of vanilla, a sprinkle of cinnamon, and a drizzle of caramel syrup.

I wipe the nozzle with my towel, smiling at my work. A flight of four different coffee concoctions sits in front of me, ready for Dahlia to taste—just as I hear her begin to unlock the front door. I can make out her form through the glass windows, the barely risen sun in the distance accenting her confused features.

She hesitates as she opens the front door, peeking her head inside and glancing around, no doubt curious as to why the lights behind the front counter are on. "Um...hello?"

"Hi. It's me." I step out from behind the counter, making myself visible. "Elena."

"Oh." She breathes a sigh of relief, entering the building and shutting the door behind her. "What the heck are you doing here this early on a Tuesday?"

Dahlia's shoulder-length blond hair sways as she shrugs off her jacket, tossing it onto one of the tables beneath the front window. I walk back behind the counter and slide the flight I made across it so that it reaches where she's standing at the end.

"Was hoping I could interview for a barista position. You plan on opening in a month, right?"

Dahlia's brows rise as she studies the drinks. She lifts her head, and I can make out the amusement on her face. "I thought Everett offered you a job months ago and you declined?"

I shrug. "Wasn't his job to offer, was it? I figure, you're the owner—it's your call. I'm not interested in pity from my siblings, so I thought it best to prove my skills and let you decide if you'd like to make a new offer."

"I'm impressed."

"I know." I nod before pointing at each one of the drinks in front of her. "I've got a classic drip coffee, vegan latte, a vanilla almond white mocha, and a Dirty Everything."

"Dirty Everything?" she asks, picking up that one first.

"Yep. Like an everything bagel, but it's a dirty chai. Two shots of espresso and four ounces of spiced chai. Steamed milk of choice, two pumps of vanilla, a dash of cinnamon, and a drizzle of caramel."

She brings the glass mug to her lips, taking a small sip. Her blue eyes widen in shock as she swallows. She takes another sip before saying, "Fuck. That's good."

"I recommend developing four to five solid drinks and ensuring all staff can make them to perfection. It's great to have a specialty, fun-named option that's exclusive to the business, and eventually we can play with more ideas, but far more people are going to order something tried and true like a latte or a mocha. If we nail those, with our own small twists, it'll go far with customers."

Dahlia takes her time sipping from each of the drinks I created, loving every one. "You know you didn't have to do this, right? I don't even know how you got in here." She laughs. "I would've offered you a position because you're family, and because I trust your brother when he said you have the skills I need."

"I don't want handouts from my brother," I say.

"I get it." She takes the Dirty Everything between both hands, and I decide it must be her favorite. "It's hard to accept help when you don't feel you're worthy of the support."

"I didn't say that."

"You didn't have to." Dahlia shrugs. "You remind me of myself sometimes."

That catches me by surprise. "How so?"

"I used to only be capable of focusing on my shortcomings too. All the ways I was failing others, all the ways that life had failed me. Eventually, I realized I wasn't damaged beyond repair, just dented enough to give me character."

I let out a dry laugh at that. "How did you find that mindset?"

"I finally opened myself up to receive love I never thought I deserved." She smiles to herself, and my mind drifts to my brother. All those feelings he wears on his sleeve—all of his conviction and purpose to care for others—were exactly what Dahlia needed. She meets my eyes, and that smile forms into a grin, as if confirming my very thoughts. "You're loved too, Elena. In case you need to be reminded."

I don't want to be reminded. It's not the lack of knowing whether I'm loved that makes me feel undeserving; it's the fact that I'm harboring secrets from the people who love me. Secrets that make me unworthy of it.

When I don't respond, Dahlia continues, "I need you to work at least twenty-five hours per week, and mornings would be preferable. You can work more if you want, of course."

"I don't."

She smirks. "I figured. I've already hired two other baristas, but I'd love for you to spend the next few weeks training them and helping me finalize the coffee menu so Peggy can focus on the bakery." Peggy is the pastry chef Dahlia brought in to assist with bakery operations.

I nod. "Deal."

"Okay." She walks behind the counter, pushing open the double doors that lead to the kitchen. I watch her through the service window as she grabs an apron off the hook and ties it around her waist. "I'll talk to the other two employees this week and get a schedule put together so you can start on Monday. For now, clean up all that." She winks, waving at the mess I left across the coffee counter.

"Yes, boss." I salute, feeling lighter—more accomplished—than any time in my recent memory.

I spend the next few hours cleaning the kitchen before assisting Dahlia with a few recipes for the bakery menu, and helping her pick out paint colors for the cafe. We decide on a shade of baby blue that complements the bright orange, yellow, and pink accents of the decor, fitting for the retro vibe she's going for.

I think Dahlia will make a great sister-in-law, not that I'd have a choice in the matter either way, but she's perfect for my brother. She challenges him, she gives back as much as she takes, and their relationship is built on friendship first. I've always been a little afraid Everett would be taken advantage of the first time he fell in love, because I know better than most just how giving he is. I think he may know it, too, and maybe that's why he kept his heart guarded for so many years.

But it's easy to see that Dahlia loves him just as fiercely as he loves her. Everett didn't need multiple tries to get it right. He may have waited his whole life for it, but he only needed to find love once. I guess that's true for both of my brothers, and it makes me wonder how I got things so incredibly wrong for myself.

That thought plagues me as I leave The Wicked Wildflower and head two doors down to Heathen's Surf Co. Bells on the door chime as I enter, and I'm greeted by bright shades of blue, green, and orange. Surfboards hang from the rafters. There are tables spaced throughout the store with all different types of apparel, as well as racks of clothing hung along the walls. One corner of the store is reserved for skateboards and accessories. Neither of them will admit it, but Leo and Everett both had an intense skateboarding phase in our teen years, and they both fucking sucked.

A nostalgic laugh bursts from my throat as I think back on it, and it garners the attention of Everett, who's standing at the front counter folding T-shirts. He smiles, though his eyes spell confusion and concern. "Hey, Lele. I did not expect to see you here this morning."

I glance around at the ocean-inspired murals accenting the walls, and the massive canvas behind the register showcasing both of my brothers sitting on twin surfboards while laughing. There is a display in the corner of the store with more blown-up photos of the two of them dressed in apparel from a campaign they began last year with a surfwear brand.

Heathen's is the quintessential West Coast surf shop you'd expect to find in a quaint beach town like Pacific Shores, and that's probably why I don't come often.

It reminds me of Zach. The quintessential West Coast surfer boy who wanted so badly to be something different, and died in a surfing accident just as he was beginning to accept his roots. He never even got to see Heathen's up and running. He'll probably never know the inspiration he provided this place, but I can see him painted all over the walls here.

Everett clears his throat, and I lift my eyes to meet his. His brows are drawn, head tilted as he waits for me to respond.

"I was actually at the bakery with Dahlia."

A surprised smile lifts at his lips. "Really? What were you doing there?"

"Interview," I say absently as I step behind the counter and begin helping him fold T-shirts. "August offered to let me rent one of his spare rooms, and I think I'm going to take it. I know you offered me a job a few months ago, but I wanted to make sure Dahlia and I were going to work well together before I accepted a handout like that."

"Wasn't a handout." He doesn't look at me, and we continue working in tandem. "I love you, and I'd do anything for you, but that bakery is Dahlia's livelihood now. It's her legacy, and I wouldn't risk that for a pity job offer. You have the skills she needs, and I think you'll add value to the operations of the cafe. Trying to set you up with a position there was as much a favor to Dahlia as to you."

I shrug. "Well, I thought Dahlia should be the one to decide."

"And what was it she decided?"

"I start Monday."

"I figured." He chuckles, eyes lifting to meet mine. "And you're going to move in with August? Are you sure that's a good idea?"

Not at all.

But I don't see myself having many other options, and some primal part of me, maybe the piece of my soul that craves pain, actually yearns to be in his presence. I try to shove that voice so far down she's forgotten, but she's proved impossible to ignore.

"I think it'll be fine," I murmur.

I sometimes picture him—his voice, his touch, his eyes—when my hand is between my legs, and I'm chasing pleasure. So, it kind of turns me on when he narrows that emerald gaze in my direction. When he's kind to me in a rough way, like he doesn't want to be, but he can't help it.

I left August, I cut him out, I drowned myself in liquor and warm bodies to try to forget him, and it didn't work. Seeing him in the flesh, living beneath his roof—it doesn't amplify any feelings I've forgotten. They've always been here, haunting and tormenting me.

Perhaps dancing with that ghost up close and personal can serve as the punishment for all the sins I can't seem to outrun. I'll torture myself with his eyes and his voice while I'm forced to be deprived of his touch.

"The things he said to you the other night—" Everett begins, but I cut him off with, "I deserved them."

His head snaps up, eyes narrowed. "Why do you think that?"

I pluck the last shirt from the pile, folding it and setting it on the others, smiling at my brother and ignoring his question. "I'm going to head back to your place and start packing my things. Will you be around later to help me bring them over?"

He sighs defeatedly before nodding. "Yeah. I'll be home after Lou gets out of school, around three."

I pat his hand, but he doesn't look at me when I smile at him.

As I make my way toward the front door, Everett calls out, "I don't think this is the healthiest living situation for either of you, Lele."

I turn around, pressing my back to the handle as I push it open. "There isn't anywhere for me to live that is healthy, but at least this way, those of us most damaged will be out of everyone else's way."

Chapter Thirteen

Violet

"Talk" - Hozier

"You think that having Elena move in with you is the best option?" my therapist, Kelsey, asks.

"I mean...it felt right at the time I asked." I rub the back of my neck with a hand. "But now everyone is telling me it's a bad idea, and I'm rethinking my decision."

When I came in for my session today, I didn't intend to tell her anything about Elena. I've never mentioned Elena's name to Kelsey before. I've hardly uttered it inside my own head over the last four years. But somehow, once I was on the couch and all the events of the last couple of weeks fell down on me, the words spilled from my mouth of their own accord.

All of my friends think it's a terrible idea, even without them knowing the true depths of our fractured relationship. The fact that we haven't spoken in four years—and that our friendship was unable to survive my brother's death—was enough for them to encourage us to steer clear of each other.

Darby suggested I bring it up in therapy today before my session. I told her it wasn't something worth talking to Kelsey about, and yet here I am.

"Who has told you it's a bad idea?" she asks.

"I mean, Darby and Leo both expressed concern, and I know Everett is planning on telling the same thing to his sister. Plus, you don't sound thrilled."

She laughs under her breath, shaking her head as she types into the iPad in her lap. "I'm intrigued that you thought my question was presented as a concern. I was genuinely asking how you feel about it. That's what matters to me."

"Like I said, in the heat of the moment, it just felt like the right decision. I don't really know how to explain why."

"Does there need to be a reason?" Kelsey asks. "Maybe you should trust your instincts."

I shrug. "Maybe."

"Do you want to talk about Elena more today? I understand you two grew up together, she dated your brother, and that ended poorly." She crosses her legs, gently placing her hands in her lap. "I suppose what I'm struggling to understand is how her relationship with your brother and his passing has had such an adverse effect on your relationship with her. I assume there is something I am missing?"

So many things.

"I'm not quite sure I'm ready to go there yet," I admit reluctantly.

"That's okay. Baby steps." She smiles. "You've made great progress over the last few months. Do you think it's had any kind of effect on your day-to-day life?"

"I do."

A few months ago, I don't think I could've been in the same room as Elena. I couldn't have said her name or looked her in the face. Granted, being around her is still a torment and a challenge, but I haven't burst into flames quite yet—at least not literally.

Therapy has helped me compartmentalize my brother's passing, my grief, my relationship with him, and with others in ways I wasn't able to do before—and somehow, that's helping me unravel where she fits into all of it. I'm beginning to realize I'm entitled to a wide range of emotions and feelings—whereas before I thought that space was only reserved for guilt and blame.

"We're coming up on time for our session today, but I think things went well. Is there anything else you'd like to cover before we end?"

I shake my head, though part of me wants to ask her about the raging attraction I still have to Elena—about the way that I get aroused when she argues with me, and how I can't stop thinking about her in the filthiest of ways whenever I close my eyes.

I want to ask her why I feel like that, what it says about me, and how the fuck I get it to stop, but I'm too afraid of the answer. I fear she may tell me I'm sexually deranged, bound for hell, and doomed to eventually succumb to my most base desires and fall victim to the sorceress herself.

"Nope." I force a smile. "I'm feeling great."

I'm tired as hell when I get home from my session. I decided not to go back to the shop today since Maggie is there, and I have two other freelance artists onsite. There is no need for me, and it can be hard to readjust after therapy.

I know Elena will be home, but she's typically already down for the count by this time of day. It's been two weeks since she officially moved in. Just as I claimed we'd be, we act as nothing more than passing ships. In theory, avoidance should be effortless. If I kept her out of my sight, she'd be out of my mind. Though, I must've forgotten just how deeply burrowed into my brain she truly is. It doesn't matter if she's standing right in front of me, or on another planet entirely, I'm thinking of her, dreaming of her, sometimes dreading her.

Even in the moments I'm convinced I hate her, I'm fighting the urge to seek her out. To look at her. Touch her. Know her.

She's been working early mornings with Dahlia at the bakery, and I don't get home most evenings until after nine. I think she sleeps through most of the day and scurries around at night like a fucking cat before working her shift at the bakery, then comes home to crash after. I stay up late, too, and while I can hear her soft footsteps above my head when I'm lying in the dark, we don't speak to each other. She's gone when I wake in the mornings, and I'm at work by the time she gets home.

I'm earlier than usual today, but it's late enough in the

afternoon that I'll likely be able to avoid her. To be safe, I'm quiet when I enter the house, shutting the front door softly and heading straight into my bedroom. Sometimes therapy feels like the washing away of dark clouds that weigh me down, and I like to take a shower afterward to truly cement that feeling.

As I'm stripping off my clothes, I hear a soft, incessant buzz coming from somewhere in the house.

It doesn't take me long to realize the low vibration is coming from above my head. The sound bleeds through the floorboards from the room directly above mine. Elena's room. Assuming it might be a toothbrush or some weird white-noise machine she uses when sleeping during the day, I do my best to ignore it, unbuckling my jeans and shucking them down my legs.

Then, she moans my fucking name.

It's the all-too-familiar mewl that's been imprinted on my bones for years. She's coming. It's a breathless, muffled scream, but the three syllables that make up my name are unmistakably present in her voice.

Just as the sound passes, that buzzing stops, and silence rains down on me like acid.

She was right above me, chasing pleasure with my goddamn name on her lips.

The thoughts plague me as I stomp into my bathroom, slamming the door hard enough that she likely heard it. I crank on the shower, turning the temperature up as high as I can possibly bear. The water sears my skin as I step inside. I lean against the wall and let the heat pound against my chest, my mind reeling.

It's that soft yet rough sound that echoes in my head every time I fuck my fist. It's what I've heard since she moaned my name for the first time all those years ago. I close my eyes and watch hers rolling back. Remembering the tremble of her thighs, and the contented sigh that left her mouth when I touched her in the right places.

That alluring sound is like a spell pulling me in, even though I know damn well she'd fucking kill me if I ever allowed her to get near again. It's pure torture to know that every time I close my eyes and see her face, she may be doing the same.

Suddenly, my cock is in my hand. Raging and desperately hard. I'm pumping myself to the point of pain, knowing I shouldn't be having these thoughts. Not now, not with her above me.

The one solace I'm supposed to have in this harsh reality is that she's let me go. That's the only truth that allows me to believe I'll someday recover from her. She's infected every fiber of my soul, a slow-spreading disease that I spent my entire life exposing myself to, the symptoms only developing in her absence.

If I let myself entertain any kind of hope of healing between us, I'll end up obliterated by her again and knowing that she's getting herself off while imagining me is detrimental to my delusions.

I want so badly to hate her for it. For all of it. So often, I wish that we'd never experienced the brief love affair we had. I wish I'd never felt her lips on mine, that I'd never touched or tasted her, that I'd never felt her body beneath my hands, or her skin on my mouth. I wish I'd never heard those three words uttered from her lips.

Sometimes, I wish I'd never met Elena at all.

Because on the darkest nights, in the farthest depths of despair that I fall into, I know that if I'd never loved her, I never would've known love period. I used to believe it a blessing that I could've stumbled upon the girl of my dreams as a young boy, that I'd get to spend my entire existence loving the same person—but now I know it's nothing but a curse. A vast, numbing emptiness.

In these moments, I almost wish I'd never experienced her love to begin with.

It's that thought that has me halting my movements, my hand tightening around my aching cock before letting it go. I rub the water from my face, refusing the urge to continue fucking myself.

Those fantasies I used to chase in the dark are no longer viable, not when she's living here. Not when she's doing the same.

There is a siren standing in my kitchen.

Back turned to me, her smooth legs seem to extend for miles beneath the hem of the oversized tee she has on, likely since she's not wearing a goddamn thing beneath it. Her hips sway to the sound of Lana Del Rey filtering through the speaker on the counter.

She must've heard the slam of my door and the shower. She must know I'm home now. Though I'm not sure she realizes I'm standing right behind her as she moves to the soft music, dipping pretzel sticks directly into a jar of peanut butter while the kettle on the stove finishes boiling.

My cock throbs in my sweatpants as I stare at her.

"I know you're standing there, Augustus," she says nonchalantly, a catlike purr to her tone that boasts no trepidation.

She's riding a post-orgasm high and has no idea that I heard her while she found it.

"Do you not own a pair of fucking pants?" I mutter, walking over to the fridge and grabbing a soda from the top shelf.

"I didn't think you'd be so offended." She laughs snidely. "It's nothing you haven't seen before."

"Doesn't matter."

She's like a demon. No goddamn mercy, torturing me with her lush body, her endless eyes, and her siren-song of a voice.

"I'm surprised I still have such an effect on you, considering you hate me now," she murmurs. I can't tell if she intended for me to hear it or not.

The kettle whistles, and as she takes it off the stove and pours her tea, I slam the fridge door. "I don't have to like you to—" I stop myself, realizing the comment I'm about to make can't lead anywhere good.

Spinning on my heel, I intend to leave the kitchen, but the rattling chime of ceramic on quartz has me halting. Elena stands beside me, gaze narrowed as she leans over the steaming mug on the counter in front of her. "No, please go ahead and finish that sentence."

There's a taunting tone to her sultry voice, and a challenge inside her fuck-me eyes that screams *show me* rather than *tell me*.

My fingers flex, flesh blazing with need to bend her over that counter and show her exactly how I feel about her attitude, her bare legs, and the way she moans my name.

I thought we'd had a moment a few weeks ago, some brief unspoken understanding of where we stand. The pain we may have mutually caused, the blame and guilt we both carry, and the silent agreement that neither of us can be asked to hold the other's burden.

I don't understand her sudden insistence on messing with me. It was a broken girl I allowed into my home, whom I offered that room, but the ferocity standing in front of me now is all too familiar to the spitfire I fell in love with.

Though, I can't help the deep satisfaction that rushes through me at seeing that spark in her, even if it's been ignited by her instincts to drive me to the brink of fucking insanity.

Regardless, my fractured soul must be spared.

I need to get the fuck out of here.

I give her a once-over, forcing a look of boredom on my face before I pass her. Our shoulders brush briefly, igniting flames across my skin.

She lets out a breathless laugh. "Everyone thinks you're so soft and fragile, that I'm crazy and reckless...but I know you better." That has me pausing, and she waits a beat before continuing in a faint voice, "Deep down, you're just as spiteful as I am."

Spiteful? When she barreled back into my life in need of rescue, I did that. When she showed up on my doorstep drenched in rain, I offered shelter. I allowed her to wreck my heart and soul until I was nothing but shattered fragments of a human being, and still, I opened my door for her when she came knocking after years of silence.

I've given her every piece of me, and it seems as if that's still not enough.

Those flames across my skin spread to my head and my heart until I'm raging. If she wants my spite, I'll give her that too.

I whip around and step in front of her. She arches her back against the kitchen counter, looking down at the place my chest now presses into her crossed arms. I grip her chin, forcing her head upward until that deep brown gaze is locked on mine.

"You say that like you want me to show you how spiteful I can be. You say that like you want to be punished by me, Elena. Is that what you want?" My voice comes out a near growl. I'm at my breaking point with her fucking games, reaching the limit of her teasing, unable to stop myself from throwing it back.

Her lips pout, eyes erupting with challenge as those long lashes flutter, and her pert nose scrunches in vexation. She's so goddamn beautiful it fucking aches.

"Go fuck yourself."

I smile, knowing that's the response she offers when she's been cornered, when her clever comebacks run dry. It's what she does when she's flustered and bested by her opponent. "Like you did earlier? Your toy between your legs when it was my name you were moaning?" A flash of surprise in her eyes gives her away, though she tries to quell it. "I got home early, and your room is right above mine."

"Don't flatter yourself. I..." Her lashes flutter as she looks around the room, anywhere but at me. "I was thinking about someone else."

"You're a terrible fucking liar." I laugh. "You know how I know you're lying, Elena?" My hand still on her chin, I turn her head again, forcing her to meet my eyes. "Because you say my name differently when you're coming. It's breathier. Raspier. Deep. It's fucking primal." I drop my mouth, allowing my breath to skate across her cheek as I purr, "You don't say anyone else's name like that."

I tilt my head, my nose just brushing against hers as our

mouths align. We're close enough to share the rapid breath leaving our lips, and if I stood still, I'm positive I'd be able to feel the tandem pounding of our racing hearts. Her gaze rapidly flutters between my lips and my eyes, and I can see the desperation building in her dark irises.

I lift my thumb, brushing it across her bottom lip, savoring the feel of its softness. "I see the way you still tremble beneath my touch." I watch her mouth part in anticipation as I whisper, "But you'll never feel it again."

Chapter Fourteen

Vice

"Master & A Hound" - Gregory Alan Isakov

I frown at the blinking cursor on the bright, blank screen in front of me.

I hadn't been lying when I told August I was taking a break from writing, but somehow, having a job has actually become freeing when it comes to the pressures of putting fingers to the keyboard again. Before, it was like something I had to do. It had only been my full-time career for about a year before I stumbled into my crumbling depression, but writing is something I've done my entire life. It was an escape for me, a place where I was always safe, and could confidently and openly portray myself through the lives of fictional characters.

Plus, I'm self-aware enough to know that I love playing God.

I could live a thousand lives and experience every type of love story the universe had to offer—not only through the stories of others, but my own too. When it was passion and pride that fueled me, I found immense success.

But after moving back to Pacific Shores last June, it felt more like a chore. It had been my career, and I had lost it, and it seemed like the natural thing to do to get it back—to get myself back on track—was to begin writing again. Except, the words wouldn't come. The pressure grew too heavy because it was no longer an escape, a passion, or a safety—it was a necessity. It was as if I were being forced into it, and that, paired with my depression and poorly processed grief, was enough to drown me.

Now, if nothing else, it's not a hard requirement for me to get by. I have a job, a reason to get up every morning and do something with myself. While my depression isn't magically cured, and I still have a lot of shit to work out inside my brain—shit I don't particularly feel compelled to deal with and very likely never will—I at least can pay my bills, even if I never type another word again.

And somehow, that makes me want to write.

All day while I'm at the bakery, I daydream of a thousand different storylines, developing characters and imagining all the places I can take them. But sometimes, when I sit down to try to type, that imagination gets lost. The stories exist inside my head, but when it comes to expressing emotion, I can't seem to find the words to properly portray...feeling.

Any kind of feeling. Love. Lust. Hope. Happiness. It's all lost to me.

Pain, guilt, and shame shine through just fine. But even the most broken characters deserve their happy ending by the time the last page is written, and I no longer feel qualified to provide them that.

Sure, I don't have to write romance. I don't have to write a happily-ever-after, but if I make that pivot, if I stop writing love stories, I think I'll be discarding the last shred of the person I used to be. Because the young girl who daydreamed—who stayed up late at night handwriting poems and teaching herself Italian—she was destined to tell stories about love.

I was so sure I'd given up on her, so sure she died that day, too, but if I give up writing romance in pursuit of other genres—that somehow feels like dropping her coffin into the ground, burying her in soil. I don't think I'm ready to do that to her just yet.

Since it's unlikely I'll find the words I'm searching for tonight, and sleep will evade me as well, I leave my bedroom and head downstairs for something to eat. I did skip dinner, after all.

August and I have gone back to nothing more than passing

glances and muttered responses to basic questions, keeping as much physical distance between ourselves as possible. We almost crossed a line in the kitchen last week, and I hate to admit how much it killed me when he ended our interaction with the upper hand—how his venomous words shredded through my puckered scar tissue, and when he walked away victorious, I felt like I was left bleeding out.

There was a bit of satisfaction that came with that near-slipup, though. August can taunt and tease me all he wants, but he forgets that I once knew him better than anyone else on earth. I've spent hours—days—studying his face, his expressions, his reactions. He's just as weak for me as I am for him, and I have no doubt that knowing I was chasing pleasure with his name on my lips, right above his head, sent him spiraling too. I knew by the way he spoke of it, the way his eyes flared when he touched my face, that he'd done the same under the cover of darkness.

He imagines me, dreams of me, even if it kills him to do so.

I've stuck to using nothing more than my hand to get off since, not wanting to risk him hearing me again. But sometimes, I'm tempted to torture him more. Leave my door open, scream his name, beg him to get me off himself.

It's demented and fucked up, and I don't know what it says about me that the thought of driving him to the brink of insanity turns me lust-crazed.

I tiptoe quietly down the stairs. It's late and very unlikely August is still awake. Regardless, until I get my disconcerting reactions to the man under control, I'm avoiding him like the fucking plague.

I watch the kettle like a hawk, ready to catch it before the whistle so it doesn't wake him, drumming my fingers against the counter. It's like when you're waiting for the water to boil, it takes so much longer than when you're distracted by something else. That's kind of how August and I feel sometimes. We're slow-simmering, popping bubbles, raging with heat. When I search for signs of our combustion, it always feels too slow. But I know the moment my control slips, the moment I drop my guard, we're going to boil over, and I'm terrified of what the outcome will be.

A shriek slices through the silent night, piercing my ears and rattling my bones. Gasping, I snatch the kettle off the stove, but the screaming doesn't stop. Hair stands on the back of my neck as I whip around, scanning the house.

In the dim light, nothing moves, and the noise ceases. Only one lamp in the living room is still on, but nothing else appears out of place. Trepidation rises in my throat as I glance around. I can't tell if the noise came from outside, but it sounded close. It sounded like someone facing pure terror.

Walking through the living room, I check the television to see if August left it on, but he didn't. My body trembles with uncertain fear, and just when I'm convinced I made it up, another yelp tears through the quiet room.

Tracking the sound is much easier this time. It's definitely coming from inside the house, and I follow it through the den to August's bedroom. I hesitate outside his door, wary of invading his space. Until I hear him scream again. It's unmistakable, the sound of raw pain coming from his familiar voice. It rushes through me, settling in my chest and causing a full-body wince, like his voice alone is force enough to sucker punch me.

"August?" I ask, easing the door to his room open.

It looks the same as I remember it, though it's been over four years since I've been inside. A large bed sits at the center of the room, to the left of the door, forest green comforter crumpled and tossed aside. To my right is a dresser, littered with socks and belts. A walk-in closet is directly in front of me, with a bathroom door beside it.

I drag my gaze to where August sits upright in bed, startling because he's staring directly at me. Air swooshes from my lungs on an exhale, and while our eyes lock, I somehow know he's not seeing me. Shock and fear war within his green irises, but whatever he's seeing, it's not this room.

His chest heaves nearly uncontrollably, like no matter how

hard he tries, he can't catch his breath. I watch him grab the base of his throat before another scream echoes off the walls of the silent house. "No, no, no." His legs flail, and he scrambles back against his headboard, like he's crawling away from something. "I didn't! I didn't!"

He falls back on his pillow, eyes fixed to the ceiling now. He's still clawing at his neck, panting hard.

It's agonizing to watch him like this. Nausea twists my stomach, and my eyes fill with tears as I slowly step toward the bed. It must be a night terror, because this appears far worse than any bad dream could be. Leo used to suffer from night terrors the first few years after my family took him in. It was PTSD from witnessing his mother's death, according to doctors.

Leo doesn't talk about it often, mostly because he can't remember having them. They stopped when he was a teenager. My mother said it was because night terrors were far more common in children than adults, but I suppose it's not impossible for August to be suffering from them, with the trauma he bears.

From what I remember, you're not supposed to wake someone in the midst of a night terror; you're only supposed to coax them back to sleep. Tears drip from my jaw and to the floor as I tiptoe toward his bed, holding back sobs at the sight of him like this.

"August," I whisper, choking on the word.

He looks so broken, the deepest pits of darkness in his mind rising to the surface in a catastrophic wave. Bearing witness to the devastation is wrecking me—his screams like claws tearing through my flesh, his fear like a knife piercing my heart, his pain like black hole swallowing me whole.

I slowly climb onto the bed, sitting on my knees. My first touch is featherlight, fingers sweeping over the hair on his forehead, matted with sweat against his skin. He gasps at the contact, but I hush him. "It's okay, Augustus. It's me."

I don't say my name, because I no longer know if his subconscious will recognize it as a savior or a foe.

He begins to tremble, and I hesitate once more. I don't know if my presence is causing more distress, amplifying whatever battle he's already fighting in his mind.

I lean away, extending one leg off his bed and planting it to the floor, but the moment I do, he yelps again, screaming, "No! No."

I know he isn't talking to me. I know he's not in the room right now. Wherever he is, though, is a place much worse, and I don't want him to be alone when he returns.

I think my leaving him alone may be the reason he's facing this.

The reason he's so broken.

With that in mind, I lift my knee back onto the bed, gentle as I crawl across the mattress and to his side. He's still flailing, and I have to dodge a rogue arm as I sit back against his headboard, nudging my own arm behind his neck.

My movement causes him to roll right over, his head falling onto my lap as his heavy arm drapes across my thighs. I run my fingers through his curls, hushing him again. "I've got you. It's okay. You're safe, I promise."

Finally, he exhales a shuddering breath, hand tightening on my thigh. He turns his face to me, and his eyes are finally closed. His breathing evens out, and his lips part slightly as heavy huffs of air filter through, though, not as frantic or panicked as they were before.

I continue brushing his hair while my eyes trace the outlines of his face. He's so beautiful; it feels like an eternity since I've allowed myself to savor it—savor him. His long lashes cast shadows over his freckled cheeks, strong nose, and perfect lips.

Tears pour from my eyes like rainfall now, watching the person I once loved beyond words find rest in my arms. I fight to quell my broken sobs, not wanting the rise and fall of my chest to disturb his finally found sleep.

"How did we get here, huh?" I ask the darkness cast over us. "It wasn't supposed to be like this." I brush my thumb over his temple. "I'm so sorry."

His hand slides up my thigh and over my hip, tucking beneath the hem of my shirt and resting on the bare skin of my stomach. The caress is warm and familiar, like coming home. His entire bed smells like him. Rain and pine. Everything I used to associate with comfort and safety and belonging, it swallows me. I feel blanketed in it—his touch and presence. It's the kind of wholeness I know has been missing from my life, the kind of feeling that might just heal me.

I'm flooded with memories of all the ways he's saved me throughout my life.

At thirteen when I bled through my pants at school, and everyone knew I'd started my period. He tied his sweatshirt around my waist before wrapping me in his arms and telling me it'd be okay.

At fifteen when I was stood up for prom, he snuck me out of the house in my dress and danced with me under the stars in our field of violets.

At nineteen when he rubbed my back as I cried myself to sleep after my brother left for his first World Surf Tour, and I knew I wouldn't see him for months.

At twenty-one when I self-published my first book, and it felt as if he were the only person who truly understood my excitement.

Every time his brother broke my heart, August pieced it back together, keeping my soul intact, repairing every fracture and healing every wound.

His constant assurance, quiet confidence, unbreakable love—it saved me time and time again. In return, I failed him. Broke him. Left him.

It wasn't my intention; I was blinded by my grief and guilt, too focused on wallowing in my own pain and all the reasons I didn't deserve recovery. I never considered he might be doing the same, never thought about how my absence would've destroyed him.

Maybe, deep down, I thought he deserved the hurt too. Maybe that was my grief talking—I don't know anymore.

All I know now is that as I study his beautiful face, he's still my best friend. The love of my life. He never stopped being either of those things to me. I only stopped being worthy of them. Worthy of him. I thought that notion had been clear, but I can see now that I was wrong.

I watch him, and I'm stricken with the realization that the person who sleeps before me now is merely shattered remains of the boy who once loved me so fiercely, and I'm the monster who took a sledgehammer to his soul.

❧

A soft groan rattles through my consciousness, and as I float back to reality, I realize how fucking sore my neck is.

I match the sound with my own, forcing open my exhausted eyes, blinking against the daylight. Fuck. I fell asleep in August's room.

I'm still sitting mostly upright, my back rigid and aching against the headboard. My legs are numb beneath his weight. I drop my head. August is still lying across my lap, his fingers flexing against the skin at my hip, and it's impossible to ignore the low-burning blaze that sets off in my core at the feel of his touch.

He groans again, eyes fluttering heavily as he stirs. He blinks rapidly, and when his gaze catches mine, his thick brows furrow. Sliding off my lap, he pulls himself into a sitting position beside me on the bed, scrambling to the edge of it as he tilts his head in confusion.

His lip trembles, and I almost think he's going to speak, but he doesn't. I wonder if he doesn't know what to say, or if he can't decide if I'm really here. I wonder if he's still lost inside his dreams.

I wonder how often he dreams of me.

"Hey," I say softly. "Did you get some sleep?"

His eyes aren't terror-stricken as they were last night. He appears somewhat rested, his hair mussed from my fingers running through it for hours. My hand twitches, wanting to brush his curls from his forehead, but I freeze, thinking better of it, placing my hand atop my thigh instead.

August watches my movement, rearing back, almost as if any touch from me would be venomous. His lip curls, emerald eyes narrowing, unnerving in their cold assessment. "What the fuck are you doing?"

His sharp words slam into me with enough force to send me flinching, like a physical blow right to my guts. Whatever remnants of the soft boy who slept in my arms is gone, replaced by anger and accusation.

"You...you were having a night terror. I..." My voice shakes as I try to explain myself, because he stares after me like my mere existence is a violation. "I heard you, and..." I tremble as I force the rest of the sentence from my mouth. "You looked...sounded... It scared the fuck out of me."

He scoffs, revulsion dripping from his lips as he spits, "So, you took it upon yourself to invade my space? Crawl into my fucking bed?"

There is so much loathing in his face it rocks me to my core. I slowly climb out of his bed, feeling like an intruder, like a trespasser. Backing toward the door, I'm unable to stop the moisture that's building behind my eyes from spilling over.

"I'm sorry. I was trying to help. It killed me to see you like that, August."

He laughs, lifting off the other side of the mattress. "Do you know how long I've been having night terrors?" He begins pacing, hands sliding through his hair. "Years. Years that you abandoned me. Years that you didn't give a fuck about what I was going through." He stops, head lifting, eyes setting raging flame to my very soul. "So, no. You don't get to care now that you've been a witness to it. You don't get to manipulate me with your fucking tears. Crawl into my bed, thinking you're doing me some kind of favor. Do not try to convince me that you are concerned for my well-being now, because when I needed you most, you weren't fucking here. I've learned to take care of myself now. I don't need you. I do not want you."

There is no manipulation in my reaction to his venom—the trembling of my limbs and the streams cascading down my cheeks. It's all real, because his words are like weapons, obliterating me from the inside out.

"I've long wished I could forget you, and I've failed every time I've tried. You're like a goddamn parasite, embedded in my brain and feeding off my soul since the day I met you. Sucking the life from me little by little until I'm nothing but a corpse." He swallows hard, as if an attempt to calm himself, though it does no good. "I've tried drinking you away. Sleeping you away. Fucking you away with other people. Nothing works. I can't get rid of you. I've tried to numb you with needles on my flesh, with ink and metal... but you're still right here." He taps his temple. "You're always right. Fucking. Here."

With every twist of his knife, every stab into the center of my chest, anger bubbles up my throat like the blood he'd gladly watch me choke on.

Yet, he presses on, like he won't be satisfied until he's obliterated me into nothing but charred fragments of a once whole person. "You're like a drug, and the moment I think I'm clean, you're forcibly injecting yourself right into my veins. A fucking vice that I cannot escape from. You're already inescapable inside my mind, so the least you could do is ensure you're not the first thing I fucking see when I open my eyes, too."

I blink at him, stunned that these words could be falling from his mouth. My voice is vicious as I seethe, "You invited me to move in. You asked me here. Who the fuck are you to put that blame on me?"

"I also asked you to keep your goddamn distance!" he snaps. "Ships in the night, remember?"

"What the fuck did you expect me to do when your screams were like spears shooting right through my sails? Ignore them?"

"Yes!" He's damn near shouting now, chest heaving, face flushed with anger. "I did not invite you into my bed, or into my life. I invited you to rent a room. You are a stranger, Elena, and I don't want you to be anything more than that. Never again."

"Fuck you." I grasp the door handle, throwing it open. Hot, indignant tears free-falling from my eyes, my words choked by the emotion clogging my throat.

"Sometimes, I think that'd be easier," he murmurs, the sentence barely audible, but loud enough for me to hear it before I step through the threshold of his room.

"What did you just say to me?"

He'd turned toward the bathroom, but at the realization I didn't leave, he spins, eyes snapping to mine. Irate flame pierces through me. "I still think about fucking you, and I hate myself for it. I detest my desire for your body, but I can't stop myself from wondering if the reminder that you're nothing more than flesh and bone, just like me, would help rid myself of this soul-eating compulsion to know you."

Like the final rip of a cord, any light left inside me winks out at those words.

That choked anger, that bubbling sensation—it boils over. Like a match sliding across red phosphate, I catch flame. It's not sensical, the destructive craving that takes me over, the urge to make him burn and bleed and crumble to pieces just the way his words have done to me.

I still think about fucking you, and I hate myself for it.

Sick satisfaction rushes through me as I watch the kernel of fear spark to life in his eyes when I flash him a feral smile. He thought he found strength in the words he just spewed to tear me apart, but that slip-up was a showcase to his weakness.

Turning on my heel without another word, I slam his door behind me—hard enough to rock the foundation of the house we share.

Chapter Fifteen

Violet

"Cherry" - Lana Del Rey

Trepidation hangs heavy on my shoulders as I slide the house key into the lock.

Yesterday was Sunday, which meant it was family dinner day, and was supposed to be my day off. Except, after waking up and finding Elena in my bed, I went straight down to the boardwalk anyway. I couldn't spend the entire day in the house with her, and the only place that felt safe was the quiet solitude of my office behind a locked door with an audiobook and my sketch pad.

I ran into Darby as I arrived, and she mentioned that, for the first time since moving back to California, Elena had agreed to join dinner. I wasn't about to be the person to ruin that for her, or for the rest of them, regardless of how much she'd pissed me off. So, I mentioned that I was covering for someone and couldn't make it.

I made sure to arrive home before she did last night. She was gone for work when I woke up this morning, and I haven't seen her since she left my room with tears streaming down her face.

I know I overreacted. Badly. I was way out of line in what I'd said to her, though my tongue held no lies. I meant every word, but the delivery in which I spewed that vitriol was so fucking wrong. She didn't deserve that, even if it felt like a breath of relief when I finally let it out.

I know I have night terrors, and I know they're awful to

witness. I have no doubt I scared her shitless, and she did the only thing she knew to calm me.

But the truth is, for one split second when I opened my eyes yesterday morning and saw hers staring back at me, I convinced myself I was living in a different reality. One where she was mine, where she would wake in my bed because it was hers too, where my brother was alive, and we were happy.

When actuality slapped me in the face as the world set in around me, I lost my mind.

It hurt too much, it was a gutting moment of realization, and I took all of it out on her.

I sigh deeply, knowing that if she hasn't locked herself away for the evening already, I'm going to have to swallow my pride and apologize to her. Every moment with her feels like a battle—some enticing, some challenging, all of them stirring up feelings in my otherwise numb existence. Other moments are painful, bringing to the surface all the hurt we've ever caused.

I know it's best to avoid her, but sometimes I can't bring myself to do so. Sometimes, when we've gone days without crossing paths, I even find myself missing her. Hoping that I'll find her in the kitchen or descending the stairs when I open the front door.

Like, even though I'm constantly reminded of all the agony she's caused me, my baser instincts long to be near her—the pull I've felt my entire life.

As I push open the door, convincing myself I'm ready for whatever I find on the other side, I'm caught completely off guard—utterly unprepared for the sound that meets me.

That unmistakable, sultry, cock-pulsing moan that's forever branded into my memory, echoes through the quiet house, accented by the familiar buzzing of her vibrator.

All the guilt that's followed me the last twenty-four hours simmers to molten anger, liquefying into blazing heat that settles in my core. I slam the door behind me, loud enough to grab her attention.

The sounds are clear enough that there is no way her bedroom door isn't open, and the torment is nothing but personal, because she knows exactly what time I arrive home from work each day.

Confirming my suspicions, the vibrator doesn't shut off after I make my presence known. It continues, and a soft yet loud, "August" echoes off the walls of the house.

She's doing this on fucking purpose.

What's worse, is that I understand why. I know she's toying with me after those fucked-up comments I made about my desire to fuck her out of my system.

She's taunting me for revenge, and I deserve it.

That knowledge doesn't dissolve the exasperation funneling through me as I climb the stairs, each step louder than the one before it, making damn sure she knows I'm coming.

Her proximity has been chipping away at my composure day-by-day since she moved in. I'm fighting a constant battle between rage, lust, and longing. It's taken every ounce of strength to keep her at arm's length, but waking to her in my bed and now hearing her moan my name has obliterated my self-control.

Perhaps I'm a weak man, but the moment my name left her lips, I lost the fight at denying us both the touch of each other's body.

Sure enough, her door is wide open as I turn right at the top of the staircase. Elena's sprawled out on the center of her bed, legs spread, head thrown back on the pillows, framed by her dark, wild curls. The head of the serpent snaking around her thigh seems to taunt me, the crescent moon beneath the center of her breasts a cruel reminder of a past life, just like the violets on her arm. She holds a wand to her core with both hands, arms bracketing her chest so her bare tits press together, the bars through each of her nipples glinting in the moonlight filtering through the window with each rapid breath.

My heart pounds in my ears, all the blood in my body rushing straight to my cock at the sight of her. In a god-like show of strength, I refrain myself from approaching, simply leaning against the doorway and crossing my arms.

"Yes, Daddy...please." She sighs, and I'm certain she knows I'm watching.

The title sets my blood boiling, my cock aching with need as I watch her open legs tremble, her perfect fucking body on display—a goddamn offering. Her lashes flutter, full lips parted in a silent *O* as she chases pleasure with my image in her mind.

"You're a fucking brat."

She lets out an all-too-dramatic gasp, head snapping up and eyes fluttering open. They go wide, but it's all for show. "Oh, Augustus." She pants. "I didn't know you were home."

"I'm so sure," I growl. Her eyes sparkle with mischief as her knees drop, spreading her wider, revealing her pussy. My restraint snaps, and I launch into her room. "Fucking cock tease, you are." I stop in front of the bed, and she playfully bites her lip, extending her foot to the center of my chest. I grasp her ankle. "You are torment personified, you know that?"

A feline smile curves her lips as she shakes her leg out of my hold. "And yet you can't stay away. Came running the second you heard me call your name."

I fucking hate her. I swear, I fucking hate her.

"Like chasing a bad habit." I grab her knee, hooking it around my waist as I lean over her mattress. "You say I come running, but here you are...practically begging for it. You think I can't see the way your cunt started dripping all over the bed the second I walked through that door? Needy for me, Elena? Desperate?"

"Hmm." She sighs like my words hold no bearing. With her other leg, she pushes against my chest, forcing me upward as she slides her foot down my stomach, toes dipping into my waistband. She drags down my sweatpants, voice like silk as she murmurs, "Looks like you're desperate too."

I don't stop her, and she unhooks her leg around my waist, sitting up to help tug my bottoms to my knees, my cock tenting my boxers. She licks her lips, eyes fixated on it, like she's remembering what it tasted like in her mouth.

Her eyes navigate across the rest of my body, pausing on

my tattooed thigh before snapping to my face. "Does it cause you pain? Seeing my name every time you look at your skin?"

Her words rip through my chest like bullets. I fall forward, one hand landing on the bed beside her, the other fastening around her neck.

If she insists on killing me, maybe I'll take her to hell too.

"Does it cause you pain? When you bite your tongue and swallow the urge to call out my name each time you're fucking someone else?" My breath skates across the tattoo on her neck. "Dreaming of an experience you never got to have?"

She gasps, and her legs wrap themselves back around my waist, flushing our hips together as if she's desperate for the friction. Her fingers curl around the base of my neck.

"I could ask you the same," she whispers. "I don't imagine it'll be too difficult to get you to fuck me now, would it?"

As I pull back, she smiles softly, like she believes she just won a match in this fucked-up game between us. I don't see it that way. We're both tortured souls who've become so numb we're chasing any feeling we can find.

Despite that understanding, I refuse to let her come out of this interaction on top.

I take my grip off her throat and let her legs fall until I'm kneeling between them on the bed. "Spread your lips and show me your pussy, Elena." Her back arches at the sound of my voice, hips lifting in my direction, but I deny her what she's searching for. "I want your vulnerability, the same way you took mine. Invite me in. Ask me for it."

At first, she smirks, moving her leg toward my chest again, thinking she can toy with me until I grant her what she wants. I grasp her ankle and throw it back onto the bed.

The action causes her lips to part—long, dark lashes fluttering as she finally relents, sliding a trembling hand down her bare chest. Moving between the valley of her breasts and across her stomach—over the tattoos I put there years ago—she hovers at the apex of her thighs. Slowly extending her pointer and middle finger, she opens herself for me, and the sight of her wet, glistening pussy is damn near enough to make me come.

A deep groan tears from my throat. "Beg."

Rage and desperation war within her eyes. She wants to fight me. She doesn't want me to know just how badly she needs me, but I see it all the same.

"No," she attempts to say, but it only sounds like a moan.

I slide my hand up her leg, fingers dancing along her thigh. The heat of her flesh and the goosebumps on her skin tell me how much she craves my touch.

"Stop fighting me, Little Vice." Her eyes flare at the name. My palm glides along the dip of her waist, but I don't go near the place she needs me most. Moving to her breast, I brush my thumb across her nipple piercing. "You're no better than I am." I hover over her, bending down so that she can feel my breath against her skin when I murmur, "You know how badly you want to be ruined by me."

"August," she cries, body jerking as I flick my tongue over her nipple, the metal of the barbell cool against my lips.

"Beg, Elena," I demand once more.

"Please." The word comes out a breathless whisper, but it's all the surrender I need. The submission that reminds us both she's fucking mine.

"Please what?" I ask.

"Please..." Her breath hitches, eyes glistening in the moonlight filtering through the window. "Fuck me."

I laugh against her flesh, relishing in the feeling of having her exactly where I want her. Needy and at my mercy.

I rise off the bed, kicking off my underwear and stepping out of my joggers. The air hangs heavy between Elena and me, standing before each other without clothing.

Not naked, not bare, because both of our walls are higher than ever. We're guarded and untrusting, merely chasing sensation with physical touch because we've both reached the point of combustion in the other's presence. If we don't find some way to pierce this tension, we'll crumble entirely.

I kneel on the bed. "Keep showing me your pretty cunt, Little Vice."

Her eyes fall closed, head falling back as she rolls a peaked nipple between her fingers, back arching when she spreads her fingers wider, exposing herself to me, and I'm fucking aching.

"Tell me what you want," I command, voice gruff and strained.

"I want you to fuck me, Augustus," she whispers.

"Why do you cry my name when you come? Why do you see me when you touch yourself?" She moves two fingers over her clit, rolling them in slow circles. I press my hand against them, halting her movement and adding just enough pressure over her most sensitive place to make her tremble. "Answer me."

Her eyes snap open, blazing through me with equal parts lust and longing. "The last time I remember feeling anything at all was when I was wrapped up in your touch," she admits, her tone timid and soft. "I can't help it if it's you I picture when I'm chasing euphoria."

Her answer sends insanity barreling through my veins, my vision damn-near blurred with rage. Because it's her fucking fault she's so numb—that we're both so numb. Her fucking fault we've been reduced to nothing but dust and desperation and daydreams.

She destroyed us, and now she's returned, taunting me with remnants of everything she left behind.

"You know what your touch reminds me of?" I slide my hand up her stomach, closing it around her throat, squeezing hard enough to make her gasp. "Pain."

I finally drop my hips to meet hers, feeling the slick slide of her arousal as my cock nestles itself between the lips of her pussy. I don't allow myself to sink inside her, though.

"You once said you loved the pain I cause," she chokes out, voice vibrating against my palm.

"I do." I smile, thrusting so that the head of my cock flicks against her clit. She gasps, hands latching onto my forearm as her eyes roll back. "And I sure as fuck am going to enjoy punishing you too."

"Are you going to fuck me now?"

"No." I huff a rough laugh, and her brow furrows. "I'm not stupid enough to sell my soul to the devil. I'm not going to fuck you, Elena." I pump again, still refusing to notch myself inside her, but allowing my cock to move between her slit, adding pressure to her clit and coating myself in her wetness. "But I'll still make you cry my name."

"God," she groans, throat tightening in my grip.

"God's not here, Little Vice. You pray to me now."

I move my cock between her thighs, pulsating at the feel of her slick skin, her pussy lips wrapped around me. Her tits bounce with each thrust, the jewelry through her nipples glinting in the moonlight. I'm going to fucking come like this. I don't even need to be inside her. I don't need her mouth or her hand. Just her flesh grazing mine is enough to send me over the edge.

One of my bars notches against her clit, and she inhales swiftly, eyes blowing wide. "Fuck," she cries. "Are you pierced?"

I nod, panting through clenched teeth as I fight back the urge to well and truly fuck her. My self-control is hanging by a thread, and I deserve a goddamn medal for the restraint I'm expressing in this moment.

"How...many?"

"Why don't you count for me?" I slow my movements, dragging the first bar of my ladder against her clit. "Out loud, Elena."

Her legs tremble at my waist, and I know that she's tightening around nothing—so fucking desperate to have me inside her. "One?"

I nod, inching my hips forward.

"Two," she gasps.

"Good." I thrust once more. "Almost there."

Her eyes roll back, nails digging into my back. "Three."

I nod again, moving faster but keeping my base firmly

placed over her clit so she can feel them with each thrust. I know it's heightening the sensation for her; I can see it in the way she quivers uncontrollably. She's fighting to hold it back, but she's on the brink of losing herself.

"Ask me when, Elena. Ask me why." The words are hardly audible through my clenched teeth, as I hold on to my composure, hot need barreling down my spine and gathering at the base of it.

I drop to my elbow, bringing our faces closer together—close enough that my forehead rests against hers. Her eyes rage and glisten, near-black with lust, lids fluttering in a fight to stay open. She slips a full lip between her teeth, and I'm so entranced by her ethereal beauty that I damn near forget the question I was asking.

Damn near forget why I want to hate her so badly.

She's the kind of allure, the kind of touch and warmth, that makes you want to fall in love instead. Let her demolish and destroy and obliterate you only so you can thank her when it's done.

With her so fucking close—lips full, plush, and inviting—I'm pulsing, aching. But more than anything, I just want to kiss her. I want to remember the simplicity of her mouth and the ease of her lips against my own. The way Elena kisses me feels like wrongs being righted, like the world tilting on its axis in a way that makes the sun shine brighter. Like her lips could alter reality and unravel the fabric of the universe itself.

It's been years since our last kiss, but I still feel it in my mouth and on my tongue—with every word I speak, every breath I take. It's inescapable, it's torturous, and I never want to let it go. Wrapped up in her body, feeling her writhe beneath me, whimpering my name—I want nothing more than to kiss her again. To be reminded of light after an eternity in darkness.

"When?" she asks, voice a timid whisper, breaking me from my enchantment. "When did you get your piercing?"

My eyes snap to hers, and I realize I've slowed my tempo, hardly moving my hips as my cock nestles between her slit. It's throbbing, and I know all she'd have to do is clench her thighs to make me come, but I'll be damned if I get off without her doing the same.

"January thirteenth." I begin thrusting through her lips again. "Four years ago. That was the first one." Her breath hitches as I knock one bar against her clit, sliding my hips upward so the next one brushes it too. "The second one I added exactly one year later."

Her features twist in recognition, that realization warring with the pleasure I'm sending through her veins as I rub my bars against her.

She knows exactly what the date January 13 means. I woke up that morning flooded with texts by her brothers attempting to make sense of what had happened. I didn't care. I had received her message loud and crystal clear. I turned off my phone, drove down to San Diego, and spent two weeks staying with my former mentor, Jensen.

That day, though, nothing was going to numb the pain she'd caused. Nothing was going to distract me from it. I knew that, but in an attempt to chase the hurt, I pierced my cock. Pierced my tongue, too. Had Jensen start a rib piece—whatever body modifications I could imagine causing me the most amount of pain, whatever I could do to drown out her absence.

I thrust my cock an inch higher, finally resting that last bar over her bud. "Third one I had done on January thirteenth, too. Last year."

She gasps, and her hands grip my waist, twisting in the fabric of my shirt as she flushes us closer together. She begins to move her hips in sync with mine, meeting me with each pump. Sparks fly up my spine, electricity humming between us like a living current.

"Why"—she pants between words—"didn't you add a fourth one last month?"

I slide my hand from her neck, bracketing her jaw and brushing my thumb over her full bottom lip, her tongue flicking out in anticipation, briefly meeting my skin.

"Because you're home now. Under my roof," I rasp, slipping

my finger into her mouth, and she moans, accepting it. "Where you fucking belong."

Like a dam being demolished, Elena bursts. Head flying back, my name crawling out of her throat on a cry. Her body shakes uncontrollably, nails digging into my ribs as she loses herself. Despite not being inside her, I feel her release gushing over the base of my cock, dripping down my balls, her thighs clenching and quivering.

I fucking explode, my tip pulsing as cum spurts between her pussy, spilling onto her stomach. My forehead falls against hers, both hands twisting in her hair behind her head as my strength gives out. We become a mess of tangled limbs, broken tension, and sated sighs.

I couldn't count how many times I've orgasmed over the last four years—whether by my hand or someone else's, but what I do know is that none of them could compare to this feeling. Elena's breath, her touch, her endless eyes. Being wrapped in her is a sensation beyond description, beyond language. Nothing I could chase—pride or lust or greed—would measure up to her.

She is the ultimate vice, and there is no escaping it.

No cleanse to rid me of the addiction, the habit, or the craving. I'm not sure I see a point in trying anymore. Maybe I don't mind being infected; maybe I've only ever been meant to chase her anyway.

Deafening quiet blankets over us, the only sound our mingled breath and the drumming of our hearts. Elena's hand snakes underneath the hem of my shirt, fingers tracing my back, gliding over my sweat-slicked skin. I tremble at her touch, savoring the moment before I know it's no longer appropriate to be collapsed on top of her, and I have to pull away.

She sighs as I do, almost like she wishes I wouldn't.

I sit back on my knees, unable to stop myself from running a finger through the release pooling on her stomach, gliding it across her skin and between the valley of her breasts.

Elena watches with rapt attention. "You made a mess of me."

I bring two fingers to her mouth, nudging at her lips. She opens, allowing me to dip them inside as she licks my cum away. "Now you know how you make me feel all the time."

Her eyes flare, but she doesn't respond when I remove my fingers from her mouth, stepping off the bed and putting on my pants and underwear. She stays in place as I dart into her bathroom, wetting a cloth and returning to the bed, wiping my release from her stomach and between her slit.

"Did you get it out of your system, Augustus?" she asks as I toss the cloth in the hamper beside her bed. "Have you been reminded that I'm nothing more than flesh and bone?"

No. I've been reminded that you're absolutely everything.

"Is the game over now?" she continues, crossing her legs and propping an arm behind her head as she watches me.

"Nah, baby," I taunt as I reach for the door. "We're just getting started."

Chapter Sixteen

Vice

"Ribs" - Lorde

"Do you think I could do this upside down?" Leo asks.

I drop my book, glancing at him from the other end of the couch. He's got his feet against the wall, head dangling off the end of the sofa as "California Love" blows through the Bluetooth speaker on the desk in the corner. A blue glass bong sits in front of him, and his eyes are narrowed in deep concentration as he attempts to flick his lighter and stretch his neck so that his mouth can cover the pipe.

"I can't fucking believe you're about to be a dad," Everett mutters from the chair across the room, offering Leo the same perplexed expression I know I have.

Miraculously, my brother gets his lips around the mouth of the bong while simultaneously lighting the bud, inhaling a perfect hit before using his free hand to push the bong away from his head and blow out a cloud of smoke.

"First of all, fuck you." He points at Everett. "I'm going to be a great dad. And secondly, fuck you." He swings his legs sideways, damn near taking me out in the process. I shove his shin out of my face and off the couch as he moves into a sitting position beside me. "You know I have actual fears. How dare you exploit them like that."

"What fears?" I ask, closing the book in my lap. There is no way I'll get any reading done so long as they're here.

I got off work this morning at eleven, and about four hours later, both of my brothers let themselves into August's house, waking me from my nap and asking me to join them for a smoke session in the sunroom.

I haven't ventured in here much since moving in, but it's a nice enough space. Clearly, August uses it as some kind of studio with a makeshift tattooing bench and a worktable sprawled with canvas paper and pencils. There is a couch against the back wall, facing out into the backyard through the wall-to-wall windows across from it, and a lounge chair in the corner.

Supposedly, Darby kicked Leo out of the house for a few hours this afternoon because he's smothering her. He says he's not, and we all know that isn't true. He smothers her on a good day, when she's not pregnant. The way I'd describe him now is more like he's attempting to crawl inside her skin and carry the baby for her.

I don't blame her for telling him to get out of her face and settle down before coming back home.

"My dad abandoned me," Leo continues. "I mean...he loved my mom, but he couldn't do it without her, and when he had to, he just gave up." He speaks of the situation casually, but the distant look in his eyes and the way he chews on the inside of his cheek tells me it's something he battles with often. "What if something happened to Darby, and I ended up the same way?"

"It's not something in your blood, Leo," Everett scoffs. "That kind of shit is learned behavior, and that asshole didn't raise you. Carlos and Monica Ramos raised you, and they did a good fucking job. The only thing in your genes is a susceptibility to alcoholism, which is why you smoke weed." Everett nods toward the bong. "You're going to be a good dad."

Leo sends him a grateful smile. "You're a good dad too."

"I know."

"Do you guys think I'll be a good mom?" I ask.

Everett inhales so sharply he begins coughing, and Leo looks at me like I just kicked a dog. Their heads swivel frantically between me and each other, eyes wide, mouths gaping, unsure how to respond.

I burst into laughter, the sativa Leo brought beginning to kick in. "I'm kidding. You know I don't want fuckin' kids."

Everett lets out a sigh of relief as Leo rubs a hand down his face.

"You have all the qualities of being a good mother, but your lifelong adamancy of not giving birth kind of threw me," Leo says. "You will be a cool-ass aunt, though."

"Oh, absolutely." I nod rapidly. "I'm going to be super mysterious and edgy. I'll teach them all tarot and how to put a man in his place. I'll show them where to find the sluttiest fanfics on the internet, and I'll introduce them to Lana Del Rey so they never forget who our Lord and Savior really is."

They frown at me, and I'm so fucking happy that both of my brothers are girl dads. I laugh again, falling back onto the throw pillow behind my head and tossing my legs into my brother's lap.

"I like hearing you laugh, Lele," Everett admits. "You seem like you're doing better, and Dal said you're doing a great job at the bakery."

"Tell my boss not to talk about her employees to her boyfriend. It's unprofessional and none of your fuckin' business." I kick a leg out, pointing at him with my big toe.

The grand opening of the bakery was this past weekend, and it went amazingly. People came from all over the region to celebrate it. Turns out Dahlia's background in marketing, graphic design, and social media did wonders for promoting the bakery and the boardwalk as a whole. I worked three twelve-hour days in a row, the entire family along with me, and I can't remember the last time I was so fucking exhausted.

It served as a good distraction after whatever the fuck happened with August in my room last week. I've hardly seen him since, having just one wordless run-in in the kitchen on Thursday.

When I decided to masturbate with my bedroom door wide open, right around the time he gets home from work, I knew that I'd inevitably cause chaos because of it. I thought he'd sulk, slam doors, and maybe yell at me later on. I did not think he'd appear in my doorway for a front row show, but once he started playing the game, I didn't have the strength to call time-out. I joined right in, and something far too real erupted from that pent-up frustration.

It was rough and wild and painful, but soft and tender and raw at the same time.

Emotionally exhausting and spiritually fulfilling, all while providing a desperately needed release I've been craving far too long.

Nothing has ever felt like that—like him.

It's equal parts terrifying and addicting, and I want to do it all over again. I want more of it. All of him. The yearning to feel him inside me is agony—a constant gnawing urge I can't relinquish on my own. The need festers beneath my skin.

I'm hot just thinking about it.

"Elena?"

My eyes snap to my twin's, face flushing. "What?"

"What are you thinking about?" Leo nudges me with his knee.

I don't bother lying. "An orgasm I had last week."

"Jesus Christ," Leo mutters, shoving my legs off him and curling his lip at the same moment Everett groans, "Why the fuck would you say that to us right now?"

"You asked?"

My brother rolls his eyes. "I was trying to be fucking sentimental. Goddammit!" He runs a tattooed hand through his hair. "Can you not allow me to live in a blissful ignorance where my sister isn't a sexual creature?"

"Why does it offend you so much?" I ask. "I don't yell at Dahlia when she yaps about how big your dick is, no matter how disturbing I find it. Stop conforming to gender norms, Everett."

"You shouldn't have said that thing about his dick," Leo murmurs. "He's going to be annoying now."

"I didn't need the reminder. I'm well-fucking-aware." Everett smirks. "And I'm a feminist. We know this, don't insult me by insinuating otherwise. I don't think it's wrong. I just don't want to hear about it. You're like a baby to me."

I smile innocently. "A baby who was so thoroughly ravished—in filthy, derogatory ways, just so we're clear—that she's still thinking about it, even a week late—"

"Hey, Auggie." Leo flashes a shit-eating grin, eyes raising to something behind me.

My mouth clamps shut, words stuck in my throat as I slowly turn my head, finding August towering in the doorway. Of course, he's just gotten home from a run, so his white T-shirt is sticking to his toned chest, a lickable bead of sweat falling down his temple. He's fighting to maintain his composure, but when his eyes flash to me, I find a heat that could match the flame in my cheeks right now.

He heard every fucking word.

"Am I interrupting?" he asks softly. He's not wearing his glasses, so his green eyes are clear and smoldering when they meet mine, burning holes through my fucking face. "I heard commotion and figured you both must be here."

"My wife told me I had to leave the house because I'm a stage-five clinger," Leo chimes.

"I'm not surprised by that in any capacity." August smiles playfully before lifting his shirt to wipe the sweat from his forehead, revealing his lean stomach and golden skin. The pronunciation of his abdominals could've been carved by Michelangelo himself. It's actually insulting to look like this. It pisses me off, in fact.

A frown tugs at my lips as my gaze catches on an unfamiliar tattoo along his ribcage. It's fucking huge and heavily detailed. The art is beautiful but heartbreaking. Literally. A human heart spans the length of his side, framed by unmistakable violets, exactly like the design along my forearm. A knife pierces the heart from top to bottom, blood dripping down the blade.

Some kind of script or writing is faded behind the heart, but before I can attempt to make out the words, he drops his shirt, breaking my stare. When I lift my gaze to his face, his eyes are on me.

"You did interrupt," Everett says, filling the awkward silence. "Our sister here was just telling us all about her orgasms. So, I'd like to thank you for your timing, actually."

August fights to keep his expression neutral, but I don't miss the slow rise of his brow beneath that gold hoop pierced through it. The near imperceptible tilt of his lips as he eyes me once again.

"Well, unfortunately for you two"—he nods at my brothers—"I've got to take a shower. So, I'll leave you to Elena and her orgasms." He smirks, giving me a final once-over before he spins off the door frame and disappears down the hall.

I can only pray that the color of my face doesn't match the heat licking up my cheeks. My stomach turns over on itself, butterflies clog my throat, and my pussy fucking throbs at the weight of that interaction.

I swallow, willing neutrality into my features.

"So, how's that going?" Leo asks.

My eyes flash to his, and while he studies me intently, there's no accusation in his gaze or in his tone. I glance at my twin, who's oblivious as always, staring down at his phone.

"How's what going?"

"You and August. Are you good? Friends again? You haven't talked to us about what living together is like, and I want to make sure you're comfortable here. Not feeling like you need to stay here out of necessity."

Everett perks at that, and he slips his phone into his pocket before leaning on his knees.

"Living here is fine. We mostly stay out of each other's way." I pick at my nails. "We'll never be friends again, but we coexist like two roommates should."

Everett hums contemplatively, his foot tapping against the floor.

"What?" I ask, looking at him. "What is it you want to say?"

I can always tell when he wants to say something but is too afraid, or otherwise feels like he can't.

"You seem to be doing better." He shrugs. "I thought August may have something to do with it, that's all."

"He gave me a place to stay," I respond. "So, that's something, I guess. But I don't really need the rest of you holding out hope for anything more. Too much has happened, and we've outgrown each other." Those words burn like acid as they crawl out of my throat. My soul wants to scream wrong, wrong, wrong but I continue, "We won't be friends like we used to be."

"I think it's more than that, Lena," Leo chimes in. "If you've ever loved someone, in whatever capacity that may be, you never fully stop. A little part of you always hopes for their well-being. I think just knowing he's here, that he's safe and okay, after everything we've been through... It's helping you, even if the relationship isn't the same anymore."

I only shrug.

Of course, he's not wrong. I've always longed for August to be safe and healthy. Maybe not happy, not in my deepest moments of despair when I needed someone to blame, but I savored whatever information my family would share in passing. The confirmation that he was breathing was something I couldn't function without.

"I mean...the first two days Darby and I drove from Kansas out here, she didn't even speak to me." Leo laughs to himself. "There was so much tension, so many secrets, we were completely untrusting of each other, but it was like..." He shakes his head, taking a breath. "Just knowing she was under the same roof I was, even if in different rooms, I felt settled. I felt whole. That if she needed me, I was nearby. That I knew where she was and that she was safe. After so many years of asking questions, or fear I'd stumble across her name in an obituary or something like that... the knowing, it helped."

"Yeah," I breathe. "It does."

"Yeah, well..." Everett sighs. "I still think you should be seeing a therapist."

Everett has been pushing therapy to me since the day Zach died, but even harder in the last six months. They tell me everyone is going to therapy now, at the insistence of Dahlia. Even August has one, a fact which took me by surprise.

But even with the distraction of living here, the distraction of having a job, the urge to write again—that heaviness in my bones remains. That guttural exhaustion and self-loathing rest beneath the surface of my skin. Therapy would mean pulling it out, addressing its existence, and I've just learned how to pretend again. Therapy would mean speaking of my past, opening up wounds I'm still attempting to bandage.

Seeing a therapist would mean telling the whole story, and maybe it's not rational, but I'm terrified of the chance that they may look me in the eye and confirm all of my fears.

I am the villain, I am to blame, and there is no hope for me.

"I don't need therapy." I laugh, dodging the concern as I settle back into the couch and throw my legs on Leo again. "I have books, weed, and good orgasms. I'm doing great."

I smile at my brothers, lying through my teeth.

Chapter Seventeen

Violet

"imgonnagetyouback" - Taylor Swift

"You know we have that gallery auction up in Venice Beach this weekend. I'd love it if you came." Everett wraps his arms around the back of Elena's head as he tugs her against his chest.

She locks her hands around his lower back. "I'll think about it."

He laughs, pulling away. "That's better than no."

She's swallowed up next by Leo, who presses his lips to the top of her head. "They always donate a portion of their proceeds to ocean conservation efforts. But they're also working with the Hayes Foundation for this event, so some of the money will be donated in Zach's name too."

When Elena steps out of his arms, she blinks hard, eyes fixed on the floor. The information clearly rocks her, and she takes a brief moment to compose herself before responding.

"It's black tie," I blurt, forcing the attention from her to me.

All three of them turn my way. Elena swallows, studying my face, though I can't read the expression on hers. Finally, she blinks and shakes her head. "That's really cool of them. I'll definitely try to come, okay?"

Leo gives her a closed-lip smile, and both of them say goodbye before heading out the front door. She lets out a deep sigh before padding into the kitchen and digging through the pantry.

"Don't get their hopes up like that," I say, though I didn't mean to.

I'd definitely had the thought—that the moment Elena heard my brother's name, she'd have nothing to do with the event—but there was no need to voice it.

She peeks out of the pantry door, bag of pretzels and a jar of peanut butter in hand, slamming it shut with her foot. "What do you mean by that?"

I shake my head, rubbing a tired hand down my face. "I don't know. Sorry."

I've been running a lot, and I pushed myself especially hard tonight. I'm fucking exhausted. It's the only thing I can do to keep myself out of her fucking bed. This past week has been torturous. Despite my promise that we were only getting started, I've been doing my best to stay away.

Whatever happened that night in her bedroom was an awakening—for both of us, I think. I don't want to see the aftermath of what happens when we cross another line, because it would surely be enough to kill me. It damn near did when I overheard her refer to the night as ravishing, admitting she'd been thinking about it all week. The satisfaction that coursed through my veins at her words could've set my fucking blood on fire. It took all my strength not to let the reaction show in front of her brothers.

Lusting after Elena is one thing, but actually having her is something else entirely.

It's detrimental, and I would not survive.

"No, Augustus. Explain yourself," she presses, her nose scrunching in the way that puts my cock on high alert. I have to grind my teeth to keep from telling her how fucking adorable I find it. Her lip juts out, pouting, and fuck, I want to bite it so badly.

"We all know you're going to bail," I mutter, unable to deny myself the urge to piss her off, just so I can see her pretty face twist in vexation. What the fuck is wrong with me? "So, why bother pretending otherwise?"

She scoffs. "What makes you say that?"

I pop a brow, looking her up and down. She's wearing a maroon crewneck with a dagger in its center, the words *Feeling Stabby* in cursive lettering are over the top and bottom of the image, paired with mismatched blue cotton shorts covered in... tigers?

"You're lazy, you rarely leave the house, and you hate being social." I nod toward her outfit. "Plus, you live in clothing like that. Do you even own something black tie?"

Her brows rise, massive, alluring, want-to-die-inside brown eyes blinking at me in disbelief. Tongue in cheek, she tosses her snacks onto the counter, swiftly closing the distance between us until her toes meet mine.

She bats her lashes, my skin flames, and my cock is hard enough to break through brick when her lips tilt into a saccharine smile. She places a hand at the center of my chest, the prick of her touch sending shivers down my spine, causing me to bite back a moan at nothing more than the goddamn brush of her fingers over my clothed skin. Fuck. I am so ruined.

She drags her hand down, hovering dangerously close to my cock. It pulses, knowing that she's nearby, desperate for her to touch it, take it out. Hold it, suck it, bite it. If she dropped to her knees in front of me right now, I'd throw every ounce of my well-fought caution to the wind, and if she sucked my cock, I'd chant her name like a god I'm praying to.

She doesn't, though. She doesn't do anything but leave me hard and arching when she whispers, "You're going to eat your fucking words, Hayes."

The glare she cuts me has me choking on my breath, and satisfaction simmers in her gaze as she drops her hand, stepping back and snatching her pretzels from the counter before turning toward the stairs.

I watch her perfect ass sway with each step she takes, and I can't help my smile.

"I don't doubt I will, Little Vice."

"Baby girl, I told you not to be lifting heavy shit in your condition," Dom, Everett and Leo's friend, says as he steps away from me and finagles a large box out of his wife's hands. "Sorry, I'll be right back."

"No worries," I say, lifting my glass of whiskey to my lips. "Do you need any help?"

I came early to the event—an auction at an art gallery named Muse—because it's partially happening in my brother's name. The Foundation's name. My parents aren't attending, though, not able to make the drive from Palm Springs.

I talk to my mother often, but our relationship has been notably distant since my brother died.

My dad fucking hates me and refuses to acknowledge my existence.

It's why I had no part in the Foundation when they started it, and why I've never attended the events they've put on. But tonight's auction is in large part due to Everett and Leo and the relationship they have with the gallery's owner. They were insistent that I attend, that I be involved in the Foundation and my brother's memory.

Unsurprisingly, once that was made clear, my parents were conveniently unavailable.

So, I arrived early, because as the only member of the Hayes family in attendance, I felt like I should. Though, everyone keeps treating me like I'm fragile, like I shouldn't lift a finger. I want to scream that it makes me feel out of place and like a burden, but I don't know them that well.

"It's not a condition, Dominic," his wife, Macie, snaps. "It's your spawn."

He laughs affectionately before kissing her forehead. "Okay, fine. Please don't strain yourself while you're developing my spawn."

She huffs, placing a hand over her rounded stomach before facing me. As if she can read the discomfort in my features, she smiles softly. "Come with me. I'll have you help Leo with the lights he's setting up over the front doors."

I set my drink down on one of the standing tables that outline the perimeter of the showroom. Macie leads me through the large, open space and to the front door, where Leo stands on a ladder, stringing small fairy lights over the top of the frame while his wife watches from below.

He pauses, glancing down at Macie and me. "How's she cookin', mama?" he asks, nodding toward her stomach.

Macie drops her head, looking at her body before her gaze swings to Darby. She closes the distance between them. "I'm not as ripe as you are," she says, placing one palm on her stomach before extending the other to Darby's. "But she's baking."

"I hope they're best friends someday." Darby giggles.

"Maybe if we, like...press our bellies together, they'll absorb each other's energy or something." She steps into Darby, bumping their midsections in a way that sends a fit of giggles echoing throughout the room.

I grab the string of lights hanging in the center of the doorway and walk them to the side opposite Leo, tossing them over the frame and latching them into the hooks that line the door.

"Thanks, Auggie," he says.

Macie turns, hands on her hips as she examines our work. "Perfect." She claps. "It gets pretty dark in here after the sun sets. We want to keep the lighting low and calm. These will definitely help with ambiance."

"I don't need to make a speech or anything, do I?" I ask.

"Nope." Her blond curls bounce as she shakes her head. "Not unless you want to."

"I don't."

She laughs. "It'll be pretty low-key. Local collectors and buyers, plus the artists and their families, will be in attendance. Everyone is free to silently bid on pieces they're interested in. Next week, I'll contact winners and coordinate delivery. A quarter of the proceeds go to the artist, a quarter to Muse, and the other half is split between the Hayes Foundation and a variety of other conservation charities. There will be an open bar and hors d'oeuvres. Feel free to mingle and talk with buyers about your story and the Foundation. They'll probably be willing to bid higher if you do."

I chuff awkwardly, rubbing the back of my neck. "Honestly, I'd rather not do that, either."

Macie shrugs. "That's fine. I can do it. I'm great at talking to people, and there's nothing I love more than getting a man to open his wallet."

"Are all the buyers men?" I wonder.

"No. But most of them are married to one, and if there's one thing I love even more, it's getting a man to spend exorbitant amounts of cash on his spouse."

"Damn right," her husband chimes as he saddles up beside her.

"Please," she scoffs. "You love spending money on me."

"Yep." Dom nods, kissing her temple. "Turns me on."

I chuckle as they both step away, Dom's hands all over his wife while she laughs into his shoulder. I finish helping Leo with the lights, briefly greeting Everett and Dahlia as they arrive. I spend the next hour silently bidding on a number of Carter's photographs up for auction that I think would look good in the shop.

He's a landscape photographer who's worked all over the world but specializes in the

West Coast and Hawaii. I learned after speaking with him briefly at Darby and Leo's wedding last spring that while he and his girlfriend, Penelope, are primarily based here in Los Angeles, they split much of their time between their hometown in Oregon and where his mother lives on Oahu, so most of his work is shot between those three regions. Lucky for him, considering they're three of the most beautiful places on the planet.

Several of his pieces are of Pacific Shores in particular, though. One shot of the boardwalk catches my eye, another of a grassy knoll overlooking the coastal cliffs, the image washing me in a sense of déjà vu because it looks suspiciously similar to the cliffside Elena and I spent so much of our youth lying on while we studied the stars...and each other.

I assumed Elena wasn't going to attend when she didn't leave her room once this morning before I took off. It was cemented when Dahlia and Everett arrived without her. She would've had to get a ride from one of her brothers, or from me, considering she doesn't have a car of her own.

Even so, as the night goes on, I keep watching every person who walks through the door, wondering if—possibly hoping—it could be her.

I force my eyes away again as another pair of strangers enter the gallery, dragging my attention back to Darby and Leo. Soft conversation hums all around me, but I can't focus on any of it. I'm standing next to a table, elbow propped with a fresh glass of whiskey in my hand. Darby sits on a chair beside me, legs thrown onto Leo's lap, her heels abandoned on the floor as he rubs her swollen feet.

"I told you that you didn't need to help with setting up, Honeysuckle. Look at your poor feet, baby."

I glance down. Her eyes are closed, head tossed back as she holds her growing belly, golden hair falling around her shoulders. She's wearing a black cocktail dress that hugs all of her pregnancy curves, though it looks fairly uncomfortable. I know Leo had insisted she wear flat shoes and not spend so much time on her feet. She didn't listen to either recommendation.

"It's fine." She sighs. "That's why I have you."

The front door whooshes open as city noise and outside air pour in, but I refuse to look this time. I keep my eyes fixed on my friend as she takes another sip of her water, but when I hear someone gasp, "Damn" nearby, my head snaps up.

I don't know exactly who said it, but Macie is standing closest, so it must've been her. Darby and Leo's heads snap the same way mine does as my personal hurricane of nightmares blows into the building.

Just like she promised, I'm choking on my fucking tongue.

Elena saunters into the room looking like the personification of a painting you'd find hung up in this gallery. Fuck that, actually. The Louvre. Two straps of plum-colored fabric, just wide enough to cover her ample breasts, rest on Elena's shoulders, creating a deep V before they meet at her navel, the crescent moon and dripping stars I tattooed beneath her sternum when she was twenty-two on full display. A thin, silver chain wraps around her waist, and the dress flows down below it like liquid satin, pooling at her feet. A massive slit rides up one side, almost to her hip. Each step she takes into the gallery has the fabric swishing, revealing the entirety of her left leg, and the serpent around her thigh. My eyes get caught there, and the damn thing seems to wink at me each time the dress slides aside and reveals it, like it's fucking taunting me.

Her skin is smooth and glowing, seeming to sparkle in the soft gallery lighting. Dark curls tumble down her shoulders, swaying over her breasts with each movement she makes, and I'm suddenly desperate to have the strands between my fingers—wrapped around my fist.

It's almost as if she's fucking backlit, the art on display, the creation to be admired in this room. Everything else goes blurry, outside my periphery and nonexistent. There is only her.

As if summoned, her eyes snap to mine. She gives me a once-over, stare snatching onto my gray suit, brow lifting in slow assessment. The feline smile that has my cock stirring to attention spreads across her full, cherry-painted lips.

Hungry? She mouths before tossing me a wink.

Like a sucker punch, all of the oxygen is swept from my lungs, and I begin to choke on nothing. A moment later, a crash echoes, startling me and breaking my stare. I glance down to find shattered glass around my feet and whiskey soaking my shoes.

My gaze snaps to Elena again, and she's smirking at me before turning toward the bar and sliding into one of the stools.

"Fuck," I mutter, squatting as I begin to pick up the broken glass.

"How did she get here?" Leo asks as Everett murmurs, "Why is she wearing a fucking loin cloth?"

Leo huffs, kissing his wife's ankle before standing and setting her feet in his seat, Everett trails behind him as they go in search of their sister. The view of them walking away is blocked by Carter as he bends to his knees in front of me with a small trash bin, plucking shards from the ground.

"Sorry."

"No worries, man. Happens." His lips tilt slightly as he pauses, studying my face. "I know she's their sister, but where do you fit into the equation?"

"I don't, really," I lie. "She's my roommate."

He cocks his head. "That it?"

"We used to be friends," I murmur. "When we were kids."

"Used to be?"

I grunt in confirmation, and as we finish picking up the glass, he drags a rag across the floor to soak the spill before tossing that in the bin.

"I get it." He smirks as we stand.

Across the gallery, Leo, Everett, and Elena speak in hushed tones. My attention is pulled away when Dahlia steps up behind Darby's chair, saying, "You know, Penelope told me that the rooftop has a gorgeous view of the city. I was going to see if I could sneak Everett up there for sex."

Darby's nose scrunches, lip curling as she gazes up at her sister, offering a perplexed and disturbed expression.

"Um...why don't I give you my key, then?" Carter says awkwardly. "Door locks from the outside, and that way, we can make sure you don't accidentally traumatize any of my other tenants."

"That would be great." She smiles, snatching it from his outstretched hand with zero shame. "August." She turns her eyes to me. "We should be about a half hour or so. You know..." Dahlia shrugs. "In case you'd like to have any conversations out of the eyes of nosy, overprotective brothers."

"Coincidentally, I was just going to ask Leo if he could come help me with a few boxes I left in my apartment," Carter adds.

Dahlia winks before striding across the showroom floor and intercepting Everett as he and Leo walk back toward us. She whispers something in his ear, and a grin spreads across his face. He spins on his heel, and follows her like a damn dog through the backdoor and into the stairwell.

Carter stops Leo before he reaches us, nodding in the same direction Everett and Dahlia just disappeared. "I need you to help me get a few things upstairs."

"Oh." He pauses, glancing back and forth between Carter and his wife. "But Darby...and her feet..."

"I'm fine." She waves him off. "I can survive fifteen minutes without you."

"I got her." Penelope smiles as she returns from walking a number of buyers through the gallery.

He sighs, relenting as he steps up to his wife and plants a quick kiss on her lips, hand on her belly. Carter winks at me before they both head toward the apartment units above the gallery's main floor.

"Go say whatever it is you need to say."

"I have nothing to say," I mutter, glancing down at Darby.

"That's not true. You both have left far too much unspoken, and I know for damn sure she didn't wear that dress for anyone else tonight."

I exhale a heavy breath as my gaze darts back to Elena. She leans over the bar, arms propped on the counter, sparkling eyes and a beaming smile fixated on the bartender. He studies her, open with interest, his gaze lingering on the soft skin spilling from her neckline. Nausea rolls in my stomach as I watch the encounter.

Skin that was on my hands, in my mouth, only days ago.

Fuck her for doing this to me. Fuck me for allowing it to

happen.

Darby's right. She didn't come here for anyone else tonight. She came here to taunt me, to win the next round in whatever deranged game the two of us seem to be playing. She wore that dress, perfectly curated to show off every inch of ink I've drawn on her flesh, for me. To torture me, drive me mad, and make me wild. Maybe we're both reaching the point of insanity, a place we won't return from, but fuck it. If she thinks batting her eyes at another man and wearing a dress tailored to my deepest desires is going to obliterate my self-control—if that's what she wants from me—I'm going to give her exactly what she's asking for.

Chapter Eighteen

Vice

"Love Is A Laserquest" - Arctic Monkeys

"What is it you call this garment?" my brother mutters from behind me.

I glance over my shoulder. "A dress?"

"Made of what? One singular window curtain?"

I scoff, rolling my eyes as I turn back to the bar.

"How'd you even get here, Lena? You said you weren't going to come today." Leo's voice breaks in next. He enters my periphery, blond hair and blue eyes burning a hole into the side of my face as he props an elbow on the bar.

"I wasn't going to be ready before you both had to leave, so I took an Uber."

My brother's eyes bulge hard enough to pop a vessel, I'm sure.

Everett shoves his way between Leo and me. "You took an Uber? From Pacific Shores?"

I nod.

"How fucking much did that cost?"

"About one-fifty."

"Jesus Christ, Lena," Leo murmurs.

Yeah...it's a lot of money to prove a point, but watching that glass shatter at August's feet, watching his jaw drop and his eyes flame, was worth every cent. I'm definitely not in a position to be throwing away that much cash, especially now that I'm paying rent, but I'm doing okay with what I make at the bakery.

"What?" I ask, turning to face them both. "You told me you wanted me to be here for support, so that's what I'm doing." I swipe a hand down my dress. "It's a black-tie event. I'm dressed for the occasion, and provocative has always been my style, so please stop acting so scandalized. It's not like I'm out here flashing my tits."

I grab a cocktail napkin, placing it in front of me as I wave the bartender over. Glancing at my brothers once more, I find them both staring at me slack-jawed.

"Can you give me some goddamn breathing room? I'm going to grab a drink, take a look around, and talk to Penelope about a painting she's been doing for me."

"How do you know Penelope?" Leo asks.

"I met her at your wedding."

I spoke with the girl briefly when I first arrived and she was helping me find my brothers. I don't remember how it came up, but she mentioned she's an artist in her free time, outside of earning her PhD in archaeology from UCLA and traveling the world. I was blown away by her ability to maintain a hobby while being a full-time student and adjunct professor. Especially considering I couldn't get out of bed most days at that point.

She showed me some of her work, and I don't know...it felt kind of like magic. Her art made me want to make something of myself again. Be someone worthy of looking at it.

I asked her if she could create a painting for me. I didn't care what, just something I could hang up in my room and look at on days I couldn't get out of bed. Something that might give me motivation to try.

Somehow, she understood exactly what I meant by that.

She texted me a few months ago to tell me my piece was ready, but I had fallen far too deep in my spiral to care, and I never responded.

I mostly came tonight to torment August—somehow, he's become that motivation, even if it's for all the wrong reasons—but I want to see Penelope too. Apologize. Check if she'd still be willing to sell me the piece she made for me.

"Are you sure you should be drinking?" Everett asks. "You've been sober since you moved in with August, right? Do you think maybe it would be better if you stayed that way?"

I close my eyes, jaw tightening with the urge to snap at him.

I know I'm getting defensive, and I know his concern is warranted. He's right—I've been sober since moving in with August just under two months ago. I've replaced alcohol with other vices—green eyes, soft hands, and harsh words. I know my mind seeks distraction to quell the storms raging inside my head at all times, to hold me back from slipping into that darkness that tears me limb from limb.

I'm still not convinced that I have a real drinking problem, or that I need to remain sober for my entire life, though. Alcohol is used by thousands of people every day to cope with their anxieties, their fears, their trauma. I'm no different.

"If I order a Diet Coke, will you stop treating me like a fucking child?"

My twin's nostrils flare, agitation simmering in his eyes. "I'll stop treating you like a child when you mature beyond the level of the eleven-year-old I have at home."

I scoff, but he says nothing, bristling as he walks away from me. My gaze flitters to Leo, who remains at my side. "You two are too alike sometimes. Stubborn as fuck." He smiles softly before kissing my cheek. "We just love you, okay? We're happy you're here." He nods back toward Darby. "I'll be rubbing my wife's feet if you need me. And don't take another fuckin' Uber. Get a ride from someone."

I snort, turning back to the counter just as the bartender steps in front of me. He smiles, and it's somewhat mischievous, certainly going beyond basic customer service. I glance down—my nipples are clearly visible through the thin fabric of my dress. The way his eyes won't stop bouncing, I know he sees it too. Figures.

He's cute but in a bland way. Nothing about him stands out. He has no edge. He seems like the type of guy who goes down on a woman for all of five minutes—zero percent chance of finding her clit—and then comes up for air, asking if it's his turn yet. He probably grunts "Who's fucking you like this?" while delivering backshots so shallow you can't help but wonder if he even has it in.

Hard pass.

"Has anyone told you that you're the best-dressed person at this event tonight?"

I drop my chin into my hands as my elbows rest on the bar, batting my lashes at him. "No, but you're about to."

His brows rise, but he covers it with a laugh. "Yeah. I was."

He licks his bottom lip, opening his mouth like he's going to continue, but I don't allow it. "I'll have a vodka soda with lime and a splash of grenadine. Oh, and two cherries."

The bartender stares. I stare back, impatiently tapping my nails against the bar top.

"Do you have a tab you'd like me to add that to?" he asks.

"Yeah, you can put it under the last name Graham."

"That your boyfriend?"

I smirk, grabbing my glass. "Brother."

He sinks his teeth into his bottom lip. "Good."

As I move to lift my drink to my lips, pressure clamps around my wrist, holding me in place, forcing my fingers to uncurl from my glass. The scent of rain and pine invades my senses, and I know it's him before I see him. Long, olive-toned fingers push my drink back toward the bartender.

"She won't be needing that." His voice is gruff, raking along my bones and putting all of my molecules on alert, causing a hum beneath my skin. "I know you're not about to start drinking, Little Vice," he whispers low enough that only I can hear.

"I'm not sure why you'd think that's any of your fucking concern," I rasp, tilting my head so that our mouths nearly brush, faces close enough to share breath.

His green eyes are a panic-inducing kind of beautiful, causing my heart to thrash inside my chest as they focus on my lips.

"Everything about you is a concern to me," he rasps but not with affection.

"That doesn't mean you can tell me what to do."

I turn back to the bar, but his breath follows, tickling my ear as he whispers, "Oh? But you like it so much."

I shiver as his words skate down my spine, the caress of a wicked promise. Still standing behind me, August rises to his full height, nudging my drink even closer to the bartender. Part of me wants to continue pushing him—snatch it back and down it in one gulp. Another part of me feels drunk enough off his touch and his skin to deem the alcohol unnecessary, and a third—my sanity, I presume—thinks it's better to not drink at all, knows I shouldn't have ordered it to begin with.

"Is he your boyfriend?" the bartender asks, giving August a wary assessment.

August smiles down at me, like he's expecting an answer to the question.

I don't.

"Look, man, she doesn't seem to be interested in you. Why don't you walk away?"

"Oh?" August leans an elbow on the counter, blocking my view of the bartender and cutting him out of the conversation entirely. "Why don't you tell him whose roof you live under, Elena? Who you invite into your bed?" He smirks, giving me a once-over. "Better yet, tell him who you wore that dress for tonight, and then remind us both who will be taking it off you later."

Those words seep into my flesh, melting through my bones and settling deep in my core. Rage and lust war beneath my skin, setting me ablaze. My teeth grind, my cheeks heat, and I can only stare after him, dumbfounded.

His emerald gaze sparkles mischievously behind his glasses. "Go ahead, baby. You let him know. I'll give you two minutes, and then I better find you in the bathroom waiting for me."

"For what? My punishment?" I mutter, mostly to myself.

Just as I think August walked away, either not hearing or not caring about what I'd said, I'm startled by a rough hand sliding around my neck. He sweeps my hair over my shoulder before dropping his head and whispering against my skin, "Is that what you're hoping for, Little Vice? Are you wet just thinking about it?" His other hand lands in my lap, gliding alarmingly close to the center of my thighs. My heart beats wildly, and I wonder if he can feel it when his palm brushes over my collarbone. Embers burn deep and low in my belly, erupting to flame the closer his hand gets to my center. "Thinking about the way you'll bite your tongue to muffle your cries from everyone in this building as I spank your ass red for being such a cock tease? Are you making a mess all over your thighs right now as you imagine it?"

"My God." My eyes flutter shut, and it's a battle to keep my composure as my body wants to forget we're in a room full of people. Of our family. I know our pose looks like nothing more than August standing behind me, playing with my hair. Nobody can see the hand he has beneath the bar, twisting in the fabric of my dress like he wants to tear it off me. Nobody knows what's going on here but him and me, and somehow it makes me frantic with need.

"Remember who you're a slut for, Elena. Not for him," he rasps, nodding toward the bartender, who's now huddled at the far end, pretending to ignore us. "He can't give you what you need. Only I can do that. So, close your fucking tab and remind him who you belong to, then meet me in the bathroom so I can remind you too."

His hands leave my body, and I'm aching.

"The longer you make me wait for you, the longer I make you wait to come."

Fuck.

I slump against the bar, all of the oxygen held captive in my lungs being set free. My heart is racing, my body trembling. I know I've soaked right through my panties, August was correct about everything. The only thing he got wrong was me having an open tab. So, I don't say another word to the bartender, or anyone at all, as I slide off my stool.

Glancing around the gallery, I make no note of either of my

brothers or Dahlia. The only two people I recognize are Darby and Penelope, still sitting at the same table Darby was at when I walked in. They're deep in conversation of their own, but as I drift across the gallery floor, Darby glances back briefly, gaze locking with mine. She smiles slyly before turning back to Penelope.

I know August and Darby are close now, so if he has no fear about her knowing what we're up to, then I don't need to either.

I don't even know what we're up to, honestly.

I don't know what he's going to do, all I know is he's desperate to get me alone, and that's enough. He may lift my dress over my hips and fuck me against the sink, or put me on my knees and slip his cock down my throat. I'm drenched at the thought of it.

His rough words are complemented by soft hands, like even when he's dominant and rugged, his touch is laced with care. Pleasure is the ultimate goal, even when we both want it wrapped in a bit of pain.

It's addicting.

There is a small alcove at the back of the showroom, tucked behind the main gallery. As soon as I turn the corner, I find August leaning against the wall with one foot pressed against it and his arms crossed at his chest. He flicks a brow, eyes dropping to the watch on his wrist. I know damn well it didn't take me two minutes to get here. He must read the challenge in my expression, because he simply pushes off the wall, glancing around to ensure we're not being watched or followed, before opening the bathroom door and allowing me to slip inside.

He follows, letting it fall closed behind him. I spin, our gazes clashing in a simmering blaze as he clicks the lock into place—the sound of it echoing inside the room like a salacious promise. He nods toward the sink. "Sit."

His tone doesn't invite argument, and as much as I love to defy him, something about it has me complying. My heels click loudly as I make the two steps and hoist myself up. The bathroom is immaculate, more like something you'd find in someone's home than a public space. The counter spans the entirety of the front wall, with one sink at its far end. Terracotta-colored towels and rugs accent the sky-blue walls, and it smells like cinnamon and vanilla.

August closes the gap between us, standing in front of me as his hands fall to my knees. They spread for him of their own accord, and his palms slide up my thighs, dragging my dress with them as his eyes sear through my own. His emerald irises hold so much—lust and passion and need, but also rage and pain and fear.

I wonder if mine tell the same truth—the one neither of our lips can.

As much as we may fight it, as much as we may run, nothing will ever feel like this. It's the craze we've been chasing all our lives, only ever finding it in the brief period we belonged wholly to each other, and that the tragedy of our past will forever prevent us from experiencing it again without the guilt and the pain.

That maybe these stolen moments are all we have left, and maybe we're terrible people for taking them, but that fact alone isn't enough to stop us. We're more than a force of nature; we're cosmic. It's gravity that pulls us together, and the outcome may be a detrimental collision of planets, but it's not enough to stop us from chasing the stars we only find in the other's eyes, from touching the clouds only felt on the other's flesh.

I cup his face, bracketing his jaw as my thumb reaches for his lip. His eyes fall closed, and he trembles at the touch, but doesn't pull away. Every fragment of my shattered soul begs me to kiss him, and I'm determined to do just that as I slide my palm behind his neck, fingers tangling in his hair. I tug him against me, and his strong arm loops around my waist, flushing our bodies together.

My lips brush his, but the shuddering breath he lets out against them has me halting. His fingers dig into the skin of my back, like he's anchoring himself to my body, and his forehead presses against my own. Our mouths are nearly touching, the blaze of it hot against my lips.

"Kiss me, Augustus," I whisper, but it rises from my throat like a plea.

"I can't."

Those two words are a reckoning, and my hand slips from his neck as he falls to his knees in front of me. He grasps my ankles, sliding his palms beneath the hem of my dress and pulling it up my legs, revealing my skin inch by inch. I shiver when his tongue swipes his bottom lip, the ball of his piercing gliding across his mouth, curious how it'd feel against my own flesh.

"Why?" I ask.

He doesn't answer until his hands are at my hips, my body bared to him, his gaze fixated on the center of my legs, only covered now by a sinful strip of black lace, that I know he can see has been soaked through.

"Kissing you will kill me." Finally, his eyes flit to mine, lust-laced and starved. "And I'm not ready to go yet, not before I get another taste of your hot little cunt. Not before I give you your thorough punishment for fucking with me tonight."

Chapter Nineteen

Vice

"Acquainted" - The Weeknd

A whimper escapes my mouth, my toes curling at his obscene language, my core clenching around nothing—desperate for him.

"I never could get this out of my head," he murmurs, fingers dancing across my skin until he reaches the apex of my thighs. He slides his thumb through my slit, cursing at the wetness, before pressing it to my clit and moving in tight circles.

My head falls back against the glass, back arching into his touch.

He takes his time, torturing and tormenting me until I'm writhing.

"Do you see how it feels, Elena?" He moves a finger to the crease between my thigh and pelvis, slipping beneath the hem of my panties and pulling them aside. "To have something you want so desperately, and watch it hover just out of your reach."

I low moan escapes my lips, followed by a strained, "Fuck you."

All too quickly, his hand is gone, I'm hauled off the counter and flipped around. My dress is hiked above my hips, and a resounding slap echoes throughout the bathroom just a second before a flaming sting flashes across my ass. I jolt forward, but his grip on my hips holds me in place as I struggle beneath them.

"Don't be a brat."

"August." His name rips from my throat on a growl.

"That's better. Say my name." He snakes an arm between my legs, roughly spreading them open. "Fuck. These thighs. This ass." He dips into the waistband of my panties, tugging them down my legs until they bind at my ankles. "And your pussy—pretty as ever."

I clench at his words, my core flooding with arousal. My eyes are screwed shut, unwilling to face my own reflection in the mirror. Unwilling to address the lust I'd find in my gaze.

"Do you want me to touch your pretty pussy, Elena? Should I check to see if it's weeping for me?"

Some sound leaves my lips, but it's not an admission. I'll never say the words out loud to him, but I respond with a shallow nod.

He slips his hand between my aching thighs, and my entire body trembles as his fingers meet my flesh, parting me open and brushing over my soaked center. The pad of his thumb makes contact with my clit again, moving in delicate circles that do nothing but tease me further.

I buck my hips in a desperate search for sensation.

"Look at this greedy cunt, so wet for me." He moves down, barely slipping one finger inside me. Just enough to put me on edge, but so far from providing what he knows I need from him.

I press into him, attempting to force his finger farther, but he pulls back just as much. His palm smacks across my ass again, causing me to jump and moan as the burn rages through me. "Use your words, Little Vice. Ask me for it."

A mix of frustration, humiliation, and pure need expands inside me, causing a broken whimper to leave my mouth.

August places his thumb back on my clit, moving faster, causing that spark to ignite low in my belly. My legs tremble as he whispers against my flesh, "Say: 'Daddy, I need you to eat my needy cunt. Please, let me come.'"

"Never," I bite out on a moan as his thumb speeds up, sending fire through my blood and shockwaves through my body.

He stops suddenly, and another cry of frustration leaves me.

"I have no problem teasing you until you're a withered puddle on this bathroom floor. I'll keep you here all night, drenched and leaking down your legs." His thumb continues again, mouth hovering just over my ass, breath hot against my skin. "Or, you can beg me for what you so desperately crave, and I'll show you just how much you've missed me."

"August," I groan.

"That's it. Tell me the rest."

I swallow, tears stinging my eyes as he keeps me right on that edge, punishing me thoroughly. I'm craving him as desperately as he claims. Because everything I've locked away comes flooding back when I'm with him, and I might combust without the release and escape I know only he can provide me.

"E... Eat my needy cunt." I breathe. "Let me come...please."

He smiles against the back of my thigh.

He shoots to his feet, grasping my hair and pulling hard enough to force my eyes open, locking with his in the reflection of the mirror. He presses his body against mine, and I feel the hard length of his cock resting on my lower back as he drops his head so that his mouth hovers right over my ear.

"Look at you. Flushed and trembling. Watch yourself when you tell me that I'm the only one who can make you feel this way."

I can't look at myself, I'm too drawn to him. My breath is rapid, lips parted as I pant, but words don't leave my mouth. August smirks, using his free hand to slip off his glasses, bringing them around my body and holding them out in front of my face.

He tugs on my hair again. "Say it, Elena."

"Only you," I whimper. "Only you can make me feel this way."

"Good girl." He nudges the temple of his glasses to my lips. "Now, open your mouth. Hold onto these while I eat your pussy, yeah? Gotta keep you quiet somehow. I know how much you like to scream my name."

He slips the tip into my mouth, and I bite down on it with my front teeth as he pulls his hand away. The view I present in the mirror is purely erotic. Blown pupils, flushed cheeks, glistening skin, mascara running down my cheeks from the tears brought on by his teasing. August's glasses hang from my mouth, making me appear every bit the desperate pet he brings out in me. He smiles when my eyes flare as that realization sets in, because fuck, we both know I love it.

August drops back to his knees.

"And what are you going to call me while I'm feasting on your cunt?" he asks, hooking both thumbs inside me, spreading me open and exposing me thoroughly.

"Daddy," I murmur, voice muffled.

He groans. And then his tongue is inside me.

"Fuck. I couldn't forget this if I tried. Addicting." It's almost as if there's longing in his voice when he whispers against my flesh, "My Little Vice."

I collapse over the counter as he swirls his tongue, reaching deep enough that I'm clenching around it as his piercing applies a pressure to my inner walls—an intense sensation I've never experienced before. The pressure heightens everything, I spiral and buck against his face in an attempt to push him further.

He slips out, leaving me empty as his tongue slides up and settles over my clit. He flicks at it fast and firm, forcing my moans to reach a crescendo that has me biting the temple of his glasses so hard I fear they may crack. All of my energy, my buzzing atoms and flaming blood, rush to that place at my center, readying to peak and crash over him.

The ball of his piercing glides over my clit in a steady, fierce rhythm that has me reaching that cliff quicker than ever before, but as I jump into the freefall of bliss, he stops.

My fist slams against the counter, a guttural cry clawing from my throat, stifled by my closed mouth and clenched teeth. I'm fucking throbbing, so desperate for release that it's painful.

August only laughs before grabbing my ankle and lifting my foot, slipping my panties off before repeating the movement with my other leg. I stand straight, glancing behind myself and down at him.

He lifts his gaze to meet mine. "We both know I can't taste your pussy without coming in my pants." He flicks the button on his trousers, unzipping them. "So this time, I think I'll use yours instead."

He pulls out his cock. It's hard and raging—pre-cum leaking from its tip, the barbells of his ladder reflecting off the overhead light. My throat dries at the sight of it, and I want it in my mouth so goddamn bad. I'd be the one coming from taste alone.

He wraps the black lace of my underwear in his fist before taking hold of his length and pumping hard. With his free hand, he grasps my thigh, lifting my leg and bending it. "Put your knee up on the counter and give me better access, baby." I immediately comply, willing to do anything at this point to reach release. "Good girl."

A whimper escapes me. I can't decide if I'm more addicted to his degradation or his praise. Or maybe it's the way he can so deliciously deliver both at the same time.

I watch him pump himself once more, his eyes zoned into the center of my legs. He groans, like the feeling and the sight has him losing his mind the way I am.

It's enough to have my head falling forward again, a twin sound leaving my lips.

Suddenly, another slap sounds, and my ass is flaming.

"Eyes on that mirror, Little Vice." He smiles against the back of my thigh, teeth grazing my sensitive skin. "Keep pretending you hate me while you watch yourself come on my tongue."

I lift my head, and meet my reflection. A flush runs from my cheeks and down my chest, my gaze black with lust and need, my hair falling wildly around me, the ends of it swaying with each heave of my rapid breath.

My eyes fight to stay open as August's tongue begins lapping at my clit again. Long, languid strokes that have my entire being vibrating as he flicks that piercing over my bud. He's relentless in his pursuit of my body, and that pent-up anguish from his torturous edging has me already finding that wave, my legs trembling as it begins to crest.

My hands curl at the edge of the sink, clawing into it as he slips two fingers inside me. He presses against my walls in the same tempo he sucks my clit, and I'm immediately breaking. Free-falling off the cliff, drowning beneath the wave, shattering inside the stars.

There is something fiercely erotic about watching myself come, heightening the sensation to nearly unbearable levels of pleasure that cascade over my skin like a rain. I look impassioned and crazed—a mess. Yet, that mess is beautiful and catastrophic and euphoric. I rarely feel that way about myself, and for a brief moment, accepting wild nature feels like a kind of satisfaction I've ever known.

A low groan vibrates against my center, and I'm pulsing at the feel of it. August roughly moans again as he removes his fingers from inside me, and his mouth from my clit. "Fuck," he mutters, lips moving up my thigh and to my ass before he sinks his teeth into my cheek, giving it a firm slap. "All you have to do is drip for me, and I'm coming."

Another whimper escapes me. I brace my hands on the edge of the sink, lowering my leg, and dropping my head as I try to catch my breath. He pulls away, and fabric rustles as he tucks himself back into his pants. I straighten my spine, expecting him to stand, but instead, his hands glide back up my legs, taking my dress with them, until I'm exposed once again.

"But I'm not completely satisfied yet, Little Vice." He grabs my ass in each hand, and my breath hitches as he spreads me open. "I need to know if any other man has ever played with this ass—been inside it."

I swallow hard. "N... No." The word snakes through my teeth, choked and trembling.

He grunts in approval, clearing his throat just before he spits between my spread cheeks. I gasp, body flying forward, but his arm wraps around my front, holding me steady. He slowly stands, his body brushing against mine with the movement.

His eyes meet mine in the mirror—sated and blazing. His jaw clenches, studying my reaction as his hand slides between my cheeks, circling around my tight, now wet, hole. I can't catch my breath as he teases it, my jaw trembling as it strains to stay shut.

In a flash, he grabs his glasses, pulling them from my mouth. "Stick out your tongue."

I watch myself comply, and it's almost as if I'm floating outside my body, a mere spectator to the show that he and I put on. I realize he is still holding my panties, eyes widening as he replaces his glasses, slipping the fabric past my parted lips.

"I need you to watch yourself come this time, but we can't risk anyone hearing us, can we?"

I shake my head.

His laugh is smooth against my skin as he slides his glasses back on before dropping his head and grazing my jaw with his teeth, hand sliding down my neck to take my throat in his grasp. He squeezes once—hard enough to make me sputter around the fabric between my lips before he loosens his grip.

Saliva pools in my mouth, and I taste the mix of my arousal and his release. It's thick as I swallow, and I know he feels my throat bob beneath his palm.

"How do we taste?"

I moan because I can't answer any other way.

"I know, baby." With his other hand, he presses into my ass with one finger, just lightly. "I want your ass, Elena. I want what no one else has ever had."

His breath fans over my ear, sending a shiver down my spine that pools in my core. Our eyes lock in the mirror, there are unspoken words behind that sentence—words that neither of us want to address aloud.

"I want to stretch it, fuck it, come inside it and watch my release drip from you afterward. Do you think you'd like that?"

I don't know, honestly. I've never tried ass play. Never trusted anyone enough to do so, but fuck, I want to try everything with August. I want to submit to him wholly, offer him my body, because he's long owned my soul. I want to relinquish my control to him. Let go of the shackles tied to my desires, because in our basest form, he's as depraved as I am. Inside our own darkness, we're safe enough to embrace it.

Maybe we were made for each other after all.

I nod frantically.

"Do you think you can come like this?" he asks, pressing his finger deeper.

A cry leaves my throat, muffled by the panties in my mouth. I nod again.

His lips brush the shell of my ear, dragging down my neck and resting at the tattoo he placed on me so many years ago. "I'm going to add a second finger. I want you to slip a hand between your pretty thighs and play with your clit for me, okay? We're going to watch through the mirror as I make you fall apart while I finger-fuck your ass."

I groan, my head lolling against his shoulder as my lids flutter, all the sensation in my body rushing to where he presses inside me. His broad hand squeezes my neck again, and I'm gasping, eyes flying open.

"You've gotta look, too, baby. Now touch yourself like I told you to."

He slowly adds the second finger, giving my body the time to stretch around it. I'm incredibly full—blazing and buzzing—as he begins to pump his fingers inside me. My hand slides between my legs, strumming over my hyper-sensitive clit. I know it won't take much to make me come again, and as August and I match each other's pace, bringing me back to the edge, I focus my gaze on his face.

His full lips parted, the breath that filters through them is warm and heavy as it lands at my neck, chills biting my spine at the feel. His emerald eyes burn through a thousand shades of green behind his glasses as they bore through mine. I'm transfixed by him—his beauty, his touch, his taste. The contrast of rough dominance and soft caress, the whiplash of his dichotomies driving me to the brink of delicious insanity.

"Get there, Elena," he rasps, still fixated on my face. His tone is almost begging when he continues, "I want to see you break for me."

I circle my clit faster, and as my tempo rises, he matches it with the movement in my ass. Pleasure pools deep inside me, heat coiling before my body goes taut, and that ecstasy bursts. The moment it hits me, my legs buckle, but August's knee falls between them, keeping me in place. My body goes slack, muffled screams clawing their way out of me. My hand slows as I ride out my orgasm, and August eases his movements before pulling his hand from my ass. I slump in his arms, entirely drained.

"Atta girl. So good for me." He drags his lips over my tattoo, nipping at the skin. Moving his hands to wrap around my waist, he holds me up, becomes my strength. "My chaos. My addiction. My little vice," he whispers.

I preen at his praise, suddenly desperate for more of it. His touch is soft when he gently grabs my chin, directing my gaze back to the mirror. "Look how pretty you are after I've made you come. How breathtaking you look when you submit to me."

I swallow as he pulls my panties from my mouth and takes a step back, pocketing them. He makes quick work of washing his hands, smoothing down my wild hair, and adjusting my dress. Nothing is going to hide the flush in either of our cheeks, but he swipes a thumb under each of my eyes to remove my smeared makeup.

"You've always been the most beautiful woman I've ever seen." That hand cups my cheek, and he brushes over my lip. "But you're beyond words when you're wearing the glow only I can give you, the beauty that belongs only to me."

Chapter Twenty

Violet

"Cinnamon Girl" - Lana Del Rey

Her lashes flutter, and the effect I have on her only deepens the iridescent radiance in her eyes. They're heavy and half-lidded, swimming in passion. It's a flawless match to the flush in her cheeks, her skin illuminated by perspiration from being so thoroughly ravished.

By me. Ravished by me.

I've spent a lifetime dreaming of ways that I could see her in this kind of light, hear her say my name in that erotic and breathy tone, feel her skin come to life beneath my hands. I only began to discover the ways I could make her melt during our brief affair those years ago, and when I lost her then, I never thought I'd have another chance to explore her. To explore all of our depraved desires and deepest cravings.

Part of me wants to run away from this. From her touch and her heartbeat and the look she's giving me right now, knowing the way those brown eyes can kill.

Losing her then brought me as close to death as I've ever been, but staring at her now may be the most alive I've ever felt.

It's a terrifying tightrope to walk, watching her stand there on the other end with a knife in hand. There is no way of knowing if she's going to sever that tie and send me plummeting, or if she's going to grab my hand and pull me in, cementing us in a permanent embrace.

Whether I'm in her arms, or on the line, I feel ruined.

"Do you want to go home now, Little Vice?" I ask, still cupping her cheek.

Her lips tilt softly, but she shakes her head. "No, I need to go buy a painting."

She must see confusion drift across my features, because she laughs lightly, grasping my wrist and pressing her lips to my palm. She drops my hand, brushing past me as she heads toward the door.

"You'll come find me when you're done, and I'll be taking you home."

She peeks her head around her shoulder, a smirk on her pretty lips as she dips her head. "Yes, sir."

My cock jumps at the sultry tone of her voice, and just as she grips the door handle, a pounding comes from the other side. We both jump, eyes locking as my breath catches and my stomach lodges itself inside my throat.

"Look, I'm not trying to interrupt whatever you two are... working out in there, but I am six months pregnant, and I need to pee!"

I immediately blow out a relieved sigh at Darby's voice.

"I'm trying to do you both a solid right now, but if you don't get the hell out of this bathroom, I'm going to grab my husband and make him kick you out of here."

Elena throws the door open. "Are they out there?"

Darby stands in the doorway, swaying on her bare feet. "No. Leo is still upstairs with Carter." She cuts us a glare. "And apparently that...endurance is a family trait, because Everett's still on the roof with my sister."

"Ew." Elena huffs. "Well, sorry. Bathroom is all yours." She moves past Darby before pausing briefly. "And thank you for um... covering."

She smiles as Elena walks away before turning to me. "Leave."

"Yes, ma'am." I shuffle past her, pausing briefly to kiss her cheek. "Thank you, Darbs."

"Yeah, yeah. You're welcome." She sighs, moving to close the door, but just before it shuts, she says quietly, "She still loves you, by the way. Don't think she ever stopped."

I turn back to her. "What makes you say that?"

"I can see it on her face." She smiles softly. "I know the look well."

Without waiting for a response, Darby shuts the door. I leave the alcove that houses the bathroom, moseying through the rest of the gallery, talking briefly with our friends. But my eyes are always focused on where Elena is, who she's talking to, and what she's doing. She spends most of the next hour in deep conversation with Penelope, who introduces her to another couple. A Black woman with long, braided hair—the only person here dressed almost as immaculately as Elena—and a brunette white man. She laughs at something he says, and it makes my gut twist, though it's clear the woman next to him is his wife.

I don't know what it says about me that I want to own her so badly I'm unwilling to let her gift another man with something so simple as a laugh.

After that, Elena disappears for a while, but I have to pretend it doesn't make me frantic while I'm in conversation with Dahlia and Everett, because he doesn't seem concerned about his sister's whereabouts. Finally, she returns from the stairwell at the back of the showroom, a narrow rectangular box beneath her arm and Penelope at her side.

Her face is brighter than I've seen it in years, and in a move so unlike her, Elena initiates a hug with the red-headed artist.

As they pull away, she glances around the room in search of something, and when her eyes find mine, her lips tug into a wide smile. The exact kind of smile I vividly remember seeing that very first time, because it made me question the chances of an eleven-year-old boy going into cardiac arrest after my heart took off in a gallop so fierce it could've knocked me on my ass.

It's racing like that again, like a blow right through my chest, and I almost feel the need to stumble back and clutch my ribs.

Elena beelines straight toward me, ignoring all the commotion around us. She stops just as her toes meet mine, head lifting. "I bought a painting."

She says it like she's proud of herself, like she's the one who made the art. I understand the feeling, though. When you've shut yourself out for so long, neglected care and joy and connection, taking it back feels monumental. It is monumental.

I know it's hard for her to feel accomplished in the things she thinks she's supposed to be achieving—her job, her writing. She's likely still drowning in debt, and who knows when she'll be able to afford a car or a place to live on her own—but right now, she's fought back enough financial independence to get herself to this event tonight, to buy herself a gift.

Even if it was to spite me, she got out of bed today, she got herself together, and while she doesn't need the frills of elegance to be the most beautiful person in the room, I know it's done wonders for her confidence. She is always breathtaking to me, but right now, she knows it too, and that assurance on her face is a beauty beyond description.

My heart swells with something a hell of a lot like pride.

"I can see that." The smile I give her back is effortless. "What's it of?"

She shrugs. "I don't know yet. It's a surprise."

I offer a bemused expression, but she only laughs, brushing past me in the direction of her brothers and their wives. "Ready to go whenever you are, Augustus," she chimes over her shoulder as her perfect ass sways with each step she takes.

I follow her, feeling somewhat like a dog—her leash around my goddamn soul.

"I'm hitching a ride home with Augustus," Elena says as she reaches them.

Darby and Dahlia shoot me mischievous, knowing smiles. Leo smiles, too, but it's softer. More hopeful, and a pang of guilt slams into me like a freight train. He thinks I'm taking care of his sister, reviving the friendship he knew us to have.

He and Everett are still in the dark when it comes to our many, many secrets. The old ones, and even worse, the new ones too. I doubt that Darby or Dahlia realize the depths of them either. If they did, they wouldn't be grinning at me right now. They'd be disappointed in us both.

They all think that Elena and I are simply attempting the slow rebuild of a platonic connection we shared once upon a time. Darby knows more; I've disclosed my feelings for Elena to her, but never the true depths of them, or what she felt for me in return. Nobody knows what happened the day my brother died, or any of our final words to each other.

Elena and I are devious. We're liars.

And while the bed she lies in at night, the hands that touch her body, are none of her brother's concern, I know they see her as fragile. If they knew what was happening between us, understood how reckless I'm being with her when I can't even understand it myself—they'd never forgive me.

We say our goodbyes, and that guilt slices deeper when Everett whispers, "Thank you" as he hugs me. I force a smile back at them all before I follow Elena out of the building.

My truck is in a garage across the street, so I keep my hand on the small of her back as we cross the busy road and lead her to where I'm parked. I set her painting in the back of my Bronco before opening the passenger door and holding her hand as she hauls herself inside of it.

It's quiet as I drive out of the city and onto the interstate that will lead us back to Pacific Shores. The world around us is dark, highlighted only by the lights of the towns we drive through, and the low glow of my dashboard. I steal far too many glances in Elena's direction, having my attention stolen by the urge to watch her rest her head at the window.

"Do you think we should feel guilty?" she whispers once we're well on the road.

I suck in a sharp breath, wondering how she does such a damn good job at reading my thoughts. "Guilty for what?"

I take my eyes off the road for only a fraction of a second, catching her gaze as her head whips to the side. "It was a memorial event for him." Her features are withdrawn, conflicted. "And what we did..." She trails off, sighing.

As awful as it is, I don't think my brother crossed my mind for a single moment since Elena walked through those doors tonight.

While I'm happy to raise money for good causes, and appreciate the help that our family and friends put into the event, nothing is ever going to bring him back.

No amount of charity, no amount of guilt, none of our mutual self-loathing.

So... "No, I don't feel guilty," I admit. "Maybe that makes me terrible."

"I don't either, and I can't decide if it makes us terrible or not." She chews on her lip, resting her head back on the window. Each pass of the truck under a streetlight casts her face in a soft, golden hue, revealing the tragic beauty of her tormented expression. "I once heard that the human brain stays active for up to seven minutes after death, and it's believed that in that time, the person who died replays their life. Like a highlight reel."

I swallow, turning back to the road. "I don't know if I believe that."

"If it were true, what do you think he saw?" Her voice turns hollow, and she shifts in her seat, turning to face me, but I don't have the strength to do the same. I don't know what has compelled her to talk of him tonight. I don't know why it seems like neither of us can say his name.

"Only good things," I whisper.

She's quiet for a long moment before she murmurs, "Sometimes, I can't remember if there were good things."

My grip tightens on the steering wheel, matching the sensation swelling in my throat. "There was. He was a happy person." Suppressed emotion builds in the pit of my stomach, forcing itself to the surface, but somehow, I don't want to stop this conversation from continuing. "And because of you...he knew what love was."

I finally allow myself a brief glance at Elena, needing to know her reaction. She's already staring at me, her eyes misted with unshed tears, bottom lip trembling.

"You showed him what that looked like," I continue softly. "Regardless of everything else, it couldn't be doubted that you did love him, you know? And being loved by you, Elena..." I exhale deeply. "There's nothing like that. That love is the highlight reel, always worth the pain."

I face the road again, but I hear the gulp of air she takes as she attempts to stop herself from sobbing. I hear the rattled breath falling from her lips, and the heave of her chest. I don't know exactly what her last conversation with my brother was like, but I know it didn't end well. He'd said things to her that he knew he'd regret later, and for the first time, I realize she may not be aware of that fact.

He knew he'd regret them. He knew he'd forgive us. He just hadn't been ready yet.

Determined to compose myself long enough to get us home, I blink back the tears that want to free fall from my eyes too. Elena attempts to cry quietly, but late in the night, in the quiet cab and the near-empty freeway, it's impossible to focus on anything else.

I reach across the seat, clasping a hand over her thigh, unsure of how to comfort her any other way. I brush the fabric of her dress out of my way so I can caress her bare skin, moving my thumb in gentle circles.

"He told me that, you know. He told me he'd forgive us eventually. That he knew we made more sense than the two of you ever did." She places her hand over mine, her breath calming. "He was mad, he felt betrayed, but even in that moment, he had every intention of making things okay again."

"You never told me this," she whispers, the words broken.

I turn to her, tracking the tears that stream from her glistening eyes, wishing more than anything I could wipe them away. Longing to finally provide the comfort she never allowed me to years ago. "You never gave me the chance."

Her eyes fall closed, head tipping against the back of the seat. She doesn't say anything else, but her hand stays atop mine.

"Did you ever fall in love again?" she asks, startling me after a long bout of silence.

"No," I say. "I think I was destined to love the same person all my life."

She lets out a bereft laugh. "She must've been a real bitch to let you go."

"I don't think so." I shake my head. "I think she had her reasons..." I squeeze her thigh. "I just wish she'd told me what they were."

"Sometimes, I wish she had too." She curls her fingers around mine, squeezing back. "You were never the villain in her story. You're always her highlight reel."

My head whips to her, and the lights outside flash over her face, revealing glimpses of red-rimmed eyes and swollen lips. Removing her hand from mine, she settles into her seat, and I finally watch her eyes flutter closed.

Her breath slowly grows heavier, and I wonder if maybe she had fallen asleep earlier. I wonder what thoughts might have been floating through her psyche that woke her, compelled her to ask me if I've been in love since her. I wonder why she'd even entertain it, when it's always been clear that I was created with her soul in mind.

Wherever our beings began, ours were beside each other; that much I'm certain of.

Something scattered them to the wind, forced them to find each other over and over in each life lived, and maybe in other lifetimes we got it right. In different realities, it's always been us.

But this one became twisted and tortured—it tore us apart.

That's the thing about magnets, though. They find their way back together, even if they have to cut through other substances to do so. Sometimes the moon orbits the Earth from a farther distance, but it always returns, even if that means eclipsing the sun.

Elena and I may be destined, but what does it mean if that destiny includes the detriment of others? The obliteration of ourselves?

Is the guilt that swallows us warranted? Is it the punishment for our crimes? Or do we get a pass because we're meant to be? Is happiness beyond this pain still possible? Or are we cemented in the gray reality we've seemed to create for ourselves?

The questions pound against my mind like the pattering of rain on a roof, fogging my brain as I finish the drive home. By the time I pull into the driveway and kill the engine, Elena is fully asleep.

I gently tap her shoulder, whispering her name, but she hardly stirs. Remembering what she's like when she's woken without proper rest, I decide it may be safer to carry her inside without waking her at all. Stepping out of the car, I'm quiet as I shut my door and round to her side, opening hers.

She whimpers as I reach over her body and unbuckle her before scooping one arm beneath her knees and the other around her back, pulling her from the seat and hoisting her into my arms. I shut the door with my foot and adjust her weight as I reach the front of the house to unlock it and get us inside.

She begins to fidget as I make my way up the staircase, groggily asking, "What're you doing?"

"Didn't want to wake you," I whisper. "So, I thought I'd carry you to bed."

She curls against my chest, placing a hand right over my heart. I know she means nothing by the gesture, but that doesn't change the fact that I feel everything at the sight of it.

"But you hate me."

I halt, pausing to look down at her. Elena's eyes remain closed, her lips forming the perfect pout that makes my knees buckle, lashes fanning out over her soft cheeks. I can't help but watch her in quiet restfulness as I reach her room.

"I wanted to hate you. But I don't," I admit softly as I lay her down upon the bed. "I needed to escape you. But I can't." Hovering over her, I trace the peaceful features of her face, brushing my thumb over her cheek. "You're so deeply etched into the fabric of my being, the depths of my soul, that I find I'm incapable of doing anything but loving you." I press my lips to the top of her head, whispering, "My favorite vice."

I move to the end of the bed, unstrapping her heels and setting them on the floor. I know the dress will be uncomfortable to sleep in, but I don't want to go so far as to undress her while she's mostly asleep.

I toss the comforter over her shoulders, stealing a kiss against her forehead. I never allow myself to be so gentle—so affectionate—with her. Not for the sake of boundaries or because I don't want it, but simply because it pains me to do so. To let myself believe, for even the briefest of moments, I could have her that way again.

It's why I won't kiss her. Why I don't fuck her. I'll tease us both with touch and taste, but the true connection of our souls is far too painful. There are too many secrets kept, too many words left unspoken, because the truth is, I don't fucking trust her. I don't know if it's possible for that foundation to be rebuilt, and without it, Elena and I are nothing more than flesh and bone.

I straighten, and as I turn to leave her room, a small, soft hand snatches out to wrap around my wrist. I spin, finding two espresso-colored eyes blazing back at me. I don't need to ask—the heat inside them tells me she heard every word that escaped my mouth.

"Stay," she whispers.

"I can't." My tone is low and tortured. "I'll never leave if I do."

"So don't." Her tone is a plea. "Stay with me. Please."

I pull my wrist from her grasp, sliding my palm up to hers and lacing our fingers together. "Not until you find yourself again, Elena. Not until you open up to me. I can't stay until I know why you left. Why you were happier without me."

"I was never happier without you, Augustus." Her gaze is fixated on our hands. "Not for one moment."

"Then why did you leave?"

Her throat bobs as she swallows, and she refuses to meet my eyes as she pulls her hand from mine and rolls over, murmuring into the darkness, "I don't deserve happiness."

More than her touch, more than her distance, more than the loss, more than the pondering of alternate realities, it's that sentence that kills me. Like blades slicing through the center of my gravity, everything turns upside down.

How she could ever think such a thing about herself baffles me, makes me wonder if I haven't done a good enough job throughout my life showing her that she deserves everything.

I pull off the blanket covering her, and she turns to face me again, brows knit in confusion.

"Take off your dress," I demand before stalking over to her dresser, kicking my shoes off by the door. Opening the top drawer, I grab a pair of cotton shorts. I pull open the next two drawers before finally finding an oversized tee and grabbing that too.

When I return to the bed, she's lying on her back, watching me curiously. She's completely naked, but it's not the playful tease I'm used to finding. It's raw exposure—more than her body. It's the unspoken understanding that I know her deeply enough to see her this way, to recognize the difference between moments of intimacy and those of vulnerability.

We're silent as I loop the bottoms over her feet, sliding them up her legs and fastening them around her hips. She sits up slightly, just enough to lift her arms above her head as I drape the T-shirt over her. I step back, stripping out of my own clothes until I'm left in nothing but my boxers.

She moves over a few inches, and I crawl into bed behind her. I snake an arm over her waist, tugging her flush to my chest as I slip my other arm beneath her neck. She places her hand in my open palm, running the pad of her fingers along my own.

"You deserve happiness, Elena."

She doesn't respond, but I hear the soft sniffle of her emotions. I feel the silent tears that drip from her cheeks and onto my arm. I don't know how many times throughout my life she's lain beside me in the depths of night, crying herself to sleep over thoughts of my brother. I don't know how many times I tried to save her from that pain, and how I could've failed us both so miserably.

I don't know how we'll ever escape it now.

Chapter Twenty-One

Vice

"Older" - Lizzy McAlpine

Another stab of pain slices through my lower abdomen, and I groan, bracing my arms on the counter as I drop my head between my shoulders.

I grind my molars as I ride out the wave, the pounding in my temples not helping things, and the obnoxious fucking song echoing through the cafe worsening all other symptoms.

I normally don't mind Dahlia's taste in music, but whatever pop anthem is blaring through the speakers right now is about to make me fucking violent.

I take a deep breath, glancing around to ensure there aren't any customers who need to be helped before I duck into the break room and grab my bag. I locate my bottle of ibuprofen and my CBD-infused essential oil roller before returning to the register.

I take two pills, chasing them with my third iced coffee of the day, before rubbing the essential oil over each of my temples. The smell of lavender and eucalyptus invades my senses, immediately calming my racing heart.

Years ago, when I was first diagnosed with PMDD, my doctor told me that overconsumption of caffeine could worsen the condition, and I don't doubt that's true, but if my head is going to pound and my uterus is going to try to fucking kill me, iced coffee is a necessary evil.

I was placed on hormonal birth control to help with the

symptoms, and it somewhat has, but my luteal phase is still a monthly thorn in my side—literally.

After so many years doing sedentary work, I've forgotten how straining seven hours of standing and moving can be when I'm experiencing a flare-up. I've only been working for three hours, and I'm not sure I'm going to survive the rest of my shift, but as of now, I'm the only barista working. Peggy, Dahlia's pastry chef, is in the kitchen baking, and I've been covering the early morning shift for Dahlia while she and Darby are in Kansas.

Their father was finally tried for his long, long rap sheet of embezzlement and fraud, and they both wanted to travel out there for the sentencing. It sounds like it has been a rough year for them since Dahlia handed over evidence of his crimes to the authorities, essentially severing whatever family ties they may have had left.

I don't blame her. In fact, I probably would've done worse if he were my father.

Both of my brothers encouraged them not to go, but they felt they needed the closure of facing their dad and telling him just how terrible he was to them, and how much better off they are now that they've escaped him.

Unfortunately for me, with Dahlia gone, I'm not due to be relieved by another barista for two more hours, which means I have no choice but to tough it out behind the counter.

There was a rush earlier, but as I glance around at the buzzing cafe now, all patrons appear to be happy. It's a beautiful day beyond the bakery's front windows, the sun shining down on the whitecaps past the pier, making the water look particularly turquoise this morning. Surfers dot the horizon, and a few people stroll along the boardwalk outside, but it's still early in the season, and things are fairly slow. I take advantage of the easy morning by pulling a barstool behind the counter and flopping myself atop it, resting my head on my arms.

Sometime later, a familiar, muffled voice comes from behind me before my brother filters through the back door. I knew Everett had a meeting at Heathen's this morning with Leo, August, and the small business initiative—I had him pick me up on his way in. I typically walk to work, but when starting so early in the morning, I don't have the damn energy, not to mention the flare-up hitting me today.

I was uncomfortable on the drive over, and when he asked me what was wrong, I told him it was just a headache. I'm not surprised he decided to come back and check on me after his meeting. He's a fucking mother hen if I've ever known one.

If it weren't Everett, it'd probably be my mother. I'm glad he's the one who ended up with a kid—he got all of Mom's nurturing nature. I've never known that woman to be a coffee drinker, but she seems to be stopping by almost every day. If it's not to check on me; it's to check in on one of her many, many other children who work on the boardwalk.

She may have only birthed two of us, but she claims all six.

They likely feel it's the only time they can see me. I know it's my fault for being such a nightmare. I know that they worry, and I know that I shut them out. Even before...everything, I've always been somewhat reclusive. A homebody. I love my family, but too much social interaction overwhelms me, even with the people I love most. It's an awful trait to have, but it's how I am.

Before I moved to New York, I had a routine of meeting up with my parents about once a week or so, and I know I've gotten much worse at that since being back in Pacific Shores. It's certainly something I can make more of an effort on, though I have dragged myself to two Sunday dinners in the last three months, which seemed to make my family happy.

The back door swings shut behind Everett, and his eyes narrow the second he takes me in. I try to force a smile at my brother, lifting a hand to wave, but concern floods his features, and he picks up his pace, reaching me in just a few steps.

"So, it is a flare?"

I nod, and he places a hand on the center of my forehead.

"You don't feel warm."

"No." I shake my head. "Just bad cramps and a killer

headache." I rarely have a fever when I'm experiencing a PMDD flare, but it has happened before.

My premenstrual syndrome became progressively worse throughout my teen years and into my twenties. On top of the physical symptoms, I began experiencing terrible mood swings, anxiety, and panic attacks, even depressive episodes. I either couldn't sleep at all or couldn't get out of bed.

Since being diagnosed, every month is different, and the severity of the flare-up varies, which makes it hard to manage my life around the condition. When I was twenty-two, August finally convinced me to talk to a doctor about my symptoms. I was often unwilling to discuss what was happening with anyone besides him, so I'd shut myself in my room for several days until I felt better. It wasn't abnormal for the rest of my family to not hear from me for a little while, especially if they thought I was deep into my writing, but August was the exception. When I would go MIA, he'd know something was wrong, and when he checked on me, he'd see how I was truly feeling.

It took three months for the doctor to diagnose me and put me on birth control. Diet, exercise, fresh air, and meditation are also known to help, as is therapy—but all of those things feel too hard to manage.

It's an odd realization—to know that you're suffering but still feel the pain you're experiencing is less daunting than just simply doing the work to be better. I'm not sure what makes me like this, or if it's possible to escape. I'm too tired to try.

"Let me take you home," Everett says.

"I can't." I sigh. "Nobody else is coming in for another two hours."

Everett chews the inside of his cheek, head swiveling around the cafe. Without a word, he walks behind the counter and through the swinging doors that lead to the kitchen.

A few minutes pass before he returns with my purse and my sweater in hand. "Let's go."

"But—"

He spins, walking backward toward the back door. "Peggy called in one of the other baristas early, and she'll cover until they arrive. The coffee bar will be totally fine, but you are not. I need you to take care of yourself right now."

His tone invites zero argument, and I know he's not wrong, so I slide off the stool and follow him out of the building. My brother helps me into his Jeep, and once we get home, he leads me inside and sets me up on the couch rather than having me climb the stairs to my room.

I don't tell him that I'll need to make it up there before August gets home anyway, because we haven't spoken since I woke up with him in my bed four days ago, and I'm not ready to see him yet.

I woke up that morning brewing with anxiety, and while his touch may be the best cure for it, not even having him beside me could quell it. I locked myself in the shower until long after I knew he'd woken and left my room. From there, my mood plummeted. I did my best to keep my distance, not wanting him to blame himself or think that our night together was the cause of it—though at first, I was unsure of that myself.

My diagnosis has caused anxiety for years now, but my life has given me more than enough reason to have all those symptoms on my own. It can be hard to wade through what might be a flare-up, and what is just me. My trauma.

But as the next two days went on, I began feeling nauseous, lost my appetite, and then the frequent headaches set in. Knowing I was coming up on my period, I figured it had more to do with PMDD than anything August and I had done last week. My symptoms have been getting progressively worse the last twenty-four hours, but today is by far the hardest.

My head is pounding so hard that my vision is dotted with flashing lights, and all I want to do is try to fall asleep. I set an alarm for thirty minutes before August normally gets off work while Everett fills up my water bottle, grabs my heating pad from my bedroom, and turns on old reruns of *Real Housewives*.

"I have to take care of some things at the garage and then

swing by Lou's school because she forgot her lunch at home. Do you want me to stop by later to check on you? Or I can send Leo after he finishes his surf lessons?"

I shake my head, pulling my knees to my chest as I lie sideways on the couch.

"Well, I'll call to check in on you later regardless." He kisses my forehead. "Please communicate with one of us, with Mom—hell, even August—if you need something, okay?"

"I will, I promise." I yawn. "I'm just tired, so I'm going to try to take a nap."

My twin nods, looking down at me solemnly. Everyone says we have the same eyes, but I think his are much kinder than mine. He takes a knit blanket off the top of the couch and drapes it over me before heading to the door.

"Love you, Lele!" he calls.

"Love you too," I grunt through gritted teeth.

I tug my knees to my chest, wiping away my tears with a shaking hand. I'm staring at the kettle on the stove, and it feels like it's taken eons for the water to heat, and all I want is a fucking cup of chamomile. It feels like someone held a fork over a flame and is now repeatedly stabbing me in the center of my gut with it, twisting it all about to ensure I feel every one of the prongs.

I want to lie down, and I want to shower, and I want tea. I want to scream at the kettle to heat faster, I want to scream at myself to stop being so fucking crazy, I want to scream at my body for making me feel this way. I want to throw coffee mugs across the kitchen, craving the shattering of something that isn't me.

My jaw clenches tight enough to ache as the scream lodged inside my throat attempts to force itself out of my mouth like a battering ram. Dropping my face into my hands, I find the strength to hold back that roar, but I'm too weak to accomplish much else. Tears soak my palms, my chest heaves with sobs, and my body trembles beneath the weight of it all.

I didn't sleep at all. I absent-mindedly stared at the television for some undetermined amount of time before I couldn't take it anymore. I needed something. A distraction, a blunt, a fucking drink. The surge in that craving was enough to get me off the couch and to the kitchen, attempting to make a cup of tea in hopes it'll calm the urge.

Finally, the whistle of the kettle blows just as the front door slams, and the clash of sounds sends me spiraling.

I know rationally, I should stand up and remove the kettle from the burner, but instead, I just cover my ears and hope all the noise will diminish on its own.

"Elena?" The voice is muffled through the screaming and my covered ears, then a sudden silence sweeps over the house. "Elena," he whispers, much closer now. "Look at me."

My head lifts, and emerald eyes behind black-framed glasses come into view. His brows draw together as he tilts his head, a rogue chestnut curl falling into his face.

"You're home sooner than I expected. I wasn't going to leave a mess for you."

"I don't care about your mess." He cups my cheeks with both hands, shaking his head. "Leo told me you left work early."

I nod, swallowing. "Cramps."

He gives me an unconvinced expression. "Have you started yet?"

I shake my head.

"So, it's a flare-up?"

I nod again.

"They're not always like this, are they?"

"Most months aren't this bad, but this whole week I've..." I trail off as my emotion clogs my throat, tears erupting once again. "I've been fucking crazy, August. I don't know what the hell is wrong with me."

"Shh." He hushes me. "Nothing is wrong with you. You're not crazy." He brushes away the hair falling loose from the bun atop my head. "Can I touch you?"

I nod, and August slips his hands down my shoulders and beneath my arms, hauling me into him. I throw my hands around his neck, and he scoops beneath my ass, lifting us both as I hang off him like a fucking sack of potatoes.

"Wrap your legs around my waist, Little Vice."

The low vibration of his voice rumbles against my neck, sending a blaze to my core. I know he didn't mean it salaciously, but it doesn't stop a surge of heat from flooding my body as I tighten my thighs around his hips.

He carries me out of the kitchen, but doesn't start up the stairs the way I expected him to. He goes past the staircase, through the living room and the library, and straight into his room.

"What're you doing?" I ask.

"You don't have a tub in your bathroom, but I do."

He nudges the bathroom door open with his shoulder, lowering me onto the edge of the tub. I lift my head, blinking around the dark room. It's huge. A double-sink vanity with opulent mirrors sits across from me, with a standing shower and a toilet in the corner beside it. I turn slightly toward the deep, oval tub. Candles line the sides. August picks up a small wicker basket from the edge, sorting through bath bombs, salts, and soaps.

"You get a lot of company in this tub, Augustus?"

A smile tugs at his lips as he sets aside two candles, a bottle of bubble bath, and a small bag of salts. "Nope. Just you." His eyes meet mine when he turns the faucet on, testing the temperature of the water. "You know I like baths, Elena."

The heat in his gaze steals the breath from my lungs, memories flashing through my mind. My old apartment on the harbor had a big, beautiful bathtub like this. It was only a few short months that August and I spent wrapped in our secret love, but many of those nights together took place in that tub.

One night in San Francisco had been my favorite of them all.

It feels like a hundred different lifetimes have come and gone since that brief one we had the privilege of living inside. I wish we could've stayed in that life. I wish we'd never left that hotel room.

I wish I'd never left him at all.

August breaks eye contact, pouring a generous amount of soap into the water, followed by a shake of the salts. "Strip and get in," he says. "I'll be back with your tea and a lighter for the candles." He stands, watching me expectantly, but I don't move. "Do you need me to undress you too?"

Yes.

I shake my head.

He nods. "Want me to grab your e-reader?"

"No." I sigh. "My eyes hurt, so I don't feel like reading right now. Can you grab my laptop so I can watch something instead?"

"Sure." He turns to walk out of the bathroom, leaving the door wide open. "Now, get naked for me, Little Vice."

"Are you doing that on purpose?" I shout in his direction. "Saying things you know will turn me on?"

I only receive a deep, echoing laugh in return.

When August comes back a few minutes later, he's holding a steaming mug of tea in one hand, with my laptop tucked beneath his other arm. I'm fully submerged in the near-full tub, bubbles covering the majority of my body.

I still have pain, but the muscle soreness I was experiencing on top of my cramps has faded substantially, and my headache has gone from full roar to dull throb. August sets everything down on the vanity counter and bends over to rummage through the cabinet below it.

He pulls out a long wooden tray and a small white pillow. The tray sits perfectly across the tub, resting on the edge of either side. August then motions for me to sit up as he slides the pillow between my back and the side of the tub.

"Damn." I sigh, settling back. "You really do love baths."

He laughs, setting my tea and my laptop on the tray before sitting on the edge of the tub. "They help with my panic attacks."

"Panic attacks?" I ask. "How long have those been happening?"

He tilts his head, offering a sorry smile. The kind that tells me there is no point in answering. They're another one of the many aftershocks from the earth-shaking catastrophe the two of us caused.

"I'm sorry," I whisper.

He shakes his head, dipping a hand into the water to run his fingers along my thigh. We're both quiet for a moment, watching the water ripple past his hands as he brushes my skin. "I'm going to warm up some clothes for you in the dryer, then I'll come back and check on you."

"Lucky day for you to get off work early, huh?"

He gives me a bemused expression as he lifts off the tub. "I didn't get off early. I left when Leo said you weren't feeling well."

"What?" I ask. "Why would you do that?"

"I know you don't like your family seeing you like this." He leans against the door, crossing his arms. "I know I'm the only person you allow to take care of you. Even though you don't want to, I'm the person you trust to know what you need without you having to voice it. You need to be taken care of today."

Those all-too-familiar black threads of guilt creep over my shoulders and slowly tie themselves around my throat. I've been wrapped up in work, in my family—in August. I've started to forget all my sins. I've forgotten the reason I shut myself out to begin with, the reason I didn't allow myself the distractions of love, friendship, self-worth. I've allowed myself to forget that I don't deserve any of this.

"How many panic attacks—how many night terrors—have you experienced over the years that you had to handle on your own? That I wasn't here to care for you?"

"And how many flare-ups did you go through on your own?" He swallows, rubbing a hand over the stars tattooed on his wrist. "You left me to crumble beneath the weight of my pain, but I see now that you forced yourself to suffer too." He lifts his eyes to mine. "I just want to know the why of it all."

Chapter Twenty-Two

Violet

"Unknown / Nth" - Hozier

The bathroom is dimly lit by candles and the glow of her laptop where it plays what I instantly recognize as Season Four of *Real Housewives of Beverly Hills*. I've rewatched it with her so many times it's now impossible for me to miss the two women fighting back and forth about hexing one another.

Elena's head is tilted back against the pillow, a washcloth covering her eyes. She didn't answer my question earlier, and I knew she wouldn't. She simply stared at me with quiet trepidation until I finally left the bathroom and went to get her things ready.

Now, candlelight flickers against her golden skin, casting a soft glow over the moisture glistening on her chest. She's still mostly covered by bubbles, but they've diminished enough that I can make out the two peaks of her pierced, honey-colored nipples.

My fingers tighten around the fabric of her robe with a sudden itch to sketch her like this. Her body is a masterpiece, meant to be re-created through multitudes of mediums, forever immortalized. She's the kind of beauty that should be remembered. Studied. Cherished. She's art.

It's been years since I've allowed myself to draw her, and the way it hits me as I watch her in this light is enough to knock me off my feet.

I must have made a sound, because she's suddenly sitting up, the cloth falling off her face and into the palm of her hand. Her head whips sideways, eyes meeting mine.

"Hi." She blinks.

"Sor... Sorry," I stutter, realizing how fucking weird I must look, being caught staring at her like this. She smiles knowingly, and heat crawls up my neck. "I grabbed your fuzzy robe from your bathroom and warmed it up in the dryer for you."

"Thank you, Augustus." She grips the sides of the tub, pulling herself from the water.

I'm dumbfounded, slack-jawed, struck stupid, as she rises. Water sluices off her perfect body in thick rivulets, cascading over her flawless, smooth, golden skin. Thick suds of bubbles slide down her thigh, over the serpent tattoo that wraps around it.

I love that tattoo. I love her thighs. Fuck. I'm hard.

A bead of water rolls between her perky, hard tits, dripping down her stomach like the stars I inked on her sternum years ago. I'm fighting the urge to fall to my knees and crawl to her. Beg to lick every drop off her body, until I'm the only cause of her wetness.

What does it say about me that I'm jealous of the fucking water? I'm disgustingly envious of every drop that runs down her skin, wishing it were my hands instead.

She steps out of the tub, and I'm damn near panting when my eyes get stuck on her pussy, almost as if I can feel it flooding my senses. Her taste, the way she smells, how it feels when she's clenching around my fingers and my tongue. I involuntarily lick my lips at the sight of the ruthless temptation.

"Augustus?" Her sultry voice has my eyes snapping to her face. She flashes me the sly smile that makes my goddamn knees buckle. "My robe?"

"Sorry," I breathe, holding it open.

She turns around, and I bite my tongue to keep from groaning at the view of her perfect ass as she slides her arms through each of the sleeves, and I let the fabric slip from my hands and onto her shoulders.

I've seen her struggle with PMDD for years. I remember her periods being bad in middle and high school, worse than they seemed to be for other girls. She battled with the pressure of being judged—told she was faking the severity of her symptoms for attention, or to get out of gym class. Not just by other students, but by teachers too.

I knew her better, though. I could see how much pain she was in, even back then.

In her early twenties, it got worse. The symptoms started weeks before her period and lasted long after. They were paired with anxiety attacks and mood swings. She'd sometimes go days without leaving her bedroom. She wouldn't eat, couldn't sleep. Couldn't focus on her writing.

Her flare-ups would sometimes coincide with her on-again, off-again relationship with my brother, and he loved to use words like crazy and insane and too-fucking-much. He didn't believe her either, because she couldn't understand what was wrong with her, because not every month was the same.

But like always, I knew better. I saw what no one else could.

Elena spins, tightening the robe around her body. Her eyes flutter upward, playful and taunting and such a contrast to the haunted vacancy I found in them earlier. "I like it when you stare, by the way. Feel free to continue doing so."

She smiles as she steps away from me and back into my bedroom before halting. I know she's taking in the made-up bed, overflowing with pillows I brought down from her room. The television turned on and set to the same episode of *Real Housewives* she was watching in the bath. A fresh pair of sweatpants and her favorite crewneck sit folded at the edge of my mattress. The table on the opposite side of the bed from where I sleep has her e-reader, a fresh mug of tea, and her dinner sitting beside it.

"It's the red lentil soup from Fred's deli. I had it delivered. I also made you grilled cheese, and that tea is raspberry leaf. I read it helps with symptoms, but I can make you another cup of chamomile if you don't like it.

She turns around, brows drawn deeply as her lips cluster at the corner of her mouth. "You said you didn't want me in your room."

I take a careful step toward her. "Thought tonight could be an exception."

I want you right beside me.

She seems to hear the words I don't speak, causing her eyes to soften.

"I don't want to be anyone's charity case, Augustus."

"You are not my fucking charity case." I take another step toward her. "You are the only person who doesn't treat me like I am one myself."

Her breath hitches as I close the distance between us. "What are we doing here, August? What is all this?"

"You've always been my undoing," I whisper, bringing my hand to her cheek. "Sometimes I fear you may be my detriment." Her eyes fall closed as I make contact with her soft skin. "But right now, Elena, you are my salvation."

She exhales a shuddering sigh, leaning into my touch before nodding.

I let my hand drop from her face, sliding down her neck and between her breasts until it lands on the knot of her robe. Making quick work of untying it, the fabric falls open, revealing her flawless body to me. She allows me to take it off her shoulders, her skin now mostly dry.

I dress her, and she watches my every movement with rapt attention. We're both out of breath by the time she's covered up, and I know there is a part in each of us that wishes I'd strip her bare again, though tonight isn't the right time for whatever physical steps we'll inevitably take next.

Because I wasn't lying when I said I fear she'll be my detriment, but I also realize now that there is no force strong enough to keep me from her. Our grandest sins, our deepest pain, our tortured souls—they all resulted in the two of us ending up right back here.

We may destroy one another until we're both ground to dust, but there's no doubt we'll be doing so wrapped in each other's arms.

"Get in bed, Little Vice," I murmur as her sweater falls over her body.

She listens, pulling back the sheets as she crawls inside, inching toward her end of the mattress. Her end. A dangerous thought for me to be having.

I press play on the television, folding the covers back over as I sit beside her, propping myself against the headboard. She's beneath the blankets, and I'm on top of them, though I'm not sure what the point of that is when every boundary I've attempted to place between us has been obliterated.

She matches my position, pulling the soup into her lap and swirling half her grilled cheese through it before taking a bite. She moans, and my cock immediately jumps.

Adjusting my position to hide it, I clear my throat before asking, "When I grabbed your laptop, I noticed you had a document open. Are you writing again?"

She cuts me a glare, slowing the movement of her chewing. "I told you weeks ago I was writing."

"I thought you were lying." I shrug.

"No." She sets her sandwich down, covering her mouth as she laughs. "I never stopped writing. I always find my fingers moving in some capacity. It's just that everything that comes out of me now is depressing...or very poorly written." She sighs. "The things that used to come naturally to me don't anymore. I'll never stop being a writer, but...I don't think I'm an author anymore. Maybe I was never meant to be one, and my career was a short-lived fluke...I don't know."

"You were," I rasp, fiercely enough that her head snaps in my direction. "You are meant for it, Elena. Your words are important."

She offers a forced, closed lip smile and a small lift of her shoulder. "I'll keep trying, then."

"That's all you can do." I shrug. "Are you feeling better?"

Her smile grows. "Yeah. Physically, at least. My stomach and my head feel better, my muscles are less sore, but my brain...that's still a mess." She snorts. "Although, I'm not so sure that's from the

PMDD. I used to be able to spot it, you know? I could piece apart when I started to feel..." She chews her lip as if searching for the right word. "Crazy, I guess. I knew exactly what was coming, and my anxiety was a tell-tale sign of how bad my symptoms would be that month. But the last few years, I have felt crazy all the time." She laughs snidely. "I don't even really track my cycle anymore. I'll start my period and think, oh, so that's why I was exceptionally insane last week."

"What about therapy?" I ask.

Her eyes flash to mine, lip curling before she takes another slow bite of her grilled cheese. "Hard pass."

I roll my eyes, biting back a laugh. "I swear by it, Elena. It's done wonders for me, truly."

"Stop trying to peer pressure me, Augustus," she mutters with a full mouth.

"Have you ever thought that maybe your grief exacerbates your PMDD, or vice versa? That your diagnosis might be affecting you differently than it does others?" She drops her eyes to her lap but doesn't respond, so I continue, "Maybe a therapist could help you sort through that. Get you on antidepressants or something that could help." Her jaw tenses at that suggestion, and I know she's about to get defensive, so I put my hands up in surrender. "I know years ago you said they didn't make sense for you and that you didn't want to take any medication like that, but...you're suffering differently now, and that's okay. It's also okay to treat yourself differently too. You deserve a little grace."

Her jaw relaxes, but she still doesn't address me as she continues eating. Elena reminds me of a wounded animal. Defensive and vicious, but it's only a mask for her fear and pain. Coaxing her into accepting care is like she's finally let me examine her wounds without biting, and that's enough for tonight. I stop pressing, settling against my pillows and allowing her to eat and watch her show in peace.

A half hour passes in silence before she asks, "Therapy has helped you?"

"Yeah." I smile softly. "It really has, I think. Some days are still bad, and I'll be working through this shit for the rest of my life, but...it doesn't feel as heavy as it used to."

She's on her side, facing me, cheek pressed against her hand on the pillow as she nods. The dim light of the lamp on my bedside casts her in a warm glow, but her eyes are withdrawn and cold. Her dishes are stacked atop the table on her side, her tea now tepid and forgotten beside them.

Because old habits never die, I throw caution to the wind and pull my hoodie over my head, tossing it to the floor before flicking off the light and the television, and crawling into bed beside her.

"Can I ask you something else?" she whispers into the darkness.

"You can ask me anything."

She shuffles closer to me, and on instinct, I open my arm so she can rest her head on my chest. I don't think either of us meant to let it happen, but cosmic forces seem to be at work when it comes to Elena and me. We don't have any control over it.

"Did you ever feel like it was your fault?"

The question unsettles me, sends my chest spiraling into the pit of darkness where my soul used to rest. Only the feel of her hair sliding between my fingers keeps me grounded to earth, to this room, and this bed with her.

"Yes."

"Did therapy help with that?"

I inhale deeply, buying myself time. I know the unspoken question she's asking, but what I don't know is how to answer it. Her eyes bore holes through the side of my face, but my gaze remains fixed on the ceiling.

"I think so. Therapy has helped me separate reality from the hauntings of my own mind." Emotion wells in my eyes, and I bite my cheek, breathing through my nose to quell the burn in my throat. I don't want her to hear it. "There are things I could've done differently that would've resulted in a different outcome, and I'll never escape that, but therapy helped me understand the difference between intention and impact. The impact will always haunt me, but I've learned to understand my intentions, and at the very least, I can accept those."

She's quiet, and I wouldn't know she was crying if I didn't feel the wet prickle of her tears as they drop against my chest.

"Can I ask you something?" My voice breaks on the question.

"You can ask me anything." Her voice breaks too.

"Do you think it was my fault?"

Trepidation chokes me, hard enough to sever my throat as I wait for her response, for a voice to the truth I've been terrified to hear.

"No," she whispers, her tone steady. "I've never thought that."

Pressure lifts off my neck, my airways opening once more, and only now do I realize the weight pressing down on me the past four years. Only now do I realize that I've been living without oxygen—that her empathy is my atmosphere.

"I do think that we're both responsible, though," she admits quietly. "In our own ways."

"I think that too."

Her hand brushes over my chest, like she's searching for hope beneath my skin. I run my fingers through her hair before cradling the back of her head, like I'm searching for healing in her arms. Solidarity in a catastrophe only the two of us can understand.

"Can I ask one more thing?" Her voice is low, hollow, and distant after sitting in silence.

"Always."

"Do you think I'm crazy?"

A surprised laugh escapes me, and she tenses at the sound. I'd do anything to root inside Elena's mind, to understand her thoughts and how they surface, how she finds the courage to voice them all, her unrelenting curiosity—a force more powerful than any fear she has or the reaction it may garner. "Maybe a little."

I expect her to laugh back at me, but she doesn't. Her voice is stoic in the darkness of my room as she asks, "Is that why he never loved me? Why nobody can?"

I turn my head, finding her eyes blazing through me, still wet with the tears she just stopped shedding. New ones brew behind her lids, glistening in the hazy moonlight slipping through my curtains.

"No, Elena." I kiss her forehead. "I think we're all kind of crazy—wild—with the right people. He was never your brand of wild, but that doesn't make something wrong with you. Just wrong for each other."

"So, if I'm crazy..." Her delicate throat works as she swallows. "Does that make you crazy too?"

"I don't know how else I'd describe any of this, Elena," I admit, stroking her hair. "The complexity of wanting to hate you, and love you, and fuck you all at once." I trace the outline of her beautiful face in the darkness, halted by the way she bites her lip as she watches me. "I want to run away from you and hold you closer at the same time. There are moments I wish I'd never met you, while painfully aware that I'd die without your existence." My hand finds her jaw, thumb resting on her bottom lip and pulling it from her teeth. "I miss you even when I'm right next to you, and I loathe you when you're far away. But one thing I always know for certain is that I'll take you any way you come, any pain you cause, no matter how brief the moment, because simply experiencing you...it's more valuable to me than the air I breathe."

I expect her to react with surprise, to gasp or widen her eyes at my heart-wrenched confession, but she doesn't. She blinks, eyes glowing with something like understanding, like she already knew those words because they came directly from her soul too.

"Is it wild that I feel the exact same way?" she asks, bringing her hand to my face.

I choke on a laugh. "Yeah."

"So, we're each other's brand of crazy?"

She makes the same motion to my lip that I did with hers, and I wonder which one of us will cave first. Who will finally put us both out of this unending misery by replacing their hand with their lips.

Neither of us do.

"Yeah," I finally respond, feeling her thumb bounce against my mouth with the movement. "We always have been."

She nods, moving her hand over my chin and down my chest, back to the same spot it was resting before. She traces the tattoo of raven wings beneath my sternum.

"I should go to my own room, Augustus."

"No," I rasp. "Stay here with me. Please."

She lifts her eyes to mine, uncertainty shining in her chocolate-colored irises.

"Just tonight," I beg. "One last time."

"Just tonight," she echoes. "One last time."

Chapter Twenty-Three

Vice

"Born To Die" - Lana Del Rey

"*Il mio angelo*," my mom exclaims before the bells on the front door to the coffee shop even stop chiming. She immediately breaks several health code violations as she walks around the counter and takes my face between her hands. "You look so much better today."

"I'm feeling better," I say, lips pursed between squished cheeks. "It only lasts a few days."

"Monica, get out from back there," my dad grumbles. "You don't need to get Dahlia slapped with a fine."

"*Ti darò uno schiaffo*," she snaps back.

He watches her with affectionate amusement, and the glitter in my mother's brown eyes matches it. They've always had the kind of playful, easy-going marriage that I hoped to find for myself. They met young and realized quickly that they'd never need anyone else again.

It was easy to get caught up in the idea of simplistic eternity when it was the primary example of love you spent your whole life witnessing. Now, I watch them in astonishment, unable to comprehend how two people could've possibly gotten every decision right the first time around, or if there are darker aspects of their story they've kept hidden from us.

I wonder if dark people like me even deserve that kind of happiness.

I didn't used to think like this, and that's probably why I can't finish a manuscript to save my fucking life.

"What're you two doing here?" I ask, sliding to the end of the counter so the other barista, Aimee, can take over.

"Grabbing an overnight bag for Lou from Dahlia. We're going to pick her up from school, and she's going to sleep over at our house. Everett's taking Dal away for the night to celebrate her birthday."

"Fuck. It's Dahlia's birthday?"

I've been working with her for the last five hours, and nobody said a goddamn thing.

"Everett texted the family group message three times yesterday to make sure nobody forgot," my dad chimes.

I've had the family group text muted for years. Dammit.

"I feel bad," I say as my mom tosses me a serves-you-right look.

"It's fine." Dahlia flutters through the double doors that lead from the kitchen. "I don't like to celebrate my birthday, anyway." She smiles at me as she hands a backpack to my mom. "That's why I didn't say anything."

"None of that!" Mom swats at her before pulling Dahlia in for a hug. "Today is tied for my top six favorite days of the year. Don't insult me by belittling it."

"Top six?" I deadpan, glancing at my dad.

"She thinks the best days of the year are the ones where her kids and grandkid were born." He smiles at her adoringly. "Notice how my birthday isn't on that list, but it's fine."

Both of my brothers come through the front doors of the cafe, smiling as they greet our parents. "Thanks for watching her," Everett says as he pulls away from my mom's embrace.

"You can pay me back with more—"

"More grandbabies. I know. I know." He laughs, scratching his beard. "I'm doing my best, okay?"

"All you have to do is not pull out." I tilt my coffee mug in his direction before taking a sip.

"Yeah, dude. If you can't perform, just say that." Leo tosses him a shit-eating grin.

"You're fuckin' annoying," Everett mutters.

"Aye, man. At least I planted my seed."

"Don't say you planted your seed." My lip curls. "That's disgusting."

"Yeah." Everett nudges Leo. "Say cream pie. It's much classier."

"No cream pie jokes!" our mother snipes.

"Oh, my God," Dahlia groans, wiping a hand down her face. "I'm going to trespass you guys. You're making the customers stare."

I glance around; the shop has gone quiet. I also realize our dad has migrated to the back of the bakery, pretending to look at the artwork along the walls as he creates as much distance from the rest of us as possible. I don't blame him.

"You can't trespass me. I own this—" Leo's stops when the bells on the front door chime again, and we all turn to find August and Darby entering together. His face brightens immediately. "My Honeysuckle. How are you feeling?"

"Like a planet." She sighs as his arm snaps out, tugging her against his chest.

He plants his lips against the top of her head as his hand splays across her ever-growing belly. "Oh, no, baby. You're not a planet. You're the whole goddamn universe."

Darby laughs as Leo spins her so that her back rests against his front, resting his chin atop her head, swaying in place. "How was your session, Auggie?"

August's eyes meet mine, just briefly. They look clear, and he smiles softly, though I can't quite make out the meaning behind it. "It was good."

I force a smile back. He was persistent in his encouragement the other night for me to seek therapy, and my instinct was to shut it down. I won't tell him—any of them—this, but his words stuck with me the last three days since I fell asleep against his chest.

I haven't slept in his arms again, haven't been back in his room. I called out from work the next morning, my symptoms still pretty severe, but I didn't allow August to take care of me like that again. It was too vulnerable, and I needed time to process. By yesterday morning, I was feeling myself, but we've been working opposite schedules, so I haven't seen him much.

We have a lot we need to address, and both of us keep tiptoeing around it.

"Are you going home now or going back to work?" Everett asks August.

"Work," he says. "I promised Maggie I'd finish a thigh piece of hers I've been working on, but we've been busier than expected so I haven't had the chance, and she's been asking for months."

A slow ache builds in the pit of my stomach at the reminder that August spends most of his days touching other women's bodies, but I know it's not right of me. That's his work, and his art, and he's professional. I'm well-fucking-aware just how strict his sense of professionalism is when it comes to his business.

Plus, I don't have a claim on him. Other than the fact that anyone out there who gets him naked is going to be subjected to seeing my name all over his thigh.

That gives me a sick sense of satisfaction.

"Oh, Maggie, huh?" Leo raises his brows. "How's that going?"

What. The. Fuck.

August's eyes flash to mine, assessing, before turning back to my brother. "That's nothing."

"Is 'nothing' a new code word for fucking? Because Dahlia doesn't want us to cuss in the coffee shop?"

"I didn't know that was a rule," August muses, lips twitching. Like the jokes about him fucking some random girl right in front of me are funny?

I take back my former thoughts, that ache rising to the surface of my being like a molten rage. I may not have a claim on Augustus Hayes, but I never signed up to be a fucking side piece. I think back on every conversation we've had since I moved in with him, and he never mentioned seeing someone, but he didn't mention not seeing someone either.

And if he's tattooing her...

Fuck. Rage clogs my throat, tears stinging the corners of my eyes. I know how intimate inking someone's skin is when you're emotionally attached to them. How vulnerable it is to claim someone's body that way when it's also a claim to their soul. I know what it means to August to connect with a lover in that capacity and...fuck.

I feel sick.

I've made regrettable choices in my past where he is concerned, but I never allowed someone else to touch me with a needle. Especially not someone I'd fucked. Because that's all it ever was—fucking. There was no emotion, no care, no love. I didn't think it was possible to create art on someone's body when you're having sex with them without attaching all of those other things.

My family continues to hold conversation around me, and I can feel his stare burn into the side of my face, but I ignore it. Pulling off my apron, I mutter, "Well, my shift is over."

I have half an hour left, actually, but if Dahlia notices, she doesn't voice it.

"Do you want to stay and have lunch with us?" Darby asks innocently.

I swallow hard, forcing the emotion in my throat back down. Deep, deep down. I raise my head, faking a smile. "I actually have a date tonight that I need to go get ready for."

"A date? Really?" That's August's voice, but I refuse to meet his gaze. His tone is cold and accusatory. The sound of it makes me bristle, but I hope he's feeling even one-tenth the way I am right now, even if I'm lying through my goddamn teeth.

"I hope it's not the filthy, derogatory orgasm guy from a few weeks ago," Everett murmurs under his breath.

"Nope. He was a total douche, actually. Won't ever go near that mess again." I finally cut my gaze to August, and he's seething. Nostrils flaring, there's a simmering rage in his eyes that I'm certain matches my own. "In fact..." I flash my teeth at him. "I'm probably going to have even filthier, more derogatory, need-to-seek-a-priest-afterward orgasms with this new guy."

"I am standing right here," my mother mutters.

August looks at me with a clenched jaw and eyes blazing bright enough to set the building on fire. The rest of my family looks at me like I should be committed.

I hitch my thumb over my shoulder, in the direction of the back door. "Well, I better get going."

"We have to go too," Everett drawls, watching me with concern. "Everyone tell my girlfriend happy birthday."

"Happy birthday, girlfriend," we all mumble in alarming unison.

Leo kisses my head, and my mother hugs me before following the rest of my family out the door—Everett and Dahlia to their weekend away, my mom and Darby off to lunch, and Leo back to the surf shop.

August stays, watching me with that scorching stare. I ignore him, stalking through the doors to the back of the bakery and grabbing my purse. When I return, he's still there, arms crossed, waiting.

I shove past him and out the front door, taking a right on the boardwalk. He follows, reaching me in a few quick steps. "The fuck was all that about?"

"Don't you have an appointment to get to?"

He pauses, barking a laugh before catching up to me again. "You're fucking jealous."

"I'm not jealous, but I find it appalling that you'd be..." I trail off, unsure of how to describe whatever the hell has been happening between August and me since I moved in with him two months ago.

"What, Elena?" August stops on the boardwalk, grabbing my arm and halting me too. "What claim do you so desperately want to have on me that the mere mention of another woman's name next to mine sends you into such a spiral?"

My teeth grind, skin heating where he holds my wrist. The world warps around us—people passing by, the squeal of seagulls above our head, the sea breeze floating through my hair and the distant crash of waves against the shore—but all I can focus on is his flaming emerald eyes and the pressure of his touch.

"Are you...dating another woman and then coming home and holding me in the middle of the night?" I ask. "Toying with me the way you have been, while entertaining someone else at the same time?"

August bursts out an unhumorous laugh, jaw tight as he glances at our surroundings. Only now do I realize we're standing directly in front of Heathen's, and he must notice it too, tightening his grip on my wrist and dragging me around the side of the building.

Before we make it to the parking lot behind the boardwalk, August spins abruptly, pushing me against the wall of my brothers' surf shop. His chest is heaving, brushing against mine with every angry inhale. Green eyes blazing behind his dark-rimmed glasses, his nostrils flare as he studies my face.

"You are... You are delirious, woman." He slides his hand up my arm, leaving goosebumps in his wake. "So frustratingly blind." His long, strong fingers wrap around the back of my neck, tightening in my hair. "Impulsive. Reckless." He inches into me. "But fuck are you beautiful when you're envious." His eyes linger on my lips before they snap to mine, blazing and breathtaking. "For you to think I've ever seen anyone but you—it is endlessly infuriating." He huffs another flat laugh, nodding toward the parking lot. "Go get in the truck. I'm taking you home."

"What about your appointment with Maggie?" I snap back.

"If you want to act like a brat, I'm going to treat you like one. If you want to throw a fit, I'm going to punish you for it. Now get your ass inside my fucking truck. Wait for me while I go cancel with her."

All of the heat radiating across my skin floods right to my core at his insinuation, and I can't hide the triumphant smile that spreads across my face.

I have an irrational, intense, ruthless hatred for whoever the fuck this girl Maggie is, and I don't care how crazy that makes me. I'm dripping at the thought of him walking inside his shop right now to tell her that he can't work with her today because he'll be busy with me instead.

We are so fucking toxic.

"Yes, Daddy," I whisper into his neck as I press off the wall, not missing the way he shivers. He damn near growls as he watches me walk away.

His Bronco's top and doors are taken off, so I'm able to climb in easily, warm spring air breezing over my heated skin as I wait. It only takes a few minutes before the back door to Boardwalk Tattoo opens and August slips out. His features are hard and rough, and I'm concerned about what it does to me to see him angry like this.

He doesn't say anything as he hops into the driver's side and starts the ignition. We make the short drive home in silence, sexual tension permeating the air between us, thick and hazy. Once he pulls into the driveway and kills the engine, August unbuckles himself, but I make no move to do the same.

"Are you seeing her?" I ask.

"No."

"Why did Leo say that then?"

He sighs, running a hand through his dark curls. "She's been interested in me for a while, and your brothers are under the impression I've been suffering from a...dry spell. They've been trying to convince me to go out with her for years."

"Who the fuck is she?"

"She works for me."

Goddammit. Nope. I don't like that at all.

My face must give me away because August shakes his head, hiding a smile before licking his lips. "I like seeing you jealous. It makes my cock hard. Feels like a fitting punishment for the torment you've been providing me all these years."

"Torment?" I ask incredulously. "I haven't been around!"

"Oh, you don't need to be, Little Vice." He hops out of the driver-side before rounding the Bronco to where I'm sitting in the passenger seat. "You can destroy me from three thousand miles away."

"You say that like you witnessed me trying." I throw off my seatbelt and hop down from the truck, but August pins me against the side of the hood before I can shove past him. I look up at him, narrowing my eyes. "You talk about the claim you think I want to have to you, but you seem to be the one trying to own me."

He drops his head so his gaze meets mine, his arms bracing against the truck, boxing me in. I feel so small beneath him, and he watches my face like he knows it too.

"I've never wanted anything more than to own every piece of you, Elena."

"Then why'd you let me go so easily?"

There is a war within his gaze, and his mouth twitches, lips trembling with hesitation. Like there are words he wants to say, but he can't get them out. He swallows them down, and whatever secret he's harboring has me shoving against his chest.

"No, you don't get to do that. Whatever you're hiding, say it. I can fucking take it."

"It wasn't easy," he rasps. "It destroyed me, waking up that morning to find you gone. The night before, seeing you at my door, taking you to bed—it was the first time I allowed myself to have hope."

My breath shortens at his admission, tension and trepidation coiling tightly at the base of my stomach. He closes his eyes, like he doesn't want to look at me. Suddenly, I'm grabbing his face, pulling his forehead against mine.

He exhales with trembling breath before he continues, "You don't get to talk about jealousy to me when I had to watch you walk into that Manhattan apartment with another man's arm around your waist. When I had to watch him twirl you in the street and watch you laugh at something he said. You don't get to be jealous when I had to witness that. When I had to walk away."

My chest seizes, his words wrapping around my lungs and squeezing impossibly tight. "What..." I pull back, blinking. "What do you mean?"

"I came after you," he whispers, eyes still closed. "I came to New York, and I saw you with a man. With friends. Happy and carefree and fine." His voice cracks on the word. "I didn't let you go easily, Elena." His lids finally flutter open, burning right through my soul. "I never let you go at all."

I imagine the drumming between our chests could be heard for miles, and the haze of tension between us begins to dissipate, revealing the most clarity I've had in years. I inch my thumb along August's jaw, feeling the short, shallow bursts of breath escaping his lips. Running my thumb over it, savoring its soft feel against my skin.

"Elena," he rasps, and I feel the vibration against my palm. Multitudes of green dance in his eyes, like the color of the Earth. Grass beneath my feet, palm leaves whispering in the wind, the sparkle of glittering water when the sun hits it just right. Gravity.

He's my gravity, my atmosphere.

A yearning hunger radiates inside that gaze—a need, a question.

I don't make him ask it aloud as I snake my hand behind his head and bring him to me, answering. His lips meet mine, soft in the way they feather between my own. Tasting, and teasing, and testing the waters of this rebirth between us.

It's not enough.

I twist my fingers in his hair, pulling hard, and he groans as I force us closer together. I'm brazen in my pursuit of our connection. I need his touch to know I'm still breathing, his mouth to remind me what I'm living for.

As his mouth opens, I slip my tongue inside, seeking claim. He meets me halfway, allowing them to dance together. The ball of his piercing flicks against my lip, earning a surprised moan from me. He matches it as our mouths continue to move in sync. One hand leaves the hood and lands on my lower back, splaying across it and pressing me harder into him.

Our hips flush, and we swallow each other's moans as he

grinds his length against my core, giving me a tease of every inch I've been craving. None of it feels like enough, and I'm not sure how anything else ever will again. It's all I can do to bring us closer—merge our beings.

Both of his hands find my ass, scooping me higher as my legs wrap around his waist. I feel the vibration of my name leaving his mouth, and I swallow it with hope I'll trap his voice inside me forever.

We're a clash of teeth and lips and tongue, hard lines and soft hands, trembling limbs and impassioned whispers.

He takes me off the hood, and I cling to him like he's my tether to the very orbit of the planet as he carries me up the front porch steps to the door. He holds me against it, his lips moving across my jaw and down my neck, before falling off my shoulder as he looks down to fumble with his keys. The door falls open under our weight, and August stumbles us inside.

We're a mess of breathless caressing, and I work to catalog every movement of his body and every sound leaving his lips. It's one of those moments that feels deeper than real, brighter than color—it's innate and all-consuming. The kind of moment that tilts your axis, restructures your being, and alters your soul.

He devours me—hand sliding up my spine, teeth nipping at my lips, the wet slide of his tongue against mine, his dizzying taste flooding my senses. The twist of his hair beneath my fingers and the grind of his body against my own. My breath catches as his teeth drag against the hollow of my throat, and I'm entirely unaware of the place he's taking me until he sets me down against a bookcase in the den.

It's the kind with an expansion at hip-height, providing a wider countertop space and a cabinet beneath, the shelves above it lined with a colorful array of books. My back rests against the spines as August stands between my legs, hands falling from my thighs and to the counter where I'm sitting, boxing me in the same way he was before.

He pulls back just enough to meet my eyes, allowing me to

catch my breath, even though I don't want to. I don't survive on oxygen anymore. He's all I need for my heart to beat. Our staccato breathing is the only sound in the otherwise silent house—a sensual purr.

His lips part with rapid breath, pupils blown as his eyes track the movement of my hands when I glide my palms down the center of his chest, dipping underneath the lapel of his flannel and moving down his arms, taking it off him. He works with me, sliding it off and allowing it to fall to the floor. Our foreheads press together, and both our gazes fall to see the way my black tennis skirt has ridden up my legs, revealing bare skin wrapped around his hips.

"You couldn't find the word earlier," he rasps breathlessly, fingertips inching up my thighs.

"What?" I ask, voice shaking at the tease of touch.

"Earlier, you stopped short when you were searching for a word to describe what this is. What we've been doing all these weeks."

I nod.

"The word is falling," he says softly, slipping his hand beneath the hem of my skirt. "We're falling, Elena, and I'm so goddamn tired of pretending I'm still standing on the ledge trying to make a choice when we both know that I dove headfirst the minute you showed up on my doorstep."

"August." My head drops back against the shelves, his name leaving my throat in a whimper.

He lifts an arm, cupping the back of my neck and forcing me to look at him again. Those green eyes blaze behind his fogged glasses, and in desperate need to see him clearly, I raise trembling hands to his face, pulling the frames off him.

"I want to see your eyes when you finally speak the truth your mouth has been too afraid to voice," I whisper. "They're always honest, even when you live in lies."

"What's the truth?"

I set them down beside me before bracketing his jaw, pulling him close enough that I can feel his breath, but keeping enough distance that I can watch his emerald irises catch flame when I say, "You still belong to me."

They flare as his lips feather over mine. "This is the last first time, Elena."

Every atom in my body comes to life at the rough promise.

"The last first time," I echo back, claiming his mouth again.

Chapter Twenty-Four

"Movement" - Hozier

I slide my hands up her plump, golden thighs. Continuing my ascent, I slide beneath the hem of her cut-off sweater and help her lift it over her head until Elena's sitting in front of me in nothing but a threadbare, lace bra, and a black tennis skirt bunched above her hips.

Her skin is glistening, reflecting the fading sunlight shimmering through the window with every rapid heave of her chest, looking like the ultimate personification of heavenly sin.

I've seen her naked before, but this is something else entirely.

Before was reluctant vulnerability and desperate caretaking, or the slow exploration of two people trying to determine if their connection was worth setting the entirety of their world on fire.

The flushed cheeks, swollen lips, and passion-hazed eyes staring back at me now are that of a connection deeper than outside influence—something so intricately written in the stars that even when it's wrong, no outside force was going to stop it from happening.

We're two people who've watched our world turn to ash, and have finally realized that even the charred remains of our past can't keep us from finding our way back together.

The suspended chord of time that's paused the Earth's orbit, allowing us to stare at each other, goes taut before launching into hyperdrive. Suddenly, her mouth is on mine again. We're a clash of caressing limbs and discarded clothing. We're touching, feeling, and tasting every inch of skin available to our hands and mouths.

My tongue licks the seam of her throat as her hands dip into the waistband of my jeans, flushing us tighter together. Elena's a mess of moans as she unbuckles my belt and unzips me. My lips don't leave her skin as I stumble out of my pants.

She's pulling down her panties, and I'm taking them from her hands when they reach her knees, slipping them off and throwing them behind me. Soon enough, we're both completely bared, and my palms are digging into the flesh of her flawless ass, pulling her to the edge of the counter and angling her hips upward, just enough for my cock to notch at her entrance.

The soft, "Please" that leaves her lips is all I need to push myself inside her.

Both of us go still, all of the air stolen from my lungs. I watch her eyes as her pupils blow, and the radiant caramel of her irises are swallowed by black. Elena's full lips part as her breath hitches with a silent moan. Her nails dig into my shoulder and my lower back as I press deeper.

The slide inside her is so fucking wet—soft and warm. Yet, she's impossibly tight, gripping around me like a silken vise. I don't want to leave her face, watching her eyes go half-lidded and her throat move with her moans, but I'm desperate to know what I look like sinking inside her.

"Elena," I rasp, reaching behind her head and knotting my fingers in her hair. I pull her close, pressing our foreheads together. "Look at it, baby. Watch us become connected." I thrust another inch, and the first of my piercings slides against her inner walls, causing her to whimper. "Watch us become one."

"August," she cries as I inch deeper.

Her mouth falls open as I thrust to the hilt, and I catch her astonished gasp with my lips as my cock pulses at the perfect spot, causing her body to spasm around me.

I tangle my tongue with hers, flicking the ball of my piercing against her lip and clattering against her teeth. Her nails dig into my flesh like she's desperate to force us closer. Her moans taste like a teenage dream come true.

Pulling away, I drop my head so we can both watch me retreat before plunging back in. With each thrust of my cock, the tight grip of her soaking pussy follows me, and the sight is fiercer than erotic, wilder than obscene. It's undeniable proof of two bodies created to be joined together.

"Do you see how you grip me, Little Vice? It's like you don't want me to leave."

"Never," she breathes, nipping at my mouth. "Stay right here." Pulling away with a slow tug on my lower lip, she whispers, "Paint your name inside me."

My cock throbs at the insinuation. I begin pumping faster, savoring the slick, wet slide of my cock through her arousal, the way she tightens when my piercings hit the spot deep enough to send her spasming, and the lock of her legs around my back as her nails slice through my skin.

"Remind me that my body is your favorite canvas."

I groan, dragging my tongue along her jaw. "Be fucking clear, Elena. Tell me exactly what you want." I rock my hips to hit her deeper, quickening my pace until she's panting—practically crying—into my mouth.

"Fill me..." She pants through each thrust. "With your cum. Please."

"Fuck." My head falls forward as I latch my teeth onto her shoulder.

She lifts her hips to meet my movements. My fingers grip her thighs, digging into her flesh with enough pressure to leave bruises, like she's my anchor. Her tether wrapping around my soul, keeping me in this moment with her.

There's nothing outside the two of us, no force that could unbind our beings now. Every lie ever told and every secret ever kept is freed by breathless moans we swallow, by the untamed words whispered into sweat-slicked skin.

"Are you sure?" I ask against her neck.

"Yes," she whispers. "Be the first."

My cock fucking throbs, body tightening and needing release, desperate to claim her the way she's pleading for. I rock her hips against me, moving us faster. Harder. What was first a slow, steady rhythm becomes a chaotic cadence of our bodies slamming against the bookcase. The spines rattle, threatening to fall down around us, but I can't stop the ferocity of my movements.

"The only," I rasp, fingers flexing, digging into her skin.

"Yes. The only." Her eyes fall closed.

The furniture shakes violently, like the rupture of the world around us, but we hold each other through it. The universe itself could rip open right now, and we'd sink into it without care, so long as we're doing so in this embrace.

"Grip the shelves, Little Vice," I groan through clenched teeth. Elena lifts an arm, clamping onto the edge of the bookshelf with her hand. I fold my palm over it, using our limbs as leverage to fuck her harder. "Look at me," I rasp. "Go with me."

She lifts her head, lust-laced gaze blazing through me. "I'm with you, baby." She uses her free hand to cup my face, slipping her thumb into my mouth, and I bite down onto it as my body tightens with demand to fill her. "I'm yours."

My vision blurs, release barreling through me like a bullet. I watch Elena through hazed eyes as my warmth floods her. Her pupils expand, and her lips part in a silent scream, like the sensation is something beyond words and sound. Her ankles cross at my back, hips locked around mine, pussy clenching me impossibly tight as she rides out her own orgasm.

She drops her head to my shoulder, the faint mewl of my name finally leaves her lips—the tone breathless, astonished. Utterly raw. Unlike anything I've ever heard before. A soft claiming, a verbal confirmation solidifying the binding of two souls.

I stay inside her, and she tenses around me, refusing to let me go. She's a mess of wild hair and glistening skin, hot breath fanning across my neck as she attempts to catch it.

"I'm with you, baby," I whisper against the top of her head, brushing through her strands with my fingers. "I'm yours."

She clenches, whimpering at that too.

I give her another moment to compose herself before I'm lifting her into my arms, my cock staying firmly inside her body as I carry her to the chair at the center of the den. I sit down, forcing her to straddle my thighs. Once I'm seated, she pulls back from my neck, eyeing me curiously with a sated gaze.

"We're not done yet." I grip her hips and roll her against me. "I'm still punishing you for being a brat. For questioning my loyalty to this exquisite body." I deliver a swift smack to her ass, causing her breath to hitch. "So, you're going to bounce on Daddy's cock like a good girl, until that pretty little cunt is so full of my cum that you never again wonder who either of us belongs to."

She moans as I take her nipple between my fingers, rolling the bar of her piercing. I'm still half hard, but when she straightens her spine, leaning back and bracing her hands on my knees to present a view of our joined bodies, I'm all the way fucking there again.

I'm still buried inside her, the base of my cock glistening with our mixed climax. "Look at your pussy stretched around me." The words rip from my throat viciously. I slide a palm over her stomach and down her center to the place we're joined, spreading two fingers around myself. "I wish you could see how full it is. I'm fucking leaking out of you."

"I can feel it," she whispers, and her pussy flutters as my thumb swipes over the spot our bodies connect. Gathering a mixture of our releases, I raise my thumb to her mouth and slip it between her lips. She slowly rocks her hips as she sucks on it.

"Get to work, baby girl," I murmur, urging her to move faster, her pretty tits bouncing with each grind of her body on mine.

"Yes, Daddy," she whimpers, tossing her head back and arching her breasts forward.

Planting her hands on my chest, she finds a steady rhythm with her hips, somehow moving up and down and side-to-side at the same time. She rolls forward, forcing my cock so deep we're sealed together entirely, while pumping her hips and creating a delicious friction that has us both trembling.

One of my hands splays over the curve of her ass, feeling it bounce with every movement she makes. I tease and taunt and pinch her flesh, her moans heightening with every touch. She tosses her head back, moving her chest over me, putting her pert, hard nipples in my face. I flick my tongue against one of her piercings, feeling the clatter of metal on metal.

She cries out at the sensation, bracing her hands on the top of the chair above my head. I lift my arms, sliding my palms beneath hers so she can hold onto me instead. Our fingers entwine, linking together as she digs her nails into my knuckles, rocking me hard enough to make the chair shake and sway.

"You ride my cock like it's your goddamn job, baby," I growl through clenched teeth before biting down on her nipple. She moans, arching herself further into my mouth as I suck on her skin. "You were made for this, weren't you? My perfect whore."

She drops her head, hair surrounding our faces like an otherworldly veil. Her nose skims mine, rapid breath panting in confirmation. It's not enough.

I latch onto her lip, biting down. Elena hisses at the sting. As I pull away, I whisper, "Use your words. Who's my little slut?"

"I am," she cries, grinding down on me so fucking hard I'm damn-near cross-eyed.

"Who owns your cunt?"

"You do." She swipes her tongue over my bottom lip.

"You gonna come on my cock, Little Vice? Make a mess like the needy girl you are?"

"Yes," she pants into my mouth. "You're going to make me come."

I begin lifting my hips to meet her movements, our bodies slamming together in a wet, salacious joining of flesh. Our release drips out of her and down between my legs, pooling on the seat beneath me. It's vulgar and obscene, and hot ecstasy gathers in the base of my spine at the feel of it.

I move faster, fucking her hard and deep. Her moans grow

louder, hands tensing around mine as she anchors herself to my body, chasing that peak.

"That's it, baby. Take it all. Take me deep. Let me watch you unravel. Soak me with both of us. I need to feel it when I ruin you."

"August." My name is a breathless gasp on her lips, and I swallow down the beautiful noise as she breaks for me.

Her entire body tenses, going taut and tight before she quivers wildly. Her core pulses around me, gripping tight enough that I imagine my imprint being forever branded inside her as she climaxes, flooding my cock.

"Fuck, Elena," I mutter. "I'm going to fill you up again."

"Please," she whimpers, kicking her head back and giving me a phenomenal view of her flawless body as it rocks and writhes above me. "I want to feel you dripping out of me for days."

"Fuck." I drop my face against her chest, feeling her wild heartbeat against my lips. The pulse of it matches the flutter of her pussy around my cock, and suddenly I go mindless, body fracturing, soul splitting open as my own orgasm rushes through me.

I pull back, forcing my eyes open, refusing to miss a second of her reaction as she feels my cum shoot deep inside her.

A rough moan tears from her throat, and all other surroundings go fuzzy, each of my senses solely focused on her beautiful face, the tremble of her body wrapped around me, greedily taking everything I have to give. The throb of my cock as it offers her every piece of who I am.

There is nothing left of us as individuals, only whatever being we became when fused together.

She releases my hands, and I slide them down her sides, dragging the pads of my fingers along the slick skin of her back, savoring every touch she'll ever allow me to have. She wraps hers around my neck, aligning her face with mine. Our lips touch, but we're not kissing, merely catching our heavy breath, calming our pounding hearts.

I don't know how much time passes like that, and I don't care.

I'll sit here forever, my body inside hers, her lips on my own, her hands on my skin.

I'll die of thirst, starve to death, turn to dust right here if it means she's staying—going with me.

Eventually, she lifts herself , and my body feels incomplete as I slip out of her. Sitting back on my thighs, both of our gazes lock between her thighs, watching the slow drip of my cum falling between my spread legs.

"That is..." She sighs.

"So fucking hot," I rasp. "You've never experienced this before? Only with me?"

She lifts her eyes, and they're sated as she smiles. "This is the first time I've ever had sex without a condom." Her hands slide down my chest. "I'm also still on birth control. You know...in case you were worried about any of that."

"Honestly, Elena...That's all an afterthought to me. I would've taken any risk to have the reward of fucking you bare like this."

She laughs softly. "Your therapist would probably tell you that's not a healthy attachment style."

I grip her hips, tugging her chest against mine. "I don't care. Not when it comes to you. We weren't meant to be healthy." I brush my mouth against her jaw. "Or sane. We're each other's brand of crazy, and I'm fucking tired of living my life with concern for outside forces and how they'll feel about it." I kiss her again, harder this time. "Because no matter how bad the consequences, no matter how wrong we're supposed to feel about it, we end up right back here anyway."

She nods, lips moving against mine. "I think...maybe...despite it all, this is where we're meant to be."

"That's right, Little Vice," I rasp.

I lift out of the chair, keeping her in my arms as I walk through my bedroom and into the bathroom, depositing her on the edge of the large tub.

She watches me with amusement as I flip on the faucet and plug the drain before dropping a purple bath bomb into the rising water. Elena kicks her legs over the side of the tub, sliding into the shallow water, and I follow, positioning myself behind her so that her back falls against my chest.

I take a loofah from the edge, dunking it in the water before running it over her shoulders. She sighs as the hot water cascades over her soft skin.

"I'm going to get you clean," I say gently. "Then, I'm going to take you to bed and fuck you again. This time you'll be beneath me so I can watch every face you make and every noise that leaves your pretty lips as I hit the right spot." Her head drops against my shoulder, bright brown eyes fluttering up at me, setting my soul aflame. "I'm going to memorize what you look like when I'm driving you to the edge, so I can repeat it..." I kiss her temple. "Again...and again..." I squeeze out the loofah, watching the soap suds gather and drip down her perfect body. "And again."

"Hmm." She sighs contentedly. "Don't threaten me with a good time."

I laugh, gazing down at her. She's so beautiful like this. Fearless and carefree. The wild chaos I fell in love with from the moment I met her. That beauty had been stripped from her, and it's only now that I realize I'll cross any line, commit any sin, ruin myself entirely if it means I can be the one to bring her back to life in moments like this.

Chapter Twenty-Five

Vice

"From Eden" - Hozier

"Lele?" My twin's gentle tone pulls my eyes from the notebook on the counter in front of me, the pen slipping from my fingers as I look at him.

"Hey."

Everett's attire spans from business casual to beachgoer when he's working at the surf shop, or a blue collar-style polo when he's managing the garage that used to belong to our dad. But today, he's dressed much nicer than I've seen him lately.

A white button-up, sleeves rolled to the elbow, is tucked into a gray pair of trousers. The top two buttons of his shirt are undone, and a simple gold chain sits at his chest.

"Why are you dressed so nicely?" I ask.

"Actually, that's what I wanted to talk to you about. We have dinner tonight with the mayor and some other small business owners around town." He rubs the back of his neck like he's nervous for whatever he's going to say next. "Do you think you could pick Lou up from school and watch her tonight? Mom and Dad are also attending, and she was supposed to go home with a friend after school, but she just called and told me her friend canceled."

"Yeah." I laugh. "I don't mind. I love hanging out with Lou."

"Really?" he asks, tilting his head.

"Yeah. She's cool as fuck."

Everett's lips twitch. "She is, isn't she?"

"Her mother's influence."

"She's gotten at least fourteen times cooler since I've become her dad."

"You call yourself her dad?" I ask, smiling.

"Not in front of her. Not until she asks me to." Everett shrugs, looking bashful. "But in my head, she's been my daughter for a long time."

My chest could burst at the sentiment. I can't think of three people more deserving of the

happiness my brother and his little family have seemed to find together.

"Anyway." Everett clears his throat like the emotion got to him too. "I'll leave Dahlia's keys with you, and you can take her car after work. We'll pick Lou up from August's place after dinner." He cocks his head. "Or should I say your place? Do you call it home?"

Yeah, I do, but the word has nothing to do with the walls surrounding the residence and everything to do with the person inside of it.

"I call it home," I confirm.

Leaning across the counter, he plants a kiss on my head. "That makes me happy to hear." Pulling away, he glances down at the open notebook in front of me, at the scroll scribbled across the pages. I flip it closed. I always write poetry in Italian because it feels like a layer of protection, a language most people in my life can't read.

Everett can, though.

"Are you writing poems?"

"Just here and there," I say. "When it comes to me."

Everett smiles, placing his hand over mine on the counter. "I'm proud of you."

"Don't make it a thing." I playfully bat him away. "I'm just..."

"Feeling things again?"

"Yeah," I breathe. "I guess."

"That's something to be proud of." He winks before tossing

Dahlia's car keys at me and heading out of the coffee shop.

"Can we listen to Taylor Swift?" Lou asks, fiddling with the music app on my phone from the backseat of her mom's car.

"How about Lana Del Rey?"

She's quiet for a moment, contemplating. "Okay, let's compromise and listen to 'Snow On The Beach.'"

"What's that band?" I ask.

"Oh, my God," she grumbles. "It's not a band. It's a song. I can't believe you've never heard of it. We're definitely listening to *Midnights* the whole drive home now."

I sigh in defeat as the pluck of a violin filters through the speakers a moment later. It's a whimsical, uplifting sound, but it's not entirely terrible.

"I played the deluxe version that features More Lana Del Rey," Lou says matter-of-factly.

I have no idea what the fuck that means.

We finish the drive in comfortable silence with what I feel is an appropriate amount of Lana Del Rey's voice for a feature. Though, I look forward to introducing Lou to *Norman Fucking Rockwell!* when she's a teenager.

"So, this is where August lives too?" the eleven-year-old asks, saddling up beside me as we walk up the driveway to the front of the house.

"Yep." I unlock the front door, letting her enter ahead of me. She makes a slow circle in the entryway, studying the kitchen to our left and the living room and den to our right, before turning her head to me. "Is he home?"

"Nope," I say, kicking off my shoes. "He's at dinner with your parents."

She hums, sounding disappointed. It makes me smile.

"Do you want to see our library?" I nod toward the den. "August and I both have a lot of books."

"August reads?" She's practically swooning at the revelation.

"I know." I smirk. "Hot, right?"

Lou's green eyes go wide, cheeks flushing to a shade almost as bright as her strawberry-blond hair. "I... I didn't say that."

"I know." I shrug before heading into the den. "But it's okay to have a crush on him. Your secret is safe with me. I get it."

"I never said I had a crush on him!" she exclaims. The patter of her feet follows me before halting abruptly, and though I'm not looking at her, I can tell the moment the towering bookshelves come into her view.

When I turn around, I find her mouth dropped open, head thrown back as she takes in the floor-to-ceiling shelves overflowing with books, lining the entire oval-shaped room. I track her gaze as she circles the space, running her hands along the spines.

My eyes snag on the particular shelf August and I christened a few days ago, and the chair in the center of the room. I'm trying hard not to reimagine it with my niece standing right in front of me, but the delicious memory makes it incredibly difficult. Every memory with him in the last seventy-two hours flashes across my mind.

When we're not working or sleeping, the two of us are fucking. And when we exhaust ourselves to the point of unconsciousness, we do so in each other's arms. We haven't talked about where we stand or where we go from here. It feels more like a lifetime of pent-up pining, longing looks, and soul-crushing silence, all coming to a head at once.

The only time either of us feels alive is when our bodies are joined. We're symbiotic in that way. Each of us a parasite, each of us a host too. Feeding off each other, starving when we're apart.

"Are any of these books I can read?" Lou asks, snapping me from my thoughts. "Aunt Darby told me I can't read any of your books."

"I'll give you all the good ones when you're a little older." I lean against the doorway, a smile creeping over my lips as she studies each book with rapt focus. "But there might be a couple that you'd like right now. August and I were about your age when we first started our book club."

She turns to look at me. "You and August have a book club?"

"We used to when we were kids."

I press off the door and walk to where she's standing, tracing the shelves for any of the older copies of our favorite books. Sure enough, in the corner of the room on the very bottom shelf is a full series set of *Percy Jackson and the Olympians*. I drop to my knees, pulling out *The Lightning Thief*.

"Here." I smile to myself, flipping through the pages as Lou sits down next to me. "Have you ever read this series?"

She shakes her head, taking the worn title from my outstretched hand. She flips through it, frowning. "Someone wrote all over this."

"I did." I laugh. Pointing to my annotations from over fifteen years ago, I add, "See, the neat handwriting belongs to August's annotations. Those horrid scribbles are from me."

Her eyes snap to mine. "This is August's book?"

"It was mine, and then I gave it to him, and he added notes too." I wink at her. "Maybe if you read it, he'll want to sit down with you and talk about it. He loved this series when he was young."

Her brows shoot up, the freckles across her nose seeming to glow when she blushes. "Really?"

"Yep." I laugh. "You read that first one, and let me know when you're finished so I can bring you back here and get you the others. We'll make sure August is home so you can tell him all your thoughts."

"He makes me kind of nervous," she murmurs.

"Oh, girl. He's harmless, I promise."

In reality, Augustus Hayes is the most dangerous predator to my heart and soul.

Chapter Twenty-Six

Violet

"Repeat Until Death" - *Novo Amor*

"Elena?" I call, kicking my shoes off by the front door. "How was babysitting Lou?"

Learning from Dahlia that Elena was babysitting here tonight did something to my chest. She's had a decent relationship with Lou since she moved home almost a year ago, but I know they don't spend a ton of time alone together. I think Elena has had a fear of her depression being an influence on the kid.

I think she's convinced herself that everyone in her life is better off without her. She's done a damn good job of shutting them out, and any time I watch her interact with her family, it feels like a little broken piece of her is being reformed.

Every moment she breathes life back into her old self is something I feel an immense amount of pride over.

"Good." Her voice floats to me from the den, sounding like soft, seductive music.

I follow the melody into the small library, finding her sitting cross-legged on the floor surrounded by a pile of books, flipping through them with something I can only describe as nostalgic peace on her face.

"What're you doing?" I ask, throwing myself down beside her and setting the takeout bag at her feet. Most days, if I don't feed her myself, she ends up going to bed on nothing more than raw carrots and sweet pickles. She's been a vegetarian for as long as

I can remember, but if the mood strikes her right, she'll house a well-cooked and sauced piece of shellfish, and the restaurant we went to tonight has the best shrimp tacos on the planet.

She's wearing a pair of leggings that hug her hips beautifully, and a maroon crewneck that reads, *I am the devil, and don't you forget it.*

Truth.

"I gave Lou our old copy of *The Lightning Thief* after I found it on the bottom shelf," she says. "I wanted to see what other books you've kept over the years."

"All the ones I could."

She looks up at me, smiling.

"You hungry?" I ask, and her eyes drift toward the bag at her feet. "If not, I can put it in the fridge for later."

"I actually made dinner for Lou and just ate with her. Spaghetti." She laughs. "You know, the only thing I do know how to do somewhat well." Eyes softening, she adds, "But thank you. I appreciate you thinking of me."

"I'm always thinking of you, Little Vice." I drop a kiss against her knee, snatching the bag from her feet and standing. "Plus, I plan on getting your appetite up high enough tonight that you'll need a snack once I'm through with you."

"Don't make promises unless you plan to deliver on them, Augustus," she chimes, flipping back through the pages of an old vampire romance series I remember her being obsessed with in middle school.

"You know, I have copies of everything you've written too," I call from the kitchen as I put her food away.

Footsteps shuffle across the floor as she starts searching for the collection of her titles. I have every book she's published, along with any special editions she made. I have multiple copies of many of them, in fact. When I moved into this house, I kept coming across random duplicates that somehow got thrown in with all my things.

"Well, I think a couple might be missing, actually," I say as I return to the den. "Darby scoured the collection not long ago and took copies of every one she hadn't read ye—"

My words stall, along with the air in my lungs, as I turn the corner, finding Elena on the floor again. Though this time she's not nostalgically flipping through the pages of her once-favorite reads. I can't tell what book she's holding, but she has some paperback open on her lap. Heavy, thick tears stream from her cheeks, one getting caught on her trembling bottom lip.

"Elena," I rasp, closing the distance between us and squatting in front of her. "What's wrong?"

I glance down at the page she's opened to, a red bookmark resting in the crease. Her hand trembles as she brushes her fingers over it, like it's a memory of some sort.

"He was..." A broken sob escapes her mouth. "He was reading this before he..." She swallows, composing herself. "I signed it for him when he came back from Wyoming." Bile rises in my throat at the look on her face, the fracture in her tone. "He never finished it." She shakes her head as her eyes lift to mine, glistening brown and overflowing with tears. "He'll never know how it ends."

"The book?" I ask softly, forcing calm in my voice.

She crumbles entirely, chin dipping as tears drip off her cheeks and onto the page. "Everything."

"Oh, baby." I bite back my own emotion, refusing to add to her panic, though I feel all the same grief and fear that's coursing through her too. "Can I touch you?"

She nods, and I gently take the book from her lap, setting it down beside us before leaning back against the bookcase and pulling her into my arms.

I wrap one arm around her shoulders, spreading my legs to make space for her to sit between them. Her face falls into my neck, hand knotting in the fabric of my shirt. I don't know what else to do except hush her choked sobs and brush my fingers through her hair.

I think the hardest part of grief is that it's not only unpredictable but unrelenting. No matter how much time passes, it never goes away. You're encouraged to move through it and search for some semblance of normal, but nobody talks about the way you're forced to do so while constantly tiptoeing around triggers for the rest of your life.

Something so simple like finding a book they were reading, or seeing an ad for their favorite cereal brand, hearing someone recommend their favorite movie—it can send you into an unexpected spiral, no matter how much time has passed.

It's impossible to plan for these moments, because some days we're strong and we wade through them like they're nothing more than a rough gust of wind. Other times, we're hit with a hurricane of agony, and no amount of shelter can shield us from the destruction.

"Do you remember that fantasy show he loved?" I ask hoarsely, working to keep my tone steady and gentle. "The one that took us all by surprise because he hated dragons and sorcerers and all that shit."

"He liked it because he thought that one actress was hot," she murmurs against my chest, and I rumble a low laugh at the words.

"Right." I nod, rubbing her back. "I know you didn't watch it, but the series ended a couple of years ago. I had no idea until I saw an ad for the finale come across the television one day." A stinging sensation begins to clog my throat, and I work to swallow it down, but it doesn't stop my voice from trembling as I continue, "I had a complete breakdown that day. I canceled all my appointments and stayed home to binge the entire final season. I watched the finale when it premiered that night and..." I choke on a laugh, feeling tears slip down my cheeks. "It was fucking terrible. The whole show was ruined in that final season. He would've been so pissed."

Elena lifts her head, blinking through tears. Her brows knit when she realizes I'm crying, too, and she silently lifts a hand to wipe them from my face.

"I didn't see it coming. I had been okay for months. No night terrors or panic attacks. I'd stopped seeing him in my head every time I closed my eyes...I thought I was starting to heal." I sigh.

"But that one ad, that one trigger, it sent me down a dark spiral. I missed him a lot that day, and when I was done watching it, I only missed him more. I was angry at the television show, angry at the producers and actors and directors. It felt like they were doing him a disservice, as misplaced as that anger might sound."

I cup her face and wipe away her tears too. "That night I sat outside on the back porch, and for the first time since he died, I... I just talked to him. I told him all about the ending of the show and how terrible it was. I told him how much I missed him, and how pissed off I was at our parents for the way they treat me now. Told him how much I was missing you," I admit, brushing her hair away from her face. "You can talk to him, too, you know?"

Her eyes mist over with a distant, contemplative expression before she responds with a shallow shake of her head, murmuring, "I don't think he'd want to hear from me."

"How could you ever think that, Elena?" I ask, tightening my hold on her thigh just slightly, drawing her attention back to the room—back to me. "What happened that morning?"

We've never talked about it, the morning that he died. The conversation I know he had with her just before he confronted me at the beach, though I don't know the details of it. I've never told her about the last words I spoke to him, either, or what it felt like to realize he'd disappeared from the water, the terror of watching him be pulled from it minutes too late.

That's not something I'll ever share with anyone. That is a horror to harbor on my own. I wouldn't force the terror of that vision onto another person.

She lifts her gaze, tortured espresso-colored eyes slicing through me. "I... I can't."

"Someday, will you?" I ask. "Tell me everything?"

I don't know how we'll ever make it through this—whatever this is—if she doesn't.

She nods against my chest.

"Come sit outside with me." I gently nudge her to sit up, rising to my feet behind her before I reach out my hand. To my surprise, she takes it, allowing me to haul her up too. "You don't have to talk to him directly if you don't want to, but you can talk to me. Tell me something you'd like him to know, even if it's simple, even if it's pointless."

I lead her through the kitchen and out the back door. A broad deck leads down into the overgrown lawn. I don't maintain the space out here much, other than the rose bushes I planted along the back fence when I first moved in. Lights are strung around the deck, and two lounge chairs sit side-by-side. I lie on one, patting the other beside me. Instead, she crawls right into my lap, pressing her back to my chest.

It's dark, the April air breezy and balmy, though the clear night gives way for a perfect view of the stars. "Sometimes, I think that if I'm outside, it's easier for him to hear me," I whisper against her neck. "I'm sure he'd love to listen to your voice."

She drops her face into her hands, overcome with emotion again. I let her cry it out, keeping my arms tight around her and running a soothing hand over her back. She doesn't like to cry, period, but she especially hates allowing other people to see it. I learned over the years that it's best to let Elena sit with her pain for a second. She bottles up her emotions, and when they break, they burst. She needs time to wade through them, or she'll drown within them.

I've held her like this a million times, letting her soak my chest with tears for another man. My own brother. I used to wonder if we'd ever escape it, if it would ever cease. I used to be petrified of the idea that she'd be crying on my shoulder over him for the rest of her life.

Now, I know for certain that she will. Not every moment or every day, but we'll spend the rest of our lives warring with our grief, and somehow, I find comfort in that knowledge. Maybe all those tears before were preparation for this. For all the future heartache she'd need me to soothe, and maybe a part of her won't ever stop loving someone else, but I guess I'm happy that it's him. That he was loved that way. And I'm happy it's me, that I get to offer her solace in all of it.

I think I understand it better now. Now that I know what it's like to lose him too.

"I feel guilty for crying to you when I'm missing him." She lets out a shuddering sigh.

"Don't," I rasp, choking on my own tears. "I miss him too."

"Do you think...if he can hear us, can he see us?" She tilts her head, looking at me. "Do you think he hates to see us touching like this? I feel guilty about that, too, but I don't want to be apart from you."

"He wasn't a stranger to my drying of your tears. He knew how you liked to be held. He knew you felt safest with me. I think he'd be glad to see that you're finally done battling this on your own." I kiss the top of her head. "How many times have you broken down like this and forced yourself to bear it alone?"

"Felt like what I deserved." She shrugs. "Sometimes I stop myself in moments of happiness, or when I begin to feel like I'm living again, because I remember that he's dead." Elena's voice breaks on the word. "Why should I get to move on—experience joy—when he can't? When I was responsible for so much of the darkness in his final moments?"

"I feel the same sometimes," I admit. "But I guess, on days like that, I try to feel the joy for other people, even if I think I don't deserve it myself."

"I only feel like I'm allowed to grieve. Any other sensation seems stolen to me." She's quiet for a moment before she continues, "That's why I left. Why I moved to New York. I hated seeing my family try to help me when I didn't want to be. When I came to you that night..." She lifts her head, meeting my gaze with glistening eyes. "I knew that you could be the one to do it. You could heal me. You could love me, and I didn't deserve it. I guess I was so focused on my own self-loathing, I didn't think deeply enough about how it would affect you. Or maybe I thought you deserved it too..." She presses her hands to her temples, shaking her head. "I don't know. I can't make sense of what my headspace was like back then. All

I know is..." She knots her hand in the fabric of my shirt. "You're the love of my life, but he's the boy I loved to death. How am I supposed to move on from that? Why do I deserve to?"

"The presence of grief does not equate to the absence of happiness," I say, grasping her jaw and tilting her head so that she can see my eyes. "What a disservice to the human condition it is to believe something like that. We're so much more complex, Elena."

She stares back at me, contemplative, searching my eyes for some kind of answer before finally asking, "How am I to call life happy when it ends in death? What is it to search for a happy ending if it still means there is an end?"

I search her eyes, too, but I find every answer I need. She's the answer, always has been. "Everything ends. Choosing joy with the certainty that it's fleeting is the purpose of life, I think. The ending is preexisting. Happiness is what you aim to find."

"Do you think that we could still find one?" she asks just above a whisper. "A happy ending?"

"I think we'll have to work harder for it, harder than we expected to." I brush my thumb over her jaw, watching her eyes flutter closed as I press my lips to her forehead. "But yes."

One of her tears cascades over my finger, and I swipe it away as I lower my hand, letting her head fall against the crook of my neck. I hold her there, savoring her touch as the sea breeze kicks up. A gust bursts across my face, and something rolling across the bottom step of the deck catches my eye.

One lone rosebud must've fallen off the bushes from the back of the lawn, now fluttering in the wind, as if answering in agreement.

Chapter Twenty-Seven

Vice

"Nothing's Gonna Hurt You Baby" - Cigarettes After Sex

"Augustus," I whisper, clutching his head against my chest to quell his trembling limbs. "It's okay. I've got you."

Sitting back against the headboard, I sway gently in my bed, holding him to me.

I woke to the sound of him screaming, the second night terror he's had since I moved in. It's normally his bedroom I fall asleep in at night. His bed is bigger, and he has a television and a bathtub. Plus, I like the way the sheets always smell like him.

Tonight, we fell asleep in mine, though.

He brought me upstairs after we stared at the stars and spoke of Zach, being more open about our grief and our fear than either of us have been before. I never found the courage to speak to him directly, but it kind of felt like he was part of our conversation, and after we finished, I felt settled in a way I haven't experienced before during bouts of grief.

There are many, many things I want to say to Zach, and I hope someday I'll find the courage to voice them, but I think those moments are better left between the two of us alone.

As cathartic as it was, the whole evening exhausted me. I know August hadn't intended to stay here; he merely wanted to help me up the stairs and into bed, but I found myself unable to let him go. I've done it too many times before. I can't find the will to push him away anymore.

I'm not sure if the change in sleeping location is what caused the night terror, if it was our conversation from earlier, or all just a coincidence. All I care about now is calming him.

I brush my fingers through his hair, his screaming has finally stopped. His heart still beats wildly against my stomach, and the breath leaving his lips is rapid and distressed.

"I'm right here, baby," I whisper, watching him wince with closed eyes, as if whatever is raging in his mind is causing him immense pain. "I'm here," I say again, brushing my thumb over his brow. "I'm here."

He finally begins to settle, snaking an arm over my thighs and gripping me tightly, as if my skin is his anchor to reality—my heartbeat his guide home. As his breathing evens out, I continue stroking his face, brushing my hands through his hair, letting him slip back into a more peaceful rest.

I don't know how much time has passed, my eyes drooping and my head lulling against the back of the headboard when I hear him whisper, "Elena?"

I startle, snapping my gaze down to find his beautiful face tilted toward mine, green eyes bright in the darkness of my room. "Hi." I smile. "You had a night terror."

"I'm sorry," he groans, stretching his limbs and rolling over so that I can move back down the bed. We both lie on our sides, facing the other.

"Don't apologize," I whisper. "Do you want to go to your room?"

"No." He shakes his head. "But if you want me to leave, I can. I'm sorry."

That pulls a breathless laugh from me. "I'm sorry, let me rephrase that. I'll be sleeping where you are tonight. Do you want to stay here, or do you think you'd sleep better if we were in your bed?"

His lips twitch. "We can stay here."

He takes a ragged inhale, sighing heavily as he turns onto his back and stretches out his arm, a silent request. I shuffle next to him, placing my head on his chest and molding my body against his like I was made for it.

He twirls a strand of my hair around his finger. We don't speak, but I won't allow myself to fall back asleep until he does, so I trace the patchwork tattoos over his chest, barely able to make out the art in the darkness. "Do you ever remember them?" I ask. "Your night terrors?"

"No." He sighs. "But I know what they contain."

"What's that?" I whisper against his skin, unsure if I want to know the answer.

"Him. It's always him. But sometimes I think it's you too."

Part of me wants to beg him for details, but another part doesn't want to cause him any additional distress, and truthfully, I don't want to know the depths of the damage I've caused. How thoroughly I obliterated his trust and broke his soul, when I'm the person who's always supposed to mend it.

I kiss his collarbone, over the violets he has tattooed against it.

"You know...I started writing poems again. It's been years, and it's brought back this strange sense of déjà vu. I don't have my old notebooks anymore, but it's like I can feel my old self resurfacing through new words...or something."

"Give me an example."

I contemplate for a minute, tracing his skin quietly. "I used to think love was only black and white. It was either something you had, or you didn't. You either fought to stay, or you got up and left. You were all in, or completely out. No other options. I've been reminded of that lately, but now..."

"Now you feel like you're living in the gray area?" he muses.

"No." I shake my head, lips brushing over his skin. "Now I feel like love is an entire spectrum of color. It's light and it's dark, full of multitude. It's something you have to choose, something you must fight for, but it's also unpredictable and unexpected. Felt through every sense, yet intangible. Frustratingly complicated and delightedly simple."

Green eyes study me in the darkness. He lifts a hand, cupping my face, running a thumb over my lip like he wants my words imprinted on his skin.

"I feel like love is ultraviolet," I whisper. "A color I never saw before you."

He studies my face for a long moment, caressing my skin but saying nothing. Finally, he nods, full lips forming the boyish smile that feels like home to me. "I ultraviolet you too, Little Vice."

I frown, lightly slapping his chest for making light of my revelation, but truthfully, I know exactly what he's doing. I didn't realize it myself. I often don't see my own nuances the way he can, but I now understand exactly what I was trying to say. I can't handle the words themselves, despite the fact that we've each said them a million times to the other.

They mean something different now—it feels different now.

I can't say them, and I don't know if I can hear them either, but as always, he reads the pages of my soul that are written in a language unknown by all others.

"Go to bed." I laugh into his chest, and he joins in, the sound like kindling to my soul's flame. It was his laugh I missed most in those years apart, that I've longed for desperately since finding each other again.

"I'm trying, but my high maintenance bedmate won't stop pondering life and shit."

"You're annoying." I nip at his pec. "Am I really high maintenance?"

"Yes." He grips my hair at the nape of my neck, pulling my head up. "And if you keep biting me like that I'm going to shove my cock down your throat and give you something to choke on."

"Is that supposed to be a threat? Because I'm an enthusiastically willing participant."

His eyes roll back, and he loosens his grip, head falling onto the pillow as he murmurs, "My chaos."

"Is it bad that I'm high maintenance?"

A rough laugh pierces the darkness. "Not for me, Little Vice."

"I don't like being taken care of. It makes me feel weak," I admit quietly. "You're the only person I've let take care of me before, but sometimes I think I'm a burden. I don't want to think I'm something that needs to be maintained."

"Okay." He turns his head toward me. "I won't use that phrase anymore, then. But you're certainly not a burden. I want to be the rock you lean on. The shoulder you cry on. The chest you sleep on."

"I want to be your rock too," I say on a breath. "But sometimes I don't think I do a very good job."

He nods in understanding before staring back at the ceiling. "When you left me, it broke me, but since you've returned home, it often feels as if you're all that can put me back together. You're doing a good job, Elena." He brushes his hand over the top of my head, urging me back to his chest. "You've been shouldering your own pain for years. Nobody was leaning on you, and you were refusing to lean on anyone else too. It takes time to learn that again. I've always had our support system around me."

"Yeah, well...that was my own doing." I sigh, deciding to finally voice a thought that's been stirring in my mind for weeks. "Augustus, what happened with your parents?"

"They moved to Palm Springs after...everything."

"Right." I nod. "But Everett told me they didn't allow you to be involved with the Foundation, and I rarely hear you speak of them. Earlier you mentioned something about the way they treat you now."

He swallows audibly. "My dad blames me. He hasn't spoken to me directly in years. Since the day it happened, I think. And my mom..." He huffs. "She doesn't exactly defend me. I couldn't handle the way he looked at me, the way he so clearly wishes that the roles were reversed. I had to distance myself. It was getting so bad, and I..." He cuts himself off, shaking his head. "It ate at me for a long time, but therapy has helped me wade through a lot of that. I distanced myself from my friends and from your parents for a while, too, since letting them all back in... It's filled that gap. I talk to my mom as often as I can stomach it. I'm okay. Now, anyway."

"None of it's okay." I bite back the fury in my tone, willing calmness, though I'm seething at the thought of their treatment toward him. "What do you mean now?"

"I used to struggle with the isolation a lot more. Before you came home, before I started going to therapy. The abandonment of my parents was a heavy weight—especially in terms of my father and the way he's treated me." He presses his lips against my head. "Having you back has replaced a lot of the void they left, but..." He sighs, wiping a hand down his face. "I've had some difficult moments in the past few years. Ones where I've thought about..." He trails off, and my stomach leaps into my throat at the understanding.

I push up onto my knees, crawling over him and taking his face between my hands. My heart pounds in my ears, throat seizing with pure fear as my skin goes numb.

"Do not ever think about that, August. Please." I drop my forehead to his, feeling like I'll fucking die without the warmth of his exhale against my face, the confirmation he's breathing. "I won't pretend to understand what your parents have put you through, but I cannot live in a world where you do not exist. Do you understand? Don't ever do that to me. Don't ever think that again."

"I can't help it," he whispers, brushing his hand up my spine in a reassuring caress. "The thoughts just happen sometimes...but I've never had an urge to act on them, and it's been months since I've struggled with it, anyway. I'm okay, Elena. I promise."

"Then you tell me about them, okay? You come to me, and I'll remind you how much I..." I swallow, hesitating. "How much I need you. How much better life, and the entire world is, because of you. How loved you are."

He nods, smiling softly as he presses against my back, forcing me back to his chest again.

I lie back down, settling into his side as his fingertips glide over my shoulders as mine trace lazy patterns across his chest. "I hate your parents."

"Sometimes, I do too." He sighs, kissing the top of my head. "But they already lost one son, so I'm trying to be sympathetic to the pain they hold too."

I can't offer much more of a response than a resigned humph. All I can think about is how badly I want to burn their fucking house down. He deserves so much better than them. To blame him for a tragic accident that he had to witness firsthand, to not defend your own son against the vile accusations of your husband—it's disgusting.

I can tell he's worked hard to come to terms with the sickening reality of the situation, so I swallow back all the venom I want to spew in the direction of his worthless parents. I don't want to make him feel worse.

"Is that the painting you got from Penelope?" he asks, a clear attempt at changing the subject.

I lift my head, following his gaze to the canvas hung up across my room. It's hard to see, but through the dim moonlight filtering through my curtains, I can just make out the white orb at the center of the painting, the dark blue of the horizon cutting it in half, the smattering of stars, and the white of the waves crashing against the shore.

A beach at night. That's what she painted for me.

"What does it say?" His eyes narrow, but I know the scroll is far too small to make out from this distance, especially in the dark.

In the bottom right corner of the canvas, just above her signature, three lines are written:

Just as stars illuminate their night
Just as the moon leads its tides
Beauty is found within darkness

"That's beautiful," he whispers when I finish reading. "Did she make that up herself?"

"Not sure. Maybe." I shrug. "When we met, we got to talking about how different we are from our friends and siblings. How everyone around us is like a ray of fucking sunshine, and we can't relate to that. She told me she felt more like the moon or the stars, but it was something she learned to love about herself. I told her I felt like the darkness between them." I sigh. "At the time, I saw myself as a void of just...nothing. I guess this was her reminder that I'm not."

"You know, the middle of the night is my favorite time of day." He runs his knuckles up and down my back, eliciting sparks across my skin. "I've never wanted you to be bright. I found the most peace I've ever known when I'm sinking into your darkness. Your darkness between stars feels like home to me."

"I think you are the stars," I whisper. "They feel like home to me too."

Chapter Twenty-Eight

Violet

"Superposition" - Young the Giant

"How do you guys feel about sapphires?"

"Personally, emeralds are my favorite, but sapphires are fine." Elena raises her coffee cup to her mouth, an amused smirk playing at her lips. "In what context are you asking?"

Everett half lifts from his chair, swiveling his head around the cafe in search of his girlfriend—I assume—before leaning in close to us. Dahlia's in the kitchen working on customized bakery orders while Elena takes a break from her shift. Everett and I both stopped this morning to grab coffee before heading to our respective workplaces.

He reaches into his pocket, setting a black box down on the table between his hands. His fingers tap against it anxiously as he says, "In the context of an engagement ring."

Elena's brows shoot up, her pretty brown eyes widening. "Show me now."

Everett looks around again in a failed attempt at being surreptitious before opening the box. The cushion-cut sapphire is damn-near blinding when it winks back at me. It's massive, accented on each side by two triangle-cut diamonds, and sitting on a simple, thin silver band.

"Damn," I murmur.

"Oh, Everett," Elena gasps, hand flying to her mouth. "It's stunning."

His face lights up at his sister's praise before he snaps the box shut and slides it back into his pocket. "Really?"

"Yeah." She nods. "It's very Dahlia."

He leans back in his chair, wiping a hand down his face. "Thank God. I was scared shitless of fucking this up."

"She doesn't seem like the kind of person who would care much about jewelry," I add. "I don't think you have anything to be afraid of."

"You're right." He sighs. "She doesn't. She doesn't even want a wedding, but I think a lot of it is because she's still convinced she doesn't deserve those things, you know?" Everett shrugs. "I'm trying to show her that she does."

"Do sapphires hold significance of some sort? Why that instead of a diamond?"

"Her eyes remind me of sapphires." Everett bites his cheek, appearing bashful. "Is that lame?"

"No." Elena smiles. "That's beautiful. She's going to love it."

"You think?"

She nods. "I mean...there aren't gemstones out there reminding anyone of my fucking eyes." She waves at her face, referencing her brown irises. "It's unique and sentimental. I can't imagine anything she could love more."

"Chocolate diamonds," I blurt without thinking, and the way both twins whip their heads to me makes me immediately regret saying it out loud. Yet, I can't stop myself from continuing, "Smoky quartz. Topaz." I clear my throat, taking a sip of my coffee before attempting to recover my outburst. "Those are all gems that could be compared to brown eyes, I suppose."

The words fly from my mouth so quickly there is no hiding the fact that I've spent a significant amount of time cataloging every shade of brown in her eyes and what comparisons they hold to the world around them.

She smiles at me knowingly, and I don't miss the hint of blush coloring her cheeks before those chocolate-colored eyes flutter to her brother. He watches me with curious apprehension.

"When are you going to do it?" she asks, pulling his attention from me. "And please say that I found out before Leo did."

"Of course I told you before I told Leo. That fucker can't keep a secret to save his life. He'll find out after Dahlia does."

"He's going to be pissed about that." Elena laughs, and the sound is like rediscovering a favorite song you'd forgotten the lyrics to.

Seeing her happy like this is enough to light my soul on fire.

"You're my wombmate. I needed your opinion."

I fucking hate when they call themselves that.

"And you better not tell anyone either, Augustus." He points at me without taking his eyes off his sister.

I hold my hands up, surrendering. "Secret is safe with me."

"Good." He nods before continuing, "You know I bought that live-in bus off Tyler, right? I'm fixing it up as a surprise for her?"

Elena and I nod.

"This summer I'm taking her and Lou on a road trip, up the entire Pacific Coast Highway, over to Montana, Wyoming, and back down through Utah and Arizona before we return home. We're going to try and hit every National Park in each of those states. I'll propose at some point on the trip, whenever the timing feels right."

Elena rests her face on her hands as she places her elbows on the table. "That sounds perfect. Does Lou know already?"

"Yeah, I asked her permission a while ago." He smiles. "She helped me pick out the ring too."

"You sure she's going to be able to keep the secret that long?" I ask.

"She's better at keeping secrets than you'd think." His eyes flit to something behind me. "Oh, shit. Okay, everyone shut the fuck up."

A second later, Dahlia appears beside me, bending down to press a kiss against Everett's lips. "Hi," she says as she straightens, stretching from side to side.

"Hi, Wildflower." Everett smiles up at her adoringly. "Are you taking a break? Walk me over to the surf shop?"

"Sure." She turns to Elena. "It's slow today, and I'm caught up on orders, so if you wanted to go home you can, but I don't mind if you wanted to stay—"

"Say less." Elena stands from her chair. "I'm never going to turn down a mid-day nap."

I follow suit as we all clear our table and recycle our cups.

"*Y no le hables en italiano a mamá sobre... ya sabes. Dal está aprendiendo italiano y es posible que entienda lo que estás diciendo,*" Everett lowers his voice slightly.

"*Entonces, ¿lo que estás diciendo es que deberíamos enseñarle italiano a Darby también, de esa manera podemos hablar mierda sobre Leo delante de él y volverlo loco*?" Elena wiggles her eyebrows at him, smiling mischievously.

"Exactly." He presses a kiss to the top of his sister's head before walking toward the door with his hand in Dahlia's. "Bye, Auggie. Have a good day."

"You too!" I call, a small pang of guilt swirling in my stomach because I already know the best part of my day will be when I fuck his sister later.

We absolutely need to tell them what's going on at some point, but I suppose Elena and I are still trying to navigate that ourselves, and it doesn't make much sense attempting to explain it to someone else.

I turn, finding Elena leaning against the wall with a soft smile on her face. "Would you like to be walked to work, too, Augustus?"

"I'm never going to turn down something you're offering me, baby."

She rolls her eyes, but I don't miss the flush in her cheeks or the way she bites her lip. Elena pushes off the wall and follows me to the back door, stepping out into the late morning sunshine as I hold it open for her.

"I've got a few minutes if you want to take a walk down to the pier? My first appointment isn't for another hour."

She nods, and our arms brush as we make our way down the

boardwalk and onto the pier. She links her pinkie in mine, eyes fixated on our surroundings as we stroll—though mine remain stuck on her.

The late-morning sun is just over our heads, shimmering down onto the whitecaps in a glittering display of brightness, but it holds no comparison to the way rays filter over Elena's face. Her golden skin glows, accenting the smattering of freckles over the bridge of her nose. It's when her brown eyes catch the light and morph to liquid amber, her soft pink lips tilted up into the kind of blinding smile I know she doesn't offer anyone else, that I find a beauty for which words do not exist.

I follow her gaze as she casts it over the horizon, fixating on the dozens of surfers that dot the waves. Fishermen line the pier, casting their poles into the tides below, and seagulls soar through the cloudless sky above us. Palm trees line the boardwalk, parallel to the shoreline, swaying in the salt breeze.

It's a picturesque, perfect day. The kind that draws in visitors from all over the world to witness. Yet Pacific Shores holds no candle to the woman whose finger is linked with mine. Her beauty was always unforgettable to me, astonishing and impossible to comprehend, and as I stare at her now, I realize that I've never savored it enough. I could look at her forever, appreciating every inch of skin on her body and ounce of sound that leaves her mouth, and it still wouldn't be enough.

"How late are you working tonight?" she asks when we reach the end of the pier and circle around the amusement rides before strolling back down the other side.

I've worked late the last few nights. It's been unseasonably busy, and I don't have any guest artists until early next month, which left Maggie—who's offered me the coldest of shoulders since I canceled her appointment and refused to rebook it, referring her to a different artist—and me to handle everything ourselves. We had drop-in after drop-in, and I stayed open hours after I typically do because I couldn't turn down the business. By the time I made it home last night, Elena had fallen asleep in my bed, knowing she had an early morning at the bakery herself.

Though, I didn't mind. In fact, I relished the vision of her sleeping in my bed—waiting for me.

Wanting me at all.

"I should be home earlier tonight. I'm sorry about yesterday."

"You don't have to apologize. You deserve to be busy. You're too talented not to be," she says, and I lean over to kiss the top of her head. "I just was curious, if you're home early enough, I might need your help with something."

"What's that?"

She smiles to herself. "You'll see."

As we return to the boardwalk, I pause by the back door of my shop, leaning against the wall. "What do you plan on doing the rest of the day?"

"Take a nap, possibly go for a run if I'm feeling up to it." I smile, she's been running more often lately, something I know used to be therapeutic for her when she was younger, and it makes me happy that she's finding it again. "Then I'll probably write until you get home."

"How's that going?"

"Good, actually." She bites her lip. "I've been...stuck on a few things, but otherwise, I'm really enjoying it."

"Stuck on what?" I push open the door and nod my head toward the shop, motioning for her to follow me inside. I still have a while before my first appointment of the day arrives, and I'm happy that she's offering to talk about her writing with me. I don't want to cut the conversation short.

Elena doesn't discuss her story much when she's in the midst of it. When she's brainstorming, or stuck, she opens up more. Talking it out seems to help her wade through the blocks she's facing. Over the last month or so, she's hardly mentioned it, but I've seen how much time she spends on her laptop, especially when she stays up late in bed beside me on nights she doesn't have to work the next day.

It's given me a lot of hope, that after so many years, she's finally finding herself through words again. I didn't want to ask her about it and risk ruining her groove.

As we enter my office, I shut the door behind us, and she props herself up on the edge of my desk. "I'm writing a romantic comedy." She snorts at the way my brows rise at the information. It's the last thing I would've expected from her. "The gist of it is that my main character accidentally matches with a serial killer on a dating app, and during their first date she begins to realize she's his next victim, because she's a total true crime junkie."

I nod. "Of course, she is. So, she saw all the signs."

"Right." Elena swings her feet back and forth, biting down a laugh. "So, in self-defense, she ends up actually killing the guy. Right in her own kitchen. And who's to walk in on her in the act?"

"I don't know...the town detective?"

"No! Her brother's best friend—who happens to be an investigative journalist, and the host of her favorite podcast," she yelps with excitement. "So, anyway...he has to help her cover up the murder because he's always been secretly obsessed with her, as is a requirement of romance novels."

"Of course. Yes." I smile with amusement.

"After they seemingly get away with murder, they realize that someone out there knows it was them, and is now blackmailing them for it. They have to try and figure out who, while keeping this huge secret, and of course...that's going to make them fall in love."

"I don't know how you couldn't fall in love with the person you bury bodies with, honestly."

"They burn the body," she adds matter-of-factly. "But, yeah, see? You get me."

"I always get you, Little Vice," I rasp, moving to stand between her legs. "This all sounds great, so what are you struggling with?"

"Well...it's not really the plot I'm struggling with. It's more... something new I'd like to try, something that I've never written before, but I think these characters would be into..."

"Is that so?" I ask, my voice just above a whisper as I tuck a strand of hair behind her ear.

She shivers at the contact. "Yes," Elena hisses. "And I just think I'd have a much easier time writing this one chapter if I…" She bites her lip, lashes fluttering as she places a hand against my chest, nudging me back a step.

Elena slides off my desk, turning her back to me. Her legs seem a mile long beneath her short, black denim skirt, the hem riding high on her thighs as she bends over.

"Lift my skirt, Augustus," she whispers.

I immediately comply, uncaring that we're in the office of my business. She's bent over my desk like a wet dream come true, and if she asks me to fuck her right now, I'll do that too.

I slide my hands up the backs of her thighs, gripping the denim and shoving it over her tight, perky ass. She's wearing a good-for-nothing black G-string, the thin strap banding around her hips, but what steals my fucking breath from my lungs and causes me to sputter is the bright purple jewel twinkling back at me from between her ass.

"God-fucking-damn." I bite out the word with a guttural groan.

"I've been getting myself ready for you," she rasps on a shallow breath. "I want you to take it tonight. Show me what it's like."

My cock springs to instant life at the vision below me, and I can't stop myself from taking her flesh in each of my hands and spreading her wide.

"I'm fucking throbbing, Elena," I grit through clenched teeth. "How can you possibly expect me to go through the rest of my day, knowing this pretty little ass is going to take my cock later?"

She looks over her shoulder, dropping her chin as she smirks at me, fluttering her sultry eyes. "I suppose you're not the only one who knows how to tease."

I smack her ass, causing her body to fly forward on the desk before I tug her back against me, pressing my hard length against the crease of her cheeks. "You've been teasing me for years, Little Vice. Don't get things confused." I can't stop myself from squatting, running my lips over the curve of her luscious ass before sinking my teeth into her skin. "When I get home this evening, I want you in my bed with nothing but this plug. Bring your other toys, too, and don't forget the lube."

Her breath hitches before she moans, "Yes, sir," on an exhale.

I nip at her again before standing and lowering her skirt back over her hips. I run a hand up her spine, bringing it around her neck before I grasp her throat like a collar and pull her body into mine so she's flushed against my chest. "Is that the only plug you have?"

She shakes her head, gasping as my teeth nick her ear. "It came in a pack," she says shakily. "Three different sizes. This is the largest one."

"Fuck," I hiss. "You've been wanting this for a while, haven't you? You've been stretching yourself for me?"

She nods, pulse wild against the palm of my hand. "They vibrate too. Remote controlled."

"Did you bring the remote with you today? Was this all planned?"

She nods, and my cock pulses.

"You are my perfect little whore, aren't you?" I kiss her jaw. "So clever. So needy." I lower my hand from her neck, holding it out in front of her with my palm up. "Give me the remote, Little Vice."

Her body trembles as she reaches into the front pocket of her skirt and pulls out a small black rectangle with three buttons. On/Off, an up arrow, and a down arrow.

I press the power button, and though I don't hear the buzz, the way Elena gasps and her entire body goes rigid tells me it's working.

"How's that feel, baby?"

"Oh... Ohmygod," she breathes. "I've never tried the vibration before and it's..." Her head falls back, eyes clenching shut. "Wow."

I click the up arrow twice and she folds over, slamming her fist against my desk. "Augustus," she cries. "Oh, my God, that's..."

I immediately turn it off. "Too much?"

She catches her breath before lifting her head and looking at me with espresso-colored eyes. "No, but if you keep that up, your little worker out there is going to know exactly what's going on in here." Tongue in cheek, she adds, "You well know how loud I can be, and I don't feel a particular need to be quiet when it's her who's listening."

"So jealous," I whisper, pressing my lips to hers. "Go home and get ready for me." She nods, moving to take the remote from my hand. I tsk, snatching it back. "No play time without Daddy, baby girl."

Her jaw drops, blinking rapidly. I offer her a smile, throwing open my office door and beckoning her to follow me out. While she's behind me, I pull out my phone and quickly type out a text message to her—a request for later. As I round the corner that leads from the back hallway to the main floor, I catch Maggie sitting at the front desk.

Her bright red lips pout, and short black curls bounce as she flies out of the stool behind the counter. "I didn't know you were here alread—" She stops abruptly when Elena appears behind me. "Oh. H... Hi."

"Hi." Elena tosses her a saccharine smile. "I'm Elena, by the way."

"Maggie," she murmurs, slumping back into the stool. "I've heard a lot about you."

"I know." Elena walks toward the door, crooking her finger at me to follow. I know it's a display of possession over me, and fuck if it's not the hottest thing I've ever seen in my goddamn life. I step right into her, and her eyes simmer as she runs a hand up my chest before gripping the collar of my flannel, hauling her mouth to mine. The kiss is brazen and wanton, making a loud display of her ownership of me. Running her tongue over the seam of my lips, she pulls back, but doesn't drop her hold. "I'll see you at home tonight, okay, baby?"

That's it, Little Vice. Lay your claim on me.

"I'll be there as quickly as I can," I whisper against her lips, kissing her again before pulling back and heading to the cabinet behind the desk to grab supplies and begin preparing for my appointment.

"Could've done so much better than her," Maggie mutters as I reach the desk and Elena opens the front door. The words were quiet, but not enough, pure envy and disappointment dripping from her voice.

I pause, spinning to see if Elena heard, too, and by the expression on her face, she absolutely did. If she were an animated character, steam would be funneling out her ears as all her skin turned crimson. Instead, I find narrowed eyes and a set jaw, but the look says everything it needs to.

She's a vicious little thing. Fuck. I'm hard again.

Taking a step back inside the building, Elena seethes, "I'm sorry. I didn't quite hear you. Do you want to speak a little fucking loud—" She gasps, stumbling against the door as I flick the vibrator in her ass to the lowest setting. She looks to me, eyes bulging as her mouth snaps shut.

Good girl, I mouth to Elena before I turn toward Maggie, leaning into the edge of the front counter. "You're a great worker, Maggie. I appreciate what you do, and I like having you as a staff member," I say softly. "But if I ever hear you speak about Elena again, you'll be out of a job before you can finish the fucking sentence. Are we in agreement on that?"

She swallows before offering a shallow nod, eyes fluttering to the floor.

I look to Elena, who still stands at the entrance, watching on in shock.

"Later, baby!" I call, flicking off the vibrator and tossing her a wink.

She sighs, hiding her smirk behind pursed lips before skipping out of the building and down the boardwalk. I go about preparing for my appointment, turning on the built-in stereos to avoid awkward silence between Maggie and me.

Truthfully, I should've addressed Maggie's advances years

ago when she began working here. They were unprofessional on the best of days, and uncomfortable on the worst. I may have snapped at her in a way that's not entirely appropriate for an employee/employer relationship, but the time she blatantly told me she wasn't wearing panties while bending over a table to wipe it down, in hopes I'd watch, was much worse.

Either it'll be awkward for a while and she'll get over it, or she'll quit, and I'll replace her. Honestly, I don't care much about either outcome after the display Elena just put on. It was the most incredible thing I've ever seen, and I'll be counting the seconds with bated breath and a raging cock until I can get home to her tonight.

I'm smiling as I begin setting up my work station, and my phone vibrates with a text message.

My smile drops, along with my stomach. Fuck.

I sent that text to Elena so quickly I didn't think to double check when I clicked on Everett's name instead of hers, and he just responded.

Make sure you send some pictures of that pretty little ass spread for me, baby.

Everett

Lol. Dude, that's insane. Good for you, tho.

And I would, but Dal's pretty possessive. Sorry.

Jesus. If I was in a hurry before to tell Everett I'm fucking his sister, I've definitely changed my mind now.

Chapter Twenty-Nine

Vice

"Lust For Life" - Lana Del Rey, The Weeknd

Fluttering with anticipation, I lie myself out on the forest green blanket covering his bed. Butterfly wings beat wildly in the base of my stomach, because he should be home any minute. I don't know if I want to squeal, giggle, or scream, but I do know that I've never felt like this before.

I've known sex could be playful, it could be rough, or raw and intimate. I've never known that all of those things could exist with the same person, even all at once.

When August and I fuck, it's like we're speaking a new language—something that's only known by the two of us. We communicate through rapid breath and tender whispers and gripping flesh, showcasing our most primal desires and darkest dreams. We share our emotions, our pain, and our love through the movement of our bodies, because we haven't yet reached a point where we can share them with our words.

It's complex and complicated, chaotic, and tumultuous—and I've never savored anything more.

I want to explore every impulse—the aching hunger of acts I've never had the bravery to try before—with him. There is no other person I trust so deeply, no other person I crave so desperately.

I'm laid out like an offering in his bed, nerves fluttering in my chest as the switch of the lock on the front door clicks. I showered, shaved, and moisturized every inch of my body in preparation. I complied with his demands, bringing down all of my toys from my room upstairs—though it's not many. I have a wand, a vibrating dildo, and the plugs I bought specifically for exploring with him.

I wasn't lying when I said I had certain...ideas for the book I'm writing, and I've never done anal before, but I've also never been chained to a wall in my stalker's basement while he tied a vibrator to my thigh and left me alone for hours on the edge, which I've written before too.

I don't need to encounter every sexual experience I write about, obviously, but it made for a good excuse to communicate with August that I wanted to try more anal play without explicitly saying, "Put it in my ass."

Those butterflies fly up my esophagus and lodge themselves into my throat as the stomp of feet make their way toward his room, and I'm aching with need by the time he appears in the open doorway, leaning against it.

Tousled chestnut curls fall against his forehead, green eyes blaze behind his glasses. His tongue darts between his lips as he runs the ball of his piercing over them, soaking me in.

"Look at you." His voice is low and gruff, skating over my skin in a rough caress. "Listening to me like the good girl you are." He shrugs off his flannel as he closes the distance between us. He hovers over me, pressing his lips to mine. "I thought you'd defy me so I'd have no choice but to punish you."

"I don't want to be punished tonight, Augustus. I just want to be yours."

His eyes flutter, a groan crawling from his throat as he presses his arms on the mattress and crawls over me. I move backward until we both reach the top of the bed. Once I'm back against the pillows, he places his arms on either side of my head before lifting one and slowly pulling off his glasses, setting them down on the table beside us. He follows with his shirt, tossing it behind him before he lowers his body to mine, finding the tattoo on my neck with his lips.

"You're going to be my perfect whore tonight?" His breath skates along my skin, sending chills down my spine. "My little plaything?"

"Yes," I hiss as his lips drag over my collarbone and across my chest.

"I'm going to make you feel so fucking good," he promises against my flesh, running his tongue between the valley of my breasts. The glide of his piercing is wet and rough, earning a gasp from my throat as he circles each of my nipples, flicking my bars with his.

Lifting his head, he pierces me with his lust-laced gaze. "Did you leave that plug in like I asked, Little Vice?"

He slips his hand into his pocket before pulling out the remote as I nod.

His lips tilt into an alluring smirk as he clicks the power button. A soft, low buzz lights to life inside me, causing my entire body to quiver. My breath hitches as the sensation sparks through my core, igniting a throb in my clit and a fire in my belly.

"I'm going to own that tight little ass of yours tonight." He laughs roughly before pulling back to sit on his knees. His hands run down my sides and over my hips before cupping at the back of my thighs and spreading my legs wide. "But first, I want some face time with that pretty pussy of mine. I know how needy she can be."

The unrestrained need in his tone sends a rush of anticipation through my core, mingling with the steady vibration and forcing my entire body to hum with desperation.

He falls back onto the pillows beside me, propping himself on an elbow before raising his pierced eyebrow expectedly.

"Mhmm." I lift onto my knees, putting my entire body on display. "She is a daddy's girl."

He grins, pulling his bottom lip between his teeth. August slides his arm out, moving between my thighs and resting over the curve of my ass so that I'm straddling his forearm. He drags me across the mattress, forcing me to lift my knees so that they rest on either side of his face as he pulls his arm away.

Tapping his lips, he murmurs, "Then sit right here on Daddy's tongue and let me have a taste of that sweet cunt, baby girl."

I can hardly catch my breath as I fall forward, positioning my core over his mouth. Looking down, I catch the way his eyes flare at the same moment his tongue swipes up my slit, parting me open.

We moan in unison as he mutters, "Grab my headboard, Elena, and sink down on my face. Full fucking weight. No teasing, baby. Smother me."

"Fuck," I rasp, lowering myself onto him as my hands find the upper edge of his bed frame. His eyes fall closed in an expression of pure bliss as he grabs my ass with one hand, the other splaying out across the mattress, the remote to the plug lying atop his palm.

He moves his tongue between my legs, running the length of me as he uses his hand on my ass to rock my hips back and forth. Stopping at my clit, he swirls the ball of his piercing against me, each flick sending jolts that rattle my bones and curl my toes.

A moan tears from my throat, and I grind down harder, seeking more pressure. He delivers deliciously, upping the pace of his tongue before sucking my bud into his mouth. Suddenly, the buzz inside me increases, and my entire body goes taut. The vibration reaching places I hadn't even known were there.

The plug moves in a rapid rhythm that August matches with perfect sync, and the movement of it presses against my inner walls, causing a pressure I've never felt before. It's intense and heavy, creating a fullness that damn near reaches my stomach.

"Fuck," I murmur. "Don't stop."

Leaning back, I inch my hand down August's torso until I reach the waistband of his jeans. It's a challenge to flick open the top button without looking at it, but I get it done, pulling down the zipper and slipping beneath his underwear until I make contact with his hard and leaking cock.

He groans as I grip it, pumping hard. His hot breath fans against my pussy, forcing a twin sound from my mouth. My hips buck against his face, and his teeth nick my clit, tongue soothing the sharp sting. The tempo of his mouth on me morphs against the fullness and tremor of the toy inside me, creating a pressure more intense than I can comprehend.

My body begins to tighten, and an unfamiliar, heavy urge overcomes me.

"Augustus," I whimper, lifting my hips away from him, grabbing the headboard with both hands again. "I think I'm—"

"No," he growls, dropping the remote to grab my ass with both hands and hold me to his face. "Let it go, Little Vice. Let me have it," he murmurs, flicking his tongue against me again. "Please. I'm goddamn begging. Soak me."

The plea in his tone as he sucks my clit into his mouth with enough force to rupture stars has me breaking. My cries pierce the night, light bursting behind my eyelids, colors I've never fucking seen before flashing across my vision. A release unlike anything I've ever felt bursts from me as my soul rips from my body, sending me spiraling through entire dimensions.

Like cascading through clouds of euphoria, my head swims, body falling into depths of pleasure beyond words. I don't know how long it takes me to float back to reality, but when I reach it, my eyes flutter open, finding myself slumped over August, feeling the heave of his chest beneath me, his green eyes glistening up at me through my parted thighs.

Gazes locked, I can't look away as his hand glides over the mattress, and a moment later, the vibration of the toy inside me stops, allowing my body to relax.

"I... I think..." I pant. "I think I—"

"You fucking squirted," he says on a breath. "All over me. Fuck."

I scramble off him, pulling my legs beneath me at the edge of the bed. As August sits up, leaning back on an elbow, my climax drips off his chin and cascades down his chest.

"I feel like I should apologize, but the sight of you covered in my wetness like that really does something to me, Augustus."

I run my eyes up his body as he licks his lips, savoring my taste. As my gaze clashes against his, the simmering embers of my desire blaze back to life, because he's looking at me like he's nowhere close to done.

August looks at me like he'll never get enough, and it goes far beyond my body. He craves, cherishes, and savors every aspect of who I am. The mess and the chaos—all the things no one else has ever wanted, all the things others threw away.

"I need you to tell me I'm the only man who's ever done that to you before, Elena."

"You are," I whisper. "Only you."

"Fuck," he mutters, rolling onto his knees. There's a massive wet spot over the sheets from the way I lost myself, but he pays it no mind as he points to the mattress. "All fours, baby. I wanna see that ass spread for me."

I crawl in front of him, turning my back to his front before folding my body forward and raising my hips into the air, exposing myself to him entirely.

I'm so wet between my thighs it continues to leak out of me, dripping down my skin as I spread my legs for him.

August inhales deeply, as if settling himself. His body shuffles closer before my skin sparks at the feel of his thighs brushing against mine, and the rough grasp of his hands on my cheeks.

"This is the most beautiful thing I've ever seen," he murmurs, bending over me and letting his breath caress the skin of my back. "I'd say I'm going to sketch it. I'd say it deserves to be in a museum, admired by all." His tongue drags down my spine and over the curve of my ass until he's hovering over the place my skin parts. "But I'm a terribly selfish man, Elena, and this body is all mine."

I respond with a soft mewl, the sound muffled by the pillows my head rests upon.

Keeping one hand on my ass, he slides the other between my cheeks before grasping the plug inside me. "Breathe for me now, okay, baby? I'm going to take this out of you, but I'll go slow."

I nod, inhaling as I stretch around the toy. August moves

slowly, giving my body time to adjust before he slides it out of me completely, leaving me feeling empty.

I gasp as his tongue runs the length of me, starting from my clit and sliding up to my ass, his piercing circling my tight bud. I cry out as he dips it inside me, and I'm trembling with desire.

"Elena, my God," he groans.

"I am your God, Augustus." I lift onto my elbows, turning my head to peek at him over my shoulder, meeting a blazing set of emerald eyes. "Worship me like the devout man you are."

"Fuck," he mutters, rubbing his jaw with an expression I can only describe as awestruck. "Tell me what happens next in your book."

"Oh." I'd completely forgotten that this was supposed to be a brainstorming session. Honestly, I just want him to fuck me in every way possible.

I want him to take control. To own me. He tells me I'm everything he's ever wanted, and there's nothing sexier to me than watching him take it. To forget who I am, and what both of us have been through, becoming nothing more than entwining bodies. When he leads that dance, I can finally shut off my brain, and it's behind closed doors and in his bed that I feel free.

"Umm..." I stutter, attempting to recover—remember what the fuck I've been writing. "Well, she gets herself into some trouble and is almost kidnapped. He wants to punish her for being so negligent to her own safety, so he ties her up. Teases her until she's begging, and then delivers." I bite my lip, smiling. "And she likes a bit of pain. Spanking, choking, slapping. The works."

A dark laugh rakes along my skin. "That what you want right now, Little Vice?"

"I'm game for whatever you are, Augustus."

"Hmmm." He tsks. "I don't think that works for me. I think I need you to use your words." The bed shifts, and then his hand is on me, sliding down my back in a teasing touch. "Tell me you want to be like the character in your book. Tell me you want to be restrained—at the mercy of her captor."

As his hand reaches my ass, he removes it, before delivering a slap that echoes through the room just as a flash of staggering pain ripples over my body.

"Yes," I whimper. "That's what I want."

"Say it, Elena." He spanks me again. "Grab your ass and spread it open, show me how ready you are to take me."

My breath hitches, and my face floods with heat as I brace my weight on my head and shoulders, sinking into the pillows as I reach behind myself and grasp each of my cheeks, spreading wide. I know the view I present to him now is obscene, and I'm shamelessly wet at the thought of it.

"I want you to tie me up and use me. However you want, I'm all yours."

"Mine?" he rasps. "That's what you are?"

"Yours," I repeat, though it's nothing new. "In every sense."

"Fuck." He grabs my hips, flipping me over roughly so that I'm on my back. He kneels before me, shirtless, jeans undone, and his cock hard, peeking over the waistband of his underwear. I lick my lips as I watch the pre-cum drip from his tip. "What's the safe word?"

He studies me with passion-crazed eyes, his hair wild from the way my fingers ran rampant through it while I fucked his face. He's so untamed like this, the perfect complement to my internal chaos. A mess for me.

A flawless match.

"I don't need a safe word."

"You need a fucking safe word," he bites out roughly. "What is it?"

"Violets," I breathe.

"Violets." His coarse laugh is erotic. "Hands above your head. Hold onto the bed frame, Little Vice."

He steps off the mattress and discards his clothing entirely. The full length of him is jaw-dropping, and though I'm so familiar with it, I'll never stop being astonished. My eyes find my name over his thigh, heart leaping at the ink there.

Yours is the only name I knew I'd want to die with on my flesh.

I know there must've been times over the years where he came to regret that statement, and possibly the tattoos themselves, but the way he looks at me now confirms the intention of the ink. The way he looks at me now tells me that he'll refuse to die any other way than in my arms.

August walks over to the bathroom and grabs one of my robes that hangs on the back of the door, pulling the silk belt from the waist.

He wraps the thin strip of fabric around his wrist as he returns to the bed, his face stone and serious, though his eyes smolder with pure lust.

He straddles my chest, cock slipping perfectly between my breasts as he leans over and grabs my hands, lifting both to the top of his headboard. Holding them against the metal frame with one hand, he uses the other to tie the belt of the robe around it, fastening my wrists to the bed.

He loops the silk around me three more times, until it's tight enough that I can't move, and ties a knot. A smile lifts his mouth as he glances down at me. "That's a pretty fucking sight. My cock right in between those perfect tits, and your wet mouth open and waiting."

My jaw hangs open as I stare at his powerful body above me, working to restrain mine. My eyes must bulge, because he smiles wider.

"Drop your chin, baby." I do as he says, lifting my head slightly so that my chin presses into my chest. He rockets his hips forward, sliding between my breasts as his tip reaches my mouth. I wrap my tongue around his head, sucking down all the length of him that I can. "Go ahead and spit on it for me. Get me nice and wet before I fuck you."

I moan, the sound vibrating against his cock and causing it to pulse. He leaves my mouth, staying nestled between my breasts. I spit, watching the saliva spread over his tip and expand across my own skin.

"That's it." He thrusts forward once more, piercings gliding along my slick skin, pushing deep enough that a respectable number of inches find their way down my throat, making me sputter. He pumps deeply a few times, his head kicking back as a groan leaves his mouth. "You're so fucking good at that, Little Vice."

He folds forward, placing his hands on the headboard as he pulls out of me, sliding down my body until his knees are between my legs again. Gripping the backs of my thighs, he spreads my legs and lifts my hips, exposing me once again.

"I'm going to take your ass just like this, baby, so I can see that pussy of yours as it weeps for me."

"Fuck," I breathe. "Yes."

My lids fall closed as his cock nudges between my lips, gliding through my wetness and flicking against my clit. Until a sudden sting against my cheek startles me, and my eyes snap open as he grips my jaw tightly.

"None of that," he growls. "Eyes on me. Always."

"Yes...sir." I gasp.

He licks his lips, nodding, before his gaze falls back between my legs. Leaning over the bed, he swipes the small bottle of lube. Popping the lid, he squirts a generous amount into his palm, and tosses it back onto the nightstand.

Pumping his cock and coating himself, he asks roughly, "Do you want to use a vibrator while I fuck you? Do you think that would feel good? Or do you want to try squirting for me again all on your own?"

I smile, my entire body aching with need, limbs writhing impatiently. "I'm always up for a challenge, Daddy."

"My filthy fucking girl," he rumbles. Once he's lathered himself entirely, he lifts my legs again with one hand, while guiding his cock toward my entrance with the other. "I'm going to start out slow, okay? Breathe deep for me."

I nod, taking a swift inhale as the head of his cock nudges at my back entrance.

"Use the safe word if you need to, Little Vice. I fucking mean it."

"I know. I'm okay," I whisper. My body tenses as he sinks inside another inch. There's momentary discomfort as I stretch around him and adjust to his size, but as he moves deeper, I begin to feel incredibly full.

He breathes with me, teeth gritting as a bead of sweat forms on his temple, and I want to lick it off him. The muscles in his stomach contract, and I know he's desperate to ravish me, to fuck me into another dimension.

I cry out as he notches each rung of his ladder into the rim of my ass, reaching the hilt and filling me entirely.

"That's it, baby. How do you feel?"

Like I have fucking whiplash, honestly. The drastic swing between his praise and his punishment is jarring—enticing. I don't know which I crave more of, and somehow feel like I'll fucking die without them both.

"Full," I breathe. "I need you to move."

A moan tears from his throat, and like the snap of a chain, he unleashes himself. He pulls out of me before sinking back in with enough force to cause a clap when our skin meets. He establishes a furious pace, fucking me so hard I feel the pressure in my stomach. Reaching deeper than I'd ever thought imaginable, his piercings stimulating my body in indescribable ways. It's almost as if he's inside all of me at once. My core flutters around nothing, weeping exactly as he claimed.

With my hands tied above my head, my instincts want to grab hold, touch, and cling to him. I pull at the restraints, feeling a primal heat forming at the center of my thighs as I watch his toned, powerful body pulse and flex as he works himself inside me.

His teeth sink into his bottom lip as he watches himself fuck me. Using one hand, he spreads my pussy, whimpering at the sight. "I can see your pretty cunt clenching, Elena," he rasps. "It's like she's jealous, like she wants me inside her too."

I nod, pressure building, a buzz igniting in my throbbing clit as he brushes his thumb over it.

"So beautiful like this. So obedient. Needy little whore. You don't even need to use your words, your pussy begs for me all on her own."

I don't know what kind of sound leaves my mouth next—some kind of animalistic plea. Stars begin to dot my vision, and I feel mindless as he pumps inside me. He's fucking me to the point of insanity, I think. I buck my hips, searching for his touch against my clit again.

I'm so full, and the pressure is a slow build in my deepest walls, but I need more.

I need to feel him everywhere.

"Words, Little Vice."

"Touch my clit..." I pant. "Please."

He moves his hand away, and I watch with riveted anticipation as he lifts his hand before smacking it down. A sharp burn radiates through my core, causing me to throb, but the delicious hint of pain morphs with my building pleasure, unlike any sensation I've experienced before.

"Again," I beg.

"Greedy girl." He smacks me again. "You like that?" he asks, words muffled between clenched teeth. "You like having your pussy spanked?"

"Yes," I gasp, body writhing as he delivers another slap.

He continues, the movements sharp and hard. My body bathes in flame as my being floats away from it, soaring into clouds of ecstasy so high I never knew they existed.

Jumbled, unintelligible words fall from my mouth, but I can't hear them. I only know of their existence by the vibration against my lips, my mind only catching his name.

All of my senses are hyperaware of him. His cock inside me, his hand coming down on me, again and again. His familiar smell of pine and rain mingling with the scent of sex. I'm enveloped in him entirely.

That pressure reaches the point of combustion, and the same

overwhelming sensation of fullness crashes over me. "August, I'm—"

"Yes, yes," he growls. "Drench me, Little Vice. Show me who I belong to." He flattens his hand against my clit, using three fingers to flick back and forth rapidly. The fierce tempo and flawless rhythm drive me right over that edge.

Every ounce of breath flees from my lungs as sparks explode behind my eyes. My soul fractures, splintering around me as every fabric of reality shatters, and I'm suspended in an endless moment of sheer, utter, unadulterated pleasure.

Only the sound of his voice and the feel of his lips against my neck bring me back, and my eyes flutter open to find him hovering over me. I realize my hands have become untied, and my arms immediately clasp around his back, savoring his sweat-slicked skin. His lips drag along my neck and across my jaw, heavy breath caressing my skin.

"So good, baby. So good," he whispers. His hands brush the hair from my face, reaching behind my head and knotting in my curls as he holds me to him. "My perfect girl. You take it so well." His voice is a gritted, fractured whimper, dripping with pure need. "Came so pretty for me." He moans, and the sound is so desperate and pathetic I'm fucking quivering. "Give me those big, brown eyes," he begs, tilting my head so our gazes lock. "I'm going to come. Can I come, baby? I need it so bad."

"Yes," I whisper, grabbing his jaw and forcing his lips to mine. "Come."

He opens his mouth, and I steal the breath that escapes it, swallowing down his groans of pleasure. He's still pumping inside me, cock pulsing as he barrels toward his release. Lifting my hips to deepen the angle, I lock my ankles around his back.

The soft gasp of my name leaves his lips a fraction before I feel him pause, his entire body going rigid before he drops his head to my neck, pulsating as he spills inside me. The warmth of his cum fills me, his deep groans vibrating against my collarbone, hips trembling as his orgasm rushes through him.

I stroke his back, giving him time to come down from his climax, allowing myself to savor the weight of his boneless body on top of me.

"I want you to tell me that it's never been like this with anyone else," I whisper softly. "I want to know that I'm the only one who's ever made you feel this way."

"Only you, Elena. I can't remember anything before you anymore, and I don't want to." He lets out a shuddering breath against my flesh. "You're all that matters."

I nod, sliding my hand up his neck and stroking my fingers through his soft curls. He pulls back enough that he can look at me, his hands replicating my movements as he runs them through my hair. A soft, warm glow illuminates his face from the dim lamp in the corner of the room, and his face is the most beautiful thing I've ever seen.

"You are everything," he whispers.

Three words linger on the tip of my tongue, like the heart that escaped its cage and ended up on my sleeve. I'm too afraid to say them, though. They feel like a curse to me.

Instead, I say, "You are too."

Chapter Thirty

Violet

"At The Beach, In Every Life" - Gigi Perez

"This is my writing, isn't it?" she asks, dragging her hand along my ribcage hours later.

The sun had just set when we finished, and by the time we showered together, it was late enough to have dinner. We ordered in our favorite Chinese takeout from our childhood before falling back into my bed with her favorite television show on.

I told her I hadn't watched *Vanderpump Rules* since she left, and she looked sad for a moment before realizing I had missed some huge scandal that I desperately needed to catch up on.

So, that's what we're doing now as she lies against my chest and brushes her hands across my skin. Over the tattoo of the filleted heart, the purple flowers, and the poem—written in Italian.

"Yeah," I whisper.

"Why?"

I turn my head, finding her eyes glowing with cautious curiosity.

"I was in pain. The needle numbed it."

She blinks, nodding before her eyes cast down, full lips forming the kind of pout that lets me know she's thinking deeply.

"So, you kept that poem, then?"

"I've kept all of them," I whisper, twirling one of her curls around my finger. "Everything of you."

She lifts onto an elbow, tilting her head and causing her long, dark hair to drape across my chest. "Everything?" she asks. "Every poem I've ever written you?"

I nod.

"Why did you get that one tattooed?"

I shrug. "It was the most recent one you wrote before everything happened. It was when we were our happiest. Seemed like the words were probably worth scarring my skin with."

She shakes her head, eyes widening. "You mean...you don't even know what it says?"

"No. You wrote them in a language you know I can't read. They're encrypted. I figure, if you wanted me to know what they said, you'd have written them in English."

"That's the craziest thing I've ever heard."

I smile. "On brand."

Her brows knit as she shrugs down the bed, bringing her face level with my side. Running her hand over the words again, she whispers the poem aloud:

"Maree dentro profondi occhi verdi

Tutto mio dietro occhiali dalla montatura scura

Mano ferma, sa chi sono

Togliendomi la maschera che indosso per le masse

Dipingendo immagini nel mio midollo osseo

Lo terrò l'arco, tu trafiggerai la freccia

Questa cosa, l'amore?

Sempre in bianco e nero

Ma con te, la velocità della luce

Ultravioletto"

"I could at least make out that last word," I murmur, lips tilting upward.

"This thing, love?" She translates the last verse. "Always black and white, but with you, the speed of light..." She sits up, facing me. "Ultraviolet."

I reach my hand out, cupping her face. She lets her eyes fall closed, nuzzling against my palm. "I told you I was having déjà vu," Elena whispers. "I wish I could re-read them all."

I pull myself up, swinging my legs over the side of the bed as I all but leap out of it. I'm wearing underwear, whereas Elena is still completely naked, but I don't give her time to dress as I walk out of the room, beckoning her to follow me.

I move through the darkened, quiet house, past the kitchen and into the sunroom behind it. It's cooler here than inside the house, but the spring weather is warm enough that there is no chill. I flip on the lamp in the corner, illuminating the room in a warm glow. There is a closet beside the couch that I use for storage. Mostly art supplies and some tattoo equipment for when I work at home.

There is one box on the top shelf of the closet simply labeled *Elena*.

I pull it off the top shelf as Elena watches me from the doorway, wrapping a throw blanket from the top of the couch around her shoulders.

I set it down on the workbench and pull open the lid of the box, revealing everything stacked inside. There are more items I recovered from her mother after she moved to New York, things neither of us had the heart to throw away, but I had the space for and Monica didn't. Original copies of her first publications, the raw manuscripts she'd printed out on her home computer.

There are notebooks filled with her writing—from poems to brainstorm notes to book ideas. A small box at the bottom of the larger one holds every poem she ever wrote for me, along with my own sketchbooks—ones I never showed her.

I step back, giving her space to rummage inside. "You're free to keep anything you want in there. It's all made by you or for you."

Her head snaps up. "For me?"

I bite my lip, unsure of how she's going to take the fact that I spent years of our youth drawing pictures of her, and that I never let her see the majority of them. Just one. The first time she told me she loved me, but little did she know she'd been my inspiration long before that.

Back then she wasn't mine, and it felt like something I needed to keep to myself. A daydream I was forbidden from having. Now, she feels like mine, but she also doesn't. I still feel like I'm walking a tightrope with her, constantly afraid that one wrong move or a strong gust of wind will knock us both off, and we'll never recover.

So long as we stay secret, we stay forbidden, and that's an incredibly unstable and delicate balance to maintain. I want her to know the true depths of my adoration, but somehow, I can't help but fear that sharing them would twist the knife deeper were I to lose her again.

I swallow, throwing caution to the wind like I always do with Elena. "I..." I choke a laugh, shaking my head. "I have some old sketchbooks in there, and...I suppose you've always been my muse."

Her brows rise, followed by a lift in her lips and the most adorable scrunch of her nose. Nerves rattle my stomach, and my cheeks flood with heat. Gripping the back of my neck, I watch her sort through the items until she comes across the small box at the bottom, pulling it out and setting it down in front of her.

"Those are my drawings, and all of the poems you ever wrote for me. There are a ton of others in there, though. Some of your old manuscripts too."

She nods absently, flipping through one of my books as her eyes go wide. I watch the reflection of the pages flashing in her eyes as she takes in the many, many sketches I've done.

Moments where she was in front of me—on our cliffside, at the beach, or in one of our rooms. Moments I pulled from memory—her laugh and her profile, the way she looks on a surfboard or when she's writing in her notebooks.

"I can't believe you were always right there, and it took me so long to see you," she whispers. Tears shimmer in her eyes when she lifts her head to look at me. "If I had only met you first, what would life be like right now?"

"If you had met me first, we would have just ended up here anyway." I walk around the bench, taking her into my arms and letting the blanket on her shoulders fall to the floor. "Or maybe you would've fallen for me right away, and he never would've gotten to know what it's like to be loved by you." I pull back, swiping a thumb beneath her eyes to take away her tears. "The highlight reel, remember?"

She sighs deeply, but finally nods.

Keeping her head against my chest, she turns, flipping another page of my old sketchbook. "You did all of these before... everything." She looks up at me, brown eyes glimmering. "Have you drawn me since?"

I shake my head. "I've been too afraid." I cup her cheek, dragging my thumb over her bottom lip. "You still feel like a reverie to me. Something fleeting, like you could disappear. I've been terrified to cement you like this, because it would make the pain of losing you again unbearable."

"Draw me," she whispers. "Draw me right now. Just like this."

"Elena..." I sigh as she steps back, forcing me to drop my hold. The golden light casts against her naked figure like she's being bathed in warmth. Ethereal and glowing.

"I know what I'm asking, Augustus." The plea in her sparkling eyes makes my knees buckle. "Please."

I can't pretend I don't still hold fear of losing her again, but I'm not sure I'll ever escape that entirely. The conviction in her voice pierces that fear, and I realize there is no risk with her not worth taking.

I relent, grabbing my newest sketchbook and my bag of charcoal pencils and erasers from the corner of my desk beside the workbench. "Lie down on the couch," I rasp, nodding toward it.

She saunters over, sprawling herself out and turning to face the chair that sits across from it. I sit, crossing one leg over the other as I position the canvas paper on my thigh before pulling a sharpened pencil from my bag and fastening a spare behind my ear.

When I glance up at her, she's smiling like I lassoed the moon and handed it to her, and I have no idea how or why I got lucky enough to have her look at me like that. To have her in front of me like this. To even be granted the privilege of witnessing her existence.

"Are you going to draw me like one of your French girls?" Her voice is pure silk, causing my hardening cock to pulsate.

I snort, shaking my head at the reference. "You're my only girl."

She shifts onto her side, draping her arm over the flawless curvature of her body. The other tucks behind her head, propping it up as she smiles at me with sultry eyes so molten they appear nearly caramel in this light.

She's not donning any sapphires, no jewelry at all, outside the two small bars through each of her nipples. Elena's completely bared to me, dressed only in the ink across her skin—the ink I put there.

The violets and vines on her forearm meet the serpent snaked around her thigh where her hand rests at her hip. The dripping stars and crescent moon across her sternum cup her perfect breasts, and as she bats her eyes at me, her neck stretches, revealing the cluster of stars behind her ear.

She's art personified, and I am a god among men to be granted the privilege to draw her like this. To take this vision of her and make it eternal, knowing it'll only ever be for my eyes.

"I can't believe you kept all of those things. The drawings. The poems. All of my writing."

"They're important," I respond, dragging my pencil across the page. "You're a storyteller, Elena. Each piece of art you create, or that's created with you in mind, is like a page to your own story. I'd never throw them away."

"I guess..." She sighs. "I guess I didn't think I was a story worth telling."

"Your voice is my favorite song. Your words are my favorite book." I lift my eyes to hers, studying the curvature of her hip and waist, the flare of her breasts. "Your body is my favorite canvas, and your face my favorite sculpture. You are art to me."

Her bottom lip trembles, like there is something she wants to say but can't speak. Eventually, she closes her mouth, offering me a soft smile as I continue to draw in silence.

"Would you ever tattoo me again?" she asks after a while.

"I'm always itching to touch you, Elena. In whatever way you'll have me."

"Is it the same, though? As drawing me? Or my writing poems for you? Are the tattoos the way you show..." she trails off.

"I consider it art, of course. I love doing it. I like that people offer me a piece of their skin, that they trust me to create something beautiful on it, but at the end of the day, the tattoos are for them. It's their art, I'm just helping bring it to life. It's rewarding, and it makes me feel like I matter, but it's not the same as sketching something from my own head." I sigh. "It's different with you. With you it's...possession. It's ownership. I'm taking that slice of your flesh—your body and your soul—and making it mine. I have never felt that way tattooing someone else before, but it's not the same as when I draw you. The drawings are an appreciation."

"That's so hot," she murmurs. "I like being owned by you."

I smile to myself. "I know."

"I want to own you too," she whispers.

I pause, raising my eyes to her. She hasn't moved, lying comfortably on her side as she continues her pose for me. "Is that so?"

She bites her lip, hiding a mischievous smile, and I decide that's the exact expression I'm going to put on her face when I finish this sketch. "Would you let me tattoo you?"

"You're awfully possessive, Little Vice," I drawl. "Maybe somewhere hidden, where only you'd see it, because I'm confident you'd probably do a terrible job."

"Rude." She bursts with laughter, rolling back on the couch, and I consider drawing that look instead. Her laughter is the most beautiful thing I've ever seen. "Can I tattoo you tonight? When you're done drawing me?"

I slowly raise my brow at her. "Only if you let me give you one too. Whatever I want, and wherever I want."

She drapes an arm over her side, tilting herself in a way that exposes more of her breasts and hips, tossing me a playful smile. "My body is your canvas, Augustus."

Chapter Thirty-One

Violet

"mad woman" – Taylor Swift

"You know, I haven't missed an appointment in months. You probably don't need to be my chaperone anymore."

Darby frowns at me from the driver's seat of her baby blue Mustang, blond hair whipping around her face in the wind as we cruise down the main drag of Pacific Shores. "I like coming with you. It gets me out of the shop. Plus, you never say no to any of the lunch places I want to eat."

I shrug. That's true. And she's been on a pizza kick lately, which is unfortunate for me and my lactose intolerance, because I can't turn down cheese to save my goddamn life.

"You seem to be doing well, though." Her hazel eyes flick to me from behind her sunglasses. "Is that because of therapy or... something else?"

I roll my eyes, coughing a laugh. "Therapy does help, but so does she."

Kelsey and I dove deeper into my past with Elena, and to my utter surprise, Kelsey never once made me feel guilty about it. About being with Elena then, or being with her now, about falling in love with my brother's girlfriend and refusing to let her go, even after he died.

She does think it's a complex situation, and the only way to find resolution is if Elena and I learn to be completely honest with each other, communicate better, and adopt some healthier outlets for our grief.

Today, though, she told me that she actually thinks I'm making strides in that, and it finally feels like hope is beginning to bloom.

"Leo has been asking about you two a lot." She arches a brow. "Asking what I know—if there is something going on."

"I don't expect you to lie to your husband for me, Darbs."

"I know." She sighs. "And I wouldn't. But you don't tell me much either, so I'm essentially as in the dark as he is. The only thing I know is how you feel, but I don't know how she feels or what you two are up to."

I swallow awkwardly, my cheeks heating.

She only laughs. "The guys definitely suspect you're having sex, but if it's more than that...I think you owe them a conversation about it."

I nod. I have enough respect for my two best friends to ensure they understand I wouldn't take advantage of their sister in any sense of the word, but considering our history, I think they know that already. They know I love her; what they don't understand is the depths of it.

I can't explain that to them without explaining everything, and that's where I begin to hesitate.

Someday, we'll need to sit them down and tell them the entirety of our history. It'll be painful for all of us, but I think it's the only way Elena and I can have any kind of future.

"Is it?" Darby asks, pulling me from my thoughts.

"What?"

"Is it just sex?" She parks in the lot behind the boardwalk, taking the space in front of Honeysuckle Florals before killing the engine and turning to face me. "I only ask because if this arrangement is some kind of...coping mechanism for the two of you, I worry about the outcome, were it to end. Would she turn back to alcohol if you got into a fight?" She lifts her sunglasses above her head, revealing soft, solemn eyes. "Would you begin to have your...thoughts again?"

"No. No, Darby." I shake my head. "I'm doing better about all of that, I promise. Elena is too. It is more than sex," I admit. "And I have no intention of it ever ending, but we're still trying to figure out what our version of more is. What our version of happiness looks like." I rub the back of my neck anxiously. "I think we just need the time and space to figure that out on our own before we start involving other people. It creates complications we're not yet fit to handle."

"I get it." She nods. "Eventually, though, you'll both need to address it with her family. They've been trying to hold her together for years—especially Everett. They still worry, and normally I tell Leo to stay out of things, but considering the circumstances, they deserve to be told face-to-face that she's going to be taken care of." Darby smiles softly. "She needs to do the same for you too."

"I know." I sigh, pulling my phone out of my pocket and checking the time—I still have about an hour before my next appointment. "I'm going to stop into the coffee shop real quick and see her before she heads home for the day."

Darby grins knowingly. "I'll come with you. I need to ask Dahlia a question about my baby shower."

I hop out of the passenger side and jog around the front to open her door, holding her hand as she lifts herself out. She's only about a month away from her due date, and by the way she waddles toward the back door to The Wicked Wildflower, her discomfort is growing about as rapidly as her baby girl.

The bakery is fairly busy as we walk inside. Almost every table is occupied with patrons working, reading, or quietly chatting with others. It's brightly decorated in an orange and blue retro aesthetic, with floral paintings and vintage artwork lining the walls.

My eyes find the counter where I know I'll find Elena. I do a double-take when I land on her face, because she's wearing the vexed expression I usually find alluring. The deep-set brows, narrowed and blazing eyes, scrunched nose and pouted lips that tell me she's hovering on the cusp of violence.

That look often has me fighting a battle between lust and lunacy, but in this moment, it has me coiling in fear, because my mother is the person on the receiving end of that look.

Vice

"Who do you think you are, living inside his house?"

Sadie Hayes seethes at me. Her heavily botoxed face is beet red, green eyes that match the color of her son's are scrunched and narrowed beneath pounds of eye makeup, and lips peeling back as she bares her veneers right at me.

I'm making a great effort to appear unbothered, and I think I'm failing.

I want to fucking deck her. The only reasons I don't are out of respect for the two children of hers that I deeply love, and because I don't want to cause a scene in my sister-in-law's business.

But she's a terrible fucking person and an awful mother, and the fact that she had the audacity to ruin my Thursday by showing up in my place of work to demand I move out of the house I pay rent to stay in, has me right on the edge of jumping over the counter and ripping her hair out.

"Mom?" August's voice is like salvation, and I shudder in relief at the sound.

Sadie spins, taking in the sight of her son—and Darby, standing behind him with a hesitant expression and a hand on her belly.

"Hi, love." She opens her arms, stepping toward him. His face is etched in stone as he glances at me with an apologetic expression, avoiding her hug. "I have to go to Los Angeles this weekend, so I thought I'd pop over here a day early to see you."

"You didn't think to tell me you were coming first?" he asks, eyes withdrawn as they flick from her to me. "And why are you here in the bakery of all places?"

"I stopped into the tattoo parlor, but the cute little worker told me you were out to lunch, so I figured I'd grab a coffee while I waited for you." She clears her throat. "I wanted to surprise you."

August cuts his gaze to me, unconvinced. "Elena?"

Sadie turns, eyeing me with an expression that says not a word.

Like I'd ever fucking listen to her.

"I don't think Sadie expected to see me working here when she walked in, so I caught her off guard." I force a smile, watching her swallow uncomfortably. "We're just catching up. I asked her how she's liking Palm Springs, and she told me I'm wretched and demanded I move out of your house immediately."

She scoffs, rolling her eyes as she places a hand on her hip. "I did not use the word wretched."

August's eyes glaze over in a way that makes my heart ache. Like a parent watching their child throw a tantrum, and mentally preparing themselves to pull everything together and resolve the situation, even while falling apart on the inside.

Sadie Hayes is insecure and vain. Addicted to wellness fads, loving nothing more than to toss a snide remark at anyone eating dairy or gluten, all while happy to ignore the fact she has a penchant for painkillers she wasn't prescribed. She never came to terms with the fact that she didn't reach the level of stardom as an actress that she had dreamed about when she was young. What the rest of the world saw as a woman settling down to raise a family, Sadie saw as the epitome of failure.

She resented her husband and her boys ever since, expecting constant praise and validation to fill the void left behind by Hollywood while remaining negligent and self-serving. Her husband, Alex, is just as checked out as she is, doing whatever he can to avoid her outbursts and ignore her issues.

I think all August and Zach ever craved was her approval, but she's the type of person who will never think anything is good enough. Not herself, not those around her.

She can't be pleased, and she'll never be happy.

With a tight jaw and a heavy sigh, August nods toward a table in the corner of the cafe. “Can we sit over there and talk, please? I have an appointment in a little while, but we can visit until then.”

She smiles, patting his cheek before walking over to the table and sitting down.

August looks to me, defeat and embarrassment present on his face. He steps to the counter, leaning across it. “I am so fucking sorry. I don’t know what she said to you, but I need you to forget it, okay? You’re not going anywhere, and she has no right to be speaking to you like that.” He kisses my cheek softly. “Let me deal with her so she can get out of our hair.”

“You shouldn’t have to deal with her either, Augustus. You need to tell her that the way she, and your father, have treated you is deplorable.” I take his hand off the counter and fold my fingers around his. “You don’t need to keep this façade with them. You owe them nothing.”

He offers me a half smile. “It’s easier this way. She’s been through a lot.”

“So have you.” I sigh, dropping his hand. “And that doesn’t seem to concern them.”

“My love!” Sadie chimes from across the room. “Can you order me a hot green tea, please? Organic honey and a squeeze of lemon.”

His eyes flutter with annoyance. “You do not need to make her tea.”

“I can ask Dahlia to make it,” Darby offers as she walks behind the counter. “She’s in the back office, I assume? I had a question for her anyway, but I can ask her to take over for you.” She bites her lip, murmuring, “You don’t need to be dealing with any of this” before glancing at August, ensuring he understands the message was meant for him too.

“Don’t worry about it.” I force a smile. “I’ll take care of it.”

I walk away from the cash register, not allowing either of them to get another word in as I sort through our tea shelf and begin making Sadie’s cup. I hear two resigned sighs before the door that leads through the kitchen and to Dahlia's office opens and closes, and August's clipped footsteps echo toward the back of the coffee shop.

I take my sweet-ass time making her cup of tea. I think through every drop of venom I want to spit upon her, all of my diluted rage bellowing through my bones and settling upon my skin, forming spears I want to throw in her direction.

I've never liked her. I've never thought she was a good mother, but the way she's treated August since Zach's death is unforgivable. Watching her show up here unannounced and uninvited, demanding August's attention without care for his well-being—it's repulsive.

He may get angry with me for my next actions, but I fucking refuse to be complacent.

I didn't have time to get a word in when she walked in earlier. She caught me off guard. I wasn't paying attention when I heard someone enter the building, too wrapped up in a poem I was writing. I glanced up to find her seething stare gazing down at me like I was a piece of gum she stepped in, followed by a snappy, "What are you doing here?"

Before I could answer, Sadie launched into a tirade. She said she'd recently been told I was living with August, and that she wasn't surprised to find I'd moved back to Pacific Shores and latched onto him the same way I had when I was young. That I was a manipulator, and that I'd always taken advantage of him. She told me I had a lot of nerve moving into Zach's house after what I'd done. That she couldn't believe I'd forced August back into my entrapment, and was working in the coffee shop right next to his business. Which, honestly, was the strangest take of all, considering it's my brother who owns the entire boardwalk, and my sister-in-law who owns the bakery itself.

I was ready to laugh it off, tell her it was nice to see her, and advise her to get the fuck out of my face, but after seeing August walk in, his immediate complacency and her treatment of him—I'm livid.

I finish making her cup of tea, ensuring it's made to perfection, before hanging my apron on the hook outside the kitchen door and nudging it open. "Dahlia!" I call. "I'm going to take my break if you could cover the register."

"Sure!"

Her office door swings open a moment later, and Dahlia steps out, followed by a waddling Darby. There's a forced smile on Dahlia's face as she passes me and sidles up behind the counter. "I'm totally okay if you also want to head home a little early."

"Or I can call Leo?" Darby asks. "Everett or your mom?"

I shake my head. "I'll be fine."

She sighs, hazel eyes etched with concern as she studies me. "Okay. Well, just know, I'm always here if you need me too."

The look on her face is apprehensive, like she's still trying to convince herself I don't hate her, and for some reason, it makes this moment feel significant. I step around the counter, reaching out to grab Darby's shoulder and tug her into me. She sighs softly, returning the hug, and I could swear I feel the baby kick between us, though maybe I'm just imagining it.

"Thank you," I whisper.

When I pull away, she looks at me like she might cry, but neither of us mention it before she turns and walks out the front door in the direction of her flower shop.

"She really missed you," Dahlia says from behind me.

"I missed her too," I say, turning around. Dahlia watches me curiously as I swipe the green tea from the counter and make my way to where August and his mother sit.

His eyes go wide as I drag a chair from a nearby table and plop down beside them.

Sliding the drink across to her, I smile as Sadie glares. "We didn't get to finish our conversation earlier."

August's hand finds my thigh beneath the table, drawing soothing circles, and it saddens me that he clearly feels stuck in the middle. I think he's always felt this way, because while August never shared the information, Zach would often tell me the terrible things their mother said about me when I wasn't around.

"Normally, I'd understand your feelings about me living in the home that Zach bought. It was hard for me to move in too. It was an adjustment for both of us." I nod toward August. "I wouldn't blame you for having feelings about that decision. Honestly, I don't blame you for hating me, either. I'm not a terribly likable person. I get it." I lean across the table, invading her personal space, and preen at the kernel of fear that sparks to life in her eyes. "But the guilt and blame you have placed on your son's shoulders, and the absurd treatment from your worthless husband is inconceivable. You are both shameful people, and August deserves so much better than you," I seethe, hot tears burning behind my eyes. "Zach deserved better than you, too, and he would be fucking ashamed to know what you've put his brother through." I rise from my chair so sharply, the legs of it scrape across the floor behind me. "Ashamed."

Sadie's lips tremble, her eyes misting with anger. With a shaking voice, she murmurs, "I don't know how you can be so opinionated about what our family has been through when you ran away the way you did. You left him long before I did, Elena."

"Mom, stop." August sighs, dropping his face into his hands from my periphery. "This is ridiculous. Honestly, Zach would probably fucking hate us all. We've all handled things terribly."

"The difference is that you and I"—I wave a finger between us—"understand where we've fallen short. Your parents don't seem to think they've hurt you, or that the hurt they've caused is unwarranted, and if nobody else will fucking set them straight, I'm more than happy to."

He lifts his head, and there's a bright conviction in his green eyes—something that looks a lot like salvation. A lot like gratitude. Like love.

"I know my husband has been less than supportive, and it's something I try to work on, but honestly, what would you have me do?" Sadie takes a sip of her tea. "As for me, I've never blamed Augustus for the loss of my son." Her eyes lift to mine. "I've only ever blamed you."

Like the blow she hoped her words would be, they land. Sucker punching me straight in the center of my soul, and causing me to nearly stumble over the chair behind me.

"Don't fucking say that," August snaps.

"You're like an illness to this family, Elena," Sadie continues. "Do you know how many times I watched my boys argue about you growing up? I know you all think I wasn't paying attention"—she glances at August—"but I was. And you..." She sets her sights on me again. "You were the common denominator in every fracture of their relationship. You were the last person he saw that day, and whatever you said or did to him upset him enough that he went into that water despite knowing he shouldn't have. He went into that water because of you, and he never returned."

The fight leaves my body, all that venom and all those spears fall uselessly to the floor, and I become hollow. The tears I tried to blink away win, cascading down my cheeks like liquid heartbreak.

I agree with every word she says, but I've never heard them voiced aloud before.

I've never had someone lay confirmation to the darkest thoughts that plague my mind.

"So, you'll forgive me, Elena, if I'd like to protect the one child I have left..." Her voice breaks. "From the irreparable damage of the messes you cause."

"Okay, fuck this. That is enough—" August starts.

"Yeah, so, I'm going to have to ask you to leave." August and Sadie whip around, and for the first time, I notice Dahlia hovering beside our table with her eyes pinned on Sadie.

"Me?" she asks.

"I have very little patience for my employees being harassed by customers, but I'm especially intolerant of anyone making my sisters cry." She crosses her arms and nods toward the door. "So, you can get the fuck out, and please know you will not be welcomed back."

"Ridiculous," Sadie scoffs, rolling her eyes. "August, my love, walk me out so we can continue this conversation privately." She gathers her bag, standing from her chair before tossing a final once-over at me. "I don't know what either of them saw in you, anyway."

"Me either," I whisper, too numb to feel the penetration of her judgmental stare, still bleeding from the slice of her words.

I don't look at Dahlia or August, unable to address the fact that they heard everything she'd said too. That the depths of my regret, and the secrets I've clutched against my chest for years, were ripped away and spewed out in front of us for all to witness.

I simply turn and walk out, unsure of where I'm going, because I don't think I can go home.

It was never really mine, anyway.

Chapter Thirty-Two

Violet

"Fix You" - Coldplay

"I cannot fucking believe you said that to her," I spit in my mother's direction. "Are you out of your mind?"

"Am I?" she damn near shrieks, genuine shock flashing on her face. "Did you hear what she said to me?"

"She was being protective of me, Mom!" I throw open the back door to The Wicked Wildflower, holding it for my mom to exit behind me. "She's been living with me for months. She's seen firsthand how fucked up I am. A fact you're all too happy to ignore."

"She had no right—"

"You had no right!" I shout back, causing my mother's eyes to widen in a way I've never seen before as she steps back from me. "It was vile to place that blame on her. You have no idea what kind of guilt and pain she harbors, and how much work she's been putting in to move past it. I don't even want to fathom how much your careless words today will set her back."

"August." She sighs, squeezing the tension out of her temples. "I don't have the capacity to hold concern for that girl's well-being. It's you I care ab—"

"No." I shake my head, rounding my Bronco to the driver's side. "Bullshit. You don't get to pick and choose when you care about me, and when you blame me for what happened. You don't get to decide I'm your son when it fits your narrative, or when you're attempting to absolve yourself of guilt."

My mom frowns at me, and a rivulet of sadness ripples through me at the sight. I've tolerated her apathy because I thought holding on to any shattered piece of our family would be what my brother would want—even if it meant I spent the rest of my life bleeding. Even if my parents couldn't forgive me, even if they couldn't look at me without disdain, and even if every interaction felt forced, I thought that my mother and I were on the same page.

A fractured relationship was better than none at all. A hateful father, resentful mother, and one guilt-ridden son was better than losing both of their children.

My throat constricts as I turn to face her. "I thought about killing myself. Often, actually." I swallow, tears stinging my eyes. "I know you didn't know that, because you never asked. I don't even know if you realize it, but you have never asked how I felt after he died. How I felt about my father telling me it was my fault and never speaking to me again. How I felt about living in the house that my brother bought but never got to live in, only because the guilt burns hotter when I think about selling it, even though I can't fucking afford it."

My mother watches helplessly from the walkway, makeup streaking down her cheeks.

"It was Leo who waived the rent on my suite so I could cover the mortgage." I nod toward my shop. "It was Everett who planned a memorial fundraiser because Dad wouldn't allow me to work with the Foundation myself. It was their mother who invited me to dinner every Sunday so I'd feel less alone." I clear my throat, choking on my words. "It was Darby, Leo's fiancée, who helped me find a therapist. She still goes with me to every single appointment. It was my therapist who helped me work through my suicide ideation." I wipe a thumb under each of my eyes, clearing my tears. "And it is because of Elena that I haven't had those thoughts in months. It's Elena who holds me in the middle of the night after I've had a night terror. It is Elena who makes space for all of the grief I cannot bear to hold on my own, even at the detriment to herself."

"I..." A sob bubbles from her mouth, and she clamps a shaking hand over it. "I had no ide—"

"The only blame Elena has to bear is loving me more fiercely than you could begin to comprehend. She stood up to you today for me, with courage I have never had, and in return, you destroyed her." I shake my head. "I don't value myself enough to protect myself from your aversion, but I value her enough to draw this line." I slip into the driver's seat of my car. "Do not speak to me again until you are ready to apologize to her, and until Dad is ready to apologize to me. We both deserve better than this."

With the doors and top to my truck taken off, there is nothing to cut the tension between my mother and me. Turning the key and flipping on the ignition, I call back out to her, "And Elena was right. Zach would be ashamed of what you and Dad have allowed this family to become."

She watches me with quiet tears, saying nothing as I back out of my parking spot and leave the boardwalk. Once I turn onto Main Street, I whip out my phone and shoot a text to the client I was supposed to meet with today. Luckily, he's a regular of mine, and I know he'll understand when I tell him an emergency arose, and I need to cancel at the last minute.

I have no idea where Elena went, but I know I won't function until I find her and do everything in my power to make her okay again.

I rack my brain in an attempt at figuring out where she might've gone, and I have a gut feeling she didn't head home. I can't imagine she'd have gone to the beach or to seek out her parents or siblings. I turn down Pacific Avenue, driving up the hill until I reach Fred's Deli.

Not only does this deli serve her favorite soup, but it's also one of the only places that sells the passion fruit flavor of a Mexican soda brand she loves. I pull into the gravel parking lot and kill the engine before hopping out of my truck and rushing inside. A bell chimes on the glass doors, and from across about four aisles, I catch the very top of a messy brunette bun with wild curls flowing in every direction.

My phone is already blowing up with texts from her brothers—I assume because Dahlia gave them a heads-up. I respond and let them know I found her, and I'll have her call them when she's ready.

The cashier greets me, and I toss back a silent wave as I weave through the aisles toward her. I turn the corner, chest sinking when I catch sight of her. She's staring blankly at a bag of pretzels in one hand, while she holds the bottleneck of that passion fruit soda in the other.

She hasn't noticed me yet, sniffling as tears free fall down her cheeks, dripping from her chin and to the floor, landing on her worn Converse.

"Baby," I whisper. Her head snaps up, whipping in my direction. It's when her eyes meet mine that she crumbles entirely, a broken sob ripping from her throat. I close the distance between us, wrapping my arms beneath her shoulders as she falls into me. "I've got you," I hush her. "I'm here."

I lock my arms around her waist, holding her against me. Her tears drip onto the skin of my neck as she whispers, "I'm sorry. I don't know what's wrong with me." She shakes her head. "I think I'm PMSing."

"Maybe." I sigh. "But even so, the emotion is warranted. That was awful, and I'm so sorry. I had no idea she was coming. I never would've let her confront you like that."

"Everything she said was true. I've always known it." She pulls back, turning away as she wipes her tears, like she doesn't want to face me. "I've just never had someone else say it to my face before."

"Elena," I rasp, and she drops her head. "Look at me." I snake my hand behind her neck and lift her head, forcing her gaze to mine. "None of that is true. Not one word she said. Do you understand me?"

A thousand shades of brown mingle inside her eyes, like a

tapestry of shattered glass. Beautiful in color, but broken in form. A chill bites my skin at the devastation on her face, at the realization of how such beauty could hold so much pain.

She shakes her head, and my chest sinks. My throat tightens with emotion as I tug her against my chest, pressing a kiss to the top of her head, because I don't know what more I can offer her. I don't know how to reverse this damage.

"Can you go get in my truck, please? I'm going to go pay for your snacks, and then I'm going to take you somewhere."

"Where?" she asks, her shuddering breath hot against my chest.

"A surprise. You'll see."

I slide my hands down her arms, gently pulling the soda and the bag of pretzels from her grasp. She lets them go, and when she steps back from me, I nod toward the front of the store. Elena complies, walking around the aisle we stand within. I watch her climb into the passenger side of my Bronco before I grab a soda for myself and a small jar of peanut butter.

I return to the car after checking out, setting the bag down at her feet. She doesn't say anything as I pull out of the parking lot and take a left, following the hill that leads from downtown Pacific Shores to the neighborhoods above it. I turn down the street I grew up on, Hillside Road, passing my childhood home and the tree I found Elena climbing all those years ago.

I don't know who lives in that house now, but the tree is still there, and in the prime of spring, it's blossoming brightly with the purple flowers she always loved. It gives me hope that the spot I'm taking her will also be in bloom.

It looks different now as I turn down the dirt road that leads to the power plant. Rather than a rugged knoll, it's being turned into a new housing development. Some of the homes are already built, having finishing touches put on before the new owners move in. Others are still vacant, planned to be built next.

The development is fenced off during construction, but luckily, I know the owner of the real estate company that's heading it, and he left me the code to the lockbox when I first discovered the area being excavated about a year ago.

It was right after Elena moved home. I needed air and space and open sky to come to terms with the fact that I was going to be sharing this town with her again. That I was at risk of running into her, of seeing her face, of being pelted by memories and gutted by the reminder that she is, in fact, real. I couldn't handle it back then, after not seeing her for so long.

So, I ran.

I ran until I ended up in the place that used to belong to the two of us. I was distraught to find that it was being made into housing. That someday, someone else would own the slice of land that once was my haven.

My friend Tyler, and the owner of the development company, happened to be onsite at the time, and after I told him that it used to be a place I liked to come to read, draw, and stargaze, he gave me the code to return. I never did.

Not until now.

It was never meant to be my spot; it was always meant to be ours.

And soon enough, it won't be, but for tonight, maybe it can save us.

"Are we going to the old spot?" Elena turns to me, eyes still brimming with tears, nose still red, and lips swollen. "I thought it wasn't there anymore. My dad has been complaining about all the construction they're doing up here."

"There is, but I know a guy." I force a smile, trying to hide my own trepidation.

I pull up to the fence and hop out, punching in the code on the lockbox before taking out the key, unlocking the gate, and sliding it open. I drive through before getting back out to re-lock it so I can ensure we aren't disturbed. The sun is just beginning to set in the distance, and with the lot being locked and vacant, I assume all the workers have left for the evening.

I drive past the winding rows of new houses, taking us to

the highest point of the cliffside, where construction hasn't quite yet started. Still located behind the fence line of the original neighborhood we used to sneak through to get up here, there is a large, vacant corner lot that spans out to the cliff's edge, and the sparkling ocean beyond it.

I back my Bronco in so that the bed of it faces the horizon before killing the ignition. Elena looks at me hesitantly, and I squeeze her thigh, nodding behind me. "C'mon, Little Vice. Grab the snacks."

I get out of the truck, walking to the back and opening my tailgate before lifting the compartment inside to pull out a large beach towel and a picnic blanket that I keep stashed inside. I lower the back seats before laying the towel down over the tailgate, then motion for Elena to get inside.

She still looks unsure but doesn't say anything as she climbs atop the tailgate and crawls inside, resting against the back of the front seats. I follow her movements, throwing my arm around her and tugging her head against my chest.

The view is damn-near perfect. The knoll expands in front of us, where I imagine the backyard of the future home on this lot will be. Beyond it is the Pacific. Vast and unending. The sun isn't quite flushed with the water yet, still hovering just above it, slightly to the left of where we're facing. It casts the water in glittering gold, and a temperate breeze flutters around us, causing the grass and the wild violets within it to dance.

We sit in silence for some time. I know she spends much of it silently crying out the pain she endured earlier today, and I let her do so without interruption, because I know it's what she needs to process. Every so often a sniffle vibrates against my chest, or my shirt sticks to my skin, wet with tears. I don't bother her, though. I know she'll speak when she's ready.

The sun slowly sinks past the horizon, like the water is swallowing it whole. The lower it goes, the darker the sky becomes, morphing from shades of blue to pink and orange, before twilight takes over and the deep shades of indigo and lavender arise, stars glittering overhead.

"Why'd you want to come here?" Elena whispers.

I figured that question was coming, and I've taken the time to think it through, so words flow easily from my mouth when I say, "I fell in love with you instantly. The moment I saw you. Right in front of my childhood home, at eleven years old, I knew then that I'd never love someone else.

"But your love for me grew slowly. Over years, and trust, and patience. It took time for you to see me in the light I always dreamed you would. I know a big part of that is because you fell for him first, and I know that is the foundation for much of your guilt. If only you'd loved me first, right?" I whisper against the top of her head.

She nods.

"I want you to know that I don't see it that way. No matter what you think, no matter what anyone else thinks, or what venom they spew your direction, it doesn't change anything for me. It doesn't change what happened, and it doesn't minimize the love you had for him—or he for you. If you hadn't loved him, he wouldn't magically still be here. The world doesn't work like that, no matter how much you convince yourself it does. I don't know the reason for all of it. Maybe I'll find out when I die, or maybe I'll never know at all, but for some reason he was meant to leave when he did. I think whatever force makes those types of decisions knew that already, and wanted to make sure he got to experience that kind of love before he went."

She inhales, breath picking up at my words. I lift her head away from my chest, grasping her face and turning her to face me. "Your love is a gift. To him. To me. I hate the reality where he left us, and I wish that he was here, but in every single reality that exists, it was meant to be you and me, Elena."

She blinks, and the tears welling in her eyes flow over, streaming down her cheeks. I catch them with my thumbs and wipe them away, continuing. "I loved you immediately, and you loved me slowly, but that's okay. It doesn't change anything. Not for me." Her eyes fall shut, and the exhale that leaves her lips is one of solace. "You fell in love with me right here, in this place. I picked you violets from this grass and kissed you for the first time against a sunset just like this one. So much has changed since those days and right now, but the sun still falls into the ocean, and the stars still circle above our heads, and I still love you. I need you to be reminded of that when you feel you are to blame, when you're being swallowed by your guilt—I'm as steady as the sunset and the stars and the wild violets. I love you."

Her bottom lip trembles, and as her eyes open, the last remnants of the sinking sun glow against her, causing them to catch fire. Molten amber and liquid caramel stare back at me through those eyes—the most beautiful thing in existence.

"August." She sighs, lifting her hands to place them over mine where they hold her cheeks. "I..."

"You don't have to say it back right now. I know your heart." I bring her forehead to my mouth, pressing my lips against her skin. "I feel your soul. The words don't change anything. I'm still steady."

"It's not that," she whispers. "I want to, but I'm afraid."

"Afraid of what, my chaos?"

"My love is cursed," she murmurs, lifting her head as her gaze locks on mine. "I say the words, and people tend to die."

"Elena," I rasp, shaking my head. "Every person who's ever died did so being loved by someone else. Does that mean it's all cursed?"

"I don't know."

I take a deep breath, leaning against the back of the passenger seat and sliding my hands down her body until they reach her hips. I move her to straddle me, and she follows my movements until her legs rest on either side of mine, and her hands hold my shoulders.

Tucking a loose strand of hair behind her ear, I say, "I don't think you're afraid of love, Elena. I think you're afraid of the inconsistency of it."

She tilts her head with perplexity. "What do you mean?"

"You know with certainty that you are loved by your brothers. By your parents. If you lost them tomorrow, as devastating as it would be, you would know they left loving you.

"You didn't have that with Zach. His love was inconsistent. It was always a question. You don't know if he loved you when he died. You don't know if he ever loved you at all."

Her breath hitches, eyes glossing over as the realization settles in.

I don't know the full extent of whatever conversation they had on his final day, but I do know that he showed up to her apartment the night before, after going out drinking with her brothers. I know that the next morning, he came to me in a rage after finding out we'd chosen each other.

If I had to guess, he went after Elena that night in an attempt at getting her back, and she told him it was too late. If I had to guess, they likely spat the kind of venom only they were capable of poisoning each other with. He admitted he said some things to her he'd live to regret.

Like my final moments with him, there was no closure, and no resolution. At surface level, it was disdain and fury for all of us, and I may be the only other person on the planet that has some understanding of the burden that she carries.

"No." She swallows, breath rattling. "It wasn't a question. I know exactly how he felt." My stomach drops at the hopeless tone in her voice. "The last words he said to me were: 'You are impossible to love.'"

That sinking sensation inside me plummets further, desolation icing my veins.

"Oh, Elena," I whisper, grabbing her face again. "He didn't mean it. You know that, right?" I press her forehead against mine, aligning our gazes so she can see the conviction in my eyes. "He told me he said some things he'd come to regret, and I know with certainty, he was referring to exactly that."

She closes her eyes, shaking her head against mine. "I said

something even worse."

"You can tell me, baby. Tell me what's been hurting you so I can fix it."

She takes a shuddering inhale, as if in physical pain at the memory. "I told him I wished he'd leave again. That I wished he wouldn't return."

It's like a blow to the chest, realizing all the anger and hurt of that day. The way we all damaged each other. One gone sinking with their rage, and two left behind to carry the weight of the blame.

"I said terrible things too. We all hurt each other, and he'd feel this pain if the roles had been reversed, so I have to believe that wherever he is now, he's empathizing with us.

"We never saw what was coming. We didn't know the weight the words would hold, but he'd already forgiven us by the time it was said and done."

"There's no way to know for sure, though, is there?"

I shake my head against hers, gripping the base of her neck to hold her against me. To keep her feet on the ground and her heart on the earth. Like atmosphere and gravity.

"Let me tell you what I do know," I whisper. "I love you, Elena.

"I love you as a person. I love you as a woman. I love you as a friend. I love you when you're near me and when you're far away. I've loved you when you didn't love me back. I've loved you when I wish I hated you." Tears fall from her cheeks, and I kiss them away with every confession. "You're ingrained into the fabric of my being. Your name is carved into my bones and etched across my soul. There is not a reality that I exist in where I don't love you. I'll never leave it up for debate, I'll never allow you to question it. I will never be apart from you without it being clear.

"I love you when I'm living, and I'll love you when I'm dead. I loved you when you were my best friend. I loved you when I watched you love someone else. I loved you when you were my enemy and my bad habit and my vice. There is no sin you could commit, no mistake you could make. I'll keep loving you through every single falter in your steps forward, even if it means you're walking away."

Her entire body trembles in my arms, and I feel her lips quivering against my chin as I continue to kiss away her tears. I feel them on my flesh as they move with the words she speaks. "I'm not walking away. I can't anymore. I don't think I deserve you, and I don't think I can be convinced, but I'm too selfish to let you go."

"Good," I rasp, eyes locking on her lips. "Be selfish. Let me be yours."

"I don't know if I know how to love someone anymore. I don't even know how to love myself." Her bottom lip slips beneath her teeth as she studies my face, dragging a hand up my neck and cupping my jaw. "I don't know how to say the words."

"I don't need them," I whisper. "I feel them in every brush of our skin. Every kiss." I press my lips to her jaw. "Every sweet moan of my name that leaves your mouth. You can show me your love, Elena. I'll cherish it all the same. I'll teach you to love yourself again, too."

I run my hand down her neck and over the center of her chest, until it rests atop her pounding heart. I feel the rhythm of it against my palm, steady and rapid and all-consuming.

"You touch me like my skin heals your soul wounds," she whispers.

"It does." I raise my eyes to meet hers, allowing the conviction in my soul to blaze through. Allowing her to see and sense and feel the raw fervor in my gaze, knowing that she needs confirmation beyond words. "Let mine heal you too."

Chapter Thirty-Three

Violet

"Love Song" - Lana Del Rey

I drag my hand toward her shoulder, allowing it to slip beneath the lapel of her cardigan, pushing it down her arm. She offers a subtle nod, granting permission for me to repeat the movement on her other side. I work the sweater off of her, tossing it aside before moving to her hips and inching beneath the fabric of her tank top, gliding my fingers up her stomach.

She sighs, eyes fluttering as she lifts her arms and lets me pull it over her head. She reaches behind her back, unclasping her bra and tossing it aside, too, until she's left in my lap wearing nothing but the same black tennis skirt she had on the first time I fucked her.

I hike it over her thighs, letting it bunch at her waist as I slide my hand around her backside, grasping her ass and flushing her against me. She grasps the hem of my Henley and raises it over my stomach in silent request.

I help her tug it off, and her hands are flying to the buttons on my jeans, unzipping them just enough to reach into the waistband of my underwear and pull out my already hard cock.

My eyes are glued to her hand as it grips my base, and a spark of heat erupts at the base of my spine, causing me to grit my teeth and bite back a moan.

"Augustus," she whispers, pumping me hard. "Look at me."

My eyes snap to her face—radiant with passion.

"You're my ultraviolet."

My breath hitches, cock pulsing in her hand. I swallow, panting with need as she raises her hips and positions me against her entrance. She's already fucking wet—so warm as she sinks down on me slowly. The moment my piercings brush against her walls, Elena's eyes roll back, mouth dropping open.

She removes her hand, dropping her hips so that our bodies are entirely flush, and my cock throbs at the tight, soft feel of her wrapped around me. Her body clenches as she rocks her hips against me, causing both of us to gasp.

Wrapping both hands behind my neck, she rests her forehead against mine, rolling her body, connecting us in a way that would be impossible to untangle.

It's fucking primal, the way I swallow the heavy whimpers that she feeds into my mouth with each movement.

We don't talk, but we lock gazes, allowing our eyes to speak our words. Our tongues tangle, but we don't kiss, allowing ourselves to taste each other's moans. We don't touch, we feel, hands grazing each other's skin, allowing our souls to bind.

I wonder if her flesh is laced with stardust, because this connection of two bodies can only be described as something cosmic.

We were written long ago, when the stars themselves were created.

I drag my hand up her back, feeling the sway of her hair against my knuckles as I twist it into my palm and grip hard, forcing her head to snap up. "Look at the stars, Elena. Watch as I make them collide for you."

A carnal moan falls from her lips, and I drag my tongue up the column of her neck, following her gaze toward the stars above us. The same constellations we branded on each other's bodies years ago wink back, like they've been waiting for this moment too.

I bracket my hips, driving deeper into her and setting a punishing pace.

My eyes fall closed, savoring all other senses. The softness of her skin beneath my hands, and the warm welcoming of her body as she lets mine inside her. The smell of her arousal, and the taste of the fizzy remnants of passion fruit soda left behind from her lips. The sound of her breath as she chases euphoria within my arms.

Because this isn't sex. This is love. A first for both of us.

"August," she rasps, and my eyes fly open.

She's still writhing atop me, driving herself down with every roll of her hips. The world is in full darkness now, only the light of the moon hovering above her, casting its glow upon her like a halo. She's stunning in this light, but as I lift a hand to her face, I notice the tear slipping down her cheek.

"Baby." I grip her hip hard enough to halt her movements. "Am I hurting you?"

She smiles, and another tear falls as she shakes her head. Placing her hand over mine, she drags it up her stomach and to her chest, until it's against her heart.

"No," she whispers. "I just missed you."

"I'm right here, Elena. Right here, my love."

I keep my hand where she placed it, sliding the other behind her neck to tangle in her hair. She drops her head to mine again, and her tears drip off her chin and onto my chest.

"I missed your soul," she says with heavy breath. "I missed my best friend. I often wonder how I lived life without you." She sucks in a ragged inhale, voice fractured. "But I think now I realize I wasn't living at all." She lifts her body before dropping down again, and my cock pulses as need builds in the base of my spine, hot and desperate. "I used to get so homesick, and then I came back, but the sickness stayed." With a trembling hand, I wipe her cheeks. "I think it was because I was sick over you. You're home to me."

I nod, my eyes stinging with tears of my own. "Come home, baby. I've been waiting for you."

She gasps, and her head falls into my shoulder as she grinds down, rocking her hips frantically. Her nails dig into the skin of my shoulder, pussy tightening as she begins to break.

"I love you, Elena," I whisper. "Let it all go, Little Vice. Come home to me."

"August," she cries against my neck as she loses herself. Her body goes taut, limbs trembling as her climax crashes over her.

I hold her tightly, helping her ride it out until I feel her go limp—entirely spent. She's panting against my mouth as I continue fucking her through it, chasing her orgasm with my own.

It's when the soft murmured "I love you" falls graciously from her luscious lips that the heat in my spine explodes, and my entire soul shatters like an imploding planet.

I'm mindless, gasping and moaning, driving into her with force as my release barrels through me, begging to fill every space inside her—claiming her wholly.

She continues the whispers, up my neck and over my jaw, imprinting her words deep into my skin. It's when she reaches my mouth that I allow my eyes to open, finding hers staring back at me, still glistening with tears.

There's a smile on her face now as she murmurs the soul-healing sentiment into my open and desperate mouth, "I love you, Augustus."

I surge forward, capturing her lips in a searing and fervent kiss. Our bodies are still connected, still writhing as I flush us together, kissing her hard. Her tongue drags against my lips, and I moan as it tangles with mine. What was soft and vulnerable has turned intimate and fierce.

"You're home now, Elena," I rasp into her mouth. "I'm never letting you go again. Do you understand?"

"Hold me forever," she pleads, bucking her hips against me. I'd only begun to come down from the high of my orgasm, but we both whimper as I begin to harden inside her again. I feel her smiling against my lips as she muses, "Are you going to show me your love for a second time, Augustus?"

I flip us around, laying her gently on top of the blanket in the back of my Bronco. With the roof off, she's given a perfect view of the cloudless sky—like the night cleared just for us.

Laughing into her mouth, I kiss her once more.

"Now, Elena, I'm going to fuck you under the stars you love so much."

Chapter Thirty-Four

Vice

"warm glow" - *Hippo Campus*

A tension headache pounds against my eyelids as I pull into one of the parking spots in the employee lot behind the boardwalk. Lowering the visor, I wipe beneath my eyes to clear any last remnants of my tears—profuse sobbing the primary source of my headache—before snapping it shut and getting out of my car.

I finally saved up enough money to buy myself a car. Well, to afford the down payment on a car. It's used, and ten years old, but it has decent mileage, and I'm guaranteed a lifetime maintenance warranty at Ramos Automotive on account of my last name being scrawled across the front of the building.

The most important thing was having reliable transportation for myself, because I was so goddamn tired of walking everywhere, borrowing cars from one of my brothers, or having to ask for rides. I'll be thirty in a couple of months, and I desperately needed something that could help me feel independent. I was ready to finally begin getting back on the right track.

So, I told the love of my life that I do, in fact, love him. The next day, I scheduled my first therapy appointment, and then I bought myself a car. It's a burgundy Kia, and it's kind of ugly, but I love it anyway.

My first therapy appointment was supposed to be last week, but as the day approached, I began feeling irrationally anxious and exceptionally emotional. So bogged down by my own mind,

I ended up canceling the session entirely, and had no intention to reschedule.

Then, about ten days later, my period appeared, and everything clicked into place. The anxiety-ridden distress was because of my PMDD, and I hadn't even realized it at the time. It looks so different every month, and when I'm not tracking my cycle, it can be hard to understand what's going on in my body. Plus, those days tend to feel drawn out and beyond reality—I'm fully convinced I am as crazy as I think, and my anxiety is as warranted as my mind tells me it is, so it's difficult to rationalize anything at all.

The funny thing is, in those moments, August never once suggested I reschedule my appointment. He never told me to calm down, or that I was overreacting. He came home the first night with a couple of pre-rolled joints and curled up with me in bed while showing me dozens of videos he saved on his phone that featured people being injured in the most hilarious of ways, because he knows they make me laugh when I'm high.

He made me food when I didn't want to eat, held me when I couldn't sleep, and never complained about watching my favorite television shows. He ran me baths and washed my hair. He never touched me without asking and didn't initiate sex until I did. Even then, he continued asking me if I was okay until I got borderline annoyed about it, pinned his hands above his head, and rode him so hard he went cross-eyed.

A couple of days ago, when my period ended and I was feeling much better, I told him I planned on rescheduling my therapy session, and he merely kissed the top of my head before whispering, "I knew you would."

I've never known someone to have such confidence in me. I've never known someone who knew me well enough to see through my mind in ways I myself am blind to.

Though, therapy itself ended up being far more painful than I had anticipated. First, she asked me about my childhood, my relationship with my parents, and with my brothers. But we spent most of the session talking about why I canceled before. It was easy enough to open up to my therapist, Jocilyn, about my PMDD, because it felt less heavy than all of my other trauma.

She suggested I start tracking my cycle again so I can better anticipate it, and that I see a doctor to get checked out and see if a switch in birth control may help, or potentially explore antidepressants. She validated the way my symptoms have changed over the years, and how life's stressors can contribute to the severity of the illness.

That's when she asked me about my trauma, and why I'm seeking therapy.

For some reason, I immediately broke down. I didn't know where to begin. The words spilled from me like vomit. It was wretched and painful. I gave her the surface level of my past, and the trauma that came with it, along with all the consequences I've been facing since. My poor excuse for a life in New York, my poor coping with alcohol, and my guilt for allowing the same boy I ran away from to save me.

She said there is a lot to unpack, and she looks forward to seeing me again, but that she wants me to remind myself that my grief is valid, and so is my happiness. I can feel both emotions at once, I can hold space for them, but they need not cancel each other out.

I think it's too soon to know if therapy is going to help me or not. All I know right now is that I'm fucking drained, and I don't know how I'm supposed to work the remainder of my shift after an hour of trauma-dumping all over a stranger.

Taking a deep breath, I get out of my car and head inside the back door of The Wicked Wildflower. It's a Friday afternoon, and the weather is stunning—as to be expected in early May. Dahlia finally got around to adding a few tables outside the front doors on the boardwalk, and with the sun shining down over the Pacific, the view is phenomenal. Every table out there is occupied. It's slower inside, just a few customers working quietly in the corner booths.

I walk through the swinging double doors that lead to the

kitchen before stashing my bag in the break room and grabbing an apron. As I exit, I find Dahlia standing at the large counter rolling dough for tomorrow's menu.

"Hey." She smiles at me as she continues working. "How was your session?"

"Good, but also awful?" I laugh, tying the apron around my waist. "I feel exhausted."

"That's normal. A sign that it's probably working." She winks. "I always try and do something relaxing after my sessions, like take a bath. After Lou's, we go home and make her favorite desserts, and after our family sessions, Everett and I typically take her to do something fun together, like go to the movies or surfing."

"You guys attend family therapy?" I ask.

I'd known that Darby had helped Dahlia and her daughter into therapy, and that Everett was seeing one as well to support them, but I didn't know they went together.

"Yeah." She smiles. "He wants to make her adjustment to this new lifestyle as easy as possible for her, and he thinks it helps them bond as a father-daughter dynamic, which is important to him."

"You know, he wouldn't do this for anyone else," I say. "He loves you guys so fucking much. It's sickening."

"I know." She nods, smiling to herself. "Anyway, what do you have planned after your shift later?"

"I honestly hadn't thought that far ahead." I shrug. "Probably reading." I've been hyperfocused on editing my manuscript after work most days, but after today's session, I don't know if I'll be feeling up to it.

"You should come to the beach with Darby and me. I think your mom is going to join us after she finishes her book club this evening."

"What do you guys do at the beach?" I ask.

Dahlia glances up at me, smirking. "You'll have to come with us to see."

I see Dahlia almost every day at work, and I see Darby often enough when she pops in, as well, but we don't spend a significant amount of time together outside of family dinner on Sundays. I make time for coffee dates with my mom, and my brothers will often join too.

I've never been invited to just...hang out with Darby and Dahlia, though. They're sisters, and it feels like something I'd be encroaching on. I was friends with Darby one summer years ago, but outside of that, I've always struggled to maintain girl friendships, often feeling like the odd one out.

"I wouldn't want to impose—"

"Shut up." Dahlia rolls her eyes playfully. "Sisters can't impose. It's impossible. In fact, now that I know you don't have plans, I'm going to be pissed off if you don't join. So, I'll plan to leave when you finish your shift and ask Peggy to complete tomorrow's prep, and then we'll force Darby to sneak away early too."

"Are you sure?"

"Yes." Nodding toward the front of the bakery, she adds, "Now go back to work."

"You have some serious mommy energy."

"I know."

"I guess I'm just confused about the kiddie pools."

The sand is still warm beneath my bare feet, wind whipping my hair as I toss it up into a bun and watch Dahlia and Darby lay out two small heart-shaped inflatable pools on the beach. Darby pulls a bicycle pump out of the wagon she brought down, sticking it into the inflation valve.

"Here, let me do that for you." I step up beside her and pull the pump from her grasp, standing on either side of it and beginning to move the handle up and down, slowly inflating the pool. "If you pump too hard you might give birth."

"Honestly..." She sighs, rubbing her belly. "At this point, you're probably not wrong."

"We blow them up and then sit inside them with blankets

and watch the sunset." Dahlia grabs a cooler from the wagon. "It's more comfortable than sitting on the ground itself, and we don't get sand in every conceivable crevice."

My eyes flit to Darby. "Don't you fuck on the beach like...all the time?"

"Not all the time," she grumbles, then references her belly. "Especially not since this happened."

"Speaking of fucking..." Dahlia laughs, laying out blankets in the pool I just finished inflating while I start on the other. "Can I ask you a question, sister-to-sister?"

There's a long pause before I finally glance up, realizing that she was talking to me.

"Sure?"

"Is August's dick as big as I think it is?"

I bite back the smile begging to tease my lips. "Probably bigger."

Darby blows out a slow puff of air before asking, "Pierced?"

"Yep," I reply, putting the air pump back in the wagon after I finish inflating the second pool.

"And...?" Dahlia asks.

"Yes," I respond, understanding exactly what she's asking.

"His tongue is pierced too," Darby adds.

I grin, dropping a pile of blankets into the second pool. "It very much is."

Both of their brows shoot up, and they toss each other contemplative looks before going back to setting things up.

A few minutes later, the two pink pools sit side-by-side, filled with blankets and pillows. A cooler sits between them that has water, soda, and snacks.

"We used to do wine, but obviously..." Dahlia motions to Darby, who sits beside her in one pool, while I get comfortable in the other. "Plus, you haven't been drinking, right?"

"Nope. Not since January," I say. It's not something I've brought up on my own before, but I suppose I shouldn't be surprised that they know. I'm sure that my drinking was of major concern to my brothers, and I can't be upset that they needed to talk about it with their significant others. "I don't know that I'd call myself an alcoholic or anything...I don't think? It's odd. I never felt like drinking was a problem in my teens or early twenties. It was always social, never an emotional crutch. I don't know when that changed, or what label it puts on me now, but...I just feel better without it. I don't think a glass of wine is going to make me spiral, but I suppose I just don't see the point anymore."

"I think that's great," Darby says. "You don't have to explain yourself to anyone. People choose to stop drinking alcohol for a slew of reasons, and all of them are valid."

I smile. "Thanks."

A moment later, the heavy pounding of rapid footsteps sounds from behind us, and I turn around to see Lou barreling through the sand in our direction. She's still wearing her soccer uniform, sans shin pads and shoes, with my mom trailing behind her. Two pigtail braids bounce at her shoulders as she runs, stopping in front of her mom and aunt.

"Hi," she says breathlessly, bending down to hug Dahlia before placing a hand on Darby's stomach. "Hi to you too, baby."

"Hi, bug. How was practi—"

"Elena, I'm so glad you're here." Lou cuts off her mom as she beelines to the pool I'm in.

"You are?" I ask.

She nods rapidly. "I finished *The Lightning Thief.*"

"Oh?" I laugh. "How did you like it?"

"I brought it with me. It's in the car. Can I sit in your pool with you so we can talk about it? I need to talk about it."

I glance at Dahlia, whose brows are raised, a radiant smile on her cheeks as she watches us.

"Of course." I move to the side, creating room for her as my mom reaches us. "Ciao, Mama," I say, glancing up to smile at her.

"Hi, baby!" she chimes.

"Thanks for grabbing her on your way," Dahlia says.

"Of course, my love." My mom gets into the pool on my other

side, sealing me between her and Lou. Lou goes on animatedly about her experience reading the first book in the Percy Jackson series and how much she loved it as the sun begins to set over the Pacific.

"Do you think you'll ever write a book again?" Lou asks, basically panting after the rapid speech she just finished.

"Actually, I just finished one."

"Really?" Dahlia, Darby, and my mother all ask excitedly.

A burst of laughter leaves my lips. It's been a long time since I've spoken to anyone besides August about my writing, and I forgot the giddy way it feels to talk about your books with others. Especially those who read and love them, which I know Darby does.

"Yeah." I nod. "It's very different from what I've done before. I'm finishing up some self-edits before I send it off to the freelance editor I used to work with years ago. After that, I think I'm going to begin querying agents again."

"No plans to self-publish?" Darby asks.

I shrug. "Maybe. Right now I'm not in any kind of rush. I think I'm just beginning to feel ready to dip my toes back into the industry. Maybe even activate my social media accounts again and begin interacting with readers, promoting my old work."

My mom squeezes my thigh, and when I turn my head to her, tears glisten in her brown eyes. She blinks hard, holding them back. "I'm so proud of you," she whispers, pressing her lips to my temple. "*Sapevo che ti saresti ritrovato. Bentornato.*"

I swallow hard, choking on my own emotion. "*Grazie, Mama. Ti amo.*"

"In the meantime, do you plan on staying at The Wicked Wildflower?" Darby asks.

"No pressure or anything, but please say yes," Dahlia adds.

I laugh. "Yeah. I mean...I think my ultimate dream would be to run, or even own, a bookstore. I feel most myself when I'm reading, or writing, or talking about books. I've learned the hard way that writing can be a fleeting experience. It's something that can be gained and lost, and when you lose it, it's real fucking hard to keep yourself afloat if it's all you have to rely on. I think if I would've felt less pressure to be a writer...maybe I wouldn't have been lost for so long." I sigh before smiling at Dahlia. "But the coffee shop is a great Plan B."

"You know...we have a whole empty suite right next to The Wicked Wildflower." Darby raises a pensive brow. "I have an in with the owner, might be able to get you a deal."

"Oh, my God. A bookstore. Yes!" Lou squeals.

"A bookstore on the pier probably wouldn't make much money," I say.

"Who cares?" she scoffs, leaning back against the edge of the pool and tilting her head toward the sky, closing her eyes. "The building is just sitting there collecting dust right now anyway."

"Yeah, but it would cost a ton to run it."

"Eh." Darby flutters a hand, dismissing my concern. "I'll be your investor. My husband is rich."

"You could make it a romance-only bookstore and call it Just The Tip," Dahlia muses before her eyes go wide, and she sits up straighter. "No! Between The Folds."

"Lord," my mom mutters under her breath.

"What does that mean?" Lou asks.

"Nothing," the rest of us chime in unison.

Darby giggles. "You could call it Vise Grip."

I cackle at that before it dawns on me. "No." I smile. "I'd call it Sugar and Vice. It's all romance, with a range from sickly sweet rom-coms to delicious dark romance to enticing erotica."

"Oh, that's fucking good. All that alliteration? That's a tagline right there." Dahlia nods. "You should have the shelves categorized by extreme niches, though. Instead of genres. Like a When She Calls Him Good Boy section, or Secret Tattoo, or Public Indecency."

"Mom, please stop," Lou mutters, causing us all to laugh.

We volley a few more names back and forth before the conversation merges into different topics. Darby's due date, her birth plan, and how excited she is to finally have her baby girl. We talk about Dahlia, Lou, and Everett's summer trip that he finally surprised her with a few weeks ago, and I make tremendous effort to bite back the giggle I want to let out as I think about Everett's plan to propose over the summer.

I didn't realize it until just now, but this is the first time I've stepped on the beach since moving home from New York a year ago. The first time I've stepped foot on the beach since before Zach died.

I thought I'd never do so again, or when I did, it'd be painful and sad, but right now, it feels like this moment was the exact reason I waited so long. So that I could do it with people who would make it feel okay. I know that guilt and grief will always linger, but as I watch the world cast in shades of blue and gold, and the sea air whips at my face, smelling like home, I realize that there is a life beyond that hurt.

Maybe it is true after all: the presence of pain doesn't have to equate to the absence of happiness.

Chapter Thirty-Five

Violet

"Space Song" - Beach House

Elena

I'm hanging out with Darby, Dahlia, and my mom after work. I'll be home later!

I smile, reading over the text message from Elena that she sent hours ago. It's long past dark when I lock up the building and head out to my car. I call Elena on the drive home to check if she ate with the others or if I should pick something up, but she doesn't answer.

Her car isn't in the driveway when I pull up, which has me pausing. It's well past nine o'clock, and I assumed Elena would be home by now. I try calling her again, and my stomach drops when I hear her voicemail for a second time.

I try Darby next, but she doesn't answer either.

My breath lodges in my throat, breathing heavy as I scramble to pull up Leo's contact name and try him next. If something had happened, surely, they would've let me know, right?

I sigh with relief as Leo answers on the third ring. "Hey, Auggie."

"Do you know where your sister is? Did Darby come home? She sent me a text earlier that she was going out with them, but she's still not home, and I'm—"

"Come over, Augustus." Leo laughs. "Take a damn breath and meet us at my house."

Before I can ask any follow-up questions, he ends the call. I immediately back out of my driveway and make the four-block commute to where he and Darby live. Elena's car is parked across the street, Everett's orange Jeep and Dahlia's Honda are both against the curb, and Leo and Darby's Mustang is in the driveway.

I pull behind Dahlia's car and hop out of mine, jogging up the front steps. The house looks like it could be on the cover of *Better Homes & Gardens* with the way Darby has landscaped the front with honeysuckles and hydrangeas, and the cozy elegance of the white wrap-around porch and the soft blue-painted two-story cottage-style layout.

I don't bother knocking, and it's mostly quiet as I enter. The house is painted in dim lighting, only the lamp in the front entryway illuminating the space, while the dining room to my left, and kitchen through it, are dark. The staircase directly in front of me that leads to the second floor is also dark, and a faint warm glow seems to come from the living area around the corner from the front door.

Everett startles me as he appears around that corner a second later, smiling as he holds a finger to his lips. He nods for me to follow him.

When I turn the corner, I'm taken aback by the sight that has become the living room of Darby and Leo's home. There are blankets and pillows piled high in front of the couch, and small lights strung up all around the room with tacks. A bowl of popcorn sits on the floor half-eaten, along with a pan of brownies and three bags of assorted potato chips.

Darby lies on her side on the massive, plush sofa, sleeping soundly. Two figures are just visible under the mound of blankets on the floor, but Dahlia's and Elena's faces peek out of them—both asleep as well.

Flashes of light filter over all of their faces, and I turn to realize that a movie is still playing on the television mounted to the wall.

Everett stands beside me, watching them as he smiles, and I find Leo on the other side of the room, leaning against the wall while he does the same.

"They're having a sleepover," Leo whisper-shouts, walking across the room and patting me on the back as he passes me. "Let's let them sleep. Help me build some baby furniture."

He begins ascending the stairs, and Everett and I follow him up to the second-story hallway. Leo opens the door to the room at the end of the hall, flipping on the light to reveal a pastel-yellow painted nursery. One wall is covered in a mural of flowers and vines. A crib sits against that wall, with a rocking chair in the corner, what I assume is a changing station beside it, and a small couch beneath the window.

"I need to build that dresser." Leo nods to a large cardboard box sitting at the center of the room. Everett opens the box as I begin pulling out its parts, and Leo reads through the instructions.

"I don't think Elena has ever had a sleepover in her life," I say.

"She's never had sisters before," Everett responds, and when my head snaps up, so does his. He smiles at me with something akin to pride shining in his face.

"I came home after my evening surf session and found the girls sitting at the dining room table with our mom and Lou." Leo sits down cross-legged onto the floor beside us. "Elena was showing them all how to make those crystal keychains she used to give us all the time. Remember?" He snorts a laugh. "She was going through all the different kinds and what protection they'd offer so everyone could pick which one they felt like they needed most. I guess they'd hung out at the beach all afternoon and decided to have a craft night."

"I came over when I got home and realized the girls weren't there," Everett adds. "Mom offered to take Lou for the night, and then the girls made us go sit in the garage so they could watch *13 Going On 30* uninterrupted." He scratches his beard, laughing. "We came back two hours later and all three of them were asleep."

"Elena went to the beach?" I ask.

Everett's and Leo's heads snap up, brows drawing as the realization dawns on them both.

"She's never gone to the beach. Not since..." I trail off.

Everett looks directly at me. "She's getting better, isn't she?"

"Yeah," I say confidently. "She has been for quite some time. It's been slow but steady."

"They were talking about opening a bookstore," Leo says in an astonished breath.

"Elena was?" I ask.

"Elena was...hesitantly optimistic." He laughs, running a hand through his hair. "My wife on the other hand... She was enthusiastically offering to finance the whole thing."

I chew the inside of my cheek. "If Elena wanted to open a bookstore, would you help?"

The two brothers glance at each other, offering up an expression that tells me a conversation has already been had about it, before Leo says, "We haven't considered a bookstore before. I'm honestly not sure how well one would do on the boardwalk, but... yeah. If that's what she wanted, of course I'd help."

I smile, and Leo tilts his head as he studies me. "August, are you in love with her?"

"Yeah," I breathe.

"She in love with you?"

A grin splits my cheeks so wide I have to dip my head bashfully. "Yeah."

I hear the sound of a short laugh, but when I lift my head again, it's seriousness on both of their faces. "Is this going to end with either of you getting hurt?" Everett asks.

"I don't know what answer you're looking for, but I think you know that I can't tell you with certainty that nobody will ever be hurt again." I bite my lip. "What I can tell you is that Elena's healed enough to take risks, and that's what this is for both of us. We know it's not normal, and not everyone is going to be happy with it or accepting, but we want each other badly enough that we're willing to wade through it all."

Her brothers only stare back at me like the answer I provided isn't sufficient enough.

I swallow, continuing, "I can tell you that I'm fucking crazy about her. Literally. I'd die for her, and I'm not even exaggerating, but I think you both knew that already. She's been my best friend my entire life, and the two of us are inherently better people when in the presence of the other. I can tell you with certainty that whenever she is hurt in life, whatever the reason, I'll be there to mend her broken pieces. I think I've proven that of myself by now. There are no lengths I won't go to for her, and you can think what you want of the choice we've made, but your opinion won't change it."

They blink at me, straight-faced. My ass is all the way inside my throat as I wait for their response, until Leo's dimples pop with a smirk. "I always did think you were the best person for her."

I smile back at him before turning to Everett expectantly. He looks less convinced, but his lips tilt up slightly. "I'm always going to worry about her, so don't hate me for being cautious. I think you're the best person for her too."

I nod, and Everett claps me on the back before adding, "And if it's worth anything, I think he would've accepted it too. If that's any guilt you two are harboring, I think it's worth letting go."

The words slice far deeper than Everett could've intended, because while we finally addressed where Elena and I stand tonight, there are still darker truths that they don't know. Elena and I had decided a few weeks ago we'd stop sneaking around and officially tell her family about us when the time felt right. Things have been hectic, and we've all been busy, but she and I gave each other permission to disclose the status of our relationship if or when it arose.

We haven't discussed our past, though.

It's easy enough to say that it's not of anyone else's concern, but the feeling is different. As I stare my two childhood best friends in the eye right now, knowing that I'm lying, I can't possibly imagine going the rest of my life like this. They weren't directly involved in the tragic triangle made up of Elena, my brother, and myself, but they were two existing points beside it. They weathered all of its fallout.

I can't go into it with them right now, though. Not without Elena being present. Not when Leo is on the cusp of having his first child, and so much joy and healing is taking place.

There will be time for those conversations, but it's not now.

"Thanks," I choke out, clearing my throat.

Leo smiles as Everett focuses on aligning two pieces of the dresser, holding an Allen wrench between his teeth. I begin sorting through the various parts of assembly while Leo tears down and folds the box, when Everett's head snaps sideways, and his brow furrows with concern. "Wait a fucking second, that text message you sent me a few weeks back...?"

I wince. "We should probably agree here and now that we never again talk about my sex life."

Everett's nostrils flare. "I think we need to agree that you check who the fuck you're texting before you hit send."

"I know." I grimace. "I'm sorry."

Leo frowns. "I'm scared to know."

"Best you don't," Everett murmurs.

Chapter Thirty-Six

Vice

"Love Like Ghosts" - Lord Huron

"Just make sure you keep this over it for the next few days. If it begins to peel on its own, or if your skin gets irritated, it's okay to take it off, just avoid getting the tattoo wet."

I listen to August finish up his final appointment of the day from where I rest on the leather bench he keeps at the front of the shop as a waiting area. The woman had a huge upper thigh piece completed, and while it's gorgeous, I'll never be completely rational at the sight of his hands on someone else.

It might make me crazy, but I don't care.

I decided I didn't want to go home and be without him tonight. I checked my email when I finished my shift at the coffee shop and realized I had a response from one of the agents I queried a couple of weeks ago. My manuscript isn't even finished yet, but Penelope's sister-in-law is apparently a hotshot literary lawyer and offered to float my name around to a few of her contacts after she'd read my backlist herself.

The email I received today was from my top choice agent, and I'm too fucking scared to open it, so instead of going home, I stayed at the boardwalk. I took a walk down the pier with my brothers, spent much of the afternoon in Heathen's helping them re-organize their display shelves, and then meandered down to Boardwalk Tattoo.

August was in the middle of the session when I came in, but

after I said a quick hello and went to leave again, he asked his client if his "girlfriend" could stay. Something about it was so hot. The way his hands were on another woman's skin, his focus solely on the art, all while making it abundantly clear that he belonged to me.

I've been wet ever since.

"Bye, Elena," his client, Ivy, calls as she reaches the door. "It was nice meeting you!"

"You too."

Once the glass door closes behind her, August locks it up and turns off the main lights. The space becomes illuminated only by the neon signs that hang strategically throughout the shop. He stands above me, smiling down as I lean back on the bench. Extending his hand to me, he nods toward the back of the room. "Come sit with me while I close up."

I place my hand in his, letting him pull me into a standing position before he plants his lips on mine—hard and needful, like he's been waiting all day for it. He walks me over to the bench he was just working on before he wipes it down with a cleaning solution and motions for me to take a seat.

"Have I ever told you that I think it's beautiful in here? The way you decorated, the lights, the art." My eyes track the entirety of the shop before landing on the largest of the neon signs he has hung up. On the main wall, above the majority of the workbenches, lit in fluorescent purple, it reads: *You are the artist and the art*. There are hand-drawn chalk creations all across the same wall—some from August and his staff, others from clients who come in and want to leave a drawing or a message. It's a chaotic mural of beautiful mess and, like everything else in this building, inherently Augustus Hayes.

He pauses from where he pushes a large broom across the floor, grinning at me. "Thanks."

"Don't get offended by this, but why the name?" I ask. "It doesn't seem to match the uniqueness of the business itself."

August sighs, leaning his broom against the wall before

closing the space between us. He places his hands on the bench between my legs, leaning into me until our faces align. "I had another name in mind before I opened, but by the time I did, it didn't feel right anymore. At that point..." His emerald eyes go distant behind his glasses before he shakes it off, drawing his attention back to me. "I wasn't feeling very creative. Tattoo shop on the boardwalk. Boardwalk Tattoo. Made sense."

"What was the other name?" I ask, sliding my hand up his chest and neck before bracketing his jaw and running my thumb over his cheek.

He leans into my touch, his eyes falling closed. "Violet Muse."

"August..." My stomach drops. "You were going to name it after..."

"Us." He nods.

I don't know how to respond, so I bring his mouth to mine, feathering my lips against his and hoping he can taste the desolation it brings me. He kisses me back, groaning as I slide my tongue against his, opening him up to me.

"I'm sorry," I whisper as his teeth clatter against my bottom lip, our joining painful and messy and beautiful and soft all at once.

His hands grip my hips, forcing me to the edge of the bench and flushing our bodies together. I moan as his hard length presses against me. "Don't be," he murmurs into my mouth before dragging it along my jaw and down my collarbone. "Everything happened the way it did so we could end up here, Elena," he says into my skin, kissing every place his mouth can reach. "We were meant to be together back then. We're meant to be together now."

"If you were to name it after us now, what would it be called?"

He suddenly pulls back, gazing down at me with fervent eyes. "Ultraviolet."

Time seems to suspend itself, like this moment is of some grander significance that a higher power wants us to be aware of. I'm only capable of answering by surging forward, grasping his neck, and hauling his mouth to mine, kissing him with everything in me.

He moans as I writhe against his body, whispering, "And I'm going to do exactly that. Rename this place just as soon as you open your bookstore right next door."

"I didn't tell you about the bookstore yet," I say, panting.

"Doesn't matter. You're going through with it, Elena, and we're going to be beside each other in the end. Just like it was always meant to be." He pulls back and begins untucking his shirt from his trousers. "Now, I want you to lie back on that bench and take off your pants for me."

I nod rapidly, swiftly undoing the button on my jeans, but before I can begin sliding them off my hips, a resounding "What the fuck?" echoes throughout the dimly lit room.

August and I both pause, breath catching. My eyes mirror his as they go wide at the realization that someone else is in the room with us.

He spins at the same time I sit up, peeking around his shoulder. My heart leaps into my throat when I find Everett standing at the corner of the main room and the hallway that leads to the back door. Though shadowed in darkness, I can just make out the deep set of his brows and the frown on his mouth as he crosses his tattooed arms over his chest.

"Everett, what the hell?" I ask. "Why are you standing in the shadows like a fucking creep? Have you never heard of privacy?"

"The back door is unlocked." He steps toward us, waving his hand at the front of the shop. "And there are about a billion windows that look out onto a public fucking boardwalk where anyone walking by can look inside and see what you're doing. Considering you two live together, I'd think if you'd like to have a private conversation, you'd do so in your own goddamn house."

August audibly swallows as he steps beside me, and I make quick work of rebuttoning my jeans. "Well, what do you want?"

My twin's eyes dart rapidly between August and me. "You two were together before? Before Zach died? Is that what I'm gathering?"

Fuck. My breathing hits a rapid pace as my heart thrashes against my chest, and my stomach flips with a sick feeling that must fall somewhere between guilt and shame.

"How much did you hear?" August asks.

Disappointment, betrayal, and genuine hurt all seem to war within my brother's eyes as his gaze flashes to August beside me. "Enough."

"There is a lot to unpack," I admit softly. "Now probably isn't the time, but..." I glance at August, and he nods shallowly. "We'll tell you whatever you need to hear."

"You're right," Everett's voice is cold as stone. "Now isn't the fucking time—because Darby's water broke. She's in labor."

Chapter Thirty-Seven

Violet

"Yes I'm Changing" - Tame Impala

Elena and I walk into the waiting room of the birthing center hand-in-hand, and I can't tell if my stomach is about to fall out of my ass or spring from my throat, but I do know that the unease is bone-deep after our confrontation with Everett.

The one solace of this situation is that Darby isn't giving birth at the same hospital my brother died in. A consequence of remaining in the same town where he passed, any emergency, no matter how small, subjects us to reliving the worst moments of our lives.

Thankfully, we haven't had to return to that emergency room since, and Darby and Leo found a midwife at a facility a few miles inland to have their baby. The waiting room here is serene and calm rather than sterile and cold. A fountain runs quietly in the corner of the room, and soft instrumental music strums through the speakers. The seats are plush and comfortable, and there is a large bookcase on the far wall filled with various titles, while the room is warmly lit by standing lamps rather than the blinding fluorescents of a hospital.

Any tranquility the space works to create vanishes when we find the only empty chairs in the waiting area are directly across from Everett, Lou, and Carlos, and beside Monica. Everett left my shop without another word after he informed us Darby's water broke. She's been at home for the last few days after she began showing signs of early labor, so we knew it was coming. Elena and I immediately finished locking up the place before hopping in my car and heading down to the birthing center, and we're still the last to arrive.

I take a deep breath, and she squeezes my hand as we sit down with her family. Elena takes the chair next to Monica, and I sit at the end of the row, directly across from Everett. He eyes me with quiet accusation before shifting his gaze to his daughter as she shows him something on the iPad in her lap.

The way his face brightens when he looks at her is a stark contrast to the darkness he shot in my direction. He has every right to be upset with us, and I wish the information had come out differently.

"Hi, Mama," I whisper to Monica, who beams back at me with the same expression Everett offers Lou—a gripping reassurance. "What's the status?"

"Dahlia is back there with them. Her contractions are only about a minute apart now, and she's seven centimeters dilated. We're just waiting for her to be ready to push."

"I don't know what any of that means." Elena yawns, resting her head against my shoulder. I lift my arm and wrap it around her, not missing the way Everett eyes my every move. "Just tell me when my niece is gonna be here."

"It's hard to say, love. I labored with you for thirty-six hours, but sometimes those kids just slide right out."

"That sounds horrific," Elena huffs, nuzzling her head against me. I glance down and find her eyes closed, realizing just how late it is. I press my lips against her temple.

Time passes in awkward silence, only the murmured whispers between Everett, his parents, and Lou as Elena sleeps against my shoulder. Eventually, Lou falls asleep in the same position on Everett before Dahlia finally comes out to give us an update.

She throws herself into a now-vacated chair next to Monica, huffing as she says, "She's in a lot of discomfort, and things are still moving slowly. Leo's been going on about some blog he read that stated having an orgasm while in labor can help with pain and speed things along. I left as soon as he started talking."

Everett's lip curls. "So, they're just having sex back there right now?"

"No, baby," Dahlia scoffs. "Are you going to make me explain clitoral stimulation to you right now in front of your parents?"

A loud snort rips through the room as Elena suddenly lifts her head, laughing.

Everett frowns at his sister before glancing down at Lou to ensure she's still asleep with her headphones on. "I think you and I both know how well-versed I am in clitoral stimulation, Wildflower, but I'll be happy to remind you later."

"I'm going for a walk," Monica mutters, standing from her chair as Carlos covers his laugh with a cough. "Does anyone want coffee?"

"Yes," we all say at once.

"I'll come with you." Dahlia chuckles. She stands, walking across the aisle and planting a kiss on her daughter's head before turning to her boyfriend. She wraps a hand around his throat and swiftly hauls his mouth to hers, kissing him with nothing but promise. "You better be a man of your word."

"Yes, ma'am," he says breathlessly, grinning with allurement.

"I want us to be that obnoxious," Elena murmurs against my neck.

"You are," Everett mutters, watching Dahlia walk away.

Carlos sighs, rising out of his chair and taking the one his wife just vacated. "I want you two to work this out amongst yourselves." He motions between the twins before turning to Elena. "But I'll say this: the woman I see sitting in front of me now is a glowing reflection of the girl I raised years ago. Better than I could've ever hoped you'd become. I give you full credit for your resilience, my girl, but I can't ignore the support of the hand that held you as you walked through the most painful parts of healing." His eyes flash to me. "The boys may need time to adjust. Remember, this isn't the first time they've watched her love their best friend—and they've also watched the worst possible fallout from that dynamic. Give them grace, but for what it's worth, you have my blessing. And Monica's."

"I'd never concern myself with the blessing of anyone, much less a man, but thank you." She kisses his cheek. "That means a lot, Daddy."

I inhale so swiftly that I choke on oxygen, folding over in my chair as I begin coughing.

"What?" Everett asks, eyeing me suspiciously. "Why are you having a fit?"

"No r...reason," I sputter.

"Oh, because I call August Daddy, too, sometimes," Elena says casually.

I stare at the wall in front of me, the plant in the corner, the ceiling—eyes dancing anywhere but my girlfriend's brother and father—but I feel Everett's stare burning a hole through the center of my goddamn face.

"Fucking Christ," he mutters as Carlos whispers, "Boundaries, *mi corazón*. I don't need to know that."

"Sorry," she chimes back. "I was trying to offend Everett, and you were collateral damage."

"I know, my girl." He laughs.

Elena and I have talked extensively over the last couple of weeks about our past and exactly what explanation we feel we owe her brothers. There are aspects to all of our relationships that we have no obligation to share, but we agreed that they needed to know about Elena and my history before Zach died, and our last moments with him. It's the only way for them to understand the depths of our grief and guilt, and how those complexities tarnished our ability to heal.

I think it's the only way for them to understand just how much it took for her and me to reach the point we're at now, and why the two of us are so confident that we'll be everlasting.

However, I know at this moment, she's feeling defensive and stubborn. She doesn't like the way Everett reacted, and they have a tendency to feed each other's flames.

"Why don't you come with me to get something out of the vending machine? I can't bend down to reach inside those little cubby holes anymore," Carlos says.

"Okay." Elena turns to me, smiling before she presses her lips against mine, whispering, "I love you" as she rises from her chair.

Carlos remains seated, reaching across Elena's empty seat, and landing a pat to my cheek. "*Siempre te he visto como a un tercer hijo, muchacho. No lo arruines.*"

"Was that a threat?" I ask, eyes drifting to Elena, who stands in front of me now. "Is he threatening me?"

"No," she chimes at the same time Everett scoffs, "Yes."

I'm having heart palpitations.

Everett and I descend into heavy silence as Carlos and Elena walk away. Lou is still fast asleep against his shoulder, and he gently adjusts her into a more comfortable position as I whisper, "We obviously planned to sit you and Leo down and talk about all of this. We didn't intend to keep it a secret forever. We needed time to figure things out for ourselves, but I'm sorry it came out how it did."

His brows draw together, his lips a hard line, eyes distant as he stares me down. "Why was it a secret to begin with? Were you two having an affair while she was still with him? Was there overlap?"

I shake my head. "No. I mean..." I pause. "I've been in love with Elena my entire life, so if you're speaking to feelings? Yeah. A ton of overlap on my end. She never told me she loved me back until after my brother left for Wyoming. We didn't kiss, didn't touch, until months later."

"When did you start sleeping together?"

"A few months ago."

His brows raise in surprise. "You weren't intimate back then?"

"You didn't ask if we were intimate. You asked if we slept together."

"What does that even—" He shakes his head. "Never mind.

Doesn't matter." He leans back in his chair, running a hand down his face. We've been here for hours, and it has to be close to dawn by now. "The night before...I was with him. Zach. He kept asking me about Elena's new boyfriend, and I had no idea what he was talking about. I assumed she had some casual fling happening that he was exaggerating." Everett's eyes raise to me. "But he was talking about you, wasn't he?"

I nod.

"He never found out?"

"No." I sigh. "He did. That morning. Just before."

"Fuck." Everett's voice breaks as he leans his head against the wall behind him. "She always spoke of this guilt she had, and I could never understand it. I didn't know what she had to feel guilty about. I didn't know how to fix her." His throat moves as he swallows thickly, and when he faces me again, there are tears glimmering in his eyes. "You knew, though. You fucking knew what was really wrong with her, why she couldn't get better, and you kept it to yourself."

"It wasn't my truth to share."

"It doesn't matter!" he snaps. "If I'd have known, I could've helped her!"

Suddenly, Lou stirs. Everett and I both pause as her eyes flutter open and she sits up, headphones falling off her ears. "Everett?" she asks groggily.

"Hi, Luz. I'm sorry, bug. I didn't mean to wake you." He cuts his gaze to me, eyes fierce and simmering. "We'll finish this later."

She blinks around the empty waiting room. "Where is everybody?"

"They're getting drinks and snacks. Do you want something?" He shifts, pulling his phone from his back pocket. "I can call Dad and ask him to grab—"

Monica comes flying around the corner with Carlos and Elena in tow. "They paged Dahlia while we were getting coffee. Darby is pushing!" she squeals. "They said we can head up to their floor and wait outside the room until they're ready for us."

Everett and Lou jump out of their seats, but I'm suddenly unsure if I'm supposed to go with them. I haven't been present for, well, any birth in my life. I don't know what the protocol is, but I'd assume only direct family members go inside the room when the baby is born.

When Everett stopped by the shop earlier, I was so flustered by our conversation, and by his news, that I left with Elena, but I now realize for the first time that I'm not actually sure I'm supposed to be here.

Yes, Darby is my best friend. So is her husband, and I'm dating his sister, but I'm not family. Not truly.

Lou jogs after Monica and Carlos, who are already heading toward the elevator, but Elena stands at the intersection of the hallway, tilting her head at me curiously. Everett pauses in front of my chair, glancing back. "What are you doing?"

"I don't know if I'm supposed to go. Isn't it family only?"

"Augustus, you are—" Elena starts.

Everett cuts her off, muttering through gritted teeth, "If you do not get your ass in that goddamn room to meet your niece right the fuck now, I will actually hit you."

I hold my hands up, surrendering as I rise from my chair and step in line with Everett. He claps my back, harder than necessary. "The only thing that would be truly unforgivable, Augustus, is if you ever again insinuated that you are not part of this fucking family," he whispers, separating from me when we reach Elena, who twines her fingers through my own.

Chapter Thirty-Eight

Vice

"willow" - Taylor Swift

As we walk into the spacious room, I find my brother pacing the floor, his gaze fixated on the blanket-wrapped bundle he's holding to his bare chest. His head snaps up when he hears the door open, and his eyes are red-rimmed like he's been crying, but the smile that overtakes his face can only be described as radiant.

I squeeze August's hand, the two of us entering last. I'm borderline angry with him for insinuating that he's not family and he has no right to be here. If anything, I'd argue he's more part of this family than I am. But considering the way Everett reacted earlier tonight—or last night, I should say—I don't blame August for suddenly feeling unsure of his place.

"Hey," Leo whispers, walking back over to the bed his wife lies in and gently placing their daughter in her arms before greeting the rest of us with hugs. "Come meet Willow."

I feel bad at the way Darby becomes suddenly crowded by the eight of us, not to mention the two nurses that are popping in and out of the room, but she doesn't seem to mind. Her golden hair is slicked up into a bun atop her head, and the exhaustion in her eyes can't be denied. Yet there is an iridescent glow shrouding her, a happiness so potent it's visual, permeating the air all around us.

"Okay, whoever wants to hold her needs to go wash their hands," Dahlia says.

My mother practically leaps for the sink at the back of the

suite, Everett and Lou moving to follow her. Secretly, I'm terrified of babies, and I definitely don't want to be the first to touch her, because I'm afraid I'll break her. I need to watch someone else go ahead of me so I can copy whatever they do. August stays right beside me at the foot of Darby's bed, quietly asking how she's feeling.

Leo sits at the edge on one side of her, his arm around her shoulder as he strokes back the loose hair on her forehead. My father sits on her other side, rubbing her back. "We're so proud of you, preciosa. Look at what you two made." He nods at the baby in her arms. "She's so beautiful."

"I'm taking no credit." Leo kisses his wife's head. "She's all her mama, and thank God for it."

Darby tilts her neck, glancing up at him. "No, she's definitely half heathen."

"Half heathen and all honey," he whispers. "So, she mostly got the good parts."

She lifts a hand, patting his cheek. "You're all good parts, Leo."

He smiles, and tears begin to glisten in his eyes as he tilts his head, causing Darby's palm to rest against his lips. "Thanks for giving me my baby, Honeysuckle." He holds her wrist, kissing her hand. "It's been a long while since I got to look into the eyes of someone who shares my blood."

It suddenly feels as if we're intruding on an incredibly intimate moment, so I tug on August's hand and walk us to the corner of the room.

"Are you hiding us back here to avoid holding the baby?" he whispers in my ear as Everett, Lou, and my mom rejoin the others after washing their hands.

"Of course not," I hiss.

I definitely am. A little bit.

"Do you think I could hold her first?" Everett asks, eyes fluttering to Dahlia. "I've actually never held a newborn before, probably wouldn't be bad to learn how."

Dahlia gently takes Willow from Darby's arms, transferring her to Everett and showing him how to properly hold her. He paces around the room, bouncing her in his arms as he coos at her adoringly. Our mother stands over his shoulder, watching like a hawk, and I can practically see her vibrating with desperation to get that baby in her arms.

"You're going to have to touch her at some point, Elena. She's your niece." When I shake my head, August laughs. "I cannot believe you're afraid of babies."

"I'm not afraid of them," I whisper. "I just think they're very fragile, and I don't like to be responsible for the well-being of tiny people."

He laughs again. "They're going to make you hold her."

"You can hold her, and I'll just gaze lovingly at her over your shoulder. We'll bond through eye contact."

"No, I—" His head snaps sideways, and his mouth opens as he pauses.

"Oh, my God." I'm the one laughing now. "You're afraid of babies too."

"Okay, so you're admitting you are afraid of babies, then."

"No more than you are, Augustus." I loop my arm through his, resting my head on his shoulder. "You...um...you know I don't want kids, right? Like, ever?"

"Yeah, Elena." He glances down at me, lips tilting upward. "You've been pretty clear about that for most of your adult life."

"I just wanted to make sure you knew it hadn't changed. In case..."

"Little Vice, we're both standing in the darkest corner of the room to avoid being asked if we want to hold your brother's newborn baby. I think it's pretty clear that children aren't in our future, and I am completely okay with that."

I burst with laughter again, and August's eyes ignite as he matches it. We grow loud enough that our cover is blown, drawing the attention of everyone else in the room.

"I know what y'all are doing, but you are going to meet your niece," Leo chimes.

"No, yeah. Totally. We planned on it," I say, stepping closer to the rest of them. My mom holds Willow now as Lou stands beside her, studying the baby girl. "But it looks like Lou is really excited to hold her next, so we should probably let her do that."

"Using my eleven-year-old as a human shield, Lele?" Everett asks.

"I'd never do such a heinous thing." I smile, hoping to will some lightness into the tension between us, but my twin only rolls his eyes and scoffs before helping Lou sit down on the couch beside Darby's bed as my mother places the baby in her arms.

"What's going on there?" Leo asks, eyeing us curiously.

I force another smile in his direction, not missing the way my mother frowns at the interaction. "Nothing you need to worry about right now."

Leo humphs, and I lean against August's shoulder as he sighs into the top of my head. We watch Lou hold her tiny cousin in her arms, brushing her thumb over the baby's cheek.

"Hi, Willow." She smiles before lifting her to head to Dahlia. "Mom, when you have your baby, can you name them after a Taylor Swift song too?"

Shocked gasps echo through the room as every single one of us turns our attention to Everett and Dahlia. Everett winces, biting his lip as he runs a hand through his hair. Dahlia's eyes fall closed, a deep, rough sigh escaping her lips.

"I'm sorry, what?" my mother exclaims.

I glance at Lou again, her eyes wide and cheeks flushed as she whispers, "Oops."

Chapter Thirty-Nine

Violet

"Mess Is Mine" - Vance Joy

"I'll be down in just a moment!" Darby's melodic voice chimes from the upper level of her home as I shut the front door behind me.

Elena drops her purse onto the entryway table, glancing through the dining room and kitchen before heading toward the living room. "Are we the first ones here? We're normally late."

"Not sure," I say, but by the looks of it, nobody else is around, and only Darby and Leo's cars are parked out front.

We didn't have dinner together last Sunday, since it was just a couple of days after Willow was born. Monica and Dahlia have been around often, helping Darby and Leo ease into parenthood while ensuring they're both fed, showered, and somewhat rested. The rest of us have given them a bit more space and privacy to adjust to their new life.

Everett has been working more to cover Leo at Heathen's, and Elena has picked up extra shifts at The Wicked Wildflower so Dahlia can be here to help her sister. Outside of a few brief run-ins with Everett around the boardwalk, neither of us has spoken to him much, each interaction we do have fraught with tension.

Tonight's dinner will be met with inevitable confrontation, and maybe that's why Elena and I arrived so early. It felt as if we were both sitting around the house all afternoon, just waiting to face the family, and grew antsy. Or at least, I was feeling that way.

Elena ended up obtaining representation from the top agent she reached out to, and she recently received her manuscript back from the freelance editor she hired. She finalized it today before sending it off to her agent to be pitched to publishers. On top of that, Leo asked her to create an official proposal for a boardwalk bookstore, and we've been working on that together.

We've all been incredibly busy, which is how the past two weeks flew by without any of us seeing each other for more than a few passing minutes. But Darby and Leo mentioned to Monica that they felt comfortable having the family over for dinner tonight, and she demanded everyone attend.

Dahlia reluctantly confirmed she was, in fact, pregnant after Lou's slip-up in the birthing center the day Willow was born, but they quickly stated that they weren't ready to announce it yet and needed time before sharing any additional details. I think Monica has been itching for more information from them and hopes they'll finally spill the beans tonight.

I check the clock on my phone and realize that while we are a little early, I'm pretty sure Monica told us all to come over at five o'clock, and it's four forty right now, so I'm still surprised we're the first ones here.

"I don't know where your parents are," Darby calls as her footsteps creak against the stairs. "But Dahlia and Everett are going to be late because they had to pick up Lulu from a birthday party."

She rounds the corner a moment later, holding Willow against her chest. Wrapped in a yellow onesie with a matching knit bow on top of her head, she begins to wail as Darby sinks into the recliner beside the couch where Elena and I sit.

"Baby girl." Elena pouts, leaning over the armrest to get a peek at her.

"I think she's just hungry." Darby sighs. While she looks tired, she's still beautiful, with her blond hair pulled back into a low bun, her skin still glowing and hazel eyes still radiant, even if exhaustion peeks through. Tilting Willow in her arms, she looks around the room before her eyes fix on a blanket basket beside the television stand. "Can one of you grab me that donut pillow thing?" she asks, nodding toward it.

I lift off the couch and step across the room, swiping the pink, U-shaped pillow from the basket before handing it to her and returning to my seat. Darby positions Willow atop it before undoing the two buttons at the center of her floral-printed shirt.

"How's everything at work?" Darby asks as she positions Willow at her chest, watching with pure adoration as she latches on and begins to nurse.

"It's been fine," Elena says, settling back onto the couch cushions to get comfortable.

"Good." I nod.

"Are you two ready to finally address your shit with Everett and Leo today?"

Elena side-eyes me, and I shrug.

"I've always thought it was a little insane that I spent three months here one summer ten years ago and could see the chemistry your brothers have been so willingly blind to all this time." Darby laughs. "They're acting so shocked that this relationship between you two isn't as new as they thought it was, when if they'd paid any attention at all, they would've seen it way back then."

"What do you mean?" I ask.

"Whatever weird tension was happening between you and Everett at the hospital?" She nods toward Elena. "Leo's been bringing it up, telling me neither of you will talk to him about it, and he doesn't know what happened." Darby looks at me. "And I read you like a book, August. I could tell for a while that there was more to your story than what you were telling me. And you don't have to, but I just want to make sure you can work it out with Everett and Leo and get everyone on the same page."

I smile at her reassuringly. "We'll do our best."

"Motherhood has made you very intuitive," Elena says from beside me.

"I've always been intuitive." Darby smiles. "Someone gifted

me a bunch of selenite when I was younger, and I absorbed its energy."

Elena snorts, raising a hand to flip her off.

"Better have a damn good reason for making that gesture at the mother of my child, Lena," Leo drawls as he slides through the French doors that lead inside from the back patio.

"She can redirect it at you for dripping water all over my floors," Darby murmurs.

"Baby, I can't very well strip outside when we have guests, can I?"

"I could close my eyes," Elena says at the same time I mutter, "I've seen your dick a million times."

"Augustus," Leo gasps. "That was supposed to be our secret."

I chuff, rolling my eyes as he tiptoes down the hall and into his and Darby's bedroom, surely enough, leaving a trail of puddles in his wake. He returns a few moments later in a pair of shorts and a tee, sliding down the hall with a towel beneath one foot, wiping up the water. After tossing it into the laundry room off the kitchen, he makes his way to his wife.

"That's the hungriest kid I've ever seen," he says, kissing the top of Darby's head.

"You're telling me," she murmurs. "How was your lesson?"

"Kids were great." He smiles, holding his hands out and flexing his fingers. "Is it daddy time?"

Darby glances down to check if Willow is still nursing before she nods, gently lifting their daughter and handing her off to Leo, then reclasps her blouse and tosses her pillow to the floor. Leo grabs a folded cloth from the coffee table and drapes it over his shoulder before placing Willow against it and slowly pacing the room while rubbing soft circles into her back.

"Do you think you two can stay for a little while after dinner tonight?" Leo asks Elena and me, though we already knew it was coming.

She glances at me, but we both nod as the front door creaks open. I hear it close before the sound of footsteps echoes, and a clattering sounds from the kitchen, as if something made of glass or metal is being placed on the counter.

Monica peeks her head around the corner from the kitchen a moment later, whispering, "I made lasagna. I'm going to warm it in the oven while Dad makes a salad, and we can sit down to eat as soon as Everett and Dahlia get here."

"Thanks, Mama," Leo says. "Sugar should be zonking out any minute here, so I'll get her to bed before we eat."

Monica smiles before her gaze drifts to Darby. "When is your mom flying in again, love?"

"Not until Thursday."

Monica nods. "You'll have to help me come up with a dinner idea for next week so I can make something she likes."

Darby's brows knit together, eyes withdrawn as she contemplates before answering, "You know, I'm not actually sure what she likes. I'm not even sure she knows what she likes. I can ask her." She chews on her cheek. "Or maybe I can tell her some of the things you make best, and she can choose one. Try something new."

"That would be beautiful." Monica beams before dipping her head back into the kitchen.

From what Darby has told me, her relationship with her mother was strained growing up due to the neglect and emotional abuse her father inflicted on their family. When he was finally taken down last year for a slew of white-collar crimes involving his business back in Kansas, Darby and Dahlia's mom got out of the marriage, but it's been a slow build toward a relationship with her daughters.

Dahlia is more hesitant to connect with their mother, according to Darby. Darby has grown closer to her over the last couple of years and ended up inviting her out to meet Willow not long after she was born. Dahlia and Leo are less enthused about the decision, but after the hard time Darby had getting pregnant, including a miscarriage last summer that devastated her, I think she wants to share the joy of her daughter with everyone she loves, including her mother.

A short while later, Everett, Dahlia, and Lou finally arrive. Leo puts Willow down for a nap in their bedroom while the rest of us prepare dinner and set the table, and we're mere seconds into our meal before Monica pipes up from the end of the table. "So, does anyone have anything they want to share?" Her eyes dart to Everett and Dahlia, who sit beside her.

"Mamá, tienes que relajarte. Estás siendo muy entrometida." Everett drops his fork onto his plate before massaging his temples.

Dahlia pats his shoulder reassuringly. "We didn't keep it a secret for any nefarious reasons. We just wanted to confirm a few things before we made any big announcement. Plus, we didn't want to take any of the heat off Darby and Leo's moment."

"Yeah, I didn't want you to feel inferior, brother." Everett smirks at Leo.

Leo scoffs from the head of the table opposite Monica, leaning back in his chair. "Take one look at my baby and tell me what could possibly make me feel inferior. I made the most perfect child on the planet."

Darby grumbles, shoving his shoulder.

"Sorry. We made the most perfect child on the planet." He waves a finger between himself and his wife.

Dahlia sighs, glancing at Everett, who's flashing a shit-eating grin at his brother.

"Oh, my God, just spit it out," Elena mutters. "Does the kid have superpowers or something? Four legs? Human-vampire hybrid like *Twilight*?"

"It's twins!" Lou exclaims from her seat beside her mom.

"Twins!" Monica squeals, nearly falling out of her chair.

The rest of us follow with similar sentiments, getting up from our seats or reaching across the table to offer hugs and congratulations.

"Boys." Everett grins.

"Boys!" his mom exclaims. "Oh, my God. This is the best news."

Dahlia looks radiant, glancing at Everett, whose hand slips beneath the table, no doubt placing it over her stomach. He leans into her, whispering something against her ear that makes her blush, smiling wider.

"When are you due?" Darby asks, sounding less surprised than the rest of us, though it's not unlikely she's already up to date.

"November twenty-third."

"So you're about three months along, then?"

Dahlia nods. "Fourteen weeks."

I catch Everett's eyes across the table. "I'm really happy for you all."

And for the first time in fucking weeks, the smile he offers me is genuine. "Thanks, Auggie."

Elena grasps my thigh beneath the table, and when I glance at her, she's watching all of our interactions with misty eyes and a soft smile.

I know there is nothing that means more to her than watching her brothers live out their hard-earned happily-ever-afters, and fuck if it doesn't make me more determined to ensure she gets hers too.

Chapter Forty

Vice

"Never Let Me Go" - Florence + The Machine

"I really am so excited for you both," I say, slipping through the back door and onto Leo's porch. In the distance, the sun fades into the Pacific's horizon line, streaking the sky above it in shades of orange and pink.

Leo and Everett sit on the swing, both barefoot in board shorts, talking quietly amongst themselves. Our mom is never responsible for cleaning up after dinner on Sundays, since she always cooks, but the rest of us pull cards for who gets dish duty. This week my dad and I lost, and while I was tidying up the kitchen, the rest of the family went about entertaining themselves.

I think August is with Darby, checking on Willow. It sounded like Dahlia, Lou, and my mom were in the living room catching up on some show they watch together that premieres on Sunday evenings, and Dad was going to join them when we finished.

Finding my brothers out here on the porch, I quietly shut the French doors behind me before padding over to where they sit and making space for myself between them. I pull my legs up, locking my arms around my knees as they both rock their heels against the deck to move the swing back and forth.

"Thanks, Lele," Everett says, and I know he's trying to sound soft, but his tone comes out gruff instead.

"Can we talk about this now?" Leo asks. "It's been stressing me out for days, honestly. I know you two have that twin telepathy shit or whatever, but you can't just fight inside your heads while leaving me out of the loop. It isn't fair."

I lean onto Leo's shoulder, feeling the steady movement of his breathing against my cheek. He's like a fucking rock. Not just physically, though he is incredibly toned. Leo is consistent, as reliable as the sunrise every morning. Like a walking comfort blanket that's always going to welcome me with open arms, even when I don't deserve it.

"Sorry," I murmur. Glancing at Everett, who's watching me with a pained expression, I add, "We should probably wait for August, thou—"

As if I summoned him, one of the back doors creaks open as August slips through it. I can practically feel the trepidation cascading off him with every step he takes. He stands in front of the swing, leaning back against the porch railing. He smiles cautiously, eyes focused on me.

"Do you want me to continue jumping to conclusions, or do you want to lay it all out for me right now?" Everett asks, his words aimed at August.

I sigh, rising from the swing and turning to hoist myself onto the porch railing beside August. I grab his hand, twining his fingers through mine and placing them in my lap before raising my head to face both my brothers.

I feel the thickness of emotion already beginning to coat my throat as August whispers, "We need to talk about Zach." He leans into me, planting his lips against my temple. "All of us."

"So, let me get this straight..." Everett's folded over, elbows resting on his thighs as he massages his temples. "You were always just friends, but after Zach left for Wyoming, you realized you had feelings for August the whole time?"

"I don't know," I admit on a sigh. "I guess? I always knew something else brewed between us, but I didn't think it was possible. I'd seen myself as already having chosen someone, and that I couldn't just...change my mind."

"But you did."

"Zach left me," I snap. "I was fucking broken." Leo squeezes the tension out of his jaw, looking defeated. Everett's head finally snaps up, eyes meeting mine, and a flash of understanding registers in his gaze, so I continue, "But it also made me realize that if he could do that—if he could wake up one day and suddenly decide he wants a whole new life, if he could throw me away without a second thought—why couldn't I do the same? If I realized that there might be someone else out there better for me than he was, why couldn't I chase that happiness?"

"I understand it, Lena," Leo says softly. "I guess I don't understand why you two kept everyone else in the dark."

I glance at August for explanation, because that's on him. Sure, I was somewhat jaded by the way Zach left, but regardless, I was more than ready to shout my newfound happiness from every rooftop on the planet. August was the hesitant one, and while I understand the circumstances were different from his end, and he wanted to treat his brother with respect, I decide it's not my place to voice that.

He squeezes my hand, sighing. "Honestly? It was partially because I didn't want to blindside my brother—I felt he deserved a face-to-face conversation about it. But it was also because I was afraid that the moment he came home..." August faces me. "I thought you'd just go back to him like every time before. If this whole love affair remained a secret, and I lost you, I could at least try and save my soul by pretending it never existed to begin with."

"Augustus..." I trail off, not knowing what else to say. It's easy for me to think I could reassure him with nothing but words, but the truth is, his fear is warranted. He watched me run back to his brother countless times throughout our life, and when we lost Zach for good, I ran again.

"And I did lose her." He clears his throat, turning his head to look at my brothers again. "It fucked me up in every way I anticipated it would, and the secrets kept were my futile attempt at salvaging any piece of me that didn't go with her."

"Can you tell us what happened the day he..." Leo swallows. "It's just... It's rattled my brain for years, and maybe knowing those last moments won't make anything better, but I want to understand."

I take a deep breath, tilting my head toward the sky as I blink back the tears already threatening me. "He showed up at my apartment the night before. He'd been out with you two, and he was completely shit-faced."

"I remember throwing him into an Uber," Everett says roughly before barking out a tortured laugh. "He called me a 'dumb whore' as I shut the door in his face." He swallows, shaking his head in disbelief. "That was the last thing he ever said to me."

"He really had a way with last words," I murmur.

"Tell me what you mean, Lele."

My bottom lip trembles as I attempt to force words out, but the tears come first. August untangles his hand from mine, raising it to my face and wiping them away.

"He was so drunk that night, asking questions about who I left him for, who I was with now. I just put him into bed in the guest room so he could sleep it off. I planned to call you in the morning so that we could sit down with him together before the two of you went surfing that day..." I turn to August. "But he woke up earlier than I expected him to, and he said he noticed I was wearing your shirt, and smelled like your cologne."

My mind flashes to the look on Zach's face that morning as he stood helplessly in the center of my kitchen. As the realization flashed across his face. The anger and betrayal so potent that I could taste it in the air around us. I can taste it again now.

"I couldn't lie to him anymore." The words come out of my mouth crumbled and broken, an outward portrayal of the destruction happening inside my body. I know I'm hardly understandable, heaving between wretched sobs. "I thought it was better to confirm the truth, but now...if I had just lied. If I had placated him long enough for you to get there, maybe..."

"Don't do that," Leo rasps, moving so quickly I don't even realize he's leaped from the swing until he's folding me into his arms. A rock of comfort. "Don't plague yourself with what-ifs. It's not your fault."

Watching over Leo's shoulder, I see Everett's eyes fall shut as tears begin to drip down his cheeks, his jaw quivering as he drops his face into his hands. August's palm rests at the back of my neck, warm and reassuring.

"It got really bad after that..." I choke. "I told him that I wished he'd..." I can't finish the sentence, thinking back to the foreshadowing I'd spoken into existence, the one thing I wish more than all the rest that I could take back.

For good this time?

Shivers rack my entire body at the memory of that last moment.

"We don't need to know," Leo whispers. "You don't need to remember. The last words don't negate the years of love that came before." He kisses the top of my head before pulling away. "I'll be right back, okay?"

Before any of us can respond, he darts inside the house.

August kisses my temple softly as I look to Everett and whisper, "I'm sorry."

His eyes flash to mine, like liquid amber as the setting sunlight casts over them, withdrawn and red-rimmed. He shakes his head, patting the cushion of the seat beside him that Leo just vacated. I glance at August, and he gives me a reassuring nod, urging me to sit beside my brother.

When I do, Everett pulls me into his arms, and it's a different comfort than Leo. It's something innate and biological. The first place I ever existed was right beside him, and it's that sense of belonging that rises in me when I'm held by my twin.

"Don't be sorry." I feel his chest rumble with his words as I bury my head against it. Though I'm not looking at him, I know his next words are directed at August. "I wish I wasn't in the dark for so long. I wish I could've done more for both of you. But I can't say I would've done anything differently, either. It's an impossible fucking situation. I see that now."

He rubs a hand over my hair, and there is a mutual rattle of broken breathing as the three of us silently fight through our tears while we wait for Leo to return.

"August," Everett whispers a moment later. "Have you ever talked to anyone about it?" His voice cracks. "About what you... saw?"

I lift my head from Everett's chest, catching August's face just in time to watch it fall. His eyes glaze over with a haunting emptiness, and the expression slices directly through me, gutting me so thoroughly I'm surprised my insides don't splatter to the ground at my feet.

"No," he whispers, hollow and choked. "I'll never subject anyone else to that image, even inside their own mind. That's mine to harbor alone."

"It doesn't have to be. We can carry it with you," my brother says.

August wipes a hand down his face, morphing his features from composed numbness to devastated realization, his eyes fluttering closed as the tears finally begin to free fall.

Leo reappears from the back door, now wearing a burnt yellow Heathen's hoodie, with his hands in both pockets. Nodding toward the back of his property, he says, "Do you guys want to go watch the sunset on the beach?"

Everett and I turn to August, leaving the decision up to him. He blinks rapidly, wiping his eyes before nodding and pushing off the porch railing. "Yeah, why not."

Everett helps me off the porch swing before following Leo down the steps and onto the pebbled pathway that leads through his backyard and toward the lavender-lined cliffside. I'm not sure who originally forged the trail that takes us down to the beach, but it's been there since Darby's grandmother owned the house when we were children. We used to sneak down here often to take advantage of the private cove at the base of the cliff, and though I'm now positive that Diane Andrews was aware of our shenanigans, she never ratted us out for trespassing.

Leo has had some work done to make the trail more navigable and less steep, so it's much easier to follow now than it was back then. He's also having a second, wider path put in on the other side of his property so it'll be easier to carry surfboards and beach supplies down to the bottom. That path will lead directly to the guesthouse he's having built behind the detached garage.

Everett and Leo walk ahead of me, and I reach back to grab August's arm, ensuring he's right behind every step I take down the narrow trail. Once we reach the bottom, the trail broadens as the rocky cliffside meets the sand.

Pulling him beside me, I say softly to August, "You could talk about it with us. Clearly, we all have unresolved feelings when it comes to our last moments with him, and if we finally stopped keeping them to ourselves, maybe we could understand them a little better. Maybe we'd stop feeling so alone."

He only blinks at me, green eyes shimmering with unshed tears behind his glasses. He doesn't offer a response but lifts my hand to his lips and presses them to my knuckles.

Everett and Leo sit down next to a large piece of driftwood, drawing their knees to their chests. I sit beside Everett, and August plops down next to me. The sun is fading faster now, and not much daylight remains, but the rays beam upward in the sky, and it appears as if the clouds are dancing under reflective glass, clashing together in a bright display of color.

Light skips across the whitecaps as they crest and crash against the shore, giving the whole world a soft, blurred glow that makes you question whether you've been momentarily transported to a more rose-colored reality.

"We had made plans earlier in the week to go surfing that morning. I normally check the weather app the night before to make sure conditions are good, but I'd forgotten," August says quietly, breaking me out of that golden blur and snapping me back to the only reality I've ever known. "It was windy, and the sky was dark. I knew it was bad, and I tried calling him a few times before I left, but he wasn't answering, so I figured I'd just show up anyway." I look at him, but his gaze is planted firmly on the horizon. "It was Cyprus State Park. You know the one off the highway, a few miles north of town?"

"Yeah." Leo sighs.

"I was already there when he arrived. He was so fucking mad at me. I understood why. I got it. It's hard to watch the person you're in love with fall in love with someone else, especially when you love that other person too."

The words burn. Like acid rain falling from his mouth and landing on my skin.

"I told him I understood it, but I wasn't sorry, and that his anger wouldn't change anything." August swallows, tucking his knees into his chest and hugging them. Leo shuffles sideways, forming a circle of the four of us so he can look at August head-on. "We went back and forth for a while, but he seemed to settle—to somewhat understand. He told me that it made sense, that you and I had always made sense." He glances down at me, and when our eyes meet, I know the guilt is slicing through us both, leaving him and me in tatters. "He said he'd get over it eventually, but that there were things he'd said to you..."

You are impossible to love.

"I was the one who got angry then. I hadn't known he'd been with you that morning, and he was taunting me for it. When I realized that you two had your own confrontation, that he'd said something hurtful to you..." August shakes his head, his eyes a million miles away as he relives the memories flashing across his mind. "I figured that he and I—the three of us—would end up okay. We were angry in the moment, but had a base of understanding. You were the one who got left behind, so I wanted to find you. I told him he leaves damage in the wake of his recklessness. He called after me, but I kept going. I knew I was leaving things unresolved, but I didn't care. He was my brother, you know?" He turns to us, tears streaming freely from his eyes. "Even when things weren't okay, you had confidence they would be. They always are in the end."

How many times has August watched Leo, Everett, and me fight over the years, end our conversations abruptly, and shut each other out, always having faith in future resolution? How many times did he watch those interactions, knowing he hadn't escaped one of his own?

He told me love had been a question, and that's why I was so afraid of it. It's only now that I realize the meaning of family may be the same for him.

A drumming ache erupts in my chest at that thought.

"Things won't always be okay," I whisper. "Even when they're not, I want you to remember that they are. No fight between us"—I glance at my brothers—"will ever mean more than the love that's there too."

In my periphery, I register both Everett and Leo nodding.

"I told him it was a bad day for surfing before I left, and when I reached my truck at the top of that cliff, I looked out over it, searching for him so I could tell him again." August's gaze tracks the horizon line once again. "He was already gone."

I loop my arm through August's, leaning my head on his shoulder. I close my eyes, the setting sun warming my cheeks as I face the horizon. I embrace the warmth, because I know the memory we confront next will be the darkest of them all.

"I tracked the shoreline from end to end, searching for his red board, but I came up short. That's when I immediately began bounding back down the stairs, yelling his name." August takes a rattling inhale, and I hear Leo mutter a curse beneath his breath. "Apparently someone down there had already seen whatever wave took him out. They'd called for a lifeguard, and I made it to the beach just in time to see them wading through the water in search of Zach. I ran straight to them, but by the time I was knee-deep, they were pulling him out."

I squeeze my eyes like I'm trying to rid my mind of the

image August presents, but it doesn't work. Suffocating beneath my emotion, I gasp for air. August's palm slides beneath mine, clasping our hands together and resting them on top of his knee.

"Paramedics arrived, and they were doing all they could, but I knew. Before we made it to the hospital, before the doctors confirmed. I knew the moment I looked at him that his soul wasn't there anymore."

I feel the warmth of a second palm on mine before the pressure of another lands atop it. I know it's my brothers, but I'm not ready to open my eyes yet. Not ready to face the devastation I'll see reflected back at me.

I'm not sure how long we sit in silence before Leo shakily says, "This is what I retrieved from inside the house."

I let my eyelids flutter open, vision blurry through my tears before I wipe them away to find my brother sitting cross-legged in the sand, a small black box in his palm.

"Sadie was too distraught to handle the aftermath of it, and you were taking care of her." He nods toward August, before doing the same to Everett. "You were trying to help Elena, and though I made my own attempts, I felt like there was some deeper twin-level connection I couldn't reach. I felt so fucking helpless," he whispers. "So, I helped Alex with a lot of the...logistical shit that nobody should be having to think about. I remember calling to cancel his gym membership..." He shakes his head. "I closed his bank accounts, sorted through his belongings, cleaned out his fucking car. I also retrieved his ashes from the funeral home." Leo looks at the box in his hand. "They asked me if I'd like to have them split into individual parts for loved ones to keep. I knew Sadie and Alex probably would've said no, but I said yes. I had the majority set aside for them, but I made sure to have something for each of us to keep or spread how we wanted."

A sob rips through me at the realization of what my brother holds in his hand.

"I spread mine for him in Nazaré, because he'd always dreamed of going," Leo continues. "We keep Everett's at Heathen's, because he was supposed to work there with us."

"I keep mine in a leather pencil box he made for me when he lived in Wyoming. It's on my desk in the sunroom," August whispers brokenly. "He bought that house for the sunroom. It was going to be his favorite place."

Sorrow holds me in a death grip, thrashing inside the hollow of my chest. I want to let it out on a scream, but I clamp the urge down, swallowing it with nauseating effort.

"I had these ones saved for you," Leo chokes. "I didn't think you were ready for them before, but I hope..." He's trembling as he extends them to me. "I hope you might be ready now. I think you need them now."

I take them with shaking hands. Staring down at the box, I'm unsure of what to do. I never thought I'd have any piece of Zach again—didn't think I deserved it.

"I understand the guilt you've been harboring," Everett says softly. "I didn't get it before, but I do now, and I think it's time to let it go." His eyes bounce between August and me. "We all fought, we all hated each other at times. I know for damn sure if Zach were sitting here right now, he'd be laughing at the fact that the last thing he ever called me was a whore. He'd find it fucking hilarious, and he'd probably say it again just to remind me."

He doesn't pull the laugh I know he's attempting to from me, but I toss him the best smile that I can muster.

"We were young and tumultuous. We were reckless and loud and unabashed in the way we loved each other. We always have been. There's never any way of knowing which conversation is going to be your last with someone, and I can't imagine that the last words are what I'm going to remember when I die. It's going to be a compilation of every happy moment that came before them, and I think I knew Zach well enough to say he'd feel the same."

"I think every single one of us knew, even back then, that the two of you made sense," Leo adds. "I think a lot of people are meant to be in our lives. I think we can experience love in a million different ways, but some things are just...written in the stars. I think death might be one of them, and maybe his was. I think that our souls are another, and yours are fused like that." He nods to August and me. "At some point we have to accept that there are questions we'll never know the answer to, and then we have to decide if we're going to chase contentment without them, or spend our lives tangled in what-ifs."

"I want to be untangled. I don't know how." My voice breaks as I choke on my emotion.

August presses his lips against my head as Leo nods toward the box in my hands. "Maybe figuring out what you want to do with those will help."

"I don't know."

"We have a piece of him that we can always keep with us," August whispers against my temple. "Maybe we can let this piece go. We can do it together."

"Where?" I ask.

"What does Zach remind you of?" Everett asks.

"The sun," I say immediately, causing all four of us to turn our head toward the water where it's fading rapidly, running from the horizon. "The sea. But I don't want to leave him in the same place that took him from us. He'd hate that, wouldn't he?"

"I wouldn't," Leo says immediately. "We don't hate the ocean for simply existing the way it was meant to. We wouldn't blame its nature."

"Some forces are so powerful, so vast and beautiful, they can't be tamed. We choose to thrive within their chaos. We learn to relent any constraints we wish to have on them, because they're meant to be wild," August whispers. "Zach was beginning to understand that, I think."

Watching the waves form, break, and spill against the sand before retreating home—it's reminiscent of the way it felt to love him. The world is still cast in the rose-colored hue, that ethereal softness that feels unattainable outside of Pacific sunsets. I realize if I were going to be left anywhere, this is probably where I'd want to be too.

A moment pulled straight from a kinder reality—that's where he deserves to stay.

I lift off the sand and stumble toward the water. I'm calf-deep when my knees buckle and I fall to them. Waves crash over me, soaking me from the waist down as I face the wind. I still haven't found the courage to speak to him, but as the sun bathes the sky in scarlet clouds, I feel like I'm standing in front of him for the first time in years.

"I'm sorry," I whisper, voice trembling as I slide the lock on the box with a shaking hand. "Even if I learn to live with it all, I'll never stop being sorry for it." Tears stream, dripping off my cheeks to add new drops of saltwater into the ocean below. "I'll never stop wondering what we would've looked like if we'd made it past all this. The kind of friends we could've been. I'll never stop missing you. I'll never stop wishing I could've known the person you would've become."

Inside the box is a small plastic bag filled with his ashes. I tear it open as the presence of my brothers appears, dropping to their knees on either side of me. There is movement behind me before his chest presses into my back, arms wrapping around my waist. When he rests his chin atop my head, and the beat of his heart flows from his body and into mine, I feel at home.

Tipping the box, I let Zach's ashes fall into the Pacific.

Braced by the strong arms of my brothers, and wrapped in the warmth of the love of my life, I finally find the strength to let go of the boy I loved to death.

Chapter Forty-One

Violet

"Stargirl Interlude" - The Weeknd, Lana Del Rey

Everett

Talked to Dal, and we're in. Let's set aside some time to talk about it more this week.

Thank fucking God. I close Everett's text and slip my phone back into my pocket before hopping out of the driver's side of my Bronco and walking around the back to meet Elena at the tailgate.

After the impromptu ash-spreading of my brother on Sunday, and both of our therapy appointments this past week, we're drained. Everett, Leo, Elena, and I climbed back up that cliffside in the darkness, soaking wet, and emotionally raw. We're still working out where we go from here, because the truth is, healing doesn't work like time does. It's not linear, moving only in one direction, always onward. The "ball in the box" metaphor surrounding grief is accurate—the ball starts out huge, relentlessly pressing against the sides of the box. Over time, the ball shrinks, not always hitting the pain button inside the box, but it never disappears entirely.

I think that healing can work much in the same way. Healing is the free space. At first, it's nonexistent. There is only pain. As that ball shrinks, our healed soul fills the space around it. We never lose the ball, though, and sometimes we press the pain button on purpose, because we know it's going to create more space for healing in the long run.

We spilled our truths and our lies, and all of us will be better for it eventually, but we also flooded ourselves with pain, and we've got to tread through it until we're standing on solid ground again.

I took some time to myself over the past week to envision the future I want for Elena and myself, and how I want us to keep making as much forward momentum as possible. I pulled aside Everett this week to float an idea by him, and now that I have confirmation that he and Dahlia are on board, I can run it past Elena too.

Hopefully, everything works out, because I'm already several steps ahead.

"Are we here to stargaze again, Augustus?" Elena asks, smiling mischievously as she leans against the back of my Bronco.

"Not exactly." I take her hand, pulling her away from my truck and off the gravel lot. The same lot I brought her to a few weeks ago. I walk us to the center of the field behind it. The same place we spent so much of our youth.

"You know, they're building a neighborhood up here. In a year from now, these will all be houses."

"I know." She sighs as I spin her to face the horizon, wrapping my arms around her shoulders and holding her back to my chest. "Even when it belongs to someone else, I'm still going to consider this spot ours."

The moon reflects on the ocean below us, providing a strip of white light over the rippling water. Vast darkness stretches far beyond it on either side, only the sprinkling of boat lights in the distance, a reflection of the stars sparkling above our heads.

A balmy breeze rushes over our faces, the grass dancing to the music of the palm leaves.

I can see it. Quiet nights. This view. The peaceful silence best accompanied by her soul. What I've been searching my entire life for.

"What if it belonged to us instead?"

She tilts her head, glancing up at me with glittering, curious eyes. "What do you mean?"

"What if I told you I just put in an offer for the plot of land we're standing on right now, we'll have a house built here, and you get to design it however you'd like?"

She rears back, untangling from my arms, disbelief gracing her features. "Don't lie."

"I'm not lying, Little Vice." I laugh.

"But the house...Zach."

"I've got a buyer." I smile. "Great couple. They have a preteen and twins on the way, so they'll make good use of all the extra rooms."

Her jaw drops, head shaking. "I... I don't know what to say."

"Zach wanted that house to be loud and lively and full of family. He loved that house, and it's why I haven't been able to let it go, but it's never felt like mine, and I don't think we'll ever be able to make it feel like ours." I step into her, grasping her cheeks with both hands and guiding her eyes to mine. "Now, it can have all of the things he wanted, and it can be filled with people he loved and would've loved, and we can have something to call our own."

Her long lashes flutter, eyes blinking rapidly as a blazing smile overtakes her face. "Are you being serious right now? We're going to build a house right here?"

"Yeah." I nod. "I want nothing more than to spend my whole life loving you in the same place I grew up with you. We don't need anything else. Just the two of us, and this patch of earth."

Her hands find the back of my neck, dragging me to her as she kisses me fiercely. Laced with passion and heat, her tongue slips against mine—she tastes like stardust.

"But how?" she asks.

"My mom was the co-signer on the mortgage. I called her last week and asked her to agree to sell to Everett and Dahlia. I also asked her to give me enough for the down payment on this development, until I can pay her back with the equity we make on the other house."

"I can't believe she agreed," Elena whispers.

"Well..." I chuckle, rubbing my jaw. "I may have been a bit manipulative."

Elena glances up at me with a bemused expression.

"My mom has been calling for weeks. Since that day at the bakery. She claims she wants to apologize, that she wants to sit down with my dad and me to resolve our issues. That she hasn't been able to stop thinking about what we said about Zach being ashamed of her."

Elena only raises her brows unconvinced, and I know she'll likely never forgive or accept my parents. I don't blame her for it, though.

"I was ignoring her..." I sigh. "I wasn't ready to address anything with them, but...I told them I'd come visit them soon if she helped me out with selling the house." I press my lips to Elena's forehead. "I won't ever be close with my parents, but I don't want to hate them, either. So, I'm going to keep trying, and in the meantime..." I lift my head to gaze at the stars, and Elena follows my line of sight. "At least we'll get all of this."

"And a dog," she whispers, smiling up at me. "I want a dog."

"You want a dog?" I pull back.

She hauls my lips to hers again. "I want a dog."

"Okay. I'll get you a dog." Anything she wants.

She kisses me once more, and I can feel her smile on my mouth. Slowly, her hands slide down my chest, and when I open my eyes and look down, Elena's on her knees in front of me.

"What are you doing?" I ask.

"You bought me a fucking house, Augustus." She fumbles with the button on my jeans. "I'm going to suck your dick."

"Goddamn," I mutter. "You are a work of art."

Chocolate eyes lift, giving confirmation to the sentiment. She's a fucking vision, dark hair falling down her shoulders, gaze fixed on me as she kisses the tattoo she placed on my hip bone before pulling my cock from my jeans and sticking out her luscious tongue. She runs it up the length of me, flicking against each of my bars before she swirls around my head and sucks me entirely into her warm and eager mouth.

My head falls back, a moan working from my throat as I knot my fingers in her hair and grip tightly. She bobs on my length, hollowing her cheeks and forcing me deep enough that her throat constricts around my tip, causing her to sputter.

"That's the prettiest fucking sound, I swear to God," I mutter through clenched teeth. "My girl's hot little mouth choking around Daddy's cock like that. Can you take me deeper, love?"

She moans, the sound vibrating against me and making me tremble. I inch my hips forward, feeling her jaw drop as she takes me as far as she can go. Saliva drips out the sides of her mouth and down to my base. I pulse at the feel of it. Her mouth is warm and soft, her throat tight. I could come like this, just holding myself inside her.

I retreat. "You're going to make me come, baby."

She drives forward, choking on me again as she lets out a moan of protest.

I twist her hair around my fist, pulling tight enough to make her hiss as I pull out of her mouth. I drop to my knees in front of her, before grasping her jaw and forcing her to look at me. "You're going to be a good girl and let me come inside your cunt?"

Her tongue darts out between her bottom lip before she slips it between her teeth, sparks lighting in her gaze. "Yes, sir."

Still holding her hair, I pull, turning her so that she's in front of me. Pressing my hand between her shoulder blades, I force her to drop her upper body right into the grass. I shove her leggings down her hips with my free hand, tangling them at her knees so she's perfectly restrained. Her ass is high in the air, legs spread just enough to give me a glimpse of her glistening pussy, even in the dark.

I lean over her, swiping my cock through her slit before positioning myself at her entrance. Pulling her hair to one side, I place my lips against her neck, over the tattoo of my constellation on her neck. "I love you so fucking much, Elena. You know that, right?"

"Yes," she whimpers.

"Good," I breathe against her skin. "Because I'm about to fuck you like I hate you."

I thrust home, sliding inside her easily, filling her entirely. Her breath hitches when my piercings begin to massage her inner walls as I set a quick, hard pace, moving in and out of her with abandon. She's so fucking wet, I can feel it coating me already, the sound of our joining obscene in the quiet darkness.

"My pretty whore," I rasp, lips grazing the shell of her ear. "All I have to do is promise you gifts and I've got you on your knees? Your pussy dripping, begging me to fill her?"

I lift off her, pulling her hair tighter and causing her back to arch. I splay my fingers over the base of her spine, using it as leverage to fuck her harder, hypnotized by the way her flesh ripples with every thrust.

She mewls my name, but it's not enough, so I smack her ass hard enough to make her tense and hiss, soothing the sting by running a hand over the new tattoo I gave her months ago.

"Louder," I growl. "I want my name echoing off these cliffs. I want the waves and the moon and the earth itself to know who you belong to."

"August," she cries, voice hoarse and strained. She begins pressing back, meeting each one of my thrusts with a hunger of her own. The joining of our bodies mixes with her fierce moans, creating a riveting chord that seems to ricochet off the stars themselves.

"That's it, baby. Earn it." I pause, letting her throw her body back on my cock, and the sight is fucking unreal. Flames lick up my spine, and I'm barreling toward a powerful release. "You gonna come for me nice and pretty, Elena?"

I fall forward, spreading my legs and knocking hers together so that my knees rest outside hers. She gasps at the new angle, our bodies flushed so tightly there is no space between us. It's so deep, incredibly tight. She squeezes around me, and we're both pulsing—trembling.

Bracing one arm on the ground beside her shoulder, my weight falls atop her, but I know it's a sensation she savors. I grip her throat with my freehand, rocketing my hips in a riotous rhythm, causing everything around us to blur.

It's rough. Primal and wild. Even in the midst of our untamed chaos, when I grasp her jaw and tilt her head, forcing her gaze to mine, it's raw emotion bursting in her eyes—pure love.

A kaleidoscope of brown, mixed with the light of the moon and the stars above my head, reflects back at me through those eyes. In them, I see my addiction. My salvation. My holy vice.

"I love you, Elena." I lick her mouth, taste her tongue as she opens for me, swallowing my rattled breath with each pump of my hips inside her.

It breaks her. Her restraint ruptures, and her body goes taut, a cry loud enough to rupture stars falls from her lips as release rushes through her. I don't stop. I don't slow. I fuck her through it, ride it out with her, until we lose the place where she ends and I begin.

"I..." She whimpers into my mouth, body clenching with every word. "Love you."

Her love sends me careening over the edge, scattering my soul to the sky, fusing our beings into something beyond bodies—a passion-hazed eternity.

"Augustus," she breathes, long after we've composed ourselves, now lying side-by-side atop the earth that will soon be ours. "Is this our happy ending?"

"No, Little Vice." I twirl her hair around my finger, studying the stars as she lies on my chest. "It's the start of our happy beginning."

Chapter Forty-Two

Vice

Four Months Later

"BIRDS OF A FEATHER" - Billie Eilish

"God, you two are fucking criminal," Dahlia calls, watching me from where she sits on the massive beach blanket with a hand covering her eyes. "It's actually annoying. I want you to leave."

I finish slipping off my denim shorts, kicking them aside as I adjust the triangles of my black bikini top. August snorts from beside me, and when I glance at him, I absolutely understand her sentiment. He's giving me the same kind of assessment, his eyes—barely visible behind darkened transparent lenses—track all of my exposed flesh. I'm stuck on his sun-kissed skin, the expanse of patchwork tattoos along his arms and torso, and the sculpted muscles of his toned stomach.

"We're not making anyone leave, Wildflower," my twin muses as he rubs sunscreen into his wife's ever-growing stomach while she leans back on her elbows and tilts her head toward the sun. "You're the most beautiful person on the planet, I promise. Total MILF."

Everett lies on his stomach between her legs, resting his face on her belly. We're just about six weeks out from Dahlia's due date with their set of twins, but Everett isn't wrong. She's glowing. Her sapphire ring and diamond-studded wedding band reflect the sunlight as she runs her fingers through his hair, smiling softly down at him. He proposed during their trip over the summer, and they got married in a courthouse not long after returning home. Now, they're working through the process of having Everett officially adopt Lou.

"He's right," I chime, bending over to pull a towel out of my bag. "You are a MILF."

"Whoa, whoa, whoa," Leo shouts from behind me. "What the hell is on your ass?"

I snap straight, turning to glance down at my own backside. August lets out a small laugh, leaning back on his elbows from the towel beside me, studying my body with rapt appreciation.

"It's a tattoo," I say casually.

"Is that a fucking bite mark?" Everett asks, lowering his sunglasses and staring at me with narrowed eyes.

Leo's frowning, face shaded by the umbrella he sits beneath on Dahlia and Everett's other side, rocking Willow as she sleeps against his bare chest.

I shrug, turning back to my bag and pulling out my towel, August helping me spread it beside him. I sit on my knees in front of August, tossing my hair behind my shoulders.

"Did... Did Auggie tattoo his bite mark on your ass cheek in red ink?" Leo asks.

My eyes pop open, jaw ticking with annoyance. "Yes," I hiss. "And I tattooed my lips on his pelvic bone in red ink too. Right above his—"

"Dude," Leo scoffs, directing his attention to August. "That is..."

"Super hot, honestly," Darby pipes up from her husband's other side, lowering her book into her lap.

"Honeysuckle." He gasps. "I was going to say possessive and insane."

"On brand." August laughs under his breath as he scoops my hair off my back and begins splitting it into sections before twisting it into a braid. I taught him how a few months ago, and he's loved playing with my hair ever since.

"It's definitely insane, but I can't say I'm surprised in the slightest," Everett mutters.

Our commotion must've woken Willow, because a shrieking laugh rips through the space, and when I look back at them, Leo's eyes are wide, sparkling with amusement. His daughter sits up on his chest, babbling incoherently as she places her tiny hands on her dad's cheeks.

"Yeah, sugar. Tell me all about it." He smiles contentedly as Darby leans over, pressing her lips to Willow's head before kissing Leo too. They watch their daughter, donned in the most adorable powder-blue ruffled swimsuit with a matching bow on her head. Darby's wearing a suit of the same color, and the expression on my brother's face when he looks at them feels like a definitive representation of one's dreams coming true.

"Jules finally caught the frisbee in her mouth," Lou says, panting as she runs up the beach, placing her hands on her knees to catch her breath. "She needs practice."

A fluff of brown fur barrels against August's chest a moment later as she plants her front paws on his thighs and begins licking his face. I laugh, brushing my hand through her soft pelt and scratching behind her ears.

We went to the shelter about three months ago to search for a dog, and we came across some grungy mutt with the cutest fucking face I'd ever seen. She looked like she wanted to be a border collie but couldn't figure out quite how.

They told us her name was July, and I knew then that it was kismet. If I spent my whole life with a July and an August, every day would feel like summer.

We call her Jules for short, though.

"Thanks for teaching her," I say, laughing.

Water sluices off Lou as she reaches into the cooler beside her mom and pulls a sandwich out of it, flopping directly into the sand. The dog's paws are wet, too, as she jumps on me and begins licking my cheek. It's warm enough today to enjoy the water without a wetsuit, but it's probably the last day we'll have like it for a while as the late summer morphs to autumn.

The cove beneath the cliffside of Darby and Leo's house is still brimming with summer color. The knolls rolling above it are bright green. The palm trees at the base rattle in the sea breeze, mingling with the crashing sound of the whitecaps against the shore. The azure of the sky clashes with the cobalt of the Pacific, casting the world in a hue of blue, while the sun sparkles above it, shrouding all of us in light.

"May seventh is the opening of the bookstore, right?" Darby asks me.

"Yeah." I sigh. "I wanted to open it earlier, but with my release coming up in the spring, it just wasn't going to work out. Too much going on at once."

"Yeah, but you're busy for the best possible reasons," Leo adds. "Publishing your first book in over five years, opening a bookstore, and the rebranding of the tattoo shop."

August draws circles over my shoulder blade, and though I can't see his face, I can feel him smile.

My new book was picked up by a publisher earlier this summer for a release date of next spring. When I returned to social media and began reconnecting with my readers, I was so convinced they'd all have forgotten me. That I'd have to start from scratch. Surprisingly, that wasn't the case. The support has been immense and overwhelming, and with the opening of my very own bookstore on top of all of it, I've never felt more fulfilled.

"The boardwalk will finally be filled, and it only took us six fucking years." Everett laughs.

What started out as five empty suites—the ghosts of failed businesses from our childhood, now bustling and lively, updated with paint and decor, and red rose bushes that Darby planted along each of the entrances—will soon be repurposed by all of us:

Heathen's Surf Co., Honeysuckle Florals, The Wicked Wildflower Cafe and Bakery, Sugar and Vice Romance Bookstore, and Ultraviolet Tattoo and Piercing.

"There is an author I've been chatting with online. She told me that her sister-in-law drove through Pacific Shores once and said it was beautiful. She's been wanting to visit ever since. Maybe we should set up a signing for her when the store opens?" Darby asks.

"Yeah, I'd love that."

"Well, I want those books with the sexy Canadian cowboys on the covers," Dahlia adds. "That's my request."

"You need more surfer books," Leo mutters.

"I'll do my best," I murmur.

"Hush." Darby laughs at her husband. "But I do have a great recommendation for that. It has the cutest blue cover."

"Oh, and your mom wants you to stock the series her book club has been reading. The multicultural small town one with the Latine love interests she keeps saying are to die for," Dahlia says.

"Okay, someone email me a list because I can't keep track of this, but yes. Those all sound great. Lou..." I turn my head back to look at her. "Do you have any suggestions?"

"I don't like being put on the spot like that." Her lips cluster at the corner of her mouth contemplatively. "Can I email you later too?"

"Sure, kid." I laugh.

She nods before looking at my brother. "Dad, can you take me surfing now?"

"Yeah, Luz. Let's go." He smiles, kissing Dahlia's stomach before lifting off the ground.

Leo follows suit, transferring Willow into Darby's arms. "Auggie, you wanna come with us? I brought an extra board down from the house."

"Oh, I..." August pauses.

I lift onto my elbows, placing my hand against his knee. "You should try. It's a great day for it."

Some kind of recognition flashes in his eyes, but he only brings my hand to his mouth, brushing his lips over my knuckles. "I will if you will."

"There is only one board."

"You can ride with me, Lena." Leo smiles. "Like the old days."

I tilt my head at him, a laugh bursting from my lips. "We were kids when we used to do that."

He shrugs, dimples popping. "Yeah, well I'm a professional now."

I sit up on my knees, holding August's hand as he helps me stand up. He jogs to the far side of Darby and Leo's stuff, grabbing the spare board that's propped up in the sand as I meet my brother, pulling his board from his arms.

"Not anymore, retired old man."

"Please," he scoffs, snagging it back from me.

I jog after him, and by the time we're knee-deep in the water, he's shoving me in a way that only my fucking brothers will ever get away with, causing me to tumble right into the waves.

"You're such a fucking ass." August laughs, sneaking up behind Leo and pushing him deeper too.

"Hold up, Luz. Let me go out one time with my siblings, and then I'll come back and grab you. Is that okay?" Everett asks.

"Yeah, that's fine. I didn't know August and Elena surfed too."

Leo, August, and I pause, the waves crashing over their hips and my waist. We watch Everett plant a kiss on his daughter's head. "Not for a long time, but it looks like they're going to try today."

August grabs my hand then, and when I look at him, the sun casts over his face, setting him aglow. The warmth of its light wraps around me like a familiar, long-lost embrace.

Leo, August, and Everett drag their boards out until they're all chest deep, but I've barely got my toes touching the sea floor, the water rippling over my neck.

"Saddle up, Lena," my brother says, holding the board steady. I swing my leg over, straddling the front end before crossing my legs beneath me. August is on one side of me, Everett on the other, both lying flat on their chests. Leo sits behind me on his knees, and we begin paddling toward the break.

The cove creates a gentle enclave, so the waves aren't strong here. Leo always loved this area because it allowed him consistency to perfect his form and train his body, while the waves on the open beaches in town created a more challenging environment.

It's perfect for us today, and when a small swell begins to rise, racing toward us, Leo spins our board and begins paddling rapidly back to shore. I feel the water elevate the board before my brother's movement rocks it side to side, and I know he's standing.

"C'mon, Lena," he shouts, hands gripping beneath my shoulders and hauling me up too. I plant my hands on the board, slowly bending my knees and fixing my gaze at the tip of the surfboard to hold my balance as Leo helps me stand.

He keeps his hands on my waist, and I extend my arms as we ride out the small wave. Wind whips through my hair, and saltwater splashes against my skin. I'm drenched in déjà vu as the familiar lifting sensation erupts in my chest. The feeling of meeting a force of nature head-on, and running with it, defying its power and absorbing its energy, until you find a cohesive partnership.

Like writing, surfing is an art form. A medium I've missed dearly.

We chase the barrel until it crashes beneath us, and we sink back down into the waves. The rush of water flips the board, causing Leo and me both to tumble off it.

As we both resurface and haul ourselves back onto it, my brother shakes his wet hair away from his eyes. "I'm so fucking proud of you! That was badass."

A whistle pierces the air, and my head snaps to my other brother, who tosses an arm in the air. His pointer and pinkie fingers are up, with his thumb stuck out to the side. I return the gesture before my eyes begin searching the waves for August.

Sure enough, he's just behind us, knees bent, gaze focused, gliding across the wave with one hand trailing through the water beside him. I watch him, enthralled by his graceful movement as he rides out the remainder of the wave. He'd always been a natural surfer, though like me, he didn't treat it competitively. I'm not surprised that even after years away from it, he coasts over the water effortlessly.

I press a quick kiss to my brother's cheek, whispering, "Thank you," before leaping off his board and into the water. August's board drops back into the water, and I swim the short distance between us until I reach him.

"Hi," he says, watching me curiously as I lift my upper body up onto his board.

"Hi." He inches backward as I hoist myself onto the board, straddling it backward so I can face him. "I missed you."

"Right here, baby. I'm right here."

"I know." I grab the back of his neck and tug him into me. "I'm so proud of you."

"I'm proud of you, too." He rests his forehead against mine, and I close my eyes. "I'm proud of us."

With the sun's warmth soaking into my skin, the smell of rain, pine, and seawater enveloping my senses, and the soft touch of my soul's best friend against my face, I finally return home.

Epilogue

Violet

Fifteen Years Later

"Home" - Good Neighbours

"Don't forget I'm going to be home late tonight because I'm hosting a book club at the store," Elena says as we stroll over the pier, hand-in-hand.

"I know, Little Vice." I smile, kissing her hand. The midday sun sets her chocolate eyes on fire. "I'll pick up dinner—"

"What the fuck are they doing?" she asks, interrupting me.

I look to where her gaze is fixed, catching our niece and nephews jogging down the other side of the pier, taking frequent looks over their shoulders as they hustle toward the end of it. It's clear they're attempting to be stealthy, hide from something, but they're doing a terrible fucking job.

Elena stops, spinning to watch them as they continue down the pier. It's just after noon on a Tuesday in late May, and if they're doing what I think they're doing, the lot of them are more reckless than I thought imaginable.

Willow's blond hair flies behind her as she begins running faster, holding the hand of her best friend, Allie. The twins are on her other side, and when Zander pulls his T-shirt over his head as they reach the end of the pier, it lays confirmation to exactly what they're doing.

Elena and I turn back around, catching her siblings stalking down the pier in the direction of their children, looking stern and frustrated. When Everett notices us, he calls out, "Are those shits doing what I think they're doing?"

Elena laughs, hitching a thumb in the direction they just went.

"Goddammit," he mutters as the four of them pass us, speed-walking in hopes of reaching their kids before they decide to jump off the Pacific Shores Pier.

"Got somewhere you need to be right now, or do you want to go watch the shitshow with me?" Elena asks, smiling mischievously.

"I can pencil in a shitshow." I grin, squeezing her hand and tugging her as I turn back toward the end of the pier.

Our niece and twin nephews are every bit as wild as their parents—more so, probably.

Willow climbs onto the railing, Allie joining her. A moment later, Archer steps up beside Allie and takes her hand in his, before Zander climbs on Archer's other side.

Leo calls out to them, and his daughter glances back, flashing him her own set of dimples before the four of them leap from the pier and into the water below.

We catch up, leaning over the railing just in time to find four heads popping above the surface, smiling up at us as they tread water below.

"If I get fucking fined for this, you're all working it off this summer. Unpaid overtime!" Leo shouts.

"You better start swimming before I dive in there after you!" Dahlia yells.

"I'm sorry, Mama!" Zander shouts, pushing his dark wet hair from his forehead, but the smile on his face holds no regret.

Willow winks, raising her arm to flash her parents the hand gesture that means "I love you" before the four of them begin paddling toward the shore.

Everett huffs, leaning against the railing with his arms crossed. "You'd think they'd have enough common sense to go pier jumping early in the morning before it's crowded. It's like they learned nothing from us."

"There is really no difference in what time of day you do it," Darby chimes. "It's always risky, and kids are stupid. Us included."

"Not me," Dahlia mutters. "I never jumped off this pier."

We all pause at that, glancing around at each other with unspoken realization.

Dahlia is the only one of us who never jumped off the Pacific Shores Pier. She's the only one who didn't spend a teenage summer here.

"I mean...you could try it out now?" Elena grins playfully. "I'll go with you."

"After I just yelled at my children for doing the same thing?" Dahlia pops a brow. "That would make me mother of the year."

"You did threaten to go in after them," I point out. "So, if anything...you're just following through."

"I'll do it too," Darby says. Leo eyes her suspiciously, and she only shrugs. "Dal should get to experience it, and if we wait too much longer, we'll all be too old."

Everett huffs. "Well, I'm not letting my wife go without me, so..." He pulls his cell phone from his back pocket, and the rest of us do the same, along with wallets and keys. "I'm going to go ask the hostess at the Seaside Sunset if she'll hold onto these for us." He nods toward the restaurant just behind us before heading toward it.

Dahlia leans over the edge. "Fuck, that's actually kind of a long fall."

"It'll be fine," Darby says. "We can all hold hands."

Leo stands on one end, Darby beside him. I sidle up next to her, taking her hand, while Elena grabs my other. When Everett returns, he steps between Dahlia and Elena.

Darby squeezes my palm four times, and I do the same to Elena beside me. I watch the ripple effect of the gesture, until Dahlia glances down at us from the other end, smiling.

Our lives have stretched to the farthest corners of the earth. We've watched our world burn and rebuilt it from ashes. We've been lost and broken—we've run away.

Yet, somehow, we end up back where we started. It's a settling feeling, standing at the edge of our small world, watching the waves hurl themselves against this pier. Rippling shades of sapphire and turquoise, accented by caps of white swirl together beneath, creating the rarest blue. A color that belongs to us.

Together, we leap into the Pacific, heading home.

Acknowledgments

First and foremost, I want to thank every reader who has joined me here in Pacific Shores. Those who have fallen in love with this small town, this family, and these characters. August and Elena and all of Pacific Shores are forever yours. Your endless support has made so many of my dreams come true, and I'll never be able to express my gratitude fully. Thank you for loving this series so loudly.

My husband, Bubs, for always reading the pages of my soul written in a language no one else understands. For knowing me better than anyone else and loving me more for it. For holding my hand through every bout of grief and flare and spiral. For never making me feel lesser than because of it. I love you beyond words.

My Jenna, because your role in my life goes beyond titles. You're more than a brand manager and more than a friend. Thank you for every late-night FaceTime, brainstorm session, and for holding all of my sanity in your hands. I could not function without you, and I would not be living out my childhood dreams without your support.

My team, Cassie and Page, for keeping me on track and keeping my feet moving when I feel like I can't do it myself, and for loving my stories as much as I do. I couldn't do it without you!

Lexi, the literal other half of my soul. There are a lot of reasons I believe in soulmates, but you may be the number one. Augustus is all yours because I know you could fix him hehehe.

My beta readers, Cait, Abby, Rachel, Julia, Maddy, Tori and Moe. Thank you for helping me believe in this book during the moments when I felt so unsure, and for consistently supporting it and me. Your support means everything to me!

My agent, Katie, for all your support in making my publishing dreams come true. I couldn't do it without you.

The Page & Vine Team for taking a chance on my little universe and bringing it to stores all over the world. You make me feel like the luckiest author alive.

The incredible indie bookstores and small businesses who have supported me and this series so loudly: Wildflower Fiction, Scribbles Bookshop, Heartbound Bookshop, Always

Yours Bookshop, Love and Other Books, Pages of Passion, In Bloom Fiction, Jadestone Creates, Ember Literary PR and Well Read Candle Co.

My editor, Jordyn, for taking this story and this series to new heights, for always supporting my vision and my voice, and for being as passionate about these characters as I am!

My street team. I love you, my horny little gremlins. Thank you for your endless love and excitement over these figments of my imagination. You keep me going most days, and I couldn't be more thankful for your support.

Author friends who I wouldn't make it through the day without, Bailey Hannah, Ambar Cordova, and Emily Tudor. Thank you for being in the trenches with me.

August & Elena's Playlist

Prologue — "hoax" by Taylor Swift

Chapter One — "Liability" by Lorde

Chapter Two — "I Always Wanna Die (Sometimes)" by The 1975

Chapter Three — "chemtrails" by Lizzy McAlpine

Chapter Four — "I Look in People's Windows" by Taylor Swift

Chapter Five — "this is me trying" by Taylor Swift

Chapter Six — "Fuck it I love you" by Lana Del Rey

Chapter Seven — "making the bed" by Olivia Rodrigo

Chapter Eight — "exile (feat. Bon Iver)" by Taylor Swift

Chapter Nine — "We Hug Now" by Sydney Rose

Chapter Ten — "The Cut That Always Bleeds" by Conan Gray

Chapter Eleven — "Looking Back" by Lord Huron

Chapter Twelve — "Where's My Love" by SYML

Chapter Thirteen — "Talk" by Hozier

Chapter Fourteen — "Master & A Hound" by Gregory Alan Isakov

Chapter Fifteen — "Cherry" by Lana Del Rey

Chapter Sixteen — "Ribs" by Lorde

Chapter Seventeen — "imgonnagetyouback" by Taylor Swift

Chapter Eighteen — "Love Is a Laserquest" by Arctic Monkeys

Chapter Nineteen — "Acquainted" by The Weeknd

Chapter Twenty — "Cinnamon Girl" by Lana Del Rey

Chapter Twenty-One — “Older” by Lizzy McAlpine

Chapter Twenty-Two — “Unknown / Nth” by Hozier

Chapter Twenty-Three — “Born to Die” by Lana Del Rey

Chapter Twenty-Four — “Movement” by Hozier

Chapter Twenty-Five — “From Eden” by Hozier

Chapter Twenty-Six — “Repeat Until Death” by Novo Amor

Chapter Twenty-Seven — “Nothing’s Gonna Hurt You Baby” by Cigarettes After Sex

Chapter Twenty-Eight — “Superposition” by Young the Giant

Chapter Twenty-Nine — “Lust For Life” by Lanna Del Rey, The Weeknd

Chapter Thirty — “At The Beach, In Every Life” by Gigi Perez

Chapter Thirty-One — “mad woman” by Taylor Swift

Chapter Thirty-Two — “Fix You” by Coldplay

Chapter Thirty-Three — “Love Song” by Lana Del Rey

Chapter Thirty-Four — “warm glow” by Hippo Campus

Chapter Thirty-Five — “Space Song” by Beach House

Chapter Thirty-Six — “Love Like Ghosts” by Lord Huron

Chapter Thirty-Seven — “Yes I’m Changing” by Tame Impala

Chapter Thirty-Eight — “willow” by Taylor Swift

Chapter Thirty-Nine — “Mess Is Mine” by Vance Joy

Chapter Forty — “Never Let Me Go” by Florence + The Machine

Chapter Forty-One — “Stargirl Interlude” by The Weeknd, Lana Del Rey

Chapter Forty-Two — “BIRDS OF A FEATHER” by Billie Eilish

Epilogue — “Home” by Good Neighbours

About the Author

Sarah fell in love with reading as a child. She quickly learned that books can take her to all the places she always dreamed of going, and allow her to live endless lifetimes in the one that she was given.

Sarah believes that to be seen is to be loved, and that's why romance is such an important genre. She believes romance novels offer readers reflection and relatability, ultimately helping us understand ourselves, and the world around us, a little better. She prides herself on crafting healing, raw, and uplifting stories that explore the complexities of the human spirit through the guise of love.

Sarah was born in California and raised in Southern Oregon, and still considers herself to be a Pacific Northwest gal at heart; right down to being a coffee snob, collecting hydro flasks, adamantly believing in Sasquatch, and never having owned an umbrella.

She now resides in Arizona with her husband and their pup, Rue. When she's not writing, she's reading, and if she's not reading, she's probably out searching for a decent cup of coffee or binging Vanderpump Rules for the millionth time.

Connect with Sarah on social media: @sarahabaileyauthor

Sign up for her newsletter to be the first to know about updates and announcements: sarahabaileyauthor.com/newsletter

Also by Sarah A. Bailey

Pacific Shores series
Heathen & Honeysuckle
Wicked & Wildflower
Reckless Roses
Vice & Violet

The Soulmate series
The Soulmate Theory
The Fate Philosophy
The Forever Experiment

Celestia Cove series
Coming 2026